KELLY'S REEF

James R. Burke

ISBN: 1480112089
ISBN-13: 978-1480112087

Dedication

To Catherine, Moira, and Liam who survived
and thrived on Guam.

Acknowledgements

No modern author works in a vacuum. This work is a collaboration of friends.

Linda Clare who taught me BICWOP—butt in chair, words on paper.

My writers' group: Shirley, Diane, Linda, and LeAnne who gave me the female perspective.

The Write Guys: Doug, Charley, John, Bob, and Michael, who tirelessly helped edit the work.

The Cottage Grove Harpies who corrected all the plot errors.

Frank, Barb, Ralph, Marty, and all the early readers.

My wife, who read and reread the manuscript, found every nit, typo, and misplaced comma.

A special thanks to Dr. Alder Fuller, my mentor and guru, who planted the idea that all DNA shares the same translation table. If DNA translates differently, it does not originate on this planet.

Contents

Prologue

A screeching banshee jerked me awake. Sweat stung my eyes as I shook off the dream. It was only the depth finder alerting me to a change in bottom contour.

The sun beat down, heat draining my energy, leaving me lethargic. The evening winds were still hours away, and the usual cooling squalls lay in wait on the distant horizon. A rare cloud failed to hide the sun.

Fishing sucked. The fish were smart enough to head to deep, cool water; not even a nibble despite what I considered my best custom-made lure. Charlie and TJ, my two best friends, and I drifted farther and farther south of the island of Guam without success. We were just about to give in when the damn depth finder squealed at us.

"What have we here?" I looked toward the shore and could see the landmarks on Old Wives Beach a mile off. The annoying depth gauge registered 40-60 feet under the USS *Chipmunk*, my dive boat.

"TJ, check the chart and see if there is something underneath us." I thought we should be far enough off shore to be in deep water. We had been trolling for fish along the edge of Guam's reef where the ocean floor fell to the depths.

"Nope." TJ yawned. "You been in the sun too long; musta sunburnt your fertile little imagination." He wiped the sweat off his polished ebony head, sipped his beer, propped his feet onto the ice chest, and pretended to doze off.

"Gimme a break. Just check to see if there's a reef or maybe a wreck under us." I knew his nonchalance was an act. His enormous mass uncoiled itself, and I felt the boat list dangerously.

"Yassa boss. But reminds me once more—do dah North go to dah top a de map?"

"Keep that up and I'll make sure you're assigned to teach Ebonics at the middle school. *And*, I'll tell Yale you're abusing your doctorate in English Literature."

1

Thelonious Justis, PhD, also has masters' degrees in biochemistry and evolutionary biology. He's still trying to figure out what he wants to do when he grows up and resigns from the Navy. Tormenting me seems to be high on that list; but I wouldn't have it any other way. He's been my closest friend ever since we shared space on an aircraft carrier a year ago.

"Aye! Aye! Skipper. Moreover, I'll have a fully referenced essay on why excess melanin levels are associated with superior human intelligence on your desk in the morning. Five hundred words, no more than two syllables each, okay?" He grinned perfect white teeth at me.

"While you two continue your never-ending battle of whose Mutt and who's Jeff, I, once again, did the real work of this expedition into the unknown," Charlie informed us, pointing to our navigational chart. Charlie made up the third of our trio, our friendship extending back to an adventure in Djibouti, North Africa.

"Bones, you're lost. And the North does go to the top, TJ."

Charlie blushed, but he blushes at everything—especially when he thinks he's upstaged TJ and me. Pale skin and freckles topped with a bright-red flattop and ever-present sunburn contrasted TJ's charcoal complexion and shaved skull.

He continued, "No reef. No wreck. Nothing but 600 feet of ocean below us according to the USCG navigational chart as of last year." His finger scrolled across the chart. "Depth finder must be screwy again," he concluded, giving it a whack to prove his point. It squawked back at him.

"Well, whatever it is, we just passed over it," I noted as the depth finder dial spun to 450 feet. "Let's take another pass." I swung the wheel 180 degrees and confirmed we actually had an anomaly below us. Picking up the binoculars, I identified a tower and power pole on the distant shore. This triangulated our location. "Nope, not lost. It's not on this chart. Strange. The chart's only a year old, and whatever this is should be on it," I confirmed, looking over Charlie's shoulder. TJ gave up all pretense that he wasn't interested and joined us.

Charlie was already setting up his dive gear. The guy has gills and lives to dive. "While you two continue mentally masturbating each other about whether white dicks are bigger than black dicks. I'm going to take a look." Charlie pretends to be a redder redneck than his sunburn. He gets away with it, with TJ and me—usually.

"And don't drink all the beer while I'm gone," he chided as he slid over the side.

"Last one in has to tend the *Chipmunk*," I said throwing on my buoyancy control device—BCD, and tank, slipping on fins and mask, and splashing into the tropical water. With visibility at over 200 feet, I could see a reef sitting proudly above the surrounding void. I sank past Charlie a few minutes later, and we gave each other the universal scuba WOW sign—third, ring, and pinky fingers held up on either side of the regulator mouthpiece.

Even though Charlie, TJ, and I dive together without rigidly following the buddy system, all three of us are experienced sport divers and frequently explore the same reef without direct contact. We always know, or sense, where we are in an emergency. Same Day, Same Ocean Divers. I trust my life to these two, just as they do to me.

In a part of the world where spectacular reefs are common, this was a stunning exception. Football shaped, she sat on a rocky flat at about 80 feet, rising to 30 feet below the surface. A wall of coral plunged into the abyss along her flank. The shoreward side had a small border of sand. Almost perfectly ovoid, there was a long splintering canyon into her flank. Covered with an overhang of staghorn and fan corals, the canyon formed a blind cave extending inwards far enough to turn around comfortably.

I watched her undulate with life; fish, turtles, and anemones fluttered around her. At the mouth of the cave, I glimpsed the tail of the largest green eel I had ever seen. I guessed it to be seven feet long and thick as my leg.

I looked back at TJ, who had joined Charlie and me underwater. I signaled that I wanted to take a closer look. As soon as I saw the eel guarding the entrance into the cave, I knew I had to make her acquaintance.

Eels are a common sight on the local reefs, their heads sticking out of the coral during the day or slithering through the coral at night. This reef seemed to teem with them. They are harmless if left unmolested. Most want to avoid contact. This one was aware of me, but seemed unconcerned. I didn't feel threatened by it, but knew to keep my distance.

I ventured part way into the cave, lost sight of the eel, and was just starting to back out when I sensed it slide over my shoulder. I started, my heart jerking into overdrive, and turned to find her face-to-face-to-face with me, both her mouths gaping. She just floated there, staring at me with four obsidian eyes. My first thought was that I had bad air in my tank or was getting nitrogen narcosis. A two-headed eel was impossible, yet there she was. I continued to back out, and she followed me gracefully to the entrance to the cave, but no further.

Not aggressive or acting territorial, she just seemed curious. So were my dive buddies. Charlie actually started to reach toward her, and then thought better of it. I could tell he was as surprised and shocked by her as I was. It took a couple of minutes before he thought to turn on his camera and shoot some footage. The eel seemed to enjoy showing off, swimming to the side to get a better view, but not venturing beyond the cave entrance. Then both heads turned toward each other and as if by silent agreement, turned and disappeared into the lair. I knew all three of us wanted to follow her, but swimming into a cave with a seven foot, two-headed eel wasn't something we were quite willing to try.

"Did we really see that?" TJ asked as we clambered aboard the *Chipmunk* a few minutes later. "I don't believe it!"

"We have the video to prove it," Charlie said, "but nobody's going to believe it anyway. That was too unreal."

"I'm calling her Auraka," I said.

"Huh?" asked Charlie

"That's the name of the Polynesian god of destruction," I answered.

"Okay. I suppose Sweet'ums or Tickle Bunny won't work," said TJ. Charlie thought about that for a moment and nodded.

"You know we can't tell anyone about this, ever," I said. "This reef doesn't even exist on a map, and if word of this creature gets out, it'll be overwhelmed with tourists, scientists, the government, treasure hunters, and people trying to catch it. We can't let that happen." I knew the others agreed. This was too sensational and important to make public—yet!

TJ looked at both of us. "Yeah, that's true, and I don't want anyone else to know about her until we solve this mystery. Think about it—we could become famous."

"Huh?" Charlie again.

I said, "We found a fully developed reef that's not on a chart in a region of the ocean that is well documented. And we find the biggest damn eel anyone has ever seen. *And,* it has two heads. I, for one, want to know what's going on before we tell anyone."

"My uncle said he had a two-headed calf on his ranch once," Charlie said, "but it died before anyone got to see it. And I saw a picture of a two-headed turtle once. And I read a book about a three-breasted woman. And there were those guys in Utah that got abducted on that UFO—look what happened to them." He said this with such a perfect deadpan expression, TJ and I could only stare. I swear that half the time I don't know if Charlie is a couple of bolts short of an Erector Set or putting us on. Maybe both.

"So? What's with that eel? That was awesome. I've heard of two-headed cows, but always thought that was a hoax. I don't believe I actually experienced a two-headed eel," said TJ. "Where did it come from? I mean, WOW."

"Yeah Bones," Charlie said, "I mean, how does something grow a second head?" Charlie and TJ always refer to me as Bones.

"It didn't grow a second head," I said. "I think Auraka is a conjoined twin."

"Huh?" Charlie once again. "What's a, what you call it, confused twin?"

"No, conjoined, not confused. A Siamese twin. Twins who never fully separated during pregnancy"

"But Siam doesn't exist anymore, so wouldn't they be Thai twins?" Charlie asked this with a poker face. "Mrs. Phan and her brother are from Thailand, but they don't have two heads." I still couldn't tell if he was kidding. I never know with Charlie.

I shook my head in disbelief. "Now I know you're pulling my tallywacker—you can't be that dumb."

"But how does that happen?" TJ asked.

"Once a fertilized egg starts dividing, something signals the DNA to create embryonic cells and support tissue called the trophoblast. You with me so far?" I looked at Charlie.

"The embryo has blasters? Like little ray-guns? Wow." Charlie was on a roll. TJ just rolled his eyes.

I continued to secure the remaining gear and to get the *Chipmunk* ready to motor. I stuck a peppermint in my mouth to kill the salt taste.

"Anyway, during the magical mystery trip down Fallopian Avenue, the embryo sometimes divides into two, or even three. They all have the same DNA, so they develop into identical twins or triplets."

"So your wife Emily and her twin sister Hanna split up the cells between them, huh? Who got the brain cells and who got the beauty cells?"

Charlie finished loading the gear bags and pulled out a thermos of coffee. Even with the salted peppermint taste in my mouth, coffee was ambrosia to my tongue.

I secured the anchor line and continued, "Occasionally the embryo doesn't perfectly divide, and the creature remains connected at some point. It's rare and usually fatal, but mammals have been born connected at the hip, the abdomen, the chest, and even the head. I think that happened with Auraka; the embryo partially separated, and the cranium developed into two heads while the caudal, un-separated tail portion, became the body."

TJ said, "So Auraka is twins who didn't separate?"

"Exactly, and what an incredible creature she is," I said. "That's why we need to keep her secret. If the locals find out, she'll end up a meal at a village fiesta; if anyone else discovers her, she'll end up in a jar or aquarium somewhere. We just can't let that happen to her." I looked at my friends to be sure they understood our need for secrecy.

6

"I for one do not seek fame and glory on the front page of the *National Inquirer*, so this remains between just us," I said.

TJ finished wiping the saltwater off his shiny black dome and stuck a cigar in his mouth—a sure sign that he had made a command decision. "I'm in."

"Okay, then we all need to 'pinky swear'," said Charlie, holding up his right hand with his little finger crooked. Now I knew he was putting us on. My laughter settled the question—Auraka was a secret.

"The reef needs a name," I said. We looked at each other and nodded.

"Kelly," I said. "As captain of the *Chipmunk* and senior naval officer on board, I hereby christen her Kelly's Reef." We all clinked coffee mugs to seal the deal.

Over the next month, a dozen more dives to visit Auraka, map the reef, and research the local surveys, we couldn't believe no one else knew about her. Kelly was perfect; a pristine collection of shelf corals, delicate fan corals, black corals, pelagic sharks, tortoise, octopus, and reef fish. Kelly was gorgeous, mysterious, dangerous, and deadly to the unwary. Just like her namesake—a bartender in Djibouti, Djibouti where the three of us first met.

PART 1- DJIBOUTI

<u>Somalia</u>

"Tally Ho!" I heard the pilot shout above the Village People singing "YMCA" into my headphones. The Navy helo carrying us fell from the sky while my stomach took up residence in my throat. The desert sand raced to meet us and at the last moment Low Ball, the kamikaze flying this tin can, feathered to a kitten-gentle touch down. This was the third touch-and-go he'd performed, all to confuse the Somali rebels out there waiting for us.

Three hours before, I'd been sleeping in my rack, safely on board an aircraft carrier.

"Yo, Bones. Get your butt outta bed. We gots us a boondoggle." My roommate Lieutenant Commander Thelonious Justis shook me.

Stretched out on my upper bunk, I stared at the steel pipe six inches from my head. Another day on board the USS *Carl Vinson*, CVN 70, and I had just finished my daily power nap before afternoon sick call. At sea on a WestPac tour, I was bored senseless with get up, eat, go to sick call, send the deadbeats back to work, walk around, take a nap, see more gold bricks, train corpsmen, eat again, nap some more, go to bed. Repeat tomorrow.

By way of introduction, I'm US Navy Commander Jake Matthews, MD. When asked what I do for a living, I tell strangers that I spend my days talking to naked women about sex. As a gynecologist, that's true, but it always garners attention. I was too small to be a pilot. Just as well, since I hate to fly. My wife Emily would like for me to wax the hair on my back, but I consider shaving my head sufficient depilatory activity. My passion is scuba diving.

The *Carl Vinson* is one of the navy's nuclear aircraft carriers, and I was her newest GMO, general medical officer, assigned for a year of sea duty with six thousand men. I had just completed my surgical internship and OB/GYN residency, illustrating naval intelligence at its finest. I should have been in a hospital, but here I was, anchored in the Arabian Sea, sweltering, with nothing to do. Not a woman plagued with pregnancy or fussy ovaries for a thousand miles. Once a day we would weigh anchor, float around for an afternoon while the pilots practiced take-offs and landings, then drop anchor and sweat some more.

I rolled toward TJ. "Ya knows, for someone with a degree in English, you sure 'nuff talk funny, for an officer and all. Now, go away."

He switched from street to a cultured Oxford accent. "Okay, if you're not interested in said naval exercise with the possibility of exotic adventure in a foreign country, an opportunity to serve the highest principles of your profession, and my companionship during said boondoggle, I'll get what's-his-name, the flight surgeon, to go."

TJ consumed all the space in our stateroom—a generous description of the 10 by 12 foot steel closet we shared. Well over 6'8" and three hundred pounds, he had trouble just fitting in the space. Two small folding metal desks and lockers not much bigger than a duffle bag, along with a poster of Raquel Welch from her movie *One Million B.C.* completed the *Architectural Digest* photo spread we called home. That, and a large purple pipe running through the ceiling that carried jet fuel and dripped onto the middle of my desk.

I groaned. "Since you put it that way," I said, sitting up and smacking my forehead. "Damn, I hate that pipe."

TJ smiled and shook his head. "For a doctor and an educated man, you are certainly impaired in common sense."

"Huh?" I asked, rubbing the knot on my head.

"Did you know you're the only one on board in a top bunk who hasn't duct taped a piece of foam rubber to the pipe above his head to protect his skull? We even have a pool going to see when you'll figure it out." TJ always seemed to have a pool going on something. Last week, it was the number of ingrown toenails I would treat at sick call.

"So tell me what's up?" I wanted to hop down, but instead I bent over the side of my bunk. With TJ in the room, there wasn't enough space for both of us to be on our feet.

"We just got a call from a research ship off the coast of Somalia. They have a female crewperson who is pregnant and bleeding. Their medic is asking for help, and we're the closest ship with a doctor. We didn't indicate that you might be brain damaged from self-inflicted cranial rearrangement therapy."

"Funny . . . So, when will she arrive?" I asked.

Finally, something I can sink my teeth into other than athlete's foot, crotch rot, and belly aching. Be still my bored heart.

"She won't. They are too far away to be able to get a chopper to her and back, and too small a vessel to allow a helo to land. They want us to meet her. Therefore, you have five minutes until a chopper takes us to meet a contact on the coast of Somalia. They're waiting for us on the flight deck—get packed. I'm getting our gear together."

"Do I need my dress whites? Should I take American Express or VISA?" TJ just shook his head as he left.

Fifteen minutes later, we lifted from the flight deck and cruised low across the Arabian Sea toward the coast. A diamond sun blazed on the western horizon through a filthy dust cloud blowing off the desert. The sea was a dirty glass sheet, unbroken by even a ripple. The hot air was rank with jet fuel, sweat, and dust. I looked back toward the carrier and could just distinguish the dark brown smudge of sewage slowly leaking from the starboard side. Six thousand sailors can create a mountain of poop every day. Following an incident where two seamen fishing off the fantail got dysentery from the polluted fish they cooked on a hot plate, I insisted that we not sit in sewage day after day. Daily, we would raise anchor and move a couple of miles rather than sit in a toilet bowl of our waste.

Today, as usual, there was no breeze or current. Every breath filled my lungs with a layer of crud that made me want to cough up a fur ball. I glanced across the cargo bay of the helo at Petty Officer Vignalli, a senior corpsman assigned to accompany TJ and me on this mission. He was holding his head and breathing through his mouth. Chartreuse skin was a clear indication of his fondness for flying.

"So tell me again why Vignalli is coming with us and why we can't land this thing on the research ship?" I asked TJ.

"Vignalli is available to assist you, should you need to operate on your patient, and our destination, the USNS *Swordfish* is too small to land this bird on. So, they're letting us off a few miles from the coast and have arranged a pick-up."

"Okay. And they sent you along because . . ."

"Somebody needs to keep you out of trouble." I couldn't tell from his grin if he was serious or not.

A military helicopter is just a tin can with a propeller on top as far as I'm concerned. The side door was open and functioned as the air conditioner—same as an old Ford station wagon I once owned. Every wire and tube are exposed and painted gray. Even the strap hooked to my harness to keep me from falling into the air conditioner was gray. Uniform khaki and Vignalli's green were decorative accent colors.

TJ tapped the air crewman on the shoulder and indicated that he wanted headsets. He handed both of us earphones and looked at Vignalli with a questioning gesture. TJ shook his head.

"Low Ball," TJ growled over the intercom, "if you continue to bounce this pitiful excuse for a true flying machine, I won't be responsible for cleaning up my corpsman's puke. Be advised that he ate a giant bowl of beef stew just before we lifted off."

"Low Ball? You know this pilot?" I asked.

TJ's condescending expression clearly let me know what a stupid question that was. Of course, he knew the pilot, his mother, his blood type, and how much he had in his bank account.

"No sweat, TJ," was the reply as the bird dropped two stories. Vignalli grabbed his mouth in panic. I moved out of range. "Oops, sorry 'bout that," Low Ball said into his microphone.

"Not funny," said the air crewman. "I'm gonna be seriously pissed if I have to clean up back here. This boat pussy ain't looking so good."

"Low Ball," TJ warned, "said sailor is sitting three feet from my immaculately clean uniform. Should said sailor lose it, I will make public some rather unpleasant news regarding your sexual orientation and proclivity for sheep. We wouldn't want that, now would we?"

"TJ," I said, trying to refocus on the mission, "if this woman we're going after is pregnant I might need to do a D&C. I didn't pack—"

"A sterile Dilate and Curettage tray is in our gear." He wiped sweat off his shiny 8-ball head and looked for somewhere to wipe his hand. Finding no alternative, he used Vignalli's uniform shirt. Vignalli didn't seem to notice.

"If we need blood—"

"She's A-positive, and I already have the list of blood types for the rest of the crew, in case we need a donor. I also packed the reagents for typing, and a spare bunny to see if she's actually pregnant."

"But, what if—"

"Bones," he answered before I could even form the question, "the only thing I don't have is enough drugs to euthanize Vignalli. I also did not determine whether you have sufficient clean underwear for several days, if stranded. There are limits to what I am willing to do for the success of this mission."

"TJ, what I don't understand is why we're actually here. Wouldn't it be simpler to evacuate her? Why send a team in when it's unlikely that I'll be able to do anything that their medic can't?" He shook his head, frowned, and tapped his headset indicating I shouldn't be broadcasting my concerns.

"So, Dr. Matthews," Low Ball broke in, "have you wrapped foam around that pipe in your stateroom yet? I had 34 days in that pool."

I looked at TJ who just shrugged and wiggled his ever-present unlit cigar. I think he secretly wanted to be a Groucho Marx, sans mustache.

"I hope you didn't have too big a bet in the pool," I said to Low Ball. "You know by now it was a setup, don't you?" I paused and looked toward Vignalli, who was making the sign of the cross and saying a Hail Mary, waiting for final dispensation or whatever Catholics do before they die in agony.

"I knew it," said the copilot. "Nobody's *that* thick. I had 41 days."

"Okay, TJ will cut you both in, but if Vignalli loses it because of your flying, High Ball, all bets are off," I said.

"It's Low Ball."

"Low Ball, High Ball, Grande Cojones, or Ball Less—same thing."

We continued to trade insults and gossip and flew another hour toward the rising moon before TJ pulled a small plastic patch from his shirt pocket, peeled off the backing, and leaned across me to stick it behind Vignalli's ear.

"You had a scopolamine patch in your pocket all this time?" I was truly amazed. "He's been more shades of green in the last hour than a gecko in heat, and you've been holding out?"

"Actually it's been one hour, eleven minutes. I had one hour, ten minutes in the pool, and I was the high bidder, so there's no sense in prolonging his suffering." TJ showed his perfect smile to me.

"First touchdown in five," I heard in my headset. "We're doing an insertion, so this will be a hot landing, ladies. Intel thinks there are Somali rebels coming down from the hills." Low Ball notified us to prepare to land. I looked out the open door at the sand in all directions, broken rarely by what might be generously called scrub brush. There were no lights that I could see anywhere. A flash of heat-induced lightning seared a desolate image onto my retina.

"Where are we?" I asked. Until then, I didn't consider the dangers of landing in Somalia.

"The ass-end of hell. Two guys will meet you here and drive you to a pick-up at the coast. Buckle up, we're gonna have some fun now," said Low Ball.

I looked at TJ. He smiled and rolled his stogie from one side of his mouth to the other, then spat a fleck of tobacco on the floor. Vignalli groaned.

Hot landing? Rebels? Whiskey Tango Foxtrot?

"Stick a baggie over the puke's head. We're going to make a couple bounces to throw the hostiles off, and I don't want to have to clean up after him." Low Ball planned to touch down several times for a minute or two at different sites to create confusion, an insertion technique perfected in 'Nam.

One moment we were skimming across the sand, the next my stomach jumped into my mouth as Low Ball flared and dropped to the ground. I was looking out the open door as the ground rushed up, a cloud of dust obscuring everything. Before I could look away, my sky-high stomach plummeted into my scrotum, as we roared skyward. I looked at Vignalli and hoped the scopolamine would hold. He was the only green thing for miles in any direction.

"Tally Ho!" The intercom came alive. Low Ball seemed to be enjoying himself. "Let's have some tunes to liven up this party." I am sometimes adventurous enough to get on the Dumbo ride at Disneyland; I didn't sign up for a kamikaze trip; I was not feeling the joy.

My mouth was dryer than the dirt below us. I couldn't squeeze enough spit to talk, and wondered if all the remaining fluids in my body had left my bladder to reside in my shorts. The Village People began blasting "YMCA" through the intercom. TJ's grin grew wider as he laced his fingers behind his neck and stretched out his legs. He was having fun. Vignalli was dying, and I was trying to remember if I had paid my life insurance premium. The chamber stank of sweat, fear, and ammonia. I couldn't tell who contributed which.

I heard Low Ball ask, "Again?" as my stomach did its thing—again. Down, up, off we raced.

"I'd like to get out now. Petty Officer Vignalli and I will be catching a taxi the rest of the way," I said. Hope runs eternal.

"Okay, have it your way then." I heard Low Ball laugh. "We want to thank you for your patronage and ask that you remember Low Ball Airlines for your next vacation." We fell from the sky, and the instant before we became one with Mother Earth, Low Ball flared and landed soft as feather pillow.

"OUT! OUT! OUT! Be sure to check the overheads for personal items. Remember that items may have shifted during takeoffs and crash landings."

With that, the crew dumped us unceremoniously on the sand, followed by our case of equipment and our duffle bags.

A blast of prop wash and dust was all that was left of our ride. I looked at Vignalli; he was on his hands and knees. I was glad his patch lasted as long as it did. I looked again and realized he wasn't vomiting; he was kissing the sand. He flopped onto his side, curled his knees into a fetal position, and groaned.

The moon rose higher and what little light it gave didn't dispel my growing apprehension. There was nothing as far as I could see in any direction. Nothing; no lights, buildings, K-Marts, snakes, other humans, or *anything* living, save a scrawny bush displaying an unbelievable survival instinct in this god-forsaken place.

"Well, hope you're happy, Bones." TJ surveyed our domain and sighed. "Maybe you shouldn't have asked to be let out when you did. Oh well, what's done is done. I figure Mogadishu is about 400 klicks in that general direction." He nodded into the night. "Berbera is about 50. We might be able to get there in a couple of days, maybe."

"You're shitting me, right?" I was sure he was, but . . .

"Or we go to plan B." He tipped his duffle bag, unzipped a flap, and reached inside to retrieve a small hand-held radio. A swizzling of sand caught my attention, and I turned expecting a black mamba or other slimy creature rearing up to attack. Only an emaciated lizard running for what meager cover it could find.

"New York Taxi, this is Knothead. What's your 20?" The radio crackled to life.

A blast of static replied. "About a klick out and running dark. If you see headlights, it's not us."

"Roger that." TJ stuffed the radio back into his pack and turned to stare at the desert. Something whirred past my ear before I could bat it away.

"Your taxi approaches," TJ said. "Command arranged transportation, but since we're in a hostile country we needed to arrive far enough away to protect the ship." I heard a distant sputter and popping sound that coalesced into a vintage Volkswagen camper, complete with paint-faded daisies and a peace symbol on the front. It slid to a stop in a cloud of dust, and the driver's door popped open.

15

"New York Taxi, at your service." A small wizened and bearded human, complete with a dirty gray turban and kaftan waved us over. "We can take you uptown, downtown, crosstown, to any bar, betting parlor, whorehouse, or church in our beautiful country, but I would suggest that we do it quickly. Otherwise, the assholes back there," he looked behind us. I turned and saw faint headlights a couple of kilometers off. A gunshot rang through the night, "might want to take another shot at us."

Oh shit, this is real. I'm in Somalia, and they're shooting at me.

TJ and I lugged our bags and gear case to the back, and then threw them into the cargo space. The springs creaked and sagged. Vignalli climbed in with the gear, and I started to open the front door. Our newly found host grabbed me before I could climb in and pushed me toward the side door.

"You're the doctor. You ride in back and help my friend. Your guard," nodding toward TJ, "rides up front. Can you shoot a gun?" he asked TJ.

I was whirling. "Wait a minute, who *are* you and how do you know I'm a doctor? Who else is back there? Where are we? What the hell is happening?"

"You're American. American doctors are white and have large black bodyguards who can kill people. Everybody knows that." He had an accent I would expect to hear in a marketplace in Pakistan. "The rebels back there shot my partner. He's in the back," he nodded toward a tarp on the middle seat. "Now get in before they shoot you too." He shoved me through the door, climbed behind the wheel, gunned the motor, and lurched into the night.

Having settled the seating issue, the Sultan, as I was mentally beginning to refer to him, turned back and pointed at a first-aid kit. At that moment, what I thought to be a pile of trash and rags moved and groaned. A stench emanated from the pile that was men's locker room sour and coppery sweet. I realized the pile was human, barely.

"Here's a flashlight, but keep it low, so they can't get a fix on us. A couple more kilometers and we'll lose them." The Sultan handed me a small pocket light. I shone the red lens on the pile.

"You the doc we're supposed to get to the *Swordfish*?" the pile asked, sitting upright and clutching its thigh. "Master Chief Charlie Albright at your service, Sir. Sorry about the arrangements. I had to leave my post a little earlier than expected, so we're sharing this ride." He leaned back in the seat.

The Sultan chose this moment to hit a large pothole. The Master Chief grunted through clenched teeth and leaned further back.

"Seems I fell down a flight of stairs waiting for this ride and may have cut myself. Got any Band-Aids in there, Doc?" He leaned forward and tapped the Sultan. "I need some painkillers." He was rewarded with an airline size bottle of tequila.

"Allah, forgive me, for I have participated in the destruction of your soul, giving you the devil's brew."

"Shut up or when *I* get to paradise I'll tell Allah about your still and how you already had your seven virgins." The Master Chief downed his anesthetic with a belch and wiped his mouth on the back of a huge, grimy paw.

"Let me take a look." I tried to refocus my anxiety on something I could control. I cut away the leg of his fatigues with dull scissors I found in the first-aid kit and examined his leg. A small hole at the front was oozing, but the large congealing mass protruding out the back of the leg was a dead giveaway. I couldn't see protruding bones or arterial bleeding. The pulse in his foot felt steady.

"Fell down some stairs, did you?" I sniffed twice. "I think I smell bullshit, or maybe it's just TJ's aftershave. I'd guess that you landed on about a nine millimeter when you fell. Am I close?"

"Long story, Doc." The look on his face told me not to ask.

"TJ, did you know about this?"

"Later," he said as he loaded and checked an automatic weapon.

"Never mind, let's get you patched up. I'll need to get you to a hospital soon." I leaned over the seat and asked the Sultan when we would reach our rendezvous. Before he could answer, we hit another bump. Vignalli, who had been climbing over the rear cargo seat to help, bounced against the roof and across the seat back. We finally revisited his beef stew.

"Ominous, Dominos, Padres, and Cinco De Mayo," I intoned as I pronounced the petty officer dead. I don't deal well with vomit or baby diapers.

I washed out the wound with water from a canteen and went about securing the leg in a bulky bandage, checking vital signs, and making sure my 'patient' was stable as we raced across the desert.

"Do we have an IV?" I asked.

"No," answered the Sultan, "but I do have an eight-track tape of Henry Mancini's greatest hits if you like."

How can I possibly respond to that? I've fallen down the rabbit hole and can't get out.

TJ set down the radio he had been talking into and announced we would be at the beach in a few minutes. A boat would rendezvous and take us to the USNS *Swordfish*. I looked out the back window but could no longer make out the lights following. We pulled up to a flat stretch of sand where a small group of men with a motorboat met us. Another gunshot, in the distance, let me know our pursuers weren't far behind.

"Well, time to motor on. See you guys at Kelly's." With that, the Sultan fired up the VW and started forward. He stalled a few feet away, threw open the door and came back to face me. I could smell garlic and another unidentified herb on his breath.

"I had day 63 on your pool." He slapped me on the back and was gone. I heard distant gunshots. We wasted no further time loading and launching. The USNS *Swordfish* awaited us.

The *Swordfish*

"We'll be off the coast of Djibouti in a couple of hours. I'll have the ship's commander get you to a dock where two guys from the US Embassy will take you and Master Chief Albright to the local hospital. Or at least what they call a hospital." Captain Garcia LaRouche looked like the Spanish and French heritage I would have expected from his name. A tight crop of black curls covered all but a tonsure of sun burnt skin. An olive complexion framed serious blue eyes. An immaculately pressed uniform exuded confidence and professionalism that left no doubt of his command presence.

The USNS *Swordfish* was an oceanographic and atmospheric research vessel under the command of the US Navy. Operated by a mixed crew of navy and civilian seamen, she would often have military or consulting experts responsible for various research projects on board. She would also frequently have female crewmen as well. Her gleaming white hull and fittings were clean and well maintained. Obviously, her crew took pride in her appearance. I had no idea what her job was or what she was doing in the region. An unarmed, white, research ship didn't seem to be a safe place for science geeks.

"What does that mean? Do they have a hospital or not?" I asked.

"You'll need to determine that for yourself. Half the ground floor serves as a stable for goats. However, it's the best we can do under the circumstances."

"Captain, permission to speak freely?" I asked. He nodded.

"This is a terrible idea. Your master chief needs an orthopedic surgeon, anesthesia, nursing care. I'm not qualified for this type of surgery. I was sent here to take care of a pregnant sailor."

Captain LaRouche said, "I understand your concerns, but this is how it's going to be. I can't pull anchor until my mission is accomplished, and I have no way to get my master chief to another facility. The US Ambassador is expecting you. He arranged for the local hospital to get you in and out without problems. The regional warlords track us when we're in the area. We can't let them know what we're up to."

"What, exactly *are* we up to? Why didn't we put the Master Chief on the helo and get him back to the carrier where they have proper medical facilities?" I asked.

He ignored my questions. "We have a pregnancy problem that we need your advice about. My medic will explain that to you. I also have an injured man whom you are taking ashore to help. In the meantime, I'm working on getting your security clearance so I can answer your questions. Trust me, by tomorrow this will all make sense." With that, LaRouche handed me off to an escort.

On the way to the medical spaces, the escort took me past a doorway with a dimly lit room packed with electronic gear and lab equipment. Curiosity got the better of me, and I walked in before my escort could stop me. At a table, a technician in a white coat was gingerly transferring blue, marble sized globes from an aquarium to a metal camera case. He looked startled when he saw me, but before I could say anything, a marine guard moved in front of me.

"Sorry Sir, off limits," was all he said as he shut the door on me.

"What's up with that? An off-limits lab with the door wide open?" I asked my escort.

"Don't know, Sir. Ever since Captain LaRouche arrived to head up research, whatever the eggheads are doing in there became top secret. Some kind of research on the sea floor and ocean chemistry I think."

On arrival at sickbay, a young female boson's mate sat on the exam table eating from a tray of food. Short, stout, and sporting a butch-waxed flattop, she glanced up at me and went back to stuffing mashed potatoes into her gullet. Her dungaree sleeves, rolled to her elbows, revealed an exceedingly ugly mermaid tattoo.

The female medic for the *Swordfish* explained that her patient had a positive pregnancy test three days ago and had been bleeding heavily. Twenty-four hours earlier, a moderate lump of tissue passed. The bleeding decreased, and she stabilized. Her period was two weeks late. However, since she had been at sea for six months, and well . . . I got the picture.

"What do you think?" I asked the medic.

"My guess is that she spontaneously aborted yesterday."

"Me too," I said. "Too bad I wasn't informed. I could have radioed instructions and prevented this whole evolution."

"I was planning on doing a D&C if it continued. Nobody bothered to tell me you were coming. I could have handled this one myself."

I looked around sickbay, an office with an exam table and a foldout bed. "Do you have an operating room or other medical spaces?"

"What you see is what you get, Doc. I was praying that I wouldn't have to evacuate her uterus on the mess hall dining table, but could have. We were actually headed into Djibouti to drop her with the embassy when I got the call you were less than an hour out. The medic frowned. "And now there's the 'coincidence' that Charlie was injured just before you were dispatched."

"I don't believe in coincidences," I said, "They are just someone else's plans I wasn't privy to." She nodded in agreement. "And I was told you requested the help."

She looked at me and snorted.

"I ain't pregnant," said the boson's mate through a full mouth of mashed potatoes.

The Chief spoke up. "Not anymore, you're not." She ripped the tape off her patient's arm and yanked the IV out.

"Maybe I should examine her and make sure she's okay?"

"The fuck you say," the patient said. "She already done that speculum thing and told me everything's alright. You ain't need to be poking around in there too."

"Get out of here and back to your berth. You're to report back here to me at 0600." With that the patient left, but turned around at the passageway, grabbed the remains on her dinner tray, and departed.

My carrier has an all-male crew, thankfully. Several of the support tenders have mixed crews, and their medical chiefs often consult me regarding contraception. We all make sure condoms are available whenever men go ashore, but seem entirely lost about what to do about a woman on board. Some ships don't even stock oral contraceptives. We can spend a million dollars a day to float a carrier, nuke the Middle East into a glass parking lot, but can't figure out how to get birth control pills into a ship's pharmacy?

"Sorry Sir. You certainly could examine her if you need to, but she's quit bleeding. The vaginal vault is dry; the cervix is closed, and her vital signs have been stable for the last 24 hours."

"No problem, Chief, she's your patient." I asked her, "Do you supply contraception on board?"

She looked at me as if I had two heads. "Sir, you're an officer and a physician. I respect that, but I find that question demeaning and insulting. We're not a regular Navy ship. Every woman on my ship has birth control pills. There's a box of condoms on the quarterdeck at every port, and I'll personally kick any unprotected ass I find. I've been on board for two years, and we've never had a pregnancy or single case of an STD until now."

"My apology, Chief. Don't get your ovaries in a knot, I meant no disrespect. I wish other ships did the same," I said.

"That one," she said indicating the boson's mate "didn't get the memo."

"Uh huh. Believe her?" I asked. "About not being pregnant, I mean? I've heard that before."

"Yeah, actually I do," the medic answered. "She's the second female on this ship in the last three weeks that became pregnant. I checked, and she is current on her prescription. Despite naval policy, she makes her sexual orientation clear. So no, I don't think she could be pregnant."

"You said two," I said. I waited while she poured a cup of coffee.

"I'm number two," she said and waited for my reaction. I knew better. "And it's impossible. I had a tubal ligation years ago and have been celibate for more than a year." She looked to see if I would contradict her. I didn't.

Before I could ask, she said, "And I checked the test kit for a bad batch. Both of us were positive on two different manufacturer tests, and none of the other females I sampled came up positive. The test results are good."

"Okay, I understand. I have no explanation. Do you?"

"No, I was hoping you would. Captain LaRouche is aware and warned me not to tell anyone except you about the pregnancies. In the meantime, you need to get Charlie to the hospital in Djibouti and fix his leg. Unless you want me to call the chow-hall and have them prep the OR?"

Although there was no evidence that his 'fall' had broken his femur or injured the major blood vessels, his wound did require surgical exploration and treatment. I wasn't prepared to do it on the mess hall table with him biting a bullet for anesthesia. He was waiting outside the medical spaces while I checked out the 'pregnancy problem' that supposedly brought me here.

In better lighting, I saw that he was huge—as large as TJ. A bright-red flattop accented sunburned skin and freckles. Thin eyebrows overhung green eyes. The only other feature that stood out from tattered combat fatigues he wore were his hands. He would never be a concert pianist with knuckles covered in thick red fur designed to lay waste to an opponent in a fistfight.

"Best I can do here is clean up your wound, give you IV fluids, and antibiotics," I said.

"Appreciate it," was all he said.

"Morphine?"

"Nope, rather have tequila."

"I'll see what I can do. Looks like I'm taking you to Djibouti in a few hours to repair your leg. Are you ready for that?"

I had un-wrapped the temporary bandage I'd applied in our 'taxi' and took a close look at the wound. It was clearly a gunshot, but through and through. I guessed it to be 12 to 24 hours old. No signs of infection and there wasn't any bone jutting out. There was coagulated blood and tissue protruding out the back of the wound that I took care not to disturb. I started an IV with antibiotics, but again, he declined pain meds.

"You'll do just fine, Bones. I don't need anyone else. You were the closest doctor we could find." With that, he closed his eyes and ended the conversation.

You were the closest doctor we could find? You knew I was coming before I did. This isn't about a pregnant sailor, is it? It's about you.

Back on deck, I said to Captain LaRouche, "You and I both know the Master Chief didn't fall. That's a gunshot wound. I appreciate that you've made arrangements for us to get into a hospital where I can take care of him, but again, I'll ask you what the hell is actually going on here?"

LaRouche looked down at his hands and spit over the rail into the muddy sea while he contemplated his answer. Essence of cadaver wafted past my nose from somewhere below. I hoped it was only a dead fish floating past, not an omen.

"Doc," he said turning his cold blue eyes on me, "as far as you're concerned, we are a research oceanographic vessel. My current mission is to collect data on the sea floor off the coast of Somalia. The Master Chief operated a post in the hills to monitor electronic equipment we use to locate and correlate that data. He had an accident, and we are extremely lucky you came along at the right time."

"But—" I didn't like where this was going.

Just then, TJ came through a hatch and joined us. He nodded at LaRouche, who continued, "That's all you need to know, and that is your cover story if anyone asks while you are ashore. You and Petty Officer Vignalli are to remain among the embassy people at all times until your return. Lieutenant Commander Justis is your liaison while you're there. Intel has updated him on the situation and operational parameters. I know you outrank him, but since he's a line officer and you're medical corps, he's in command from this point on."

A sailor approached and snapped to attention. He handed LaRouche a folded note, saluted, and retreated inside. I waited while he perused the message, trying to feel any breeze as we moved through a still, humid night. Not even the forward motion of the ship created enough wind to offset the sticky grime gluing my uniform to my body. A shower was a definite must in my near future.

"Okay," LaRouche said folding the note and sticking it into his pocket, "there will be an OR awaiting you. As soon as you're done, we'll get everyone back to the embassy where the Master Chief can recover. We'll plan an extraction in 24 hours."

"Wait a minute, Sir. There must be a better solution. I don't think—"

He cut me off with a dismissive wave. "There isn't. As I've explained to you, I have no way to get him to any other facility, and we can't leave until our mission is completed. Secondly, as far as anyone is concerned, your team is not even in this hellhole country. There has been no formal clearance with the local government. You're not here, never were here, and if asked, are staff working for the embassy."

"Finally, nobody, I repeat, *nobody*, can know that the Master Chief is there. And you cannot risk using drugs that could cloud his mind or judgment, in case he might say something certain people should not hear."

He continued without blinking. "Doc, you're a smart guy. I could draw you a picture, but you don't have the security clearance to get the answers you seek. We're in a bind here. You've been to trauma school; you can handle this. The Master Chief knows the score and needs your help. Now I would suggest that you get below, grab a shower, some chow, and a couple of hours in the rack. We'll be dropping you off about an hour before dawn." He turned and headed for the bridge. He stopped and turned back to me. "Do you play poker, Doc? We have a friendly game later." With that, he disappeared through a hatch. I should have just handed over my wallet.

"Here, take these." TJ handed me a green ID card and a capsule. "No uniforms, no military ID. These are your papers showing that you're an employee of the Djibouti Embassy. The ID card had my photo and a diplomatic stamp.

"So, is this my cyanide capsule, in case I get caught? You know I'll crack as soon as they hook those jumper cables to my nuts."

"Bite down and you'll taste something bitter, but it'll be over in a minute or less."

"Now you're *really* creeping me out. This James Bond shit is *way* out of my league."

TJ's grin almost caused him to drop his ever-present cigar. "It's an anti-malarial capsule, numb nuts. We didn't have time to do the entire two-week series, but we'll be back 'fore the 'sketers get ya. So let's go. You have an OR start for 6 AM, and I have an 8 AM tee-time with the US Ambassador to Djibouti."

Reality check here. I'm on a 'research' ship with a wounded 'electrician' going undercover into a foreign country, to do surgery I'm not qualified for, in a strange hospital with god-knows-what equipment, and we're not sticking around long enough to be discovered. Buckle-up Dorothy—this sure as hell ain't Kansas.

Djibouti Royal Hospital

Just before dawn, and after I had been relieved of my cash supply playing poker, the ship's launch deposited us on a decrepit pier that reeked of dead fish and petroleum oil. To the east, an anemic sky announced the dawn. Two unidentified men in black suits moved Vignalli, the Master Chief and me into an antique rattletrap ambulance and sped across town. Neither escort spoke the entire trip, even when I asked them why they wore sunglasses at night. TJ made his own way to the embassy without us.

"How ya doing, Master Chief?" I asked. His leg wound looked good before we left the *Swordfish*, but he still refused any pain meds other than Tylenol.

"Charlie." He said. "Call me Charlie while we're here. I'm not a Master Chief, just a worker from the embassy who had an accident. I realize that you have no idea what's going on, and I apologize, but nobody can know that any of us are here." His tone allowed no argument or misunderstanding.

"I'm not here because of a pregnancy on the *Swordfish*, am I?"

"What pregnancy? Of course not, you're here because I need you. Lucky you arrived when you did." He didn't elaborate.

26

"Charlie, you're right. I don't know what the hell is happening. I can live with that for now, but someday you'll owe me an explanation. Until then, I'll do whatever I can for your leg—but cut the bullshit. We both know that this is a gunshot wound. I need to explore it, clean it out, and patch you up. I'll be straight with you—I'm way, way out of my league here, and frankly, scared shitless."

"Bedside manner could use a little fine tuning, Doc."

"I'm just being straight with you. The last gunshot wound I treated was on a goat at trauma school in San Antonio, Texas. My patient ended up as stew that evening. Now, I need some straight answers."

He nodded.

"Where is the bullet? I couldn't get x-rays on the *Swordfish,* and if you are carrying a slug in your leg, it will change everything. LaRouche tells me you can't undergo general anesthesia, and that's not for medical reasons. My new friends in black up there," I nodded toward the two guys in the front, "are assigned to keep an eye on things. I get that, but there is only so much I can do using a spinal instead of putting you under general anesthesia—which LaRouche won't allow me to do."

"Understood." He looked me directly in the eye. "Do what you need to do, I'll be okay. The bullet went clean through, and I suspect it's still in the chest of a Somali rebel I tackled when the fun started. There was only one shot fired—I got a hole in my leg, and he's dead. The math is simple."

"Okay, that helps. I did a blood count on you, and you're a few cans short of a six-pack. If you lose any more blood during surgery, I'll need to transfuse you."

"No way in hell are you giving me blood from *this* blood bank. This part of the globe is dying of AIDS, and I have other plans. As far as you're concerned, I just became a Jehovah's Witness. I am not, repeat not, getting a transfusion. We wait until I'm back on board your carrier, or I use your blood. We clear on that?"

"No, we're not clear on that. You bleed out on me, and I'm giving you blood—period. You're not dying on my watch."

Charlie reached over the seat and tapped one of the Men in Black on the shoulder. "Shoot him if he tries to give me blood." Man in Black nodded. The hair on my neck stood up. Charlie looked at me, grinned, and winked.

"No anesthesia, no blood, no surgical staff, no official ID, nobody knows I'm even here—that about sum up this boondoggle? I might as well do this procedure with both arms in casts."

"That can be arranged," a Man in Black muttered. I remained silent the rest of our journey.

As the sun bled into a dull sky, we arrived at the Djibouti Royal Hospital. A short man in a white coat, chattering in French, ran out to greet us, waving his arms. Two goats looked out a first floor, open window. White Coat had a brief, heated conversation with a Man in Black who opened his coat, put one hand on a huge gun, and extracted an envelope with the other. The envelope quickly disappeared into White Coat's pocket. White Coat looked around and waved us into the facility.

I took Charlie to the OR, or at least what passed as an OR; a small room with gray, plaster walls. The door into the room was missing. In the center was a metal table with a dingy sheet covering it. White porcelain cabinets with large red crosses lined one wall. A few supplies sat behind the glass doors of those cabinets. The surgical lighting consisted of a gooseneck lamp with a 100-watt bulb.

There was an anesthesia machine and portable x-ray in the corner. The anesthesia machine was broken; the tubes and hoses rotted away.

Normally, when I enter an OR there is a team of specialists to assist; everything is sterile and in duplicate. Lab, blood bank, radiology, and pathology are just minutes away if I need them. The room smells like it looks, clean and fresh.

There was nobody waiting this morning. White Coat pointed the way for the five of us: Charlie, Petty Officer Vignalli, the two Men in Black, and me; then disappeared. The entire building smelled like a barnyard. Suddenly, operating on the mess hall table on the *Swordfish* didn't seem like such a terrible idea.

I turned to the Men in Black. "Well, don't just stand there, roll the gurney over here, and help get him on the table." They looked at each other, back at me, at the gurney with Charlie, and shrugged. But, they did manage to get him on the operating room table.

"Which one of you is going to be my surgical assistant?" I asked the Men in Black. Again, they looked at each other and back at me.

"He is," one answered, pointing at Petty Officer Vignalli. "We have orders to protect the Master Chief, not play Nurse Nancy."

Ten minutes later, we had prepared everything, and Petty Officer Vignalli had even figured out how to get an x-ray of the leg. The film he located was several years outdated and foggy, but I could see that there were no broken bones, no bullets, no shrapnel, and nobody left on base.

"Remind me to sign off on your Boy Scout x-ray badge when we get home," I told him.

"Okay Charlie, here we go." I rolled him onto his side and scrubbed his back with Betadine antiseptic. I located the space between his lower lumbar vertebrae and with shaking hands, inserted a needle into his spinal canal. Clear fluid dripping out the end told me I had found my target. I injected anesthetic, and we rolled him onto his back. Within a few minutes, Charlie couldn't feel anything from the waist down.

I got to work. I scrubbed, flushed, probed, debrided dead tissue, stitched up what needed stitching and generally made a mess of the table and floor with sterile fluids and antiseptic cleansers. Oh well, housekeeping could clean up next month when they finish mucking the stalls.

"I'm done here Charlie. You're one lucky man. Bullet went clean through and missed everything. You'll be up and around soon, but you'll need to be seen by an orthopedic surgeon as soon as possible." He nodded. "And I'm holding off transfusing you. We didn't lose any blood, and I can't treat myself if they shoot me." I looked at the Men in Black.

Before they could respond, a goat bleated and wandered into the room. LaRouche hadn't been kidding about this place.

"Get that thing out of here before he infects my patient." With that, a Man in Black pulled a large handgun from under his coat and took aim.

"Don't you dare," I screamed at him. He looked to his partner who nodded. They both looked at me.

"Okay." He holstered his sidearm and pushed the goat out of the door.

"Part of their indoctrination," said Charlie pointing his chin toward the pair, "is to have their sense of humor surgically altered. It appears the operation was a success."

An hour after surgery, we were back in the antique ambulance stirring up clouds of dust and flies as we headed to the embassy. I decided that a hurried post-op journey was preferable to risking infection from goat feces.

The Streets of Djibouti

I watched out the ambulance window as downtown Djibouti awoke. Air filled with dust and disease greeted those beginning to stir. One of the poorest countries in the region, it was a refugee camp for the overflow of anguish from Ethiopia and Somalia. The French, the Russians, the British, and the Americans all tried and failed to help. All attempts to modernize the country disintegrated in rusty heaps in the desert. Goats, camels, khat, and refugees are the main industry.

LaRouche had warned me about the poverty, but the streets and doorways of the city teeming with the homeless and hopeless overwhelmed me. Dark faces with dead eyes and dying souls watched me pass. Rags covered skin stretched thin over bones. Many of the bodies scattered in whatever shelter they could find would not awaken this morning. Perhaps they were the fortunate.

An emaciated woman in a doorway holding a naked infant stretched out a hand to another walking skeleton. Then she flopped against the wall and dropped her head onto her chest. The infant listlessly attempted to find a nipple, gave up, and accepted the inevitable. Only months old, this child knew death's call. Crusted eyes didn't blink as flies landed on them.

Several children ran alongside pounding against the ambulance windows, but they lacked the energy to pursue me. Their eyes mimicked their empty hands stretched out for something, anything. We drove past a communal well with people lined up waiting to fill pots, bottles or anything they could find with enough water to survive another day. Even with the windows up, the stench of decay, death, and despair permeated my conscience. An angry sun cooked the metal of our vehicle adding to the misery.

The world forgot these people. Relegated to the dung heap of civilization, they awaited certain death. Until then, they wandered aimlessly, all remnants of hope fading.

Hawkeye Pierce, my hero from *M*A*S*H*, whispers one-liners to me that I parrot when stressed. Black humor is my survival technique against the horrors of the world. Today, no snappy repartee quelled the grief. The desolation left my heart empty, feeling ashamed to be alive, fed, and knowing I am no more or less human than those staring back. The white man's attitude that they are only Africans, only black, only poor, stung me.

"How do you live with this every day?" I asked no one in particular.

A Man in Black said, "Live with what?" Without slowing, he honked at a man with a makeshift crutch hobbling across the street in front of us. The skin on his swollen legs was cracked and exuded purulence. My mind recalled pictures from a tropical disease seminar I once attended. I was shocked to realize he had elephantiasis, something unheard of anywhere else in the world.

I turned away from the window the remainder of the trip. I could not watch the parade of walking dead without asking if there really was a Loving God—and where was She?

TJ waited inside the embassy compound when we arrived. He looked dapper as ever, a nine-iron over his shoulder, and sweat dripping from his face.

As I helped Charlie's gurney out of the ambulance, I looked at the eight-foot mud walls topped by barbed wire. Two gardeners had automatic weapons strapped across their backs. They both stopped raking as we entered and watched us closely. One walked over and looked inside the ambulance.

"Go well?" asked TJ. I shrugged and looked away, embarrassed by my emotions and the tears threatening to overflow.

I tucked Charlie into a bedroom, feeling a disconnect between the clean linen and what I had just seen. His spinal was wearing off, and he looked pale and sweaty, pain obvious in his eyes. I hung another IV with antibiotics and was drawing up morphine into a syringe when one of the Men in Black put his hand on my arm. He just shook his head.

"Listen, I've had it with you spooks and this cloak-and-dagger crap. I know you're just doing your job, but this is *my* patient, and he needs pain medication. If he tells me who really killed JFK or where they moved the Roswell aliens, I promise to keep it safe. In the meantime, *back off*, and let me do my job." I quivered with anger—anger at them for doing their job; anger at a world that turned away from this place; anger at the arrogance that allowed this to exist.

"What did you say about Roswell?" This was the first time I'd heard this man's helium voice, and I couldn't blame him for keeping his mouth shut and letting his partner be the spokesman. He sounded like Alvin the Chipmunk, but when he took off the shades, his dull black eyes didn't joke.

"Thanks for doing such a great job on me, Doc," Charlie said, interrupting. "I know we put you in a tight box, and I won't forget this."

"Aw shucks, partner," I twanged, "'twern't nothin'." Inside I knew better. I'd pulled off a minor miracle in a place devoid of miracles, and Charlie was lucky. His recovery was still in jeopardy, however.

"It was, and I appreciate it—and thank you, I'll take something stronger than Tylenol. You weren't the only one scared shitless today." He relaxed as the morphine took effect. His lids drooped. "Tweedle Dee and Tweedle Dum there," nodding toward the door, "will make sure I don't blab any state secrets. And there *was* someone on the grassy knoll. We think it was Marilyn Monroe's cousin." He eyes closed as his breathing slowed.

"And you shouldn't talk about Roswell . . . they're kinda touchy . . . seriously . . ." He drifted off.

Kelly's World-Famous Bar and Grill

"Welcome to Kelly's, Djibouti's World-Famous Irish Bar and Grill."

Ambassador Dweck, decked out in a crisp, long-sleeved white shirt and pink polka-dot tie that accented his pathetic comb-over, made a grandiose wave. That activity loosened his coif, allowing a few straggling hairs to stick to his beefy, acne scarred forehead. The flourish finished with a self-conscious patting of the renegade hairs back into position. He then straightened the bow tie, a pocket protector, and his posture. Both Men in Black hovered nearby.

"I thought you were taking us to the Hilton for dinner?" I asked.

"You'll enjoy this more," said Dweck.

After walking through steamy back streets, heat, stink, and disreputable bazaars, I stood on what would be an alley anywhere else in the world. This was the main street, downtown Djibouti. A shallow ditch along one side, filled with something foul, served as the city sewer. A mangy dog and a small boy both contributed bodily fluids into the mix. I made a mental note not to step on wet spots.

I looked at Dweck's recommended restaurant. A wide expanse of weather-beaten boards defined a wall with two openings, one at each end. Several boards hung onto their neighbors by sheer determination. Hand painted in flaking blue paint, the single word 'Kelly' advertised our destination. Hanging from a rusty iron pipe over one door, a wooden sign displayed the fish sign—one of those Christian symbols with Darwin's legs. Over the other, the sign resembled Rudolph the Red Nose Reindeer on a bad antler day. Grungy tarps limply covered both doors.

"So," Ambassador Dweck asked, "would you like to have fish or goat for dinner?" I must have looked blank because he continued, "Oh . . . if you want fish for dinner you go through that door," pointing to the loaves and fishes sign, "and if you want the goat, you go there," pointing at Rudolph.

A car backfired, and both Men in Black grabbed for the lumps under their coats, automatically looking opposite directions down the street. Dweck looked like he released a load of trouser chili.

The weather had changed from hot, hot, and dry, to hot, hot, and muggy. The sky reflected the pallor of a medical school cadaver. Distant rumbles and a faint tinge of ozone that precedes lightning promised atmospheric drama later in the evening.

"I guess that means filet mignon is out of the question?" asked TJ, who looked like a wilted version of someone rich and famous.

I had ditched the Okie from Fenokee gardener look. LaRouche had sent me ashore in jeans and a Hawaiian shirt sporting half-naked hula girls and palm trees. Vignalli wore cutoffs and a 'Kiss Me—I'm Irish' tee-shirt. The Men in Black looked like a parody of *The Blues Brothers* with sunglasses. A small crowd of kaftan-robed locals lingered at a distance, pointing and whispering. I didn't see automatic weapons, but a concealed scimitar wasn't out of the question. I tried my killer smile and friendly wave. One of them pulled aside his robe to display his gun and smiled back. He needed dental work and an attitude adjustment. He wasn't recruiting for the local Rotary Club.

"I'll try the fresh pacific salmon," said TJ, walking through the designated door. One Man in Black followed.

"Hmm, goat tartar sounds appetizing to me. Hope it's the one that contaminated my operating room this morning," I said, looking at the other Man in Black, my designated bodyguard. I walked through the Rudolph door.

"Damn, I hate goat," he complained.

I would call Kelly's Bar and Grill understated if I wanted to sound cultured. It was a shack with a hard-packed dirt floor extension of the street outside. Ambient mood lighting came from kerosene lamps hanging from the rafters. In the center of the floor sat a stout mud oven with a flat iron disk perched on top. Oily smoke filled the room. At one end of this one star eatery stood a makeshift bar of splintered and dilapidated wood. A bucket, tin cans, and dusty green bottles completed the decor.

Hmm. No electricity or folk group playing lively Celtic tunes from the non-existent bandstand. I hope the bucket on the bar doesn't represent the men's room. Or the dishwasher.

Both TJ's fish group and my goat group convened in the middle of the single open space, and admired the establishment. Dirty rugs littered the floor. Salvation Army card tables graced the center of the space—one on each side of the oven. A third table, occupied by a group of locals eating with their heads down, sat in a far corner. One of the grizzled men turned contemptuous eyes on me, spat on the floor, and went back to his meal.

The heat and smoke from the wood burning in the oven mingled fragrantly with a barbeque aroma, reminding me I was famished. I hoped they used clean water and maybe even soap on the dishes. I didn't need dysentery to complete this holiday adventure. I discovered I needn't worry—Kelly's World-Famous Bar and Grill doesn't have plates.

"The saints be praised. It's the leprechaun with his two wraiths come to visit me poor establishment, and by the luck o' the Irish, he brings me some fine gentlemen who appear able to pay the bill this time." A female voice oozing Irish green filled the room.

Kelly was a spectacular surprise in what many would consider a hemorrhoid on the ass-end of the world. Tall and lank, decked out in a black abaya and headscarf, she flowed across the room. Deep green eyes twinkled from a face devoid of make-up. I could see wisps of auburn hair peaking around her head cover. Her robe did nothing to disguise a rack to rival Rudolph's. Vignalli grunted. I turned to him and said, "I know you've been on a ship for months, but try not to drool on the floor. And take your hands out of your pockets." We all stood mesmerized.

"What? You've all been humping camels and never seen a beautiful lassie before?" Her brogue spoke of mist on Irish meadows.

"You and the ragheads are all the same," Kelly said. "You come to the finest Irish pub on the continent, and all you can do is stare at my tits?" She gave them a boost and winked. One of her front teeth elbowed the other, adding to her mystique.

"Yo, Mohammad," she spoke to her other patrons in a quiet, civil voice. "We have real customers now, so you're done eating. You and those flea-bitten refugees get the hell out of here before I call your wives and tell them you caught a disease from my lassies." She walked over, wrapped Kraft paper around their food, pulled the card table away, and hustled them out of the door.

"Next time leave a tip, ya cheap barsturds, or St Paddy hisself will send you some snakes," she said to their departing bodies. She smiled, spit on the floor, and flipped them the bird as they departed.

"Gentlemen," She spun on us, dropping the Irish brogue. "Welcome to Kelly's. We have your reservation at our finest table." She set the card tables down in front of us and arranged enough chairs to sit. "Let me put up the closed sign to keep the riff-raff out, then we'll do a jig and kiss some blarney."

She pulled the thick, dusty tarps over the doors and yelled something into the street. As she turned back to our table, a dark, swarthy male pulled the curtain aside and started to walk in.

"Yo! Sheet head! We're closed! Or are you too illiterate to read the sign? But, of course, you are. I'd say you got the IQ of your camel, but that's an insult to such a fine animal. So please take your stinking ass out of my outstanding establishment and go blow up a car somewhere. But, try not to burn your lips on the tailpipe this time." She said all this in a soft, gentle voice, smiling brightly at him as she gently put her arm around his shoulders and ushered him out. She gave him a gentle, departing kiss on the cheek. He smiled, looked confused, and left without incident. Then, she spat on the floor.

She turned to Ambassador Dweck. "How do you say 'camel fucker' in Farsi or whatever these assholes speak in this shithole?"

"Now Kelly," Dweck began, raising his hands in a placating fashion.

"Don't 'now Kelly' me. You promised I'd be out of here in one year. That was two years ago. You make Washington get Debra and me out of here, or I swear to the goat-god these fuckers worship, I will pull that bow tie so fucking tight your eyes will bulge and your nuts will shrivel. Got it?" The lasers she shot from her green eyes should have melted his head.

"Now, now, Kelly, calm down a minute and let me introduce you to Dr. Matthews, Lieutenant Commander Justis, and Petty Officer Vignalli."

She turned the emeralds on me. "You a real doctor? Sure as my beloved Ireland is green," the brogue returned, "we need an actual doctor here, not that jerk-off who works for the Embassy," she turned back on Dweck, brogue gone, "and wants me to undress just to take my temperature."

I stepped forward and held out my hand. "Pleased to meet you, Ma'am."

Toto, fasten your seat belt—it's going to get rough in OZ.

"I ain't a Ma'am, I'm just Kelly." She stuck her hand out to me. Her grip left an indentation. She smelled exotic, or maybe that was the smoky oven?

"Well, Dr. Matthews, so long as you're here, I need to have a real doctor check something for me. Hold on." She unwrapped her head dressing and shook out a Caribbean sunset of curls.

"I hate this black robe crap, but if I don't play the game and wear this outfit, they'll have some fucking Mullah beat me with a stick. But, that would be the last hard thing he ever holds in his hand." She reached down and pulled the robe over her head in one swift motion. I heard Vignalli gasp.

"Ah," she said, "that's much better." She stretched her arms over her head displaying a pair of shorts holstering athletic legs. Barely secured in a thin white halter-top were the breasts she was certain were the center of attention in her establishment, if not the universe. Vignalli, I was sure, agreed.

She took my hand again and aimed those emerald eyes directly at me, the snake hypnotizing the mouse. Slowly, she pulled me closer to her and slid my hand under the halter-top and onto a breast.

"I have a lump. Can you feel it? Right about there," she said, pressing my hand tighter while staring at Dweck.

"Uh . . . Uh . . . Uh," was the best I could muster to counter her onslaught. I looked at TJ for a rescue, and all he could do was wiggle his cigar. "I'm not sure, but . . . but . . . I could arrange an appointment for you at the embassy for evaluation."

She leaned into me and whispered into my ear, "Just nod, look concerned, and say there might be a lump. I'll make it worth your while." She turned to Dweck. "I do have a lump. I'm gonna die, and you'll be responsible."

"Uh," I started to say. *Kansas, Toto? Hell, I fell down the damn rabbit hole—without a flashlight.*

"Kelly, damn it," Dweck interrupted, "you don't have a lump, an infection, an allergy, or any other medical reason to apply for a transfer, so I wish you'd give it up and quit pestering the good doctor. Besides, he's married." He looked at me and shrugged.

"Can't blame a girl for trying," Kelly said as she slapped my hand away. "Get your hands off me, pervert." Then, she winked one of those incredible eyes, gave a little wiggle, and roared with laughter as she mussed Dweck's comb-over into disarray.

"So, ladies, what'll it be tonight? Fish? The goat died last week and was getting pretty ripe, so he's not on tonight's menu." She stuck two fingers between her teeth and whistled.

As if by magic, a small boy, no older than twelve, materialized from behind the bar carrying a tray of pale fish. With skilled movements, he gutted and filleted the fish, throwing them on the iron platform. Plumes of greasy smoke roiled from the leftover fish guts thrown into the flames. He displayed a grin of rotten teeth as the fish began to sizzle.

"Water?" he asked, pointing at us.

"Of course," Kelly responded, "and use the bottles with seals—not the ones we filled from the faucet. Okay?" As an afterthought, she called after him, "And bring a case of Guinness."

"Yes, Kelly," and off he ran, returning minutes later with a tray of African Springs Water; seals intact as promised. I said a small thanks to Pooh, the patron saint of diarrhea. I eyed the Guinness. It was years since my last drink, but . . .

A loud banging against the walls shook lanterns and loosened dust. "Anybody home?" A voice thundered. "Got room for more hungry men?" LaRouche pushed through the curtain into the room.

"Oh my God, it's the Djibouti Cutie," shrieked Kelly, as she ran over, grabbed him by the collar, and dragged him to the table. She kicked a chair behind him, pushed him down, and straddled his lap. Being almost a foot taller than LaRouche, she buried his nose mid chest before he could protest. She then planted a big, wet, noisy kiss right in the middle of his bald spot, causing it, and most of the rest of him, to blush beet-red.

"Mrrruph, mrrrupph, urrrghh." Kelly wiggled some more, planted another wet one on LaRouche's forehead, and finally let him up for air.

"Where the hell have you been all these months, leaving me to rot while you're off sailing around the world? I missed you, you cutie, you." Before he had a chance to resist, she pulled him into another smothering hug. Vignalli whimpered.

"Give him some air, woman. You're in the land of Allah and should show proper respect for men, you shameless hussy." We all turned, and to my continuing surprise, there stood the Sultan, in a tank top, baggy shorts, and combat boots. His beard and turban were gone, and he wore a mop of dark curly hair hanging below his ears. I did a double take to be sure it was him.

"Sammy," Kelly shouted, "more fish! And break out another case of Guinness." And quick as that he had more fish baking and glasses of thick, warm, creamy Guinness in front of us.

I could almost feel the silky smoothness trickling down my throat and warming my belly. But, I could also taste the bitterness of the second, third, fourth, and tenth one along with the self–loathing tomorrow morning. *No thanks.* It had been years since my last drink, but I could still hear the foam on the glass calling seductively to me. *But hell, I could probably have one or two and be okay, couldn't I? I'd be back on board soon with nothing to drink or tempt me. Or back into the throws of incomprehensible demoralization?*

TJ cleared his throat, looked at me and then at the Guinness. TJ knew of my battle with alcohol, and that was all it took. With a sigh of longing, I pushed the glass away and took a swallow of flat African Springs. I was glad TJ was with us. That was too close, and would have been too easy to tell myself the "big lie"—I can have just one this time.

No! I can't.

"Sultani, I heard you were killed during the raid in Somalia." Kelly sprang off LaRouche's lap and hugged him. "Tell me of all your adventures. I'm bored spit-less, and our ambassador here refuses to fire me, so I can get an assignment somewhere else."

He reached across the card table and shook my hand. "Master Chief Larry Sultani, USN, at your service, Sir. Friends call me the Sultan. Sorry we didn't have much time last night to become acquainted, but Charlie and I kinda had our hands full. He's out in my love-mobile resting before we head for the airport. He's stoned on something you gave him, muttering about Marilyn Monroe and aliens." He sat down and nodded to the ambassador. A silent message passed between them.

Has it just been a day since I ran through the desert with a wounded man chased by armed bandits? Who the hell is this guy? How did I know to nickname him the Sultan? Why is LaRouche here? And just who is Master Chief Charlie Albright? And Kelly? My head swam.

"So is anybody going to tell me what is going on here?" I looked at Dweck, who was busy examining his fingernails and avoiding Kelly's stare. "And why is Charlie here? He should be recovering at the embassy."

"Bullshit. I'll waste time recovering when we get back to your ship," Charlie said, causing all of us to turn towards the door as he limped in on a set of crutches.

"You tear open my stitches, and I'm gonna be really pissed at you," I said getting up and starting toward him.

"Relax Doc, I'm fine." He refused my help, hobbled over, took a seat, and lifted his injured leg onto the corner of the table. "Neither of us wants to go back to the magnificent Djibouti Goat Hospital, so I'll be careful. Besides, we've only got two hours to get on a plane to your ship, so coming here was the best plan."

Kelly, not to lose control of conversation in her establishment, said, "So, this is the world-famous carrot-topped master spy who single handedly took out an entire legion of sun crazed Somali warlords? I'm Kelly." She stuck out her hand. "I'm easy, work cheap, and ready to join you on your next adventure—soon as the master here sets this poor slave free." Again, she scalded Dweck with her look. "So whadda ya say, sailor? Take me to the Kasbah and we'll do it all." She reached over and ran her long fingers across his cheek.

Charlie shook his head. "You hated the Kasbah. You also hated Morocco, Egypt, and everywhere else we've been together. Remember? Last time we were in Afghanistan, I had to rescue the local gendarmes from you."

Charlie adjusted his injured leg. "So, don't come whining to me about rescuing you again. That's *way* above *my* pay grade."

"Well, can you stick around awhile? At least *you* don't smell like a camel." Then her voice took on a serious tone. Her change in mood immediately chilled the room. "I'd heard that you and Sultani took some heat in the hills, and I was afraid you'd been killed. What happened up there last week? Why didn't you report in to me? Did you guys finally track him down and kill that asshole?" The room went silent.

"*Kelly*," Dweck interrupted, sitting up abruptly and scowling at her, "not everyone here is cleared for this." He tipped his chin toward Vignalli. She nodded in understanding and whistled again.

"Debra, get that gorgeous butt of yours out here. I got an assignment for you," Kelly shouted toward the rear wall. Suddenly, a petite blonde appeared from behind the bar.

Dressed in shorts and a baggy sweater, she looked to be a teenager, but her eyes carried more age than her lithe body.

"What's up, Kel?" she asked.

"Would you take our friend here," indicating Vignalli, "and introduce him to the House of the Seven Virgins? Give us an hour or so. Make sure he gets some food, and an adventure he won't ever forget. Okay, Sweetie?"

"Gottcha." She took Vignalli's hand. "Let me show you what paradise will be like—and you don't even have to be a martyr." With that, Debra led Vignalli out the back like a lamb to the slaughter.

"Make that 30 minutes. We need to leave soon; it may not be safe here," said Dweck.

Before I could question this, Sammy materialized and flung slabs of cooked fish on brown kraft paper in front of us. My mouth had a Pavlovian response to the smell. Unleavened bread and honey followed. I waited for silverware and a napkin. I must have looked stupid because Sammy pantomimed picking up a piece of fish with his fingers and stuffing it into his mouth. *Ah ha, finger food.* I stuffed a wad into my craw. The fish fell apart, dissolved, and slid down my gullet faster than a Big Mac on greased skids. *OHMYGOD. Orgasmic.*

Nobody spoke in the microseconds it took us to devour the meal, and then TJ let loose an enormous, wet belch. Before I could give him my high society shocked look, Charlie belched, followed a moment later by Dweck, Sultani, and both Men in Black. They all looked at me expectantly.

"What?" I asked.

TJ leaned in and whispered, "Bones, a belch is considered a compliment to the host on the quality of the food."

"Oh, okay," and I produced a passable compliment for those concerned. "So, if the meal was bad am I supposed to fart?" I asked.

Deadpan, TJ answered, "No—that indicates you are in love with the host's dog and want to arrange a marriage, or that you're just an uncouth infidel."

The Ambassador settled back, wiped the comb-over into relative order, and nodded to his guards. Like trained

Dobermans, they stood and took positions beside both doors.

"Commander, we need your help," Dweck began. The demeanor around the table changed subtly, and I realized that, despite his humpty dumpty appearance, he was The Man in Command.

"I contacted Washington after you arrived and updated your security clearance for what I need to tell you." He paused. "Quite a résumé you have. Finished college a year early, graduated medical school, a black belt, navy small-arms pistol championship, several medals . . ."

I was embarrassed as he recited the litany. "Yeah, and Her Majesty called last week to see if I would be 008."

"You were an excellent choice for this mission it seems."

Excellent choice? I've been set up.

I looked at TJ, who was busy examining his cigar.

Dweck continued, "A while back, we set up operations in Djibouti to follow the activities of certain terrorists groups in Somalia. I'm sure you figured out that Charlie and Sultani weren't doing scientific studies in the hills." He paused, straightened his bow tie, and looked at LaRouche. "Although the *Swordfish* and her crew are doing legitimate oceanographic surveys and research—"

"Alien hunting is what I was told," I said, trying to be clever.

"What makes you say that?" he asked, frowning at Charlie. An unspoken volume registered in that frown.

"Oh, the Master Chief here said it was Marilyn Monroe's cousin who shot JFK from the grassy knoll, and that I shouldn't talk about Roswell or aliens around you—but he was under the influence." LaRouche and Dweck both looked at a Man in Black, who shrugged defensively.

"Well, you got us," LaRouche continued. "We're on a top-secret mission to find the other three Roswell craft that we believe crashed into the oceans. In fact, part of your mission is to transport valuable alien artifacts to the carrier where they will be couriered to secret labs stateside for analysis." The Ambassador just nodded in agreement. I sensed everyone in the room looking at me.

I looked at TJ. "I know you got some scheme cooking to make money on how dumb I can be, but it won't work this time." I snorted. "Aliens, my educated ass."

LaRouche dismissed the alien theory as quickly as it came up. "Seriously, you *will* be carrying some research data and oceanographic samples back, along with one Machmuud Majeta Muhammad Alzera."

TJ again leaned in and said, "Bones, you already know that you're not here by accident." His tone turned serious. "A minor medical emergency on the *Swordfish* was a convenience, so we'd have a cover story—, but we would have brought you here regardless. Alzera is extremely dangerous, and his people put everyone involved in this mission in harm's way. We need to get this Alzera character out of here immediately, and he may not live long enough to debrief. You were the closest physician with any surgical training we could shanghai; you can defend yourself if needed and are our best chance to save him. And fortunately for Charlie, you could patch him up too." He nodded at Charlie.

I realized all eyes were on me, and they weren't kidding. "So," I sobered, "who is this guy and what am I supposed to do with him?"

Dweck took up the story. "He's a major Somali warlord whom we know has been involved in several local terrorist attacks. He's been hiding in the hills for the past three years, but coming to Kelly's the past month. Kelly has a tape of him bragging about an upcoming US operation he calls Blue Death, and I made the decision to take him out. Unfortunately, he escaped. We tracked him to the border where we tried to capture him a couple of days ago."

"And that's where Charlie 'fell down'?" I asked, cricking my fingers as a quote sign.

"They took a number of casualties too," Sultani said. "We tracked him for two days and almost got the asshole out, but when Charlie took a hit, I had to get us out of there. Fortunately, you just happened to be nearby to pick us up."

"Fortunately? *Bullshit.*" I snorted my disbelief.

Un-phased, Sultani continued, "I went back this morning and extracted Alzera. His people cut off his hand and left him for dead."

"Cut off his hand? What? He got caught masturbating?" I asked. I'd heard about such things but couldn't imagine it in today's world. But hey, these same religious fanatics stone women to death for adultery or being a rape victim. An exposed ankle is worth fifty lashes.

"They consider him a traitor who stole their honor and sold their secrets to me," said Kelly. "The traditional penalty for theft is . . ." She didn't need to finish.

"And just how do you fit into all this?" I asked.

I must have looked bewildered because she went on to explain that she runs "the greatest little whorehouse in Djibouti" as a covert arm of the CIA. Kelly's House of the Seven Virgins was one of those dirty little secrets everyone knows about, but doesn't discuss in polite company. The goal is to get information any way they can. They plant tracking devices, make videos, and spike wine with methylene blue to cause the unwary to piss bright blue for days. Tricky Dick Nixon would have been thrilled with such tactics.

"So, you have seven hookers working here?" I asked.

"Nah, just Debra and me. She wears different wigs to confuse them. We also spike the booze; that helps." She smiled. "This may look like an epicurean oasis in hell, but you'd be surprised how many of these towel-heads . . ."

"*Kelly. Please,*" Dweck broke in. "The local Islamic community is not all evil and shouldn't be called that."

"You're right," she said sarcastically, "they don't wear towels on their filthy hair. And it's not a rag. It's a tiny sheet. And if you had to put up with their holier-than-thou attitude and abuse of women in public—then watch them sneak in here at night to drink alcohol and fuck, you'd think differently about them too."

Kelly took a deep breath and continued, "I set this up to do surveillance and collect critical intelligence using sex and booze. It's now been two years, and frankly, we've done our part for God and Country. We have the goods on Alzera and his ilk. We identified a couple dozen other targets, and we turned over the photos and tapes to *Al Jazeera* and *CNN* of these assholes enjoying their virgins before martyrdom. Mission accomplished—we've done an admirable job. Now it's time to close down shop and get out of here."

"Well, you're getting your wish," said Dweck smiling and patting her hand. "I received a communication just this morning that Alzera's people plan an attack on you soon, so you and Debra are on your way to London. We need to leave immediately"

"We'll be packed and ready in ten minutes. I love you." She kissed him dead center on the comb-over and shouted for Debra to pack her knickers; the train was leaving.

"Back to the problem at hand," LaRouche said. "This Alzera character is in bad shape, holed up between here and the airport. He's not talking, and I don't know if he will live long enough to be of any value to us." He looked directly into and through me with his piercing eyes.

"We have an inbound mail flight that will encounter some mechanical problems requiring an emergency landing at the local airport," he looked at his watch, "in about an hour. You, Lieutenant Commander Justis, and Petty Officer Vignalli will pick up Alzera and get him on that plane. Your job is to keep him alive until you get him to the carrier. We need his information. But, we need to hurry; it may not be safe here much longer."

"I have a question," I said, but before I could ask it, the side of a Man in Black's head exploded into a cloud of blood and brain.

Good Bye Kelly

Books and Hollywood love to slow time in battle scenes. The reality is that events are often vague memories after the fact.

The attack at Kelly's was a series of stuttered, slow motion, mental glimpses; a montage of the obscure—a bizarre decoupage glued into the limbic system of my brain for later review. The side of a Man in Black's head exploding, which made no sense, disconnected from everything else. A Rorschach test in red along the far wall. A flash of white cloth as I bowled over backwards in my chair. My reaction; jamming my knuckles into the flesh of a neck as its owner

46

rolled over me. Standing upright on my feet. How? I just was. The other Man in Black's arm reaching into his suit jacket. A flash of light. A body falling over a table. No sounds or smells, just a picture here, an image there. Bedlam. A blade slicing through the smoke toward me. The feel of an attacker's arm shattering at the elbow and the clatter of a knife falling to the dirt. My palm connecting solidly against a face with a dark beard. A look of disbelief on that face as bone drove into brain.

Three soft pops and a scream. My first realization of sound. Kelly standing behind the bar pointing a silenced, long barreled gun. The smell of gunpowder. My pulse thumping in my ears, like an epileptic rabbit. Then, a deafening silence.

Images. Not the slow-speed hyper-vigilance or awareness my Hollywood superhero experiences. He always gets into a predicament where hundreds of enemy agents try to kill him in an ambush, but at the moment of attack, time slows. In exquisite detail, the hero pulls out his guns, knives and a bazooka, leaps across the room throwing multiple karate kicks, kills eight bad guys with a six-shooter, grabs the damsel in distress, dodges the hand grenade, and escapes unscathed. Only in a pocket book, or Hollywood.

Einstein taught me that time is relative, but it was a few moments before life returned to the local norm and the madness began to unravel. By then, my autonomic nervous system had kicked into full production—squeezing my adrenal glands empty, racing my heart to frantic levels.

I stood there shaking, trying to make sense of the scene. A Man in Black lying by the goat door, missing the side of his head. Four white robed bodies scattered across the floor; one dead from gunshots; one dead with a crushed nose; one with a crushed throat and broken neck; one gasping, his arm at an obtuse angle, fingers spasmodically opening and closing. Charlie on the floor holding the bandages on his own leg. It took a moment for me to consider his injured leg as an image emerged of him hitting a grand slam with his crutch against a head—a jumble of subliminal messages.

Dweck dusting himself off, unsure whether to straighten his bow tie or secure the comb-over. A Man in Black standing over him, weapon in hand, searching for a target.

Sultani bending over one of the assailants, unlatching a dirty satchel. LaRouche nursing a gash on his scalp, looking dazed. He looked at me and nodded. His message—I'm okay, are you? I nodded back.

Kelly walked from behind the bar holding her silenced gun. She stood over the sole surviving attacker and pointed the gun at his forehead.

"You're too late, asshole; Alzera's already gone. And don't look at me like you don't speak English." She squatted down next to him. "Your fearless leader is already out of the country and telling us everything he knows. American money was more powerful than your jihad." She made a gun out of her free hand and cocked the thumb hammer, pretending to shoot him. "I know what sewer you're hiding in and where your family lives." With that, his eyes dilated and darted around. She stooped, picked up a dagger lying next to him, retracted the blade, and slid it into the pocket of her shorts.

She walked over, nudged one of the bodies with her foot, and looked at me.

"Wow, Doc. Awesome. Looks like you took out two; one with a crushed larynx; one looks like you crushed his nose into his brain when you took him down."

Huh? Took who down? Or is it whom? Can I wake up now, before the Red Queen demands my head? Toto, help me.

"Nice move." She turned back to the survivor. "And look at this one. Busted elbow and broken nose in one punch." She poked his arm with her toe, causing a moan to escape his gritted teeth. "Not bad." She grinned at him and for added drama, spat on the dirt next to him. Then she nudged his broken elbow again.

"So what do you have you to say for yourself?" She poked the arm a third time. He drew his lips into a yellowed canine snarl. Kelly pulled her leg back as if to kick him.

His look turned from fear and uncertainty to defiance. "Fuck you."

"Oh no, it's fuck *you*," she whispered softly, walking back to the bar and retrieving a plastic bag for him to observe.

"Oh, and all that crap about paradise you and your buddies believe? I gotta tell ya—it's over-rated and none of you will ever get there." She shook the bag, rattling the contents.

"And, by the way, the last time you were here you got syphilis from a doctored condom. Guess that means your final gift on earth to your wives, sisters, daughters, and camels is the one that keeps on giving." She opened the bag in front of him and pulled out a crisp orange strip she stuck in her mouth and crunched. Her eyes never left his as she smiled and licked her lips.

She walked over to one of the dead attackers, opened his mouth, and inserted a similar rind. She then repeated the procedure with the other two bodies, finally holding one up for him to observe closely.

"This one is for you, so you won't miss partying in hell with your buddies."

"What . . . is that?" His voice broke and he coughed up the blood running down the back of his throat.

"Oh this?" She smiled, leaning in close. "This is a fried pork rind. Isn't pig a filthy animal to a true believer? Looks like your friends won't be getting a pass to paradise and all those virgins after all. I understand pig is frowned upon there." Her smile disappeared. He blanched and coughed up more blood.

"Open up." She reached out to grab his chin. He struggled away.

"No? Don't want pig flesh to be your last meal? Too bad, it's truly quite tasty."

She grabbed his hair and pulled his head back to look at her. "Here's the deal. Tell us who is funding your campaign and I might allow you to die and take your chances. Otherwise, down the hatch."

Nobody moved or spoke. Dweck found a chair upright and seated himself where he could watch. Sultani fiddled with the satchel. Man in Black reloaded ammo into a clip. A cat slinking along the wall, pounced on a cockroach, and played a kitten's version of 'Tag, you're it'.

I looked at the survivor and saw his eyes harden. He lifted his head close to Kelly and spat blood into her face. Without flinching, she slowly wiped it off her cheek, touched a bloody finger to the tip of her tongue, and grimaced.

This woman is not right; she's way off-kilter. I don't ever want her coming after me, for any reason.

"I take that to mean you don't want to cooperate?" she asked.

"Fuck you," he rasped.

"Do you believe in Allah?" Kelly asked softly. "Say hello, if you see Her." With that, she brought up her gun. Pffffft. His life ended with a look of surprise as a small red blossom flowered on his forehead.

"You really need to hone your interrogation techniques," Dweck said as he stood, dusting off his trousers, "but I genuinely liked the pig thing. Where, may I ask did you acquire a bag of pork rinds?"

"They're barbecued potato chips, but they're too fucking stupid to know the difference." She laughed. "Did you see his face when he thought about what I was doing? Priceless."

I found my voice. "You just executed that man." I didn't know whether I was shocked, scared, angry, amazed, or happy. The realization that I had killed was just reaching my conscious level—without any emotional connection. Maybe I was in denial, but I knew I would not feel guilty afterward. I wouldn't feel anything.

They tried to kill me. Those bastards tried to kill me. What did I ever do to them? What?

A deep part of my psyche wanted to cut out a heart and take a bite. Dehumanization of an enemy can be an effective justification for wartime brutality. I realized, that during Kelly's interrogation, I'd thought, "And if the pig doesn't do it, I'll piss on your grave." My shock overrode any shame about closet bigotry. Political correctness is not in the rules of engagement when it's jungle survival.

"Dr. Matthews," Kelly said, walking over and taking my arm. "We know without a doubt that this man and his thugs were personally responsible for kidnapping and beheading two Red Cross aid workers last year. They also raped and killed three teenage girls simply because their father spoke out against the local warlords." She gave my arm a gentle squeeze. "They needed to be dead. Thank you for helping make that happen."

"Alzera had plans to attack the US, which is why we need him," Charlie said. "This one was the second in command to Alzera and the one who probably cut off his hand," he added.

Sultani interrupted us, "I'd suggest we retreat while we can. The Djibouti police department ain't much, but diplomatic immunity will only go so far. And we know there are others in Alzera's tribe looking for him and us."

"And I really must get started with all the paperwork this little adventure has created." Dweck, the true bureaucrat, had his priorities.

Sultani tipped the satchel and dumped a conglomeration of objects onto the table. Sorting through them, he withdrew some documents and stuffed them in his pocket. Then he unwrapped a newspaper-covered lump of clay. Although I'd never seen any before, I was sure it was plastic explosive.

"Jeez," Sultani said, "there's enough here to take out four square blocks. These guys were serious." He began molding small lumps of the explosive like a child with Play-Doh.

"He's got a remote switch and a single detonator. It looks as if he planned to set it all off at once. I'll use enough to sanitize this place. Grab what we need and let's move out." Sultani turned back to his work.

Man in Black lifted his fallen comrade onto his shoulder. "We're not leaving him," he said in his squeaky voice.

"What about them?" I asked, indicating the other bodies.

"They'll be incinerated," said Kelly. "So if you want a souvenir, now's your chance."

Behind the building sat the flower-power VW. We crammed into her and headed down the back alley. Sultani stopped momentarily and looked through the back window. He squeezed a small device that looked like a TV remote control and the resultant explosion rocked the vehicle, throwing debris in all directions. The fireball was my last memory of Kelly's World Famous Bar and Grill. Nobody else seemed to care, but call me sentimental—Kelly's was something extraordinary.

The sky darkened to a serious threat, and thunder boomed. The hair on my arms buzzed with static. The denizens roaming the street were settling into doorways and shanties; the dust and heat remained oppressive. Being crammed in a marginally running VW van with other people and a corpse quickly raised the heat to unbearable.

"What is that stench?" someone asked.

"Death has caused the body to lose both parasympathetic and sympathetic control of the muscles of the rectal sphincter, resulting in spontaneous defecation and the olfactory sensations you are experiencing," the chipmunk voice of Man in Black explained. I turned in my seat and looked at him. He had removed his shades and was wiping a tear from his eye. He looked back at me and just said "What?"

Nobody could possibly clone something this unique. I don't know if I should be afraid of you or amazed at you.

The first lightning strike cracked the sky, freezing the tableau. The rear window exploded, and Squeaky Man in Black grunted and fell across his comrade—dead before his brain registered the bullet it stopped.

Miss Piggy

"Miss Piggy, Miss Piggy, this is Big Bird—say again."

Static. ". . . weather . . . recall . . ."

"Say again, Miss Piggy." More static. "Say again." TJ spoke into his hand held radio, fiddling with the knobs. The S-3 Dweck arranged for our rescue was a potbellied utility jet used for mail and supplies. Squat and ugly, she earned the nickname Miss Piggy.

Hell, I'll ride Kermit the Frog right now to get out of here.

We were racing through the streets away from the remains of Kelly's. A rusted pick-up chasing us sported men firing rifles from the truck bed.

At first, the dust created by our VW might have obscured their view, but the ensuing downpour turned the dust to mud and made our visibility and evasion increasingly difficult. Kelly knelt beside me on the rear seat returning gunfire. Debra, the Virgin, huddled on the floorboards next to me. I located and handed the firearms from both Men in Black to TJ.

What minimal light remained when we arrived at Kelly's had vanished, and storm clouds obscured any moonlight. I looked back at our pursuers and saw a single headlight two blocks distant. The slums around us held an occasional glimpse of a candle or lantern. Streetlights were nonexistent.

"We're going dark," said Sultani. "Maybe we can lose them."

He switched off the headlights and turned sharply down a nameless alley. The old VW coughed twice, and then found her second wind. Moments later, the solo headlight of the pursuers reappeared. They were gaining on us.

"Big Bird . . . Big Bird . . . Miss Piggy. Weather is closing down, but we will land in 30 minutes." Static. "Five minutes, tops . . ." More static.

"We copy 30 to touchdown, and five to load. 10-4." Static was the only answer.

TJ turned from his seat in the front and said, "This will be tight."

Dweck fussed nervously with his bowtie. "Considering the local government doesn't know you're even here, I had the plane declare a minor crisis so it could land. We need to get everyone aboard before anyone starts asking questions." Dweck, squeezed in the front seat between Sultani and TJ, looked back at us. "I trust we can manage that?"

"Time for plan B," Charlie said. "Who has a BIC lighter and a bullet?" He outlined a plan.

I don't like guns. I don't hunt for sport. That might sound strange for someone who won a Navy Marksman Championship, but I want nothing to do with gun violence. Even the smell of Hoppes gun oil makes me nauseous. However, I understand the weapon and how to use it safely. There is a lot in the world I think is wrong and don't like. I don't like sharks, but I know how to be in the water with them.

As a kid, my dad gave me a BB gun, and I shot a sparrow off the power line. I wasn't even trying, or aiming. It fell to my feet, twitched, gasped, and died in my hands. I threw up the tomato soup and grilled cheese sandwich my mother made for lunch that day. Then I spent the afternoon crying, inconsolable with grief. I vowed I would never touch a gun again. They were evil, and I was evil for what I had done.

Dad made me pick up that BB gun and shoot paper targets repeatedly until I realized that a gun didn't make me a killer. The gun is a tool; my mind is the weapon. My tool was Dad's .22 caliber target pistol; the only gun I own. For me, shooting is no different from throwing a bowling ball down a hardwood maple lane, or hitting a golf ball with a club; just sport.

I killed today, and the instrument was my hand. It wasn't an innocent sparrow, but a determined, ruthless enemy who wanted me dead. A nameless, faceless being who didn't know me, or my wife, or my children, or the people I help every day, wanted me dead. I can't understand that level of hatred. I can comprehend a black hole, but not the hatred that creates one. I had no regrets over his death, or killing the others who wanted to kill me. I will mourn Tweety forever, but seeing the face of pure, malignant hate, and killing it was satisfying. Maybe they saw me the same way and felt that killing me was just.

Nah, they're just religious zealots who hate based on a twisted belief that Allah will give them paradise if they arrive with the blood of an infidel on their hands. They're dead. I'm not. Fuck 'em. I won, so just go . . . I shuddered as I felt the justification of my actions. *Am I really any different?*

Survival instinct and action required to stay alive trumps philosophical debate.

Kelly placed a cold, hard lump in my hand, and I looked at her, then at the gun she handed me. "Here you go, Slick," she said. "Make that marksman medal count." It was a long barrel, .22 automatic with a silencer—a tool. I removed and checked the clip, then the action and safety.

"Ready?" she asked. "Here we go, people. Be cool. Left at the next intersection."

The VW tipped and struggled to remain upright, despite its center of gravity, as we swung left into a narrow alley. I bounced against the seat back as we skidded to a halt. Before

I had a chance to think it through, the doors flung open, and Kelly and I jumped out.

"Over here." She pointed to a stack of pallets and corrugated tin leaning against a wall. We ran to them, and as we tried to get out of sight, an ancient black face peered out of the pile. He showed no fear in his rheumy eyes as they moved from my face to the gun, to Kelly, and back to me. Kelly put her index finger to her lips and nodded at him. He withdrew further into the blackness of what he called home. As I crouched behind the pile, I saw him watching with a blank, dead-eyed stare; simply awaiting whatever fate had befallen him this time. The eyes said that if he was to die tonight, he didn't care and was ready; if he would see sunrise he didn't care and was ready; if this was entertainment, he wasn't interested.

Ahead, the VW squealed to another stop, and someone tossed out a dark lump into an oily puddle of rainwater in the middle of the street. A lantern hanging from a distant wall illuminated the package in soft contrast to the dirt of the street—not much of a target.

I set up my shot. I leaned against the pallets, raised my knees, and rested my left arm across them. I placed my right arm with the .22 across the support I'd formed and took aim. In competition, this would have been impossible to miss. But, in competition my heart rate wasn't 120, my mouth wasn't glued shut, my ears weren't ringing, and there wasn't a truck load of crazies trying to kill me. In competition, I shoot during daylight without rain obscuring my bifocals.

Okay, okay. Breathe in, breathe out. Squeeze. Breathe in, breathe out. Squeeze. Got it. Let's dance, boys.

The truck careened around the corner crashing against a pile of trash before racing toward the VW. Sultani had stopped at the far end of the street, lights off. I saw him and TJ climb out to take cover behind the van. They aimed weapons at the truck as it roared toward us.

Shit, we're in a direct crossfire. Nice plan, Charlie. My life insurance won't include death by friendly fire, in a foreign country where I'm not supposed to be. Okay, here we go. Breathe in, breathe out . . .

Just like on the target range I heard the report and felt the gun's recoil before my brain registered that I had squeezed the trigger. Missed. No, not quite. The truck's front tire obscured my target just as I fired. I must have hit the tire because the truck lurched sideways and tilted.

Without conscious thought, I fired a second round at the package just as the rear tire ran over it. Missed, I thought again. In the next instant, a blinding flash and deafening roar let me know I hadn't.

Charlie had wrapped a lump of the remaining plastic explosive around a BIC lighter and a bullet. We had to rely on igniting the fuel in the lighter and the shock wave from the bullet to do the trick. Combined with the compressive weight of the truck, it worked.

Damn. Wish I were that lucky at poker.

The truck rose into the air and rolled onto the driver's side, crushing one of the shooters under the rear fender. A second body, thrown against the wall, slid into a lump on the ground, leaving a bloody smear—his last will and testament.

As my eyes adjusted to the flash and smoke, I looked around for other shooters and spotted one crawling behind the truck, looking for his weapon. A shot from someone near the VW took him out.

I assumed the driver, hidden in the wreckage, was still alive and armed. Smoke rose to meet the debris raining down from the blast. The rain ratcheted up a notch and another slash of lightning exaggerated the scene. A hot piece of slag landed on my forehead, stinging me.

"Cover me," Kelly whispered in my ear. At least I think that's what she said. I'd lost my hearing because of the explosion. She pulled the dagger she'd taken from one of the attackers and started toward the truck before I could stop her.

"Look out," I shouted as the passenger door opened and the driver's arm emerged, brandishing an automatic weapon. The arm preceded a head with dark eyes that focused on Kelly as she ran toward him. The weapon came up and swung toward her.

Now my mind deployed the Hollywood slow-motion routine as it took forever for him to take aim. It's astonishing what adrenaline will do to the synaptic speed of the conscious mind. Equally slowly, it seemed, I considered my options. Run? Yell? Fuck it—I put a round through his neck. His head snapped back, and he dropped into the cab.

Not bad, except that I was aiming for his shoulder. Oh well, the Russian judge can penalize me for my aim.

Kelly turned and cocked her head toward me. With a nod, she gave me thumbs up and turned back toward the truck. The truck, which had been smoldering, now decided to self-immolate. A whooooooomp echoed off the narrow walls of the alley, and the night lit with a brilliant orange flame. Kelly landed on her butt as the fireball expanded. Even at a safe distance, I felt the heat wash over me. As quickly as it ignited, the flame died out and the air filled with the odor of oily exhaust and another more sinister smell. Once you've had a snoot full of burnt flesh, you never forget it. If my shot hadn't killed him, the driver was now a crispy critter. The last shooter crawled around the edge of the front bumper and collapsed, the skin on his face and neck peeled and blackened from the explosion; missing lips exposed his death grin.

I ran to Kelly and helped her up. "You okay?"

"Shit," she answered, feeling around her face. "Do you know how long it takes to re-grow eyebrows?" I saw that hers were indeed fuzzy remnants to match her blistered face, but if that was the worst of it, she was incredibly lucky.

She gently took the .22 from my hand and walked over to the truck where she put the remaining rounds into the bodies.

"That's for my eyebrows, asshole." She continued to fire on empty until I put my arms around her and took the gun back.

"Bones, I suggest we get the hell out of here." I turned to see TJ surveying the wreckage. The others were forming a perimeter looking decidedly business-like.

Sirens in the distance jerked me back to reality. I was in a foreign country without immigration papers, permission of the government, or my Navy ID. I had just killed a bunch of people, blown up a car full of locals, and helped demolish a CIA operation fronting as a whorehouse and bar. Dweck was going to have his hands full filling out all those forms in triplicate. I would have my hands full just escaping.

I looked toward the pallet hovel the old man called home, but he had pulled a can of rubbish in front of the opening—a clear 'Closed for Business' sign. His eyes stared out at the carnage, uninterested. I nodded at him and touched my forehead in a salute of thanks. His eyes disappeared into the depths.

I saw Sultani wave. "Let's go, Doc. You got a plane to catch and another patient waiting." He pointed toward the VW and said, "Go. Back up will be here for the Ambassador in a minute. Debra and I will stick around for insurance and dispose of the bodies." He tossed his keys to Kelly.

Jamal the Magnificent

"Well, that was certainly fun. What else ya'll do for excitement in these parts?" I was feeling giddy, alive. I was in denial.

Kelly, speeding us toward our next rendezvous, said, "Well, we do have a museum with *both* of the Northern Africa artifacts on exhibit. On the other hand, the zoo and aquarium have a new exhibit of Red Sea seaweeds—almost enough to fill an entire fish bowl."

"Oh be still my tourist heart," muttered TJ. He did a Groucho with his cigar.

"Don't forget the camel ride through the botanical garden," said Charlie. "Oh wait; they cancelled that when the camel ate the weeds."

What the hell am I doing here? I just killed several humans—some by pure reflex, others deliberately. How was I caught up in all of this? How did I pull the trigger and blow up a truck? That's not who I am. This isn't a joking matter, so why do I find this funny? What is wrong with you people?

A moment of silence, then we spontaneously broke into hysterical laughter. I couldn't help myself. I needed the emotional rescue after the carnage. Making fun of the enemy, his way of life, and his family is a common response to combat fatigue. We were a gang of giggling warriors in a vintage Volkswagen running from a war zone. I didn't think it would make the movie of the week, but at the time, it was hilarious. I tried to stop laughing, but just looking at anyone in the van was enough to generate more guffaws. My hysteria wasn't all laughter.

Maybe survival trumps everything else I try to do with my life?

We had no sooner settled down then Kelly pulled to the side of the road next to a small, mud brick building with a thick plank door and no windows. What I considered the front yard was a desolate strip of mud, rubbish, and chickens. A young black male in cut-offs and flip-flops sat on an upturned bucket under a tarp canopy attached to the door, smoking a hand rolled cigarette. The rain continued its onslaught, running off the edge and onto his exposed feet. Slouched against the wall, seemingly indifferent, the alertness in his dark-eyed stare told me otherwise. That, and an automatic rifle propped next to him. His arms uncrossed and he reached casually toward the weapon as Kelly climbed out. He stood to greet her.

"Jamal, how they hanging?" she asked, moving under the cover of the tarp with him.

"Not so good, Miss Kelly. Our friend doesn't look good at all." Jamal's rich baritone voice did not match his slender frame and tattered clothing. He relaxed and resumed his nonchalant guard position, leaning against the wall. "Did you bring the esteemed American physician, of whom we have heard so much? Certainly not even Sir Dweck would trust this to the embassy staff doctor. The local witch doctor makes better ju-ju than that idiot."

Kelly waved me out of the VW and made introductions. "Dr. Matthews, this is Jamal Jocuba, son of a great Zulu chieftain, heir to the De Beers fortune, and future ambassador to the United Nations. All hail and gaze in wonder at his magnificence." She made a grand curtsy, and then winked at me.

Jamal just shook his head, then my hand. "Doctor, it is a pleasure to welcome you to our poor, but honest country. Kelly, as always exaggerates my credentials." I was looking at a skinny black man with short dreadlocks, but hearing the cultured voice of a British diplomat. I was seeing a professional killer behind the façade. His eyes kept watch on everyone and everything in the area.

"He one of yours?" I asked Kelly.

"You one of them?" I asked him.

"One of whom?" they both asked. End of discussion.

"Enough idle chit-chat." He opened the hovel door into a dark, cave-like room lit with a lantern. "We'll continue sharing tall tales over high tea and crumpets at the club some other time, old chap." Jamal bent his frame at the midline and ushered me through the door with a flourish.

"You're needed inside," he said. "I suggest that you hurry. Word is there are a sizeable number of disreputable types searching the city for you, and we don't think they are planning to invite you to join the Chamber of Commerce." A radio crackled, and Jamal reached down, retrieved a hand held radio unit from under his bucket, and held it to his ear.

"Yes Sir. He just arrived—intact." He listened some more. "No Sir. The prisoner looks particularly unhealthy, in my non-medical opinion. I don't know if he'll make it, but that will be up to Dr. Matthews . . . Yes Sir, I understand. We'll get him there in time. The storm may actually help provide cover—and I have a little diversion planned for the front gate of the airport."

Long before Dr. Joseph Lister, long before the germ theory of infection, and long before sterile surgical techniques, doctors would evaluate the progress of healing by the smell. In England, the King called his Royal Physicians piss pot prophets for their diagnosis by the aroma of the chamber pot. Infections have a distinct odor that a trained nose can usually distinguish. The average person can identify bowel gas and feces. Most of us can identify a decomposing body, be it a dead rat in the wall of a house, or a corpse decaying in a swamp. Once you've sniffed a burned body, you never forget that smell either.

I would never forget the stink of this room.

I was entirely unprepared for the olfactory overload. Before I could adjust, my stomach twisted into a knot and tried to empty itself. I gagged and retched as I backed outside, caught some fresh air, and prepared to re-enter. Overlying the typical household cooking, garbage, unwashed clothes, and body odor was a malevolent cloud that coated the hairs in my nose with a foul sludge. Not the sweet, cloying smell of rotting flesh, or the insistent smell of pus that demands a second sniff—but the worst of all combined; a surprise attack on my senses. If evil has body odor, this was it.

As soon as I was sure that I could breathe without dying of toxic exposure, I looked around. On the dirt floor, slumped against one wall were four gagged men, their hands and feet trussed with plastic straps. One had a nose clearly broken and displaced onto his left cheek. All displayed bruises and blood about their eyes and mouths. Two men in desert camouflage stood guard over them. I noticed the guards were wearing surgical masks. The smell told me they had treated their masks with a mentholated salve to block the odor. As if reading my mind, one of the guards held out a jar. I smeared a small glob on my upper lip and inhaled the crisp, fresh aroma. I nodded my thanks.

"That him?" I asked them, indicating a body lying on a low stretcher.

I assumed the only other person in the room was my new patient—Alzera. He was lying on a canvas stretcher in the center of the room, breathing, but just barely. The stench seemed to swirl around him like fog as I approached. His right arm, or what was left of it, lay across his chest. A filthy rag encircled his stump, and he stirred as I tried to unwrap it. The stump was not the cleanly severed limb I'd expected, but rather, a ragged, torn wound. The arm, covered with flies, looked like a rotisserie with hanging strips waiting to become a pulled pork sandwich. The hand and lower arm were missing, and a series of hacking cuts crisscrossed the remainder. Clearly, his tormenters had taken several swings with a dull blade before successfully severing his hand from his arm. Despite the Metholatum, I could smell decay.

This didn't just happen. He's septic and developing gangrene—I can smell it. This man is going to die in a few hours if I don't amputate that arm and get him into intensive care. They brought me all the way here for this. Too little, too late.

"How long has he been here?" I asked one of the guards. He shrugged, and then lit a cigarette that he stuck behind the edge of his mask.

61

The arm was colorless and cold to the touch. The rest of him radiated fevered heat. Deep red streaks ran toward the shoulder; hard, congested vessels acting as super highways for bacteria to race into his central core. The stump adhered to the makeshift bandage and oozed a foul, yellow fluid. I turned his face toward me, and he opened clouded eyes. A thick tongue rasped across cracked lips as he tried to say something.

TJ pointed to one of the guards and said, "Grab the other end of the stretcher. Bones, we need to leave immediately. You can work on him during the flight home, but there's no time now."

Ten minutes later, we passed through the back gate of the airport. Well, not an airport; not even a landing strip—a grassy field with a shack and fuel tank at one end. Miss Piggy, a picture of Porky Pig in a bonnet painted on her side, sat short and pudgy while refueling. She wasn't much, but she was our redemption. In the distance, I could see flashing lights and hear sirens. The horizon lit up at the same time the explosion reached my ears. I suspected this was Jamal's distraction at work. The pilot was busy on the other side of the plane, gesturing and arguing with a local official.

As I boarded the plane, LaRouche handed me a small metal camera case and said, "Doc, this has to get safely back to the intelligence people on your ship." It was the same case with blue globes I'd seen on the *Swordfish*.

He raised his chin toward the plane. "Don't let Alzera die, we worked too hard to capture him. Several good people are dead because of him." He reached out and took my hand. "Thanks for everything you did for Charlie. Maybe someday we can get together and laugh about all of this." With that, he turned and climbed back into the van.

"It was fun. Have a wet dream about me." Kelly waved from the VW as she disappeared into the night and out of my life—or, so I thought.

I Hate To Fly

The pilot was back on board, and the jets were winding up as I climbed aboard. TJ secured the hatch. The airport official shouted and waved frantically as the S-3 lumbered down the runway into the storm. A vehicle with flashing lights pulled across the runway in the distance—too late to prevent escape. At the last possible moment, our pilot pulled up missing the vehicle by inches.

I made my way forward in the cramped cargo space of the S-3 to where the crew had removed a row of seats to make room for Alzera's stretcher. Small and stout, Miss Piggy carried small cargo hauls and had only six passenger seats. Sacks of mail and boxes filled much of the limited space. The plane bucked, slid, yawed, and bounced, reminding me how much I hate to fly. I tried not to think about that Twilight Zone gremlin ripping chunks off the engine.

I leaned over Alzera just as we experienced a twenty-story drop, and both of us bounced toward the ceiling. He opened his eyes and grabbed me with his good arm. A wave of rot wafted from him that made me gag.

"Blue Death," he muttered. "Blue Death." Then he died—or at least technically quit doing the usual living stuff—like breathing. I detected a smirk on his lips as his eyes rolled up. He coughed up a prodigious, filthy fur ball, the last act his lungs performed.

"Damn, I think we're losing him here. I need a laryngoscope and endotracheal tube, STAT. Somebody check for a pulse and establish an IV." I looked up at several sets of blank eyes. "And see if I can get some light in here." Vignalli broke the spell by handing TJ an IV from the trauma kit. He handed me the laryngoscope. If I slid its long curved hook with a light on the tip, into the mouth, holding the tongue aside, I could distinguish the half-moons of the vocal cords. Then I could slip an endotracheal breathing tube into the throat and voila!—we establish an airway.

Voila my ass. I'm bouncing around on a Disneyland thrill ride, in the dark, with my patient lying sideways across the cabin, his head, and airway cockeyed in the aisle. And I'm supposed to shove this tube down his throat so he can breathe? Who am I kidding?

Vignalli climbed over the row of seats, straddled him, and tried to start the IV. I stretched along the aisle at ninety degrees to the head and tried again to maneuver the scope in place. I craned my head and neck far enough to see down his throat, and manipulate the tube into place. In a well-lit operating room, with a hydraulically adjustable OR table, this is easy. After four tries and banging my head against the seats and floor with every turbulent bump, I gave up.

"Give me an Ambu bag," I shouted above the cabin noise. TJ handed me a spring-loaded bag with a facemask that I applied to Alzera's face. As I squeezed, I could see his chest rise—I had air movement. I looked at Vignalli who was still trying to get a needle into a vein. He looked at me and just shook his head.

"Keep trying," I encouraged him. I looked at a crewmember talking into his headset.

"Any chance we can land?" I yelled over the engine and storm noise. "He's going to die if I can't get him stabilized." He held up a finger and said something into the headset.

"Doc, we're over open water in foul weather, and the nearest realistic landing zone is back at Djibouti. Pilot says no can do. We weren't there." He made an air quote, "And if we go back we will never have been there . . . ya know—as in permanently disappear?" He looked at me and lifted his eyebrows in a manner that said 'I understand, I sympathize, and it ain't gonna happen—period.' "We're three hours from the flight deck, and we'll be past the worst of the weather in about 30 minutes. Best we can do."

I watched the chest rise and fall as I squeezed the bag. Vignalli gave up trying to get an IV started, and was doing chest compressions. A flash of lightning lit the cabin momentarily then plunged us into total darkness. The lights in the cabin blinked once, and we plummeted toward the ocean. I heard someone cry out in fear. It might have been me.

My mind spent a microsecond considering my fate. *Wonder if this is when I die? Wonder what version the Navy will tell my wife and kids about how I died? Wonder if this asshole is worth dying over? Wonder if plummeting into the Red Sea is what he meant by Blue Death? Wonder if that warm sensation on my leg is urine? Wonder if . . .*

Then the lights came back on; the plane leveled out, and began to climb again. The warm liquid on my leg was from the IV bag that had ruptured.

"Doc, he still has no heartbeat," said Vignalli, who had the same chartreuse color I'd seen on the chopper ride. His fingers pressed the carotid artery. "Should I continue chest compressions?"

"Wait, we started this all wrong—do it right." I reached across and shook Alzera's shoulders. "Annie, Annie . . . you okay?" I shook him again. I was losing it, but too exhausted to care anymore.

Vignalli looked at me then asked, "Do you want me to call 9-1-1?" This bit of kabuki was all that kept the horror of our situation at bay. It was a fragile grip on sanity.

I looked to TJ. He was shaking his head and rolling his eyes to the heavens.

I started to breathe for the corpse again as Vignalli restarted chest compressions. "TJ, switch places with me and take over breathing. I'll see if I can get an IV started. Maybe I can find the jugular or subclavian vein."

As soon as I said it, I realized it was impossible. I'd have to lie in the aisle on top of TJ while he squeezed the Ambu bag, breathing for the body. Then I'd have to stick a large needle in the neck or under the clavicle, hoping I didn't hit an artery. I already thought of Alzera as a body, no longer a living, breathing human. My emotional survival centers were making fun of the situation while my logic circuits were having a reality check.

I felt a hand on my shoulder and looked up to see Charlie. I'd forgotten him. "Enough," was all he said. His eyes held mine, an exclamation mark on his words.

"What do you think, Master Chief?" asked TJ.

"I think our guys got as much info as they're going to from him. We have samples of what he was planning to release and all the water data the intelligence guys need to sort it out. That's enough, because that's all there's going to be." Charlie ran his hand through the sweat accumulating on his scalp. He looked at both of us, put a hand on Vignalli, and simply stared down at the body.

"If Dr. Matthews can't do something, the mission will fail," TJ said.

I could see him mulling this over and I finally realized *this* was our true mission, not a minor pregnancy problem on a research ship.

From the beginning, our real orders were to extract Alzera. They lied to me; the story and timing of his injuries were wrong. He was tortured days ago and was dying before I got here. Someone knew it, and sent me in to try to repair their damage. I'd seen a decent man's head explode, his partner die in the back of an ancient VW van, killed men with my bare hands, shot a man in the neck, blown up people who were trying to kill me, participated, by my silence, in the torture of captured men for information they may or may not have possessed. I was facing a death sentence if certain foreign governments ever caught up with me. Oh, and did I mention flying on a helicopter with a sadistic kamikaze pilot? Did I mention how much I hate to fly?

It is rumored that Henry Stanley, the second most famous African explorer said, "Dr. Livingston, I presume?" That wasn't what he actually said, however. I suspect it was more like, "There was this lion that grabbed me by my head and was planning on making me her dinner." Then he said, "*And I didn't feel anything.*" That's a true story—really.

At times of extreme stress, pain, or near-death experiences, the mid-brain releases endorphins. These little packets of miracle molecules, thousands of times more potent than narcotics allow mammals to die pain-free. People with severe injuries describe a period of narcosis, altered thought processes, and a sense of acceptance and well-being. Runners 'hitting the wall' experience an endorphin release.

Tons of endorphins and adrenaline coursed through my veins. Stress no longer registered. I'd hit my wall, and my body's coping mechanisms took over.

"TJ?" I became very quiet. Stress or anger beyond my capacity to cope changes me to a quiet introvert.

"Charlie is right," I said. "He's gone. He was gone before I ever got to him. He was tortured days ago and lost too much blood. He was septic from an infection that spread to his central core. His heart and lungs stopped from massive shock, blood loss, and sepsis. We are three hours away from anything even approaching a proper medical facility and yes, we could do CPR until we get there, but we'd still have a dead body." I took a deep breath to quell the shaking. "I don't know what the fuck is going on here, or what genius came up with this cockamamie boondoggle, but it was too little and too late. He's dead, and there isn't a damn thing I can do to fix that. *Enough*, let's go home. *Please*."

I staggered back a couple rows, sat, and buckled my seat belt. I smelled coffee brewing somewhere. I needed some.

TJ sat next to me and leaned his seat back. "Sorry, Bones. I know you did everything you could. I also know few men who would have tried as hard to save someone who wanted to kill him. I'm also sorry I couldn't let you know what was going on. If it's any consolation, I had no idea what we were up to until we got to Djibouti and Ambassador Dweck briefed me. Not even Charlie knew we were sending in a team. It was pure luck we were en route when word came through that he was shot and running for safety with Sultani. He owes you his life."

Charlie had moved back and sat across the aisle with his leg propped up. "I do, and somehow I'll repay you." Another flash outside the window lit up his face. Through the grime, I noticed his Howdy Doody freckles.

I wish I were six years old again, eating cookies and milk, watching you on TV. I wish I wasn't here. I wish I could wake up from this nightmare.

"How 'bout just telling me what's really going on here? I think you owe me that much," I said.

"Well," TJ said, "Dweck got you clearance, but not for everything. Problem is that none of us truly knows what's going on here. Kelly is the only one who has the big picture."

"Kelly? As in the House of the Seven Virgins, Kelly? The madam who runs a government sanctioned whorehouse?"

"More than that, she's the CIA station chief for Djibouti. Kelly's Bar and Grill is just a cover for the actual work they do."

"You part of this?" I asked Charlie. He didn't respond, but his eyes spoke true.

TJ continued, "Everybody in the country: the Somali warlords, the local tribes, foreign embassies, mullahs, and the townspeople all think it's just what it looks like—a CIA front trying to get information using sex and alcohol. Anything she learns is deliberate disinformation, which is as good as real information. Nobody takes the operation seriously, which makes it ideal for doing real covert operations in plain sight. Kelly has the run of Djibouti because locals in the intelligence business think they know exactly what she is doing and why. A known spy in plain sight can spy on anything and get away with it."

"Your circular intelligence logic is making me dizzy. What does all that have to do with all this?" I gestured vaguely.

Charlie said, "She ran this particular operation from the start. What I know is that a group of extraordinarily bad people led by that asshole," nodding toward the body, "were planning a terrorist attack on the US. It had to do with something they found that would poison women if released into water. They called it Blue Death. Kelly found out about it. She sent Sultani and me to find Alzera, then all hell broke loose."

"How did Master Chief Sultani get involved with a CIA anti-terrorist plot in the first place?" I asked.

"Sultani is not a master chief; he's Special Ops," said Charlie.

"Ah, well, that explains everything. And what is it that you do, Master Chief, if I can call you that?" I asked Charlie.

"Oh, I'm a real master chief, Sir. I'm trained as a boson's mate."

"Ah huh, and what is it exactly that you do in the Navy?"

"I fix things."

"Things? What things?"

"You know. Things that get broken and need fixing."

"Like toilets on research ships? Stuff like that?"

"That, too."

"And things like broken CIA operations?" Silence.

"So," I continued, "you went in to fix what Sultani broke, got shot, and I became *your* fixer? Meanwhile, Sultani kidnaps the bad guy who wants to destroy America, but his peace loving fellow terrorists cut off his arm because they think he's in bed with Kelly—no pun intended. Now I'm here to fix this cluster fuck. Do I have this sort of right? And all for what?" I was bone tired and frustrated. I wanted a shower, some sleep, and a nutritious meal.

"For this." TJ held up the case LaRouche handed me as we boarded. I had seen the same case in the research spaces on the *Swordfish*. It was full of blue globes.

"People died today for that," I said. "What can be in that box that is worth that?"

"Blue Death," TJ let that sink in. "We think this is what Alzera was planning to release, and this is all of it. Not to sound trite, but we may have saved thousands of lives."

"Or be carrying a new weapon never before seen," said Charlie.

Holly pustules, Batman.

I looked at the box—a simple metal camera case with no radiation or biohazard stickers on it. Not even a "fragile" or "this side up" label.

"You tellin' me that we have something capable of wiping out the human race? In a damn camera case? *Are You Nuts?* What if it's contagious and infects an aircraft carrier? Or blows up and spreads radiation? Or eats the person who opens it? What the hell is in there?"

"That's just it," Charlie said. "We don't know. The brain trust on the *Swordfish* thinks it is harmless and somehow needs activation in seawater to become dangerous. They have been trying to figure that out for weeks, ever since Kelly reported the rumors of the Blue Death. The *Swordfish* is a very real oceanographic research vessel doing water, soil, and air assays. Sultani and I were looking for where Alzera found it, and who had it."

"Found? Found where? What?" The headache that had started behind my eyes began to engulf my entire head.

"That's why we needed him," again nodding to the body. "Apparently his people found something off the coast. We think we found the location but needed him to confirm it. We also needed to know if there was any more we haven't recovered."

"More? Any more what?"

"It's some type of capsule or something. We found what we believe are the last of the globes underwater near the coast. Sultani and I recovered the ones Alzera had. We don't know what they are, and that's why we had to get him and this," tapping the case TJ was guarding, "to where we can figure it out. If they found a new terrorist weapon, we need to know. Someone at the top thinks this mission is vital, regardless of the cost."

I sat back and let this sink in. I thought about seeing technicians on the *Swordfish* loading blue globes into a camera case before the marine guard ushered me out of their lab. Despite my fatigue, I knew this was something the government would hide.

"Charlie, why are you really here? Are you part of what will surely be a government cover-up?" I asked. He shook his head; a clear signal he wouldn't answer this question.

I had a cup of coffee in my hands, but no idea how it got there. I looked out the window and saw clouds and lightning. The remnants of moonlight disappeared in the distance, glinting off the thunderheads. The turbulence had abated. Nothing made sense to me, but I was too exhausted to frame more questions. The spooks waiting to debrief me on the ship would have enough questions for all of us.

"What am I supposed to put in my report when I get back on board? How do I explain him?" I asked, pointing at the body. Vignalli was wrapping Alzera's carcass in a canvas tarp.

"You won't be filling out any reports, Bones." TJ looked me straight in the eye. "And there is no body. No reports. No body. Our medical mission scrubbed because of weather, and we returned to the *Carl Vinson* to receive other orders. There was no other mission, you've never heard of the *Swordfish*, and have never been to Djibouti." TJ stopped while I grappled with what he was telling me. "Petty Officer Vignalli doesn't know it yet, but he has orders to a command where he can pretty much write his own ticket if he's smart. I also understand there was an unexpected opening in the micro-vascular surgical program you applied for last year. The Ambassador pulled strings to get you into it. We won't have to finish this sea tour."

"Got it," I said. "Be a good boy, shut up, don't rock the boat, see no evil, speak no evil, *et cetera*. We're talking about a bribe, right? A surgery fellowship for service above and beyond for my country. Better than a medal, but I don't even know what I'm supposed to cover up."

"Best consider it compensation for services rendered," said TJ.

"They can't torture it out of you that way," said Charlie. That gave me a chill.

"You said we. Do you mean . . ."

"It seems," said TJ, "that I have received approval to finish a PhD program. I dropped out of graduate school years ago, but suddenly the Navy needs a supply officer with a degree in evolutionary biology. Funny how things work out sometimes."

"Yeah, funny . . . but what about . . ."

"Charlie?" he finished. "You're taking him to Okinawa where he'll recover and then move on. He needs a medical escort, and you're nominated."

That little red warning light in the back of my mind that says 'Wait a minute, what was that', began to blink. *Okinawa?*

I turned to Charlie. "Did TJ say I'm taking you to Okinawa? That's good. They have a top-notch facility there with an orthopedic surgeon who can properly take care of your leg. But you shouldn't wait for me to get you there."

"We're not waiting," he said. I was too tired to catch the 'we'.

Two hours later, I made my first hook landing on a carrier. Looking through the cockpit windshield, I was sure the pilot would crash into the fantail. Then *twaaang*, I jerked forward as the hook caught the infamous No. 2 catch wire, that same cable that ran through the bulkhead next to my bunk, destroying my hearing.

For the second time that day, my pant leg felt wet.

Ten minutes later, a man in slacks and a windbreaker, pretending to be a civilian defense contractor, climbed aboard, took the metal case from TJ, and asked me if I had opened it.

"Are you serious? It's locked, and I won't be responsible for destroying all life on this planet."

His cold eyes and emotionless expression let me know he had no sense of humor, and that I didn't want to play poker with him.

"Didn't think so," he said flatly without moving his lips. "It's probably wired, and you'd be missing body parts if you had." Those were the last words I ever heard him say.

I turned to TJ. "Why are we carrying this stuff with us? Who is this guy?"

"Too dangerous to bring it aboard the carrier and we're the best way to get it to the eggheads that need to evaluate it. And that guy," he nodded toward the spook. "He's not here—you're imagining a government agent we need to trust with this."

Alzera, now wrapped like cargo, disappeared into the ship, probably offloading with the next garbage dump. The spook sat down, stared straight ahead, and gripped Pandora's Box lovingly.

Ten minutes later, refueling completed, the catapult attached to the nose gear and the pilot put the jets into full roar. The crew chief looked back and instructed us to put our heads against the seatback so we wouldn't get a broken neck when we launched. I thought my bladder was empty after the landing. I was wrong. I hoped I could find dry underwear in Okinawa.

PART 2 GUAM

<u>Meeting Auraka</u>

Auraka lurked out there, waiting in the dark. The full moon drew her out to hunt. That same moon pulled me relentlessly back to my love, the sea. Kelly's Reef spawned a devil that knew I was coming. I knew she waited. We had built a bond, but it was not clear who the alpha in that relationship was. The tides drawn by the moon teased her into feeding; just as they pulled me back to a reef that I named Kelly. She expected to feed. Tonight the meal would be vienna sausages.

"The suspense is killing me. Won't you at least give me a hint?" pleaded Hanna. She ran a finger across Charlie's cheek.

"Well, uh, I mean, uh," he stammered and blushed. Unconsciously he stroked the same square of cheek Hanna had favored.

This was Hanna's final test—meeting Auraka. If she survived, she would tattoo dolphins on her leg and become one of us—a Same Day, Same Ocean Diver. The three of us, Charlie, TJ and I dove together almost daily, but rarely follow strict buddy-diving safety procedures. We joke that we dive on the same day in the same ocean. The name stuck, and now Hanna was joining our exclusive little club. First, she had to survive her encounter with Auraka. She knew we planned a unique night dive for her, but didn't have a clue what that meant or what to expect.

"Tonight you will get to meet Auraka," I answered, "and you are going to see the most wondrous sight of your life. She is big and intimidating, but probably won't bite you," I continued. "Charlie and I will be there to make sure Auraka behaves herself, which is more than I expect of Charlie." I knew the eel was so unique and fearsome that most divers would panic in her presence. I knew her to be a gentle, curious monster that trusted me in her own way.

Hanna, Charlie, and I arrived on our dive site in time to watch the sunset kiss the night. This close to the equator, the moment the sun clears the horizon, there's a brief green flash. Tonight, the flash was a subtle glimpse of the universe. I felt a collective intake of breath at that moment.

The moon rose with all her majesty as we cleaned up the remains of our meal and set up the dive gear. I was excited. It was time. Auraka waited.

Silence either spooks or soothes. At ebb tide, neither the sound of waves on the distant beach, traffic noise, telephones, nor civilization intruded on our solitude. Sounds bled into the darkness of the surrounding ocean. The crisp metallic echoes of our movements as we assembled the dive gear were jarring against such quiet.

India ink black and mirror smooth, the sea reflected the full moon. To the uninitiated, just an inch below the ink awaits Jaws, Captain Nemo's giant squid, and every boogeyman known to mankind. Stepping off a boat into the blackness of a moonlit dive is to enter a surreal world few ever experience—none ever forgets.

In the distance, three spinner dolphins breached; part of a pod that hangs around the reef. I admired their grace and their intelligence. One approached the boat and eyed us as if to ask, "What's up, guys? Got any spare fish for me?"

"I'll go down and set the anchor, so it's not damaging the reef," Charlie said, breaking the reverie. Clumsy and awkward on land or in the company of other humans, yet at one with the ocean, he entered without a splash. The dolphin ducked back in the water, and I guessed it would follow Charlie to confirm the anchor was properly set.

For years of medical practice, I've made a note of a patient undergoing a routine physical that "HEENT normal: no gill slits observed." This is my short hand for an exam where Head, Ears, Eyes, Nose, and Throat are normal. I add the quip about gill slits to see if anyone ever reads the stuff—nobody does. However, with Charlie, I sometimes wonder if there aren't gill slits under the freckles on his neck.

Kelly's Reef is unique in ways we had yet to understand or fear. My best friends, Charlie and TJ, now stationed here on Guam with me after the big Djibouti boondoggle, were present when I first found her lying two miles off Old Wives Beach the previous summer. Not registered on any navigational chart, she is our personal, private reef.

"Okay, final check. Weight good, air on, pressure 3000 PSI, computer on." Hanna gave me the okay sign.

Since I taught her to dive, Hanna has proven herself a cautious, conservative diver. Nothing else about her was conservative, including the cobalt blue thong bikini she wore. It was a perfect companion to her eyes.

"Don't you ever get cold diving naked?" I asked.

"I'm not naked, I've got my BCD," she said, referring to her buoyancy control device—a vest worn to maintain neutral buoyancy, like a fish's swim bladder. On most divers, it looks like a chunk of material with stuffed pockets and accessories dangling from multiple loops. On Hanna, a fashion statement.

My dull, black, beat up, shorty wetsuit would make the Goodwill proud.

"Besides, this way, I know you and Charlie will be keeping your eyes on me, just in case." She winked.

Hanna is the identical twin sister of my wife Emily, and a naval officer working as a nurse in my OB department. She transferred here to be with her sister as soon as she heard that I had orders to the naval hospital on the island.

Admiring her backside in that thong was almost enough to distract me from preparing for a safe dive. Petite, with a blond pixy cut and a Maserati chassis, Hanna carries an air of sensuality that leaves most men defenseless. I know that her overt sexuality and the wild and crazy image she portrays are just a front; she also has a commanding presence; a cool, calm head in a crisis, and she uses all of her assets to get the job done.

In the years since I married her sister Emily, I have come to realize that much of what Hanna does is deliberate. I admire her for it. Both sisters have their quirks, similarities, and differences. Both know my heart and my life belong to

Emily. Flirting with Hanna is fun, and we've played this game since the first time they tried to do the twin switch on me.

Now Hanna has her designs on Charlie; her accidental bumping underwater; teaching him the math he needed to finish his technical diver certification while making him feel that he had done it all himself—then gushing over him about how smart he was. All calculated.

The poor lunkhead was clueless. What Hanna doesn't know is that she already overwhelms Charlie's defenses, or maybe she does? I suspect Charlie spends all of his waking hours wondering if he has any chance to be a part of her life. When he is with me, she is all he talks about.

"You know," I said, "if you keep teasing Charlie like you do, he's going to burst."

"Me? Tease Charlie? Why would you say that?" Her impish grin gave her away.

"Oh, I don't know. Bending over in front of him in your butt floss to organize your equipment. Reaching across his lap to retrieve your mask. Asking him to secure your weight belt . . . Poor guy almost forgot to turn on his air."

And he almost hung himself on his erection going over the side.

"I refuse to be responsible for any unprofessional, unsafe, or unethical behavior he might, or might not, exhibit in my presence." She giggled.

"That bikini won't pass the nursing professional ethics board. And as the self-appointed chairman, I might have to confiscate it for evidence at your court-martial. Better yet, loan it to your sister so we can play gruff sea captain and the mermaid some evening."

I spat into my mask and rinsed it with salt water. Then I dumped a mask full over my head and felt the jolt as the cold ran down my back causing the hairs to stand at attention. I zipped up my wetsuit and rolled over the side. Water temperature near Guam remains warm year round, but tonight it chilled me as water seeped under the rubber skin encasing my torso. Hanna splashed in after me, and I wondered how she always seems to tolerate the cool.

We started our descent down the anchor line. My eyes stung from the salt as my ears registered the pressure. I cleared my mask and popped my ears several times in the first twenty feet. Then I extracted my mouthpiece and swished some salt water around in my mouth to acclimate to the taste. I tried not to think about fish urine.

The reef was vibrant and alive; each fin kick left a fluorescent trail in the water from the stirrings of microbes. Everything stood in crisp relief—deep shadows against bright surface details. As we reached the edge of the reef, my hearing tuned to the squeaks, grunts, and whispers of the nightlife. The ocean is a noisy place, filled with conversations I could only imagine. The brilliant fish seen during the day nestled into the coral in deep sleep, eyes open. Octopi were abundant this night, gliding ghost-like across the coral looking for an unwary shellfish to engage in the dance of survival.

I wanted to find Auraka, but an octopus distracted Hanna. I placed my hand on a ledge nearby, coaxing. The octopus became curious enough to come out and play. She flashed from red to green to aquamarine signaling her moods, and extended a tentative tentacle to touch my finger. Despite the natural tendency to jerk away when I felt the suckers attach to my skin, I held still, and she oozed over my hand. Once she figured out I wasn't a meal, she'd had enough fun and scurried away. Auraka awaited while we played.

Around the edge of the reef, near the entrance to a small cave, was Auraka's lair. We'd agreed that Charlie would be waiting there to film Hanna when she met Auraka. I could see his video lights as he filmed the creatures of the night. Among his other talents, Charlie is a world-class underwater videographer who markets his work to travel agencies and TV stations. When we first found the eel, we agreed not tell anyone or sell images of her, knowing the harm publicity would cause. Tonight was different. Hanna was part of our cadre, and we knew she could be trusted with our secret. We also wanted to see how she would react and whether Auraka would accept her.

It was time. I opened a baggie containing vienna sausages—a special treat for a special eel.

We moved closer and she appeared, slinking around a corner of the reef at the entrance of her cave. She'd heard us coming, or reacted to Charlie's lights. At seven feet long, she is the largest green moray eel I've ever seen. I suspect she holds a record; most never come close to that length. Her chatoyant skin contrasted the color of Hanna's eyes. I hoped that would come across for viewers of Charlie's video—if it ever showed publicly.

Auraka is fearsome by anyone's definition. She has two heads, both larger than a fist. Only three of us had ever seen her, and even we couldn't believe it. I suppose we could kill or capture her for a museum, but she's a pet and part of our family; we are determined to protect her. An encounter with a giant two-headed eel is something you have to experience to believe—so Barnum & Bailey will just have to take a swim.

We have fed Auraka ever since we first discovered her. Now she expects food from anyone who approaches and has developed the nasty behavior of rushing out of the cave to get face to face with intruders. Tonight she came out of the reef and circled, slithering between my legs, and then sliding behind Hanna's neck to look directly into her mask. Both mouths gaped open, showing rows of needle-like teeth, and then snapped shut as she forced water across her gills to breathe. A giant moray eel looks terrifying, often just a head sticking out of the reef with its jaws working furiously. When I first found her, I thought there were two eels in the same coral crevice. Then both heads emerged and got face-to-facemask with me. She was curious; I activated the bladder wetsuit warmer.

Hanna startled as Auraka pressed against her mask. She jerked back but didn't bolt to the surface. Auraka edged forward, the near sightedness common to eels makes her seem aggressive when she's only curious. Hanna froze, and then tentatively moved to the side. She didn't panic and run, but she also didn't turn her back on the eel. Charlie gave her the okay sign and moved in closer to capture her expression. Auraka chose that moment to ham it up and abandoned Hanna to play Lady Macbeth for Charlie's camera. A blast of bubbles from Hanna's regulator made me realize she had been holding her breath. I wondered if she had activated *her* integrated warming device. Since she was not wearing a wetsuit, it would not have made a difference.

Auraka carries an aura of menace nothing in nature can match. Eels are docile if unprovoked, but will latch onto anything that looks like food. I don't think she can tell the difference between a vienna sausage and a finger, so I treat her with the respect she commands. Especially if she is hungry, and she is always hungry.

Hanna floated unflinchingly as Auraka continued to approach, looking for a snack. I carefully extracted a sausage and nudged it toward her, keeping my fingers well out of range. In a lightning strike, the sausage disappeared. Then another and another. I looked to Hanna, and she pointed to the baggie, then herself, then Auraka. I pantomimed the eel grabbing a finger, bending it at the knuckle to mimic a missing digit. She understood, but still wanted to feed her. Tentative at first, she quickly got the hang of it and finished off our supply.

While Auraka and Hanna became fast friends, I explored the cave with my dive light. I noted a blue green color to the water that was different from the surrounding seas. It appeared to come from a gap in the coral. Using my dive knife, I probed the area and loosened a rock. Behind it was a clutch of small blue globules. I pried them free and stuck them in a pocket of my BCD. A cornucopia filled the ocean this evening. These would look nice in my aquarium at home. I gave them no more thought.

Auraka, realizing the free dinner was over, made a few passes, allowing us to pet her. Hanna had met Auraka and hadn't panicked. She shared the awe inspired by all who knew this magnificent beast.

That's when I sensed, as much as heard, the rumble from the deep, an intense thrumming pressure behind my sternum. The pressure built in my ears and I squeezed my nose to clear my eustachian tubes. I saw the others do likewise. Charlie lowered his camera and looked over his shoulder. Auraka quit circling and looked at me with all four eyes. I thought she tilted her heads in inquiry. Then she turned toward the cave entrance and with a whip of her massive tail disappeared. In a blink, all the little fish were gone. Kelly's Reef began to shimmy.

Quake

In air, sound waves reach each ear a microsecond apart, and the brain uses that difference to echolocate the source. It doesn't work that way in water where sound velocity is muted; humans can't locate an sound origin. What I sensed wasn't as much sound, as the pressure in my chest and ears. That captured my attention.

The ocean creatures were silent—no squeaks, squawks, or chatter among them. There was nothing living in sight. Even the fish sleeping in crevices were gone.

What the . . . The rumble grew, a freight train bearing down on us. *Must be a freighter passing overhead. Propeller noise?*

I struggled to sort out the noises I felt and the sudden stillness of those missing. I looked up, expecting to see a ship's hull passing overhead, but saw only the reflection of the moon glimmering on the surface. I felt the water vibrate and churn. Sand and silt formed a low cloud stirred by millions of bubbles gushing out of the reef. Pressure in my sinuses built, and it felt like my face would collapse. My ears shot bolts of steel directly into pain central of my brain. I frantically swallowed to clear them.

I turned toward Charlie to see if he was experiencing the same—but of course, he was. He looked about frantically and appeared to struggle to see what was happening. Then, as if a giant hand grabbed him, he tumbled away from the reef and into the depths, arms flailing as he plunged. Before I could react, a massive crush of water encased me. I somersaulted backwards. The wall of water ripped the mask from my face, blinding me with seawater. I struggled to keep my regulator in my mouth as I rolled head onto, then up and over the reef.

I've been drift diving in fierce currents before, but nothing could match what embraced me. A fin yanked loose, but I managed to grab it before it was lost.

Thrown onto my back, lifted, and then bounced across the coral, I crashed into a rocky canyon. The impact squeezed the air from my lungs and ripped my regulator from my mouth. My brain screamed at my lungs to inflate, and it took everything I had left not to suck seawater into them. I reached over my head, struggled to find my regulator, and grasped the hose connection to the tank. My hand slid down the hose to my mouthpiece. Squeezing the purge button to flush, I stuck the regulator into my mouth and gulped sweet, dry air—but I didn't have time to enjoy the sensation. Again, the pressure squeezed my ears as I sensed another depth increase. I imagined I was freefalling over an abyss, but could still feel the reef surrounding me. The pain in my ears reached a crescendo as my vision went gray. I knew I was jammed into the coral; the skin on my elbow scraped as I moved to squeeze my nose.

Is this when I die? I'm not ready yet. Will someone be waiting at the end of that bright light?

Before I could clear my ears, the pressure lessened, and I realized that whatever had batted me helplessly about the ocean had passed. *What the hell?*

I lay still, taking inventory; I was breathing, aware, with no broken bones or pain. The reef had scraped and cut me. My heart thudded in my chest. The ice cream freeze pain in my ears eased as pressure equalized.

I have a heartbeat, blood pressure, and air. At sixty feet underwater, this is good.

Hanna! Where are you? Charlie? You okay? Am I okay? I had to find out, but without my dive mask . . .

A diver has limited visibility underwater without a mask. *Just open your eyes—it's okay. You've done it before.* It would be blurry, but in an emergency, I could see enough to survive. This qualified as an emergency, and I opened my eyes to a fuzzy but discernable scene. The burn of the saltwater dissipated as I looked around.

I had lost my dive light in the chaos, so I pulled out a miniature back up light from a BCD pocket and flipped it on. Charlie always carries two of everything he might need on a dive—lights, mask, knife, compass, depth meter, and peanut butter sandwiches. Although moonlight is sufficient illumination to see with a mask, I rejoiced at having at least a small light to beat back the darkness. Feeling and looking around I could tell that I was wedged on my back in a crevice. Adding a puff of air to my buoyancy compensator, I wriggled free of my coral entrapment. Rolling over, I oriented myself and kicked toward Auraka's cave—but I wasn't getting anywhere.

"Fins, dummy," I reminded myself and began to look around for them, only to find that I still clutched one in my hand. My hands shook as I tried to fit it over my bootie; I succeeded after the third try. Then I went back to basic scuba lesson number one—*Breathe in, breathe out, and repeat. Good.*

Now it was time to find my friends. I considered surfacing to see if they had already ascended, but knew they would spend time looking for me first. Surfacing without searching was not an option. Part of the philosophy and credo of being a Same Day, Same Ocean Diver is that your partner is always there. Maybe not conjoined at the hip as taught in beginning scuba classes, but as aware of you as you are of him; Same Day, Same Ocean.

Heading over the top of the reef, I realized that I was a considerable distance from Auraka's cave entrance. I saw a dim light from Charlie's camera through the surrounding murk, and kicked toward it. Sitting on a small coral head, his camera lights illuminated the area. This was good. I picked it up. Now I had more light to help me hunt for them.

But where is Charlie? Where is Hanna? What just happened?

I continued toward Auraka's cave—and there they were.

Fear manifests differently for each of us. I didn't appreciate how frightened I was until that moment. That's when adrenaline awareness occurred, my pulse skyrocketed, and my breathing became tight. Seeing my best friend swept into the depths, I feared him lost forever. It wasn't until I saw him again that I acknowledged that fear as well as the adrenaline surge my body experienced. My muscles tingled in preparation for flight or fight, my vision sharpened, and my breathing increased. I didn't have time to get over the shock of the event and beyond the denial of imagining my friend drowning; my fear of losing Hanna overwhelmed me.

I never panic, but I was on the verge at that moment. I sucked air at an alarming rate.

Calm down dammit. Breathe in, breathe out, and repeat. Slow it down.

Charlie turned toward me as he sensed the lights approaching and gave me an okay sign; at least I think that's what it was. He was a swirl of red and black in his wetsuit and BCD. I wanted to hug him; I was so overjoyed that he was alive.

I stretched my hand out and wiggled it side to side, and then pointed to my face. I knew he would understand and that I was okay without my mask. We had practiced this maneuver several times in training. Imagine my surprise when he reached toward me and put a mask in my hands—his spare. Slipping the strap over my head, I looked skyward and blew air out my nose while holding the mask firmly to my forehead. Saltwater flooded out the bottom rim with the bubbles, and I could see again. That's when I saw Hanna.

I wanted to cry out in relief until Charlie wiggled his hand and pointed toward her. He was kneeling in the sand next to her at the entrance to Auraka's cave. Feeling panic rise again, I swam around Charlie to see why he was concerned.

Ice-cold blood rushed through my veins into my ears, drowning the usual underwater sounds. I couldn't swallow. I forgot to breathe. Hanna was trapped.

Cave In

A large portion of Auraka's cave roof had collapsed, trapping Hanna's foot, fin, and tank under a pile of coral and rock. Iridescent blue sediment clouded the water. I assumed the color was something oozing from crushed coral. There was a more sinister cloud—blood drifting from her leg.

She moved, pointed to me, and gave the okay sign. This was just like her—trapped underwater and wanting to know if *I* was okay. I would have kissed her except the damn regulators were in the way. I signaled I was okay and pointed to her leg. She gave me an exaggerated shrug and a little wiggle of her hand.

Charlie and I worked frantically to move the rubble off her leg until we reached one large rock that wouldn't budge. I tried wedging my dive knife into a crevice and prying it loose; there was a slight movement. With Charlie doing the same, we moved the obstruction a couple inches but no more. Her leg remained firmly trapped. I looked around for something to use as a lever. Nothing.

I watched Charlie slip out of his BCD. He disconnected the tank straps, so his BCD was free but still attached to the tank. He then proceeded to stuff it under an edge of the rock and inflate it. Thomas Edison would have been impressed with Charlie's inventiveness. However, trying to inflate it to lift the rock didn't work. It only moved a few inches. I followed his lead with my BCD, but even the combined effort wouldn't break the blockage free. We needed more power.

The three of us looked at each other. "Oh, Shit," was the conclusion I'm sure we all shared.

Don't panic. Just breathe in, breathe out, and repeat.

We pulled our BCD's out and reassembled the gear while we pondered our next move—if there was one.

Charlie reached over and unclipped the small plastic board and pencil I use to communicate underwater. **Wait. Got idea. Back in 3 min.** Then he was gone.

I looked at Hanna, and I could see the fear in her eyes. Her breathing rate was up. I gave her hand a squeeze and looked behind her to see the condition of her tank. Trapped in the rubble, there was no way to release it. Thankfully, it wasn't her head, or we'd be doing a recovery instead of a rescue. All the while, the bloody cloud grew. I don't believe the myth that sharks can smell blood. They sense patterns of struggle from a wounded or dying fish in their neural network and come running for a meal. But, even though Hanna wasn't struggling, the idea of a wide smile of dagger-like teeth looming out of the dark sent a chill down my spine.

A small nurse shark slid past at that moment. A crustacean eater, she lacked teeth; my imagination created scores of them for her. She glided past in what I was certain was attack mode. For that, she received a sharp rap on her snout with my fist for her curiosity. I don't know which of us was more startled.

Tank toast. Ditch and buddy to surface, I wrote. She nodded agreement and began unsnapping her BCD. She switched from her first regulator to her octopus, a secondary regulator that divers carry to allow sharing air. Her octopus, being longer than her primary regulator, gave her a little more freedom. Her leg, however, wasn't going anywhere.

The octopus made me think of buddy breathing, something every diver learns during certification. That, in turn, made me think of air, and I realized we had been down the allotted time for our dive plan—not much I could do about that. I checked my integrated dive computer and saw that we had been down almost 50 minutes, and I had 800 pounds of air left. It also told me I only had a few minutes at this depth before I had to consider a true decompression stop on the way up. I looked at Hanna's computer, and although it gave her a couple more minutes before decompression, her remaining air was only 200 pounds. That computed to minutes before her tank ran totally dry. Showing the dial to her, I signaled her to calm down and breathe slowly.

Immediately I could see her usual calm return and the breathing rate slow. *Good girl.*

She pointed to her trapped leg and my dive knife, and then gave me a low air warning. She made a sawing motion across her ankle with her hand. I knew what she was suggesting—that I do an underwater amputation to save her life. No tourniquet, no anesthesia, no operating room, and minimal air—no way. I didn't even know if it was possible. The shock would kill her. We simply had to have another option. But what could I do? I couldn't leave her here and surface alone. I couldn't cut off her foot, despite what TV movies might suggest.

We were almost out of time and air. Before I had a chance to write a message that we had an extra tank on the *Chipmunk* and that I could be back down quickly, Charlie swam into view carrying our anchor. *Whiskey Tango Foxtrot?*

He pointed to the anchor, then the rock, making a circling motion with his finger. Then he pointed to his chest and indicated he was surfacing. I watched him pantomime with both hands as if he were driving a car. It hit me. What genius. He'll pull the stone free with the anchor rope using the *Chipmunk* as power. It was our last chance. Charlie had remained cool under fire, as always.

We wedged the anchor in a crevice and wrapped the rope securely around the rock. I was thankful that we had chosen an ebb tide for this dive, or we would have been fighting the *Chipmunk* to get the anchor and rope pulled to where we needed it. Apparently, whatever happened hadn't torn the *Chipmunk* free of her anchor, thereby leaving us adrift.

I indicated to Charlie to tug the anchor rope when he was ready. He started his ascent, and within two minutes, I felt him tug the rope and the slack taken up. As it strained, I silently asked King Neptune to be kind to us. He must have been listening. The rock broke free just as the rope snapped. I grabbed Hanna's leg and pulled it clear milliseconds before the rock crashed down again. That's when I saw the extent of the bleeding.

Blood in water always looks worse than it is. I could see a laceration on her calf, just above the ankle. It was bleeding freely, but no arterial spurting. I squeezed the cut with my palm, applying direct pressure to stop the bleeding. This was going to be awkward—trying to hold her leg, buddy breathe, and ascend.

I looked at her, giving the okay sign and thumbs up to let her know we were ready to ascend. She nodded and exchanged her octopus for mine, then noticed I was squeezing her leg. She paused and without hesitation reached behind her back to untie her bikini top. She pointed at her leg and the top—twice. I got it. Using the top, I wrapped the wound in a temporary bandage. Then I took my dive knife and slit a portion of my shorty wetsuit into a strip that I used to secure the wound. Now I was able to free my hands so we could start toward the surface. I reached down and released Hanna's weight belt, letting it drop out of sight.

I was again aware of the strange blue-green glow in the water, prominent now that a crevice had opened when the cave top collapsed. I glanced inside and saw more small blue globes. Something nagged my memory, but I was too busy to respond. I put my arm around Hanna to control our mutual buoyancy and ascent rate. We started toward the surface where a different world awaited.

<u>Aftermath</u>

Normally, two divers doing an emergency buddy-breathing ascent hold onto each other's BCD. Every beginning diver practices this in class. Hanna didn't have a BCD or much else to hold on to, so I just hugged her against me. Looking into her mask as we followed our slowest bubbles toward the surface, I could see dilated pupils lit with a post-adrenaline high. We both knew how close we had come to being another statistic.

I wondered briefly if I could have stayed submerged to help Hanna when I ran out of air, or panicked and rushed to the surface, only to die of a pulmonary embolus. The survival instinct trumps heroism every time. The soldier who throws himself on a grenade to save his friends is rare.

Hanna and I ascended along what was left of the anchor rope to a 15-foot depth. I knew we had pushed the envelope, risked decompression sickness, and needed a prolonged safety stop—but there was no choice. I didn't have enough air left to stop. Charlie must have considered that because there was a fresh tank and regulator hanging fifteen feet below the *Chipmunk*. Hanna and I switched regulators to the fresh tank and hung suspended, waiting for our bodies to off-gas the nitrogen we'd absorbed. I continued to hold her, not wanting to let go, needing to help her stay buoyant. *We're alive.*

While we waited, I rechecked her leg, pleased to see only minimal bleeding. She had some coral scrapes and minimal ankle swelling, so I figured her prognosis was excellent. I checked my own scrapes and scratches. I'd live too. We were starting to shiver, not so much from the 84-degree water, but a post-stress reaction. It was time to surface.

As our heads bobbed up next to the boat, Charlie reached over, locked onto Hanna's wrists, and hoisted her aboard with one smooth movement into his arms. I threw my fins and mask over the gunnels, then reached for a hand up. I floated there looking silly; Charlie was too busy fawning and fussing over Hanna to remember I even existed. I unhooked my BCD and tank, pulled myself in, and flopped onto my back, gasping. I was overwhelmed with just being alive.

"Oh my God, Oh my God, Oh my God," Charlie chanted, as if it was some special healing mantra. "What am I going to do?" He handed Hanna a towel—my towel.

His hands fluttered near her leg, then her head, then back to her leg, afraid to touch her. "Are you okay? You're bleeding. Bones, is she going to be okay?" His panicked eyes were something I have never seen; Charlie never panics.

I wouldn't have been able to stay down and drown when it came to it, but you, my friend, would have never deserted her.

"If you need a transfusion, you can have all of my blood," he blubbered. "It's really clean. I can't have Aids or anything, 'cause I haven't had sex or anything. I mean I've had sex before, but I . . . I . . ." Even in the dark, I knew he was blushing. We had almost drowned, but it was all I could do not to laugh at Charlie. Get him near Hanna and he becomes a blithering idiot.

"What about that bartender in Djibouti?" I reminded him. I was catching my breath and looking for a towel. I used his—only fair.

"But that didn't really count . . . and besides . . ."

"Charlie, shut up," I said. "I'm the doctor; trust me when I tell you Hanna's going to be fine. Get some ice out of the cooler to put on her leg. Then find a cushion to elevate it. And get the first aid kit." It refocused him on something useful before he made a complete drooling fool of himself. I would have suggested he get some boiling water, but I was afraid he'd sink the *Chipmunk* trying.

"We need to go ashore as soon as we can and find out what just happened. Let me take care of your leg first while Charlie packs our gear," I said to Hanna.

I cleansed the wound with peroxide and applied a sterile bandage. The bleeding from the gash had diminished compared to what I had seen in the water. It would require some stitches and an X-ray when we got back, but it was not life threatening. Considering how it had been trapped, I was surprised there wasn't a worse injury.

"How's that? Too high? Ice too cold? Are you in pain?" Charlie stammered. "Can I get you a sandwich or something?"

"Charlie," I snapped. "She's fine. We need to get out of here—now."

He pulled his sweatshirt over his impressive physique and managed to get it over Hanna's torso. Then she wrapped both arms around his neck and kissed him firmly, deliberately, and seriously. She didn't stop until he gave in and put his arms around her. His blush was bright enough to light the horizon miles out to sea.

"That's for saving my life. If you hadn't been there . . ." She trailed off and started to sob and shake as the reality finally hit home. Charlie just held her, and I could feel all three of us letting down, letting go. We were giddy just being alive and breathing. I finished toweling off and securing the equipment.

"So, do you two need to get a room to continue exploring tonsils or should we consider heading in to find out what the hell happened down there?"

Charlie said, "I don't have any idea what happened, but we need to get ashore to find out. The pressure and current . . ." He left the thought unfinished.

"You thinking the same thing I am?" I asked him.

The grin and the too-goofy-to-breathe routine disappeared. "That had to be a major earthquake we felt down there. I can't imagine what it would have been like on shore."

Reality struck; my wife Emily and my children were at home. Were they okay? Did something happen to them while I was diving? I needed to go ashore and check on them. I needed to get Hanna to the hospital.

Charlie finished loading the gear bags and pulled out a thermos of coffee as I fired up the outboard. The coffee was nectar.

I secured the anchor line and stopped. "If that was a quake, there may be a tsunami headed this way. We should head out to sea to be safe, but I have to be sure my family is secure."

"The fault zone that would cause a massive quake lies in the Marianas Trench a few miles from here," Hanna said, surprising me with her geological knowledge. "That means a quake would probably dissipate most of its energy in the depths. I think we may have felt a tidal surge right after the quake."

"So you don't think a tsunami is headed at us?" asked Charlie.

"Regardless, at some point we need to get ashore. I can't sit out here worrying all night," I said.

"We may have a more serious problem," Hanna said. She was staring toward the distant shoreline. "Look," she pointed.

Angel's Roost

I looked shoreward where Hanna pointed, and saw the faint outline of the southern hills backlit by the moon. A solitary buoy a mile distant rolled, its light offering a guide home. The offshore breeze carried the usual reek of mold, mildew, and garbage, rather than the flowery fragrance from earlier this evening. My eyes and my nose warned my brain there was something wrong. My ears registered the hollow clank of our movements onboard the *Chipmunk*.

"What do you see? I don't see anything out there but that buoy." I strained my eyes to make out any detail in the distance. There was simply nothing there.

"I see nothing. No lights. Nothing," she repeated. "That's weird." She was right. There *was* nothing out there. No shore lights, no road lights, no building lights. Guam was in total blackout.

I scanned 360 degrees of the horizon and saw only the single buoy light. The darkness increased my anxiety. *Whisky, Tango, Foxtrot.*

"Must be a brown out," Charlie said, referring to the common occurrence of a brown tree snake crawling up a power pole and committing suicide across a transformer, shutting down the local power grid.

The egg-sucking snake referred to as an LBB (little brown bastard) in navy jargon, was a transplant to Guam sometime during WWII. It killed all the indigenous birds, establishing itself as a major pest. An over-eager stateside magazine reporter once described the jungle as trees dripping brown tree snakes like spaghetti. That made for entertaining copy and a joke among the locals. I think the only snake he ever saw was the one he strokes in the shower, and that one certainly wasn't an ecological threat—or good copy.

"Nah, look toward Harbor Point." I pointed east. "It's out, too. Looks like an island-wide power failure to me." I stopped to get my bearings. "Whatever we experienced down

91

there affected everything on shore, as well. I'm not sure what happened, but we weren't the only ones who felt it."

"Are we gonna be able to get to safe harbor without lights?" Hanna asked, echoing my own concerns.

"I'm pretty sure we can find the channel approach if we're careful. Charlie can manage the portable spotlight to watch our depth over the reef. Since we're just coming off a high tide, we should have enough water under us." I hoped I sounded more confident than I was.

"I can see that one buoy light." I pointed. "It's the starboard channel marker for the dock. If we're careful, I can get us in. Or we can sit out here and go in by first light. I think it's worth the risk to get in now. We can always turn around if necessary."

"I agree," said Hanna. "We need to get home and check on Sister and the kids. If power is out here, we have no idea what is happening inland."

"Keep a sharp lookout for shallow coral heads and rocks," I told Charlie, who was manning a high intensity spotlight.

"Water's pretty murky. I can't see the bottom, but I think I can keep us from going aground."

Half way to the buoy, there was a snarling metal sound as the motor revved, then died. We sat in ominous silence.

"What happened?" asked Hanna.

"We ran aground on the reef. I hope we can break loose 'cause I don't want to be sitting here if . . ." I looked at Charlie and Hanna. They knew. I looked seaward, and my imagination built a twenty-story wave rumbling toward us.

Charlie and I lowered ourselves over the side, found footing, and tugged on the gunnels. The *Chipmunk* squealed and broke free of obstruction. I lifted the motor and found a bent, but usable, propeller. The engine started on the second try, and we limped toward shore.

Soon, I was able to pick out landmarks in the moonlight to guide us to the boat launch; at least what had survived.

Even in the dark, the moonlight and our spotlight were enough to see that the dock had collapsed as well as Angel's Roost, the small shack where we bought bait, ice, fuel, and other necessities. The Roost was a tin and plywood construct that blew down annually during typhoon season. Fortunately, the concrete boat ramp was still functional. Charlie swept the spotlight across the damage and at the top of the ramp stood Angel Sanchez, the facility manager, dressed in his usual ragged cutoffs and flip-flops. His torso was bare, showing off eclectic tattoos extending down both arms. Those arms were waving at us. Everyone who knew Angel knew his tattoos. The moonlight and spotlight were enough for me to see a fork-tongued snake wrapped around one arm, over his shoulder, and onto his chest where it bit his nipple. Winged dragons entwined his other arm. I knew that his back sported a giant cross with a cross-eyed, bloody Jesus. I've often wondered if Angel's tattoo artist intentionally made Jesus cross-eyed, but never had the courage to ask.

"Yo, Doc. You guys okay?" he asked as he caught our towline and helped bring the *Chipmunk* ashore. "I was worried about you being out there, but couldn't do nothin'." He tied us off to the remains of a cleat.

"What the hell happened?" I asked as I climbed out. "The dock and your shack . . ." The bait shack was a pile of rubble.

"Mother fuckin' earthquake; a huge mother. Shook like a son of a bitch forever. I got Lucy and me out just before the fuckin' store fell apart," he answered, referring to Lucy, a foul-mouthed parrot that livened up the atmosphere of his small business.

Lucy was perched on the remnant of a post a few feet away, next to a lantern. Clearly upset at being awake, she was pacing and preening her rainbow feathers. "Motherfucker, motherfucker," she squawked. "Gimme a damn cracker, motherfucker"

"Shut the fuck up," Angel snarled at her.

"Up yours," she replied and let out a loud donkey bray. Then she flapped her wings.

"Is she practicing the welcome speech for the Vice President's visit next week?" Hanna asked as Charlie lifted her out of the boat. "She might be more entertaining than the bagpipe player."

Angel flapped his arms at Lucy, who ignored him. "Power's out, phone sorta works, radio from Rota says there's lots of damage, but nobody killed. Man, you wouldn't beeeelieve it. Shook like a mother. Thought sure we was gonna die in there." He nodded at the remains of his bait shack.

"Make me beeeelieve. Show me your tits," Lucy crowed. Then she belched loudly and cackled.

"I'll make you a believer if you don't shut up," Hanna said. Charlie carried her to the truck and buckled her shoulder harness. I loaded our bags of dive gear in the bed.

"Never felt nothing like it before," continued Angel. "Thought we was dead, man. Then this humongous wave came clear up to the road." He pointed to the debris field pushed across the parking lot to where my truck sat at the far edge.

Charlie said, "Tidal surge. That fits."

An earthquake would explain our experience underwater. A tsunami, even what now seemed to be a relatively minor tidal surge, passing over us, tossed me around like a terrier's stuffed toy, and that must have been what caused the cave roof to collapse on Hanna. It would also explain the power outage.

Big mother of an earthquake. Got that right, Angel my friend.

"Any news of casualties or damage on Turner Hill?" My family lives there.

"Not that I heard of, Doc. Your house be okay I suppose, what with all that concrete and all," Angel said.

I was fortunate. Concrete block housing, provided by the Navy withstands equatorial storms, so my family was probably safe. That wouldn't be the case for everyone. I knew that I would have to report to the hospital and start damage control. I retrieved my cell phone from the glove box. No bars.

"We'll stop on the way in at home and check on my family." I didn't hear any resistance to my plan.

"Your family okay, Angel?" I asked. I knew that his mother and he lived in a shanty a mile down the beach. If the quake leveled the dock area, I could only imagine what their homes looked like. Home is a kind and a generous description of their tin and cardboard dwellings. In Oklahoma, tornados seem attracted to trailer parks. On Guam, typhoons seek the shanties. However, with FEMA money, they rebuild every year and live on the extra. Angel also has undeclared income from his various dock scams.

"Why the fuck you care?" I turned and saw Ramón, Angel's brother crossing the parking lot. "Only thing you care about is using our island to get rich, fighting your wars, and taking advantage of my people."

Short and wiry, his dark skin carries the scars of many bar room brawls. Dressed in the traditional cutoffs and rubber flip-flops, he radiates a negative vortex that sucks everyone who approaches emotionally dry.

"Is Isa okay? Your Mother?" I asked him.

"None of your fuckin' business," he said taking a step forward. Charlie moved in front of him, putting both hands up, legs spread. He took a step forward, and his bulk forced Ramón back.

"Get outta my way asshole," Ramón said, moving to the side. Charlie took a side step too and just smiled at him.

"Ramón, get outta here. It's okay. The doc and his friends are trying to help. Go home and make sure Momma and your wife's okay," said Angel.

Ramón looked up at Charlie, sneered, and then spit on the ground. Then he turned and stormed off. "Fuck with my brother and you fuck with me," was his parting shot.

"Yeah, they okay," said Angel. "Ramón got Momma and Isa out soon as she started shaking." He pondered a minute. "Sorry 'bout that. You know how he gets."

"That's okay. You sure he's blood kin? You, I know, are a homo sapiens; Ramón, I'm not so sure about," I said.

Angel shrugged. "Say, do you think FEMA gonna pay to replace my dock and store?" I could see him calculating this windfall. Running a swindle was, after all, a common and acceptable way to make a living on Guam. There was no one better than Angel at conning his customers.

"Bite me," Lucy cackled just to keep the conversation lively. From the truck door, Hanna flung a flip-flop at the bird.

"Well," I said, looking as dubious as possible while I unhooked the boat trailer, "the dock actually belongs to the Navy, but I'll make you a deal. You keep an eye on my boat and trailer until I get back, and I won't tell FEMA the dock isn't yours." A smile split his face, showing off one gold tooth and one missing front tooth. *Maybe you'll even use some of the anticipated funds to see a dentist.*

"Sure Doc. But why you not taking it now?"

"I need to make sure my family is okay and get Hanna to the hospital," I explained. I looked toward her and saw that the bandage had soaked through, "and I don't know if the road is blocked or not. Don't want to risk being stuck towing the boat 'til I know it's clear."

Hanna is bleeding, and my family could be trapped under rubble.

"No problem. And 'cause you my favorite white guy, I'll only charge you half price for the storage fee." He showed off his single, gold snaggletooth again. We both knew he got away with charging parking and storage in a lot that was government property. I didn't mind helping Angel make ends meet. He always took excellent care of us, and we knew that our cars and equipment were secure.

"Okay, here's twenty bucks," I said giving him some soggy bills that I pulled out of my cut-offs. "And there's another twenty if you'll clean the gear and the motor. Might be a couple days before I can get back. Okay?"

"No problem. I'll make sure it's all good. You got any unused beer in the boat cooler?" he asked.

"Gimme a beer. Bite my cracker," Lucy squawked.

"Help yourself. There's also some yellow tail and wahoo you're welcome to," I offered. "Need anything we can get you?"

"Nah. We be fine. You get Lieutenant Sanders in and get her fixed up real good." He reached over the back of the boat and opened the cooler, rummaging around until he found a Budweiser. "What's with the sissy soda pops, Doc?" He held up my grape Nehi.

"Don't start on me," I warned. Angel knows I don't drink, and he goes out of his way to point that out whenever he can.

"Sissy cracker. Gimme a sissy beer," Lucy intoned, continuing her tirade.

I grabbed my wallet and a few valuables from the boat as I unhooked the trailer hitch. As an afterthought, I retrieved the blue globes from the pocket of my BCD and put them in the glove box.

"What are those?" Charlie asked as I climbed in and started the engine.

"I don't know. I found them lodged in a crevice near Auraka's cave." I thought back to when Charlie and I first met in Djibouti. This wasn't the first time I'd seen a blue globe like these. The way Charlie lifted his eyebrows let me know he remembered too.

Downed palm trees and landslides delayed the drive back to the Naval Hospital. We made frequent off-road excursions. The night was still and humid. The darkness, punctuated with an occasional distant lantern, felt lonely. Some of the buildings we passed exhibited varying degrees of damage. Small knots of people milled about, uncertain whether to go inside or not. I couldn't ignore them in clear conscience, so I made brief stops to ensure there were no injuries—each delay increasing my anxiety about Hanna and my family. Other than fractured nerves, everyone seemed okay. The fortunate families had generators, allowing small pockets of lights to spring up in the hills and neighborhoods. A brief rainsquall cooled the atmosphere, leaving roads steaming.

A downed power pole blocked my way right across the intersection where I needed to turn up Nimitz Hill toward home. "Stay here," I said climbing out of the truck. "I'm going to check at that house and see if they are okay and whether there is a working phone I can use." There was.

No answer at home. No out of service message. No transfer to voice mail. Just a dead line. It was too far to walk the rest of the way up Turner Road. I dialed the Naval Hospital.

"Good evening . . . emergency . . . to report immediately . . ." Static.

"This is Commander Matthews, can you hear me? Is my family there?"

" . . . Commander, we have orders for all . . ." More Static. ". . . family . . . emergency room . . ." Then, the neighbor's phone died.

I raced back to the truck. "Shit," I said and stomped on the gas. The rear-end fishtailed as I swung us around the obstruction into the brush and grass next to the road. Both Charlie and Hanna grabbed the dashboard as I bounced back onto the pavement. The decision whether to go home or to the hospital had been made for me.

"Emily and my kids are in the emergency room."

<u>ER</u>

I pulled through the main gate to the hospital stopping at the guard station. It was the main gate only because of the guard post on the single access road.

Built originally in 1899 to serve non-active duty patients, the first hospital collapsed in an earthquake in 1903. Another earthquake in 1909 destroyed the replacement facility. The third evolution, built in 1910, survived until the Japanese invasion of Guam in WWII. The current building, dating back to the late 1940's, sits on an ocean cliff surrounded with personnel quarters, a few convenience stores, a gym, and a gas station.

One look across the low grassy field separating the main gate and the hospital building and I could see that the old structure was still standing, but appeared to have a midline crack. The main hospital, shaped as a long, three-storied H, tilted. One arm of that H separated from the other and was dark. Despite that, lights blazed in many other areas.

At least the emergency generators are working. As long as we have power and potable water, we'll be functional. Unless the damn building falls in on us.

I could see several canvas tents assembled in a parking lot at one end of the main building, so I knew staff was making emergency contingencies. Another brief squall blew through adding just enough moisture to maximize the humidity.

"Dr. Matthews, Sir." The Marine Corps Corporal guarding the gate snapped to attention, throwing a smart salute to his high and tight haircut. "Lieutenant Commander

Justis instructed me to have you report to the ER as soon as you arrive, Sir." His BDU's—battle dress uniform—were clean, pressed, and complete with body armor and automatic weapon.

So, TJ was on duty and in charge. Living less than a mile from the compound, he was usually the first on site during drills or disaster operations. He was the go-to person for all things medical. If it needed organizing, he'd already organized it. If it needed fixing, he had somebody working on it. If I needed a diaper in the middle of the Indian Ocean while on deployment, he knew where to get it.

"If I was white and lived in Chicago," he once quipped, "I'd probably be mayor or head of the Mafia." He knows everyone. He also knows where to exhume the bodies and how to get things done.

"How we doing up there, Corporal?" I nodded in the direction of the main building. "How badly injured is my family?" He remained at attention shouldering his weapon and saluting until I returned his salute. Then he relaxed. I only knew him by first name—Corporal.

"Sir, yes Sir. The Commander's family arrived and is helping with the volunteers. This Marine is not aware of any injuries to that family. They arrived with Lieutenant Commander Justis about an hour ago. Otherwise, current operations are not too bad, Sir. A few injuries, but I don't think there's anything serious. They've evacuated the west wing and some of the rooms in the middle of the building until the engineers can determine if there was quake damage."

So, my initial assessment is correct. And my family is safe.

"And the Skipper has ordered an all hands evolution." He leaned down toward my window and looked around as if to see if anyone was listening. "Problem is, Sir, the phones are down so we can't call anyone. Most of the staff just shows up like you did, Sir. Lieutenant Commander Justis put together a party of able-bodied help and dispatched them in jeeps to find other staff." The corporal reached into his guard shack and retrieved a clipboard. "I'll record that you, Master Chief Albright and Lieutenant Sanders are on base."

"Thanks, Corporal. Let any injured civilians who arrive through to the ER. I need to get Lieutenant Sanders checked in and patched up."

"No can do, Sir. We're still at threat level delta 'cause of that bombing last week. I also have orders this evening to turn back all unauthorized personnel."

A typical oxymoron. He's standing guard duty at the only paved access to the hospital compound. There's no fence or other perimeter barrier, so anyone can just walk to the hospital unhindered. This is not the time to worry about access to medical care.

"*Which* idiot gave that order? Let me guess," I said. "Were those orders directly from the Skipper, or Commander Hawke?"

I knew the Skipper would never turn away a civilian. The Executive Officer, Commander Hawke, called Hawknose behind her back, was a closet racist who would do whatever possible to prevent a Chamorro from getting help.

"Commander Hawke sent a messenger to the gate about 15 minutes ago with a note that said no one but staff and active duty was to enter."

"If you see her, call me. Better yet, just shoot her." He nodded and slid his hand closer to the trigger guard on his weapon. I hoped he knew I wasn't serious. "And if a local shows up, radio me before you turn them away. I'll override those orders." He looked relieved, obviously having considered the consequences of turning an injured civilian away from the hospital. "You won't have to take any heat."

"But Sir, Commander Hawke is the Executive Officer."

"I know. I'll have the Skipper confirm my orders as soon as I get checked in."

"Thank you, Sir" He looked relieved as he saluted again.

As I approached the hospital, I took a breath of relief. The cold fist squeezing my heart eased. My family was waiting by the emergency entrance. Benjamin, our son came bounding out followed closely by Jenny, our daughter, and my wife Emily.

Benjamin, wearing his Spiderman pajamas, oversized tennis shoes, and my fatigue cap with black oak leaf ran up to the driver's door and bounced on his toes. At eight years old, he is an unstoppable force of nature wrapped in a supernova of energy. He yanked on the door handle until I unlocked it.

"Dad, Dad, you missed it. It was . . . it was . . ." He frowned looking for the word.

Jenny, my twelve-year-old daughter, was at that magic age of potions, lotions, and motions. Too cool to be outwardly excited. She fussed with her bright pink hair. She had taken the time to put on jeans with glittery things, a boy band t-shirt and sandals. Her expression said boredom, but underneath I sensed her excitement too.

As soon as Benjamin got the truck door open, Jenny casually slipped in to be the first to get a hug from me. She trembled in my arms, and I knew it wasn't from being cold.

"Dad, can I go night diving with you next time? Please? Please? I'm ready." She had been learning to dive since we arrived on Guam and was indeed ready to dive at night with me.

Emily waited for the children to reassure themselves that I was okay and finally came over and pulled me into her arms.

"I thought. I thought, you know . . ." She squeezed me tighter, and I returned it. "The phone was out, and we couldn't . . . I didn't know what to do. I was so worried, and . . ."

"All I could imagine was you under rubble, then I tried to call here and they said something about you being in the emergency room. I don't know what . . ."

I felt the trembling again. I think it was me this time.

Charlie got out, leaving Hanna in the cab. Benjamin jabbered about glasses falling out of the cabinets and the piano bouncing across the floor. His excitement was palpable. For him, the earthquake was more fun than a day at Disneyland.

The iron fist of fear I felt when I first considered losing Charlie and Hanna finally released its grip as I held Emily longer than I needed just to feel both of us breathing. My family was alive, and that was all that really mattered.

Jenny put in her two cents worth, "We all got under the doorway, just like they told us to do in school. It was cool, ya know. Mom kept yelling, but I wasn't scared at all." She smiled at her own courage. I smiled with her.

"I wasn't afraid either, even when the bookcase fell over," said Benjamin trying to upstage his older sister. I gave him another hug and a noogie. Jenny gave me her 'don't even consider it' look.

Having assured herself that I was intact, Emily sought out Hanna. "Sister," she said. They both called each other Sister, never Sis or any other name—just Sister. "You okay? Were you underwater during the quake?" Emily leaned into the cab and hugged her twin. They both sprung eye leaks. Standing next to each other gave the illusion of a mirror. Only Emily's hair was slightly longer this week. Emily was wearing one of my old T-shirts with an Oakland A's emblem and shorts. Hanna was wearing Charlie's sweatshirt with the San Francisco Giants logo. Mine fit my wife; Charlie's hung like a tent on Hanna.

"Why are you here?" I turned to Emily.

"I figured we could be helpful, and I knew if you got home and we weren't there, you'd come here. The house is intact, just lots of broken glass. I thought it would be safer here."

"Bones," Charlie said, "let me take Em and the brats home. I'll make sure it's safe and help clean-up. You go take care of Hanna for me." I looked at her leg, which had quit oozing.

His permission to take care of the woman he loved while he took care of mine, spoke volumes of our trust in each other. Now we could each do our jobs during this emergency without guilt or concern.

"I'll update you as soon as I can." Charlie leaned in and kissed Hanna. "I'll be back to pick you up and take you home later tonight." He looked back at me. "You don't think she'll need to be hospitalized, do you Bones?" They fawned over each other like a couple of adolescents suffering hormonal rage.

"Hell no, I plan to patch her up and put her to work. With a full moon and an earthquake, I can predict the OB unit is cookin', and I'll need her help."

I wasn't kidding when I said I thought I'd be busy. I don't believe the myth about more births during a full moon, but I knew that we would have stressed pregnant patients worried about their babies. My best medicine tonight would be a dose of reassurance. Add to that military and civilian injuries from the quake, and tonight had the makings of a challenge

I found TJ leaning against the counter in the ER, chewing a thick black cheroot, giving orders, and making sense of the chaos. I never saw him smoke one of those blunt, foul looking cigars, but they always appear whenever he is in his take-charge mode. He scowls, and things happen. Towering over everything near him, that scowl carries a lot of authority. A shiny bald scalp that looked like a polished eight ball, depthless black eyes with microscopic flecks of gold, and a flat nose filling the middle of his face create a look as fierce as a tribal mask. He was clearly in charge; no chaos tolerated. Most of the exam areas had patients, and I could see a few others waiting in the triage areas.

"I smell an unwashed human who recently indulged his appetite for tuna and scuba." He didn't turn to greet me. I swear he has internal radar; nothing gets by him, or behind him.

"So, how bad is it?" I asked.

"Not bad, Dr. Matthews," he replied in his gravelly voice, finally turning toward me. Always formal, his uniform was spotless with a perfect gig line and a deep gloss polish to his shoes. My uniform consisted of a pair of ratty cut-offs and an old T-Shirt. Flip-flops completed my ensemble. "We're lucky so far; some cuts and bruises, nothing serious. There's a leg injury in OR #1 and an appendectomy in OR #2."

Well, that ties up two of my three operating rooms.

"I've had no reports from the field of anything serious." He stepped away from me and did a quick survey of his kingdom. His eyes focused on a distant field, while at the same time looked around the ER and at me. Spooky. "Hilltop Hospital is getting the few civilian injuries that have been reported."

"Hey, get your damn feet off my table," he yelled at a hapless sailor lounging in the waiting area. The poor guy nearly fell off his seat trying to straighten up. I saw the slightest quiver on the side of TJ's mouth.

"Island wide," he continued, "I'm not so sure we did as well. Main civilian generator is out, and it could be a couple months before auxiliary generators are back on line. Our back-up generators on the military bases are solid, so the hospital is good. Without island power, the pumps that bring water out of the wells aren't working. Water storage will run out in a week, and that will be a problem. Our well will give us some of the water we need, but it's going to be tight."

"How bad is our physical plant?" I asked

"One critical section right in the center. Engineers tell me we're sound, but the elevators in the middle of the building are out of commission. I've evacuated the third floor just in case and we're closing all but the essentials in the west end. Otherwise, not too serious, considering."

"And OB?"

"No problem. A couple women in labor, but plenty of staff to cover it at the moment." He paused. "We dodged a bullet. No deaths, no major injuries, some mechanical problems. Lots of broken glass, but . . ." He looked around. "Other than the few people here who need patching up, I'll probably send most of the staff home to be on-call after they check in."

"So," he asked, "is Hanna badly injured? And did she get to meet Auraka?" TJ was the only other person who had ever seen Auraka. He wasn't diving this evening because he was the on-call duty officer.

"How did . . ." I began, but he cut me off with a wave of his cigar.

"Did you forget that I'm omniscient? Nothing goes down around here that I don't know about," he said, tapping his gleaming dome.

"But how?" I tried again.

"Corporal at the gate radioed you were en route with her," he answered.

We saw Hanna wheeling into one of the treatment areas. Besides Charlie's sweatshirt, someone had thoughtfully given her a pair of scrub pants to slip on. I could imagine the stories circulating tomorrow if she hadn't.

And if Hawknose sees her . . .

"She'll be fine," I said, nodding her direction. "A nasty ankle laceration, some coral abrasions, and maybe a sprain or fracture. I'll take care of her—unless you need me somewhere else." Even though I outranked TJ and was the most senior medical officer present, I knew that he'd tell me where he needed me. I'd never question that.

"No, that's fine. Go take care of her. I'll get a hold of you if something arrives in the next hour, go on home and clean up your house. And thank Emily for her help. She and your kids were eager go-fers. Even had Benjamin pushing wheelchairs."

I did a quick check of the ER and moved into the treatment room. Already set up was a scrub tray, size seven gloves, and a suturing kit. One of my younger corpsmen looked up and asked what else I needed.

"Some 6-0 Ethilon should be fine," I said, deciding on a fine, dissolving suture that would close the wound with a minimum of scarring. Scarring those legs would be like defacing a priceless work of art. The corpsman opened a couple suture packs onto the sterile tray and excused himself to go help in the other rooms.

"Let's take a look," I said, pushing the baggy leg of the scrub pants up to the knee and remembering the bikini top we had used underwater as a bandage. "I'm glad we changed the bandage before we came in. My reputation would have been tarnished trying to explain that one." Usually an opening like that would have her teasing me, but she was strangely quiet.

"I almost died out there. If it hadn't been for you and Charlie." She took a deep breath and stopped, not knowing what to say, but speaking volumes. The dam of her lower lid finally gave way, and tears flooded her cheek.

I felt embarrassed. "That's what superheroes are for, right? Besides, Charlie deserves the credit for his idea, and you, my dear, kept your composure when most others would have panicked. It's over. Your training proved itself tonight. But it's going to be a couple weeks for this leg to heal before we can go diving again." I injected Lidocaine to numb it and scrubbed the wound with Betadine.

"I think Auraka will be cranky until she sees you again," I said as I loaded a small curved needle onto my suture holder, "providing she's still there."

"So you'll still dive with me?" she asked in all seriousness, never considering that such a close brush with death would keep her from diving again. Like all of us, Hanna was hooked on diving and someone whom we would always consider one of us.

"Sister, you're now officially a Same Day, Same Ocean Diver. You met Auraka and she gave you her stamp of approval. So I would be thrilled to go down with you anytime and anywhere. But you'll need to let this leg heal before you get your dolphin tattoo." I looked up at her, knowing she was going to be fine now. She sat partway up, threw her arms around my neck, and gave me a kiss on the cheek.

"Thank you," we said in unison, but for different reasons.

I examined her cut. It was straight and clean, like a wound from a sharp knife, but I knew that certain corals had razor edges. I closed it with a three layer subcutaneous closure and steri-strips.

"Good as new. Now drop your drawers and roll over on your stomach. Let's take a look at those coral burns your thong didn't prevent," I commanded.

"Sir, I will have you know that I am a woman of the highest moral values and a Naval Officer. What, Sir, are your intentions?" She giggled as she complied.

"Am I going to need a chaperone in here for protection—mine?" I asked.

She did her eye roll routine and said, "I didn't see any female corpsman in the ER, so you'd have to call Hawknose to be a stand by. Then she'd need protection." I envisioned Hanna holding her down while I strangled her.

"What do you plan to do?" asked Hanna. "And I don't mean about Hawknose."

"You had a close encounter with some coral and I seem to remember some scrapes on your leg and butt. Charlie's not here to kiss your boo-boo and make it all better, so you'll have to settle for an antiseptic."

"Learn that technical language in medical school, sailor?" She giggled some more. She was still trembling from her narrow escape but was regaining her playful spirit. "Ouch, that smarts," she complained as I began a vigorous scrubbing of her leg and backside with Betadine. The scrapes themselves were not concerning, but the microbes from a coral scrape could cause a nasty infection if not treated properly. I applied a topical antibiotic and decided to start her on a course of broad-spectrum oral antibiotics for a week, just to be cautious.

The door opened, and I peeked around the corner of the privacy drapes to see my corpsman putting a set of X-rays on the viewing box. "Films are ready, Doc," he reported.

"What do they show, Andy?"

"Well… the ankle and foot are tough for me to read, but I don't see any fractures."

I looked over his shoulder. "Very good. You were paying attention last week when we reviewed leg and foot films. Right here," I said pointing to the film, "is where the tibia attached to the calcaneus. Sometimes there can be a tiny chip if the tendon tears away. What do you see?"

He studied the film. "Nope, don't see anything there. Am I missing it?"

"No, you're right. Just testing you." I patted him on the shoulder. "By the way, how are the applications to medical school coming?"

"John Hopkins said no, but Tufts, UCLA, and Irvine all invited me for an interview." He broke into a huge grin, and all I could say was how proud I was of him.

"And," he continued, "I've been accepted into the Navy Scholarship Program to pay for medical school."

"That is absolutely fantastic and congratulations. And when you're done with Lieutenant Sanders, I'll need you to scrub the coral burns on my arm too."

I turned back to Hanna. "You may need something for pain later tonight," I told her.

"I'm fine."

"Well, let me give you a few Tylenol with codeine just in case." She shrugged an okay.

"Let me check with TJ," I continued, "and see if I'm really needed here anymore. Then we'll go home and finish cleaning up the mess. Why don't you and Charlie stay with us tonight? Then tomorrow we can help you get back to your apartments to see if they are livable." Both Hanna and Charlie live off base at the same apartment complex. It is inexpensive and close to the hospital. It is also a solution to the chronic housing shortage for personnel stationed here.

"Thanks. I'm not up to going home with this leg," Hanna responded. "Charlie can take me to my apartment in the morning." I could almost hear those long eyelashes batting in anticipation.

That's when the aftershock hit. It sounded like a jet landing on the roof. Cabinet doors popped open. Jars and supplies flew out. "Get in a doorway or under something," I shouted over the noise, but before we could react, it was over. Just like that. Aftershocks were to become a normal event for months to come as the earth settled down.

"Dr. Matthews, I need you," TJ announced as he pushed through the treatment room door. "The corporal at the gate called and said he was supposed to notify you if a civilian tried to get in."

"Correct. I thought it best to evaluate everyone before we turn someone away. Hawknose left orders that no one was to enter. I need to get the Skipper to override that."

"Stupid bitch," he said under his breath. "Be nice if she showed up to help, but then I'd spend all my time trying to undo her usual damage."

"Does that mean you're not sending her a valentine this year?"

He took my arm and pulled me aside. "You're right, we can't turn anyone away. I'll make sure the Skipper is aware. But it seems that Angel Sanchez is at the gate demanding that you see Isa. And . . . he has Ramón."

"Oh shit."

"Ramón has a shotgun and is threatening to use it if we don't let him in, and he won't talk to anyone but you."

Low-Rider

Angel's low-rider sat four inches off the pavement, stinking of gasoline fumes. I never understood why, on an island with more potholes than pavement, anyone would remove the shocks and springs on their truck. The deep black window tint prevented a view of the cab, but I could clearly see Ramón standing in the back, a double barrel shotgun cradled in his arms. Although Angel's brother, he stood nearly six feet tall compared to Angel's diminutive five foot four inches. At 200 pounds, Ramón isn't someone you'd engage in an argument or challenge to an arm wrestling match. His mass pushed the rear bumper the short distance to the ground. He turned to watch TJ and me approach. I could sense his eyes blazing. His internal fire can burn everything in his path; he runs on high octane. Whether an oratory for the TV cameras that would shame a Southern Baptist minister or the path of destruction left behind in a bar fight, Ramón is well, Ramón. Tonight would be no different.

TJ and I climbed out of the Jeep we'd commandeered. The marine corporal on the gate had his M-16 planted high on his shoulder, aimed squarely at Ramón's head. I knew he wouldn't hesitate to shoot at the slightest provocation. I could smell the testosterone in the air, mingled with my own sweat. The humidity hit me like a wet blanket.

Seeing us, Angel stepped cautiously out of the cab, nodded at the corporal, and waved to me. "Doc, please, you gotta help Isa. The baby's coming and she's started bleeding real bad. I think the earthquake did somethin' bad to her. She's passing out and everything on the way here. I think she gonna die."

Isa was Ramón's teenaged wife, and if I remembered correctly wasn't due for another month. Even though a civilian obstetrician was following her pregnancy, Angel updated me on her progress whenever we launched the *Chipmunk* from his dock. Although Angel and I get along, Ramón's aggressive personality strained our relationship.

"Corporal," TJ commanded, scowling and pointing the stogie, "I want you to do a double tap through the forehead of that gentleman if that shotgun so much as twitches. I want him dead, understand? Too much paperwork if you only wound him." He stuck the cigar back in his mouth and fixed Ramón with a dangerous stare. TJ was the only one not sweating. His scalp, however, steamed.

"Angel. Make Ramón put the gun down before he gets hurt," I said. I looked at Ramón. "Ramón, please don't do something dumb, okay?" I moved cautiously toward the truck, never taking my eyes off his gun.

"Not until you take care of my Isa." Although stressed, his speech wasn't slurred. "You think you can take over our island, treat us like dirt, and just let us bleed to death? We're not going to allow that. Now, you get in there and fix her before I get crazy." His hand slid toward the grip of the shotgun and then he thought better. The corporal tensed. His thumb flipped the safety off. Ramón rocked slowly from side to side.

"Ramón," I said, "cut the racist, political bullshit and put that gun down. I won't do anything with you threatening us with it. Come on. We've known each other too long for this." I swallowed to moisten the dust that filled my mouth. No such luck. My heart and lungs competed for space in my chest. The ringing in my ears filled my cranium.

"You know I'll help you if I can. I'm just going to look inside the truck. Okay?" I moved toward the truck. I didn't think Ramón would actually shoot, but I knew the corporal would—without hesitation. Ramón is skilled at stirring up emotions among the locals about "retaking their island" from the government and haoles—but oh yeah, please continue the welfare payments when you leave. He was all bluster and show—only violent when drunk. I hoped he hadn't been drinking tonight, but with Isa bleeding and possibly in labor . . .

"Ramón, pleased put that gun down; it's not helping anything." I reached for the door handle.

"Not until you fix her." I couldn't see dilated pupils in the dim lighting, but I could see him shaking.

A horn honked and I startled. Everybody turned to look, except the corporal who never took his eyes off Ramón. My rusted, blue boonie truck roared through the gate, flashed the headlights, and screeched to a dusty stop behind Angel's truck. Charlie to the rescue. He climbed out and strode toward us. Everybody stood frozen—like the moment in a horror movie just before the monster jumps out of the closet.

"Ramón, this is bullshit," Charlie said, raising his arms, palms forward. He continued his deliberate approach. He had summed up the situation and switched to his version of command mode. At times, I wonder if he isn't too stupid to breathe, but adversaries who underestimate his resolve regret it. He was speaking in a whisper, his focus on Ramón. Meanwhile, I opened the passenger side door to look at Isa.

"Ramón, you're so stupid, the only thing you're likely to do with that shotgun is shoot yourself in the shorts. Not that that would be any great loss." Charlie walked without slowing to the truck. "Gimme that." He reached up, and Ramón handed him the gun.

"And quit being such a jackass." He cracked the chamber and removed two shells.

I'm not sure what Charlie does in the military. He is a Master Chief, ostensibly assigned to the military police. He disappears for periods sometimes lasting months, and then reappears. I suspect these missions are black holes—ask, and get sucked in, never to be seen again. I know he has combat experience and figure him for some type of special ops— CIA, NSA, ABC, or some other alphabet government service. Even as close as we are, there are things he does that I know better than to question. So, I was not surprised when he calmly walked up and disarmed Ramón.

"I didn't really want to hurt no one," Ramón said, standing his ground, "but you gotta take care of my Isa, Doc."

"You numb nuts. You see that Marine?" TJ pointed, the steam coming off his bald scalp in a small cloud. "He was going to blow your fucking head off, and I would have spent hours filling out forms."

He pointed the stogie toward the marine. "Corporal, you can stand down." He slowly lowered his rifle and stepped back.

While TJ and Charlie were dealing with Ramón's chaos, I took charge of Isa. No older that 16 or 17, skinny, and dark haired, she was leaning back in the seat. A mist of sweat coated her gray skin. The cab smelled of copper, stale snack chips, and seawater.

She opened her shocked, clouded eyes in surprise as another contraction started. She doubled forward with it. "Oh . . . oh . . . oh," she moaned and collapsed as the wave passed. One hand reached across her abdomen and then fell to her side. I reached for her wrist to check her pulse. That was when I saw the blood saturating the seat and her smock. It pooled on the floor mat. Her pulse was rapid and weak, doing nothing to reduce my anxiety. She was gray and panting, from both labor and failing oxygenation to her vital systems. I began to pant as well.

"Houston, I think we have a problem," was all I could think to say. This is a disaster waiting to happen, and on my watch, too.

"Corporal," I called across the roof of the cab, "radio up the hill. Tell them we're coming in and to set up the OB ward for an emergency. Also, have them get lab there STAT, alert the blood bank, and find my ultrasound machine. Oh, and get whoever is available to help me. Have a gurney at the door, too." I couldn't think of what else to order. *Oh, yeah. Breathe in, breathe out. Repeat.*

"Yes Sir," he said, the radio already signaling.

I pushed Angel aside and climbed into the driver's seat. "I'm commandeering your truck," I told him. "We don't have time to wait for an ambulance. Get in back." Angel climbed into the bed, and we were off. Ramón came along for the ride, but I knew there'd be more military police waiting to take him into custody when we arrived. Sure enough, there were, and he went without a fight after I promised I would take good care of Isa. Angel followed the gurney and me down the hall.

"Sit. Stay." I used the same tone and hand signals I use on my three-legged beagle, Tripod. He paused. I wanted to toss

112

him a doggy treat. I also thought about sending him to get some boiling water, but the humor would have been lost. Humor doesn't always diffuse tension.

A corpsman was waiting on the ward. She helped move Isa from the gurney to an exam table. Fred Bird stuck his flat-topped head into the room, using his back to open the swinging door. As the charge nurse for the OB ward, he has as many deliveries under his belt as most physicians.

"Dr. Matthews? What's up?" Fred asked, holding his gloved hands up to keep them sterile. "I heard you have an emergency. Ralph," he stopped. "Excuse me, Dr. Zebo and I just took the last operating room for a C-Section. The remaining two rooms are occupied, and you don't have anyone available for anesthesia." He turned to leave. "Sorry."

Great, just fucking great.

The corpsman helped Isa into a gown, started an intravenous line, and drew blood. She slipped an oxygen mask over her face. The lighting blinked once and went out, leaving the ward black. A moment later emergency battle lanterns began to glow. *Wonder f'ingful. What next? A pack of rabid pit bulls?*

I said to my corpsman, "This is Ramón's wife. She's hemorrhaging, and I need to know why. Anybody else around to help?" I was mentally going down the roster and not finding much. She shook her head.

"Get a second IV going, and run in another liter of lactated ringers." I ran out the door after Fred.

"Is there anyone else here that can help?" I tried to keep the fear out of my voice.

"Just your corpsman," Fred said. "With the phones out, we're having trouble finding staff until they roll in on their own. Lieutenant Sanders' injury puts her on the bench. Dr. Zebo and I will be finished in an hour and can help." He shrugged.

Just then, Hanna turned the corner. "Just point me in the right direction and I'll be fine." She limped on her crutches the rest of the way into the delivery room, pulled up a stool, sat, and looked at me defiantly.

"Thanks, I really need your help," I said knowing better than to argue. Navy corpsmen are the finest in the world, but if I had to do emergency surgery, I needed more, much more. Hanna can flirt, joke, and wrap Charlie around her little finger, but in an emergency, she is a consummate professional. I needed her.

"What can I do to help?" I felt the swish of air as Charlie burst through the door. "Rest of your staff is nowhere to be found, so I came back." Oh, great. Charlie is here.

"Keep your hands off the Lieutenant and stay out of my way. Oh, and go boil some water." That one went right over his head, too. I think.

"I could do that, Doc." Angel looked expectantly at me. I had forgotten about him. He jittered from foot to foot in the corner.

"Master Chief, please escort Angel to the warehouse to find a case of gonorrhea and a couple tubes of elbow grease." My mouth was wisecracking, but my brain was working overtime. I'm not always aware of this automatic response.

"Aye, Aye," Charlie said. Having been on more than one snipe hunt, he was more than willing to divert the stunned looking Angel.

I finished greasing up Isa's abdomen with ultrasound gel and ran the wand over her belly and the baby. She was having a contraction, but did not react—not a reassuring sign.

"Better yet," I said to Charlie, "run to the ER and shanghai Petty Officer Rush to help me. He was gone before I could finish. Angel stood, looking blank.

"Oh, shit," I muttered quietly to myself, sweat breaking out on my forehead and soaking the pits of my T-Shirt. The ultrasound showed the baby in a normal head down position. I could see the heart beating, but no movement. The fetus just lay there. Bad fetus, no biscuit. In the lower section of the uterus was a dark, speckled mass I identified as a placenta previa. It was located well below the fetal head. "Oh, shit," I repeated, more to myself that anyone else in the room. I could smell my own sweat and fear. I hoped nobody else did.

Normally, the placenta's job is to carry oxygen to the baby and to get rid of waste products. Filled with massive blood vessels, the placenta usually attaches to the side of the uterus, out of the way of a delivery. After the baby is out, it separates and delivers. Isa's was blocking the way out for her baby, and causing all the bleeding. If her cervix dilated further, she would bleed to death.

"Doc," one of our lab techs stuck her head into the room, "the spun 'crit is only 12." That told me that Isa had lost a critical volume of blood. She continued to hemorrhage on the exam table. "They sent me up with two units of O neg until they can get you a complete match." O negative blood is a universal donor. In an emergency, transfusion risk is minimal to the recipient. If this wasn't a qualifying emergency, I don't know what was.

"Hang them," I ordered, "and get me two more. More O neg if that's all we have. Put another four on standby. Oh, and see if we can round up any donors on the premises—we may need more before the night is through." I finished my exam with the ultrasound and slipped my hands into sterile gloves. My corpsman and Hanna helped get Isa's legs bent at the knees and elevated so I could do a manual exam.

I would rather stick my hand into an electric socket or handle a live bomb than what I was about to do. A dark mass of fear roiled upward from my abdomen. Coupled with the sweet coppery smell of her blood, I felt nauseous. I could try to slip a speculum into the vaginal canal and visualize what was happening, but without stirrups and directed lighting, it wouldn't help. In addition, so much blood would hinder my visibility. If my suspicion was correct, I could potentially make matters worse and stir up even more bleeding, but I *had* to know how far her labor had progressed. I had to know if her cervix was dilating in preparation for delivery. I had to know if I had time to stall until an OR became available and the cavalry arrived. *Gently. Gently. Pay attention.*

My fingers slid along the vaginal wall toward the cervix. I felt a thin ridge at the base of the uterus and knew I had reached my destination. Ever so carefully, I let my index finger slide over that ridge. The cervix was open wide enough to loosely fit three fingers; she was dilated three to four centimeters. The soft, spongy tissue I encountered sent a chill down my spine and my heart racing. I silently prayed that I would feel the fetal scalp. I felt the placenta instead. *Not good. Not good at all. If I stick my finger into it all hell's gonna break loose.*

I looked at the paper tracing of the fetal monitor that was displaying the baby's heartbeat. The heart rate was 100 beats per minute—way too slow— slower than mine was. Moreover, in the few minutes I had been watching, the only change was a slowing to 60 beats and a very slow return to the baseline rate. Bad—really, really bad. Baby Sanchez should have a heart rate of 120 to 160. This baby was dying.

A normal, healthy fetus will show an amazing variability of heart rate in response to squeezing by contractions, its own movements, or an external stimulus. That's in a normal birth. This baby wasn't reacting to anything. This baby and I were in serious trouble. Isa was beyond trouble. The baby had a life span I estimated in minutes, not years.

"What's wrong with her, Doc? Is she gonna die?" I had forgotten all about Angel in the corner. Charlie apparently hadn't removed him. He looked as pale as I felt. Oh shit, if I screw this up Ramón will kill me.

"Angel, listen. I need your help. Isa and the baby are in serious trouble. She's lost a lot of blood and the baby's dying. I need to deliver her right now, understand?"

"Can't you reach in and use those, what 'cha call 'em, salad tong things and pull it out?"

"Not that simple. She has a placenta previa." As soon as I said it, his expression told me he was clueless.

"What do you need, Doc?" Petty Officer Andy Rush rushed in. He was half in uniform with bell-bottom pants and a surgical scrub top. His perfect flattop glistened with sweat and Butch Wax.

"I've got a previa, and I need to crash her—can't wait for an operating room. Help Lieutenant Sanders get set up." Hanna was already off her perch, opening cabinets, and retrieving wrapped bundles of sterile surgical instruments.

"No operating room?" he asked.

"Don't have one available, so right here, in the bed." I turned back to Angel.

"I don't understand." Angel moved next to the bed and looked down at Isa. I wanted to put a comforting hand on his shoulder, but I was busy scrubbing them and getting into a paper surgical gown.

"Isa's afterbirth is in the way of her baby getting out," I said, looking at her and hoping she was getting some of this. "That's where all the blood is coming from. She'll bleed to death if I don't operate." He nodded; Isa was beyond response.

"Angel, listen carefully." I looked directly in his eyes to be sure he heard me. "Go find out where they are holding Ramón and tell him what's going on. I need to do an emergency cesarean section to save his wife and baby, and I don't have time to talk to him first. You need to let him know I'll do everything I can for her."

He started toward the door. I called after him. "You know who Lieutenant Commander Justis is? The big black guy who dives with us?"

"Yeah?"

"He's in the ER. Find him. He'll help you find Ramón. Tell him it's okay for Ramón to see his baby as soon as I'm done. Go!" That got him out from underfoot. I turned back to Andy. He had finished opening an emergency C-section tray on a bedside table and was gowning-up. I didn't detect a tremor in his hands, and I wasn't going to give him time to over-think what we were about to do.

"Ready? You assisted me once before with a cesarean. Just hold what I tell you and be ready to suction out the baby's mouth and nose as soon as I pass it to you. Your job is the baby. You know what to do."

"But Doc, that was in an operating room with a lot of people and real doctors around."

"*Andy*. Everyone needs to know his limits, and when there's no one around, the sky's the limit. Let's go."

"BP's 90 over 50, pulse 110," my corpsman informed me.

"Shit. I mean okay. Check that every minute and sing out with it. And keep squeezing the blood bags and IV's."

"Lieutenant. Ready?" Hanna had set up the surgical instruments on the table. She pulled up her stool and finished gloving.

"Yes Sir." She handed me a large syringe filled with local anesthetic. Attached was a long, thin needle. Her eyes held mine. Those same eyes a few hours ago had looked at her own mortality.

I looked at Isa. "Hey there, how ya doin'?" Her eyes crept open and looked at me with a glaze like a Christmas ham. The green of the oxygen tube in her nose stood in stark contrast to the gray of her skin. She nodded weakly. "I need to do surgery to deliver your baby. Do you understand? Is that alright?"

"Don't let my baby die," she whispered and drifted off.

"Lieutenant? Andy? We agree that's close enough for informed consent during a life threatening emergency?" Of course, they were going to agree with me, but for the record, I needed to document that I had permission to do the surgery. Damn the malpractice lawyers—full speed ahead. Here we go sports fans.

<u>Cesarean</u>

I splashed a copious amount of Betadine onto Isa's belly and gave it a quick scrub. We laid out sterile towels and draped her abdomen. Then I inserted the needle under the skin and injected enough anesthetic to allow me to incise the skin painlessly. I'd add more as I dissected the various layers. I made a midline incision from her umbilicus to the top of the pubic bone and injected additional anesthetic. Reaching in with both hands, I pulled the muscles apart, exposing the abdominal cavity and her uterus. It occupied all the available space. Either Isa didn't react because of the local anesthetic I'd used, or she was too far-gone to tell I was cutting her. I hoped it was the former.

Petty Officer Rush placed a large retractor into the incision and spread the muscles. Atta boy. *Don't need to tell you what to do.* I lifted the uterus up and onto my field. It was a huge bag, thinned by the pregnancy, and clad with blood vessels along the sides as big around as my thumb. I palpated to confirm the baby's head was down.

"94 over 66, pulse 110," my corpsman sang out. "Lab's here with more blood." I looked up and nodded.

"Give her two more units as quickly as possible." The lab tech began checking ID on the bags against the patient; what

I was doing was dangerous enough without a transfusion complication.

I held out my hand, and Hanna slapped a fresh scalpel onto it. "Here we go."

I was committed to a classic uterine incision, one running top to bottom. In any other situation, I would have made a smaller lateral incision on the lower segment. The damn placenta was down there, and I didn't dare cut into it. Sometimes you can get away with cutting through a placenta if you're fast enough to get the baby out, the placenta out, and the uterus sewn shut before blood loss becomes critical. We were already at a critical level. I couldn't it.

I carefully cut high into the uterus, knowing the baby was just below the surface. Cutting a baby during a cesarean is bad form—I had enough problems without that. Slipping a large pair of bandage scissors into the small initial incision, I extended it toward the pelvis. The blunt end of the scissors protected the baby from injury. A creamy tide of bloody amniotic fluid gushed out. I had held my breath, anticipating meconium, dark green goo composed of amniotic fluid and fetal fecal matter. Meconium indicates severe fetal stress during the pregnancy. Suctioning it from the airway is critical, lest the baby takes a first breath of the toxic fluid into its lungs. There was no pea soup in this fluid. Baby Sanchez should be fine if it took that first life giving breath.

"Here we go." I reached in and lifted the head into the world. Andy slipped a small tube into the nose and mouth, suctioning fluid free as I struggled with the rest of the infant.

"Bingo. Houston, we have a boy." Someone please call *Hero Magazine* and let them know they can send that reporter now. I handed the newest inhabitant of our planet to Andy and placed clamps across the umbilical cord, cut it, and freed the baby. Andy set him on a warm blanket next to the bed and began to dry and stimulate him. The baby took in a huge lungful of air and let out a wail of moral protest for every injustice suffered by man since Adam and Eve. It was music to my ears.

So far, so good. I placed my hand into the now soft, empty cavity where junior Sanchez had resided moments before, and felt for the edge of the placenta that caused all this excitement. Finding it, I proceeded to run my hand into the zone separating mother's uterus and baby's placenta. It separated easily.

Children love to play in mud, squeezing it between fingers, and scooping it by the handful. There is something primal and sensual about that. Manually separating a placenta and plopping it out is just as satisfying.

"100 over 70, pulse 100." *Good, she's stabilizing. I'm catching up on her blood loss.* It had been no more than three minutes since the incision.

"Send this to pathology," I instructed Hanna, dropping the placenta into a bucket, "and start some Pit." Pitocin is a hormone that causes the uterus to contract, slowing bleeding. Mothers produce it naturally as oxytocin with the infant's initial suckling. Isa didn't look like she was in any shape to let Mother Nature provide the hormones at the moment. I'd get the baby to breast as soon as we're stable.

"Dr. Matthews, you better look at this," said Hanna, pointing into the bucket with the placenta. I looked closely and found a small amniotic sac with an incomplete embryo. I have never heard of a pregnancy with a viable normal infant, and a very early incomplete embryo supported simultaneously.

"Let's have path determine what that is before we say anything," I whispered. I could not imagine how I would explain this to the family. I didn't understand it. Sometimes it's better to leave well enough alone.

I continued to massage her uterus while she continued to hemorrhage. Hanna looked at me, and I knew that she knew what was happening; Isa was bleeding out. I was losing her.

"We need more blood," I said. I looked up and realized there were only five of us, six if I counted baby Sanchez. There was nobody who could stop what they were doing and get help.

"80 over 60, Doctor. I can't find a pulse." My corpsman looked stricken. *I'm not keeping up with her blood loss. I'm going to lose her.*

"Here," Hanna said, and handed me another syringe.

"Pit?" I asked. She nodded, staying with me, knowing what I needed as soon as I needed it.

I injected a small amount directly into the floppy uterine muscles hoping to start the contraction process. I felt the muscles firm in my hands, but blood continued to fill the abdominal cavity. A second, larger injection provided minimal improvement.

"Damn. Number one Ethilon on a big needle." I held out my hand, and Hanna slapped a loaded suture holder into it. A curved needle the diameter of a half dollar trailed a thick thread. I rotated the uterus to one side and pinched a bundle of massive blood vessels in my fingers. I sank the needle into the uterine wall and curved it under the bundle, grabbing the needle as it came to the surface. I pulled it through and tied the suture around the vessels, ligating them to stop the flow. I held out my hand, and Hanna slapped another holder as she retrieved the spent needle. I quickly tied off the vessels on the opposite side.

I massaged the uterus until the bleeding diminished. Lab arrived with more blood as I began closing the uterine incision. Isa and the baby survived. Fifteen minutes later, I was stapling the last layer of skin and applying a bandage. Isa was getting her fifth unit of blood, her pressure was improving, and she was awake enough for Andy to put the baby on her chest for warmth and comfort. Baby Sanchez latched onto a nipple and helped the oxytocin flow. I remembered to 'breathe in, breathe out, and repeat'. I wasn't sure I remembered that the last 20 minutes.

"Nice job, people," I complimented my staff. "Let's clean up, and we'll all go change underwear." Doing a crash C-section in a bed without an anesthesiologist is one of those nightmare scenarios I never wanted to experience, but we were now out of danger. I came close to losing a mother and baby. I held a shaking hand in front of me as the adrenaline wore off.

Ramón, Angel, and TJ were waiting in the hallway. I stood a moment collecting myself and then went out to meet them.

"Congratulations, Dad," I told Ramón. "You have a son; ten toes, ten fingers, and hung like a bull. He looks just like that guy who lives next door to you." The humor was entirely lost on him; he and Angel hadn't inherited the humor gene.

Just as well, I supposed. TJ's mouth twitched and he shook his head in amusement. I let Ramón into the room for a few minutes to see that his family was okay, and then the marine guards escorted him away.

TJ said, "Charlie took your wife home and went to round up some more staff. Soon as you're done here, I want you to get Lieutenant Sanders home and get a few hours sleep. A shower wouldn't hurt either." TJ sniffed. "Things are under control here for the moment. I'll send someone to contact you if I want you later." I realized I'd been up too many hours, survived an earthquake, an armed confrontation at the front gate, and the C-section from hell. Put me on a stick and call me a pudding pop.

The First Letter

I had spent most of the night cleaning up after the quake. The official pronouncement was an 8.1 on the Richter scale, and as I'd expected, there was no major tsunami. There were a couple minor aftershocks, however, just enough to create anxiety. Despite exhaustion to the point of being dangerous, I couldn't slow down or think about sleep when I got home. I swept broken dishes off the kitchen floor and then sat in my chair for just a moment.

A painfully short time later Emily shook me. "Sorry Jakey, you were snoring so hard in your chair I didn't wake you to go to bed. It's 6 AM, and you need to go make rounds."

"Mrrrph," was the best I could do as my system jolted into the new day.

A tepid shower did little to revive my wilted soul. I knew we would run out of water soon, so I tried to enjoy it, and failed. The drive down the hill gave me my first chance to see the damage in daylight. The concrete block bunkers we call housing had fared well. I hoped the locals and tourists did, as well. The radio played static on all frequencies.

I made early morning rounds on all my hospitalized patients, including Isa. She was recovering, with a stable hematocrit after her sixth unit of blood.

A smile lit up her pale face. "Thank you, Dr. Matthews." The baby was in her arms, nursing contentedly. "Angel told me what you did last night."

I squeezed her hand and promised to come back later. She stopped me at the door.

"We decided to name him after you guys. This is Jake Charles Justis Sanchez."

I didn't know what to say, and turned my back to her to hide my chuckle. "Thank you, that's very kind. I'll let the others know. I'm sure they will be as honored as I am." I left before I could choke up and blubber something idiotic.

The first of the letters arrived in my hospital mailbox the next morning. Plain white legal size envelope with a computer printed sheet inside. Addressed: Dr. Matthews. Nothing else on the envelope. No return address. No stamp.

I picked up the letter along with my usual stack of reports on my way to morning report, which was starting in the conference room. My role as Director of Surgical Services was to ensure the operating rooms remained functional. This meant paperwork, endless conferences, budgets, military unintelligence, and related nonsense. Every morning I reassured the Skipper and other department heads that all was well in paradise.

I was opening lab reports, bulletins, and the useless paperwork that clogs my life more than cholesterol in a fat man's arteries. I hate redundant paperwork, but in medicine the game is cover your ass and leave tracks. The letter caught my attention.

Dear Dr M

I Just wanted to let you no that I'm here on Guam. i'm living nearby and I'm real wanting to seeing you again. I hope you r3emember me. Its been a little wile since you took such good care of me and you a really busy man and all and I'm not sure you would remember everything you did to me but I hope you do becuze I'll see you soon. Until then, you watch your back and take care of yourself.

A old friend

PS- how is your nice wife and your nice children? Hope you remember me. And everthing you did to me.

There was no signature. I looked again at the envelope. *How did this get here, and what is this all about? Everything I did to him? DID . . . TO . . . HIM?*

<u>Morning Report</u>

"Jake, you with us?" asked Captain O'Brien, the hospital's Commanding Officer. I stirred from the letter. Various department heads, assistants, and junior officers filled the conference room. Group sweat from a lack of air-conditioning created the ambience of a boy's gym on laundry day.

I was so preoccupied with the letter I forgot where I was. Fortunately, I didn't knock over my cup of chow hall sludge masquerading as coffee. I realized that all the department heads were staring at me, a few with smirks. *At least I didn't fall asleep and snore.* Morning report was the Skipper's opportunity to pretend he was in charge, and he took it personally if you weren't paying rapt attention to his every word, nodding appreciatively.

"Yes, Sir. Sorry. I got a strange note in my morning mail and was distracted. Where were we?" Hawknose, the Executive Officer and number two in charge, was glaring at me. Her close-set, bloodshot eyes held a malevolent excitement. Her raptor like nose could double as a can opener in a pinch. She was dressed in dull khakis that hid her non-existent figure. The rest of the staff wore fresh white uniforms, or scruffy surgical scrubs.

She wore no make-up, sensing it would be a pointless effort. Her only concession to fashion was bright red fingernail polish on long bony fingers, completing the claw portion of her avian look.

I winked at her. That always pissed her off, and the only reason I could think of for doing it. I obtained a perverse pleasure that somehow evens our score. I felt the tension rise in the room as the others sensed yet another of our legendary battles forming.

"The Captain was asking about the armed terrorist you let through the gate last night, and why you ignored *my* orders not to allow civilians on this base. You created a dangerous situation, not to mention the publicity this stunt will cause in the local press." Hawknose smiled at me with a smugness I would've liked to shove down her throat or up a lower orifice.

"Is that a question?" Before she could respond, I pointed at my front tooth and made a picking gesture. "I think you have some carrion stuck." She had lifted a napkin to her mouth to clean her teeth when she realized all eyes were on her. The Skipper almost choked on his coffee. I figured she'd have to look up the word carrion before she knew I'd insulted her. By then, it would be too late.

"Frankly XO, I am too tired to debate this with you." I was too exhausted and worried to make up one of my usual brilliant yarns, much less put up with Hawknose's bullshit. *I need to get out of here to check on Emily. Some crank is sending me threats while you bluster.*

I knew the Skipper was up to speed on events. He'd been in-house most of the night, and I was sure TJ briefed him.

"Commander, that was a direct question as to why you deliberately ignored my orders and almost killed a civilian through your reckless decision to operate without permission *and*," her beak flared, "why you allowed an armed felon into the hospital last night?"

Oh, shit, here we go again. Haven't you learned not to come unarmed to a battle of wits with me?

I looked down at my paperwork and took a deep breath. With an audible sigh, I said, "First of all, I *was* aware that you had issued orders during a crisis without even being here. Those orders placed injured civilians in danger." I was feeling reckless. "I'll be sure you'll get credit in the local press for that."

I stood up and leaned across the table, giving her my best stink eye. I was within strangling range. I could feel my neck flush with anger. The red flag waved in the back of my mind—*careful, don't give her reason to come after you, again*—it warned. Too late—I could feel a tidal wave of self-destructiveness rolling toward the shore.

"Second," folding my index finger, "Mrs. Sanchez arrived in critical condition. She would not have survived a transfer to Hilltop. She had a placenta previa in advanced labor. Translated, that means baby coming, afterbirth in the way, Mommy dying, feces thrown into fan." Someone snickered.

"And," I continued heedlessly, "*you* weren't there to provide your *expert* opinion of the situation. Oops, I forgot that you no longer can give surgical advice." I had walked—no run—recklessly onto the thinnest of ice throwing that at her.

"That's not the point," she started, the claws crumpling the agenda sheet.

"Third," I cut her off, folding my pinky, "*I* was the senior officer at this *stunt* as you call it. *I* decided to admit Mrs. Sanchez. *I* saved both her and the baby, and *I* stand behind that decision. Had she been turned away she would be dead now and this command would be answering questions." I looked at the Skipper, letting him know the political damage we avoided. He was still dabbing coffee off his uniform. Dr. Como, our anesthesiologist, glanced around the table, and then gave me a thumbs-up.

"Fourth," I continued, "we had an armed man at the gate demanding entrance. Ramón, who has never been convicted of a felony, had a wife who was dying. I certainly didn't invite him to drop by and create havoc—as you suggest." I glanced around the table. Others were suppressing smiles or looking away. This was not the first time Hawknose and I had gotten into it.

I reached for my ring finger to emphasize the fourth point. My hand mesmerized the assembly. At the last moment, I folded my middle finger, leaving the innocent ring finger standing alone on my fist.

"And fifth," said TJ, who was sitting next to the CO, "due to incredible bravery under fire by Master Chief Albright, we resolved your 'shoot-out' without incident. He deserves a commendation for his actions last night. I think you should put him in for one." He smiled broadly at her, porcelain white on an ebony background.

Good move TJ. It's that, or the bitch is likely to court-martial Charlie.

TJ continued, "I'll write that commendation for you today, XO. Since I was there, I can document the facts for the citation better than you can. I'll have it on your desk in two hours." He added the last nail to that coffin.

"This was no big deal." I took another deep breath and sat back down. "We did the right thing and had a good outcome," I concluded. I wanted to tell her what I honestly thought of her officious meddling, but knew I was already pushing it. I could see the Skipper getting ready to break in and save me.

"And what do you mean by operating without permission? I don't need your permission to do my job or take care of my patients."

She still had to get in the last word and demonstrate her authority. "I didn't see a signed, informed consent in the chart, or consent for blood transfusion. I will need to investigate this. I expect a full report on my desk this afternoon." As Executive Officer, she could order such a report and bring charges against me if I failed to comply. She would if she could, and it was just like her to go through my patient records looking for a way to screw me rather than focus on whatever her job was supposed to be.

Needing to have the last, last word, I said, "I have some Visine in my pocket or could write you a prescription. Your eyes are bloodshot this morning from all the sleep you missed." Sometimes you just gotta poke the bear with a dull pole.

"Enough" the Skipper cut in. "A report won't be necessary, XO. I plan to interrogate Dr. Matthews about overriding your orders, which I personally countermanded, as soon as we're finished here." I could almost hear the silent chorus singing around the table *"Bitch slapped, bitch slapped, the ol' man just bitch slapped."* Coffee cups concealed several smiles.

I finished my report along with the other department heads. We concluded the earthquake was a near miss. We were lucky there were no fatalities. Civilian power would be down for weeks, and that meant potential problems pumping water from island wells, a nuisance more than anything. The last time we experienced a water shortage we collected rainwater in barrels to flush toilets, and showered in the daily torrential rains. That can be fun, but then I remembered Turtledove, the 350-pound wife of the warrant officer next door, standing naked in the backyard scrubbing the blubber in the rain. *That's a fantasy killer.*

"We're done here," the Skipper said. "Commander Matthews, I'll see you in my office." He tried to sound gruff and failed.

"Aye, Aye, Skipper."

Hawknose threw me a knowing smile. "Do you need me too, Sir?" she asked. She thought she could smell blood in the water.

"No, that's all right, XO. It'll be easier to talk about you if you're not there." He said it deadpan, leaving a puzzled look on her waxen face. I turned my head and faked a sneeze to hide my snicker.

"Well Skipper, in that case would you like me to have some donuts and coffee sent up?" she asked with a smirk. Her face was almost as bright red as her nails. This attempt at sarcasm failed when the Skipper said that was a splendid idea and thanked her.

The Hawknose
Six Months Earlier

Dr. Loeb, our resident pulmonologist, died of lung cancer a year after I arrived on Guam. The tobacco shop flew a flag at half-mast in his honor. Six months later Hawknose arrived. She had just completed a pulmonary residency, so I expected her to provide routine and emergency care for any lung problems. A sage once said, don't expect anything, and you won't be disappointed—words of wisdom when it came to Hawknose.

The day she arrived, she summoned me to her office. I anticipated the opportunity to meet a new staff member and develop a working relationship with a colleague—foolish me. We were both commanders, but I outranked her by a couple weeks commissioning date. Regardless, I expected a collegial relationship among peers. Naval physicians tend to ignore some of the rank protocol found in the regular navy.

"What's wrong with this scene?" she screeched, placing both fists on her hips the moment I entered. She was standing in the middle of a standard Government Issue office. Standard middle gray walls, gray metal desk, two gray metal chairs, and a gray metal file cabinet. Her corpse gray complexion melded right in.

"Excuse me?" I offered my hand. "I'm Dr. Matthews, Director of Surgical Services. Welcome aboard, Commander." I stood there a few more moments with my hand out until I realized she wasn't going to respond. *This is someone with issues. Swell.* I took a step forward, crowding her personal space. She flinched and stepped back. *Score one for me.*

"How can I help?" I smiled my award-winning, killer smile. She glared. I tried a slight smirk with lifted brow. She continued to glower. I switched to tucking the eyebrows tighter and looking really, serious. Her frown approached lethal.

Maybe a prescription for happy pills or hormones?

"Get me a real office. How am I expected to practice in this . . . this . . ." She waved her arm around the room. "It's *gray*. I can't work in this . . . this . . . At Tufts University, where I was the Chief Resident, the morgue had more color. This is unacceptable. My library's not here. And my personal items. I was told everything would be ready for me when I arrived."

"I'm sorry—I thought you got the message about your priority shipment." I gave her my best poker face, eyebrows lifted, and head cocked. I'm self-deluded enough to think I can make more faces than Jack Nicholson makes, and play better poker than Texas Dolly.

"What message?"

"Seems your shipment is at Guantanamo Bay. You know—one island is just like another to the shipping department." I was having a hard time keeping a straight face the redder she became. "But the good news is that they said it will only take a couple weeks to get it here—once they find it." I bit my lip, stepping back for the explosion.

"I . . . I . . ." She started to sputter and choke. I waited another moment. If she was going to be difficult, I might as well enjoy my passive-aggressive side a little.

"I'm just pulling your leg, Commander. I believe there are a couple crates down on the loading dock with your name on them."

"I don't find that at all funny, *Doctor*. Where I come from—"

I cut her off. "Hi, I'm Dr. Matthews. Welcome to our command—a fun place to work, where we all strive together in a co-operative, stress free environment." I stuck my hand out again, and she just stared at it.

"Listen," I said. "I know it's a long trip here, you're stuck in the bachelor officer quarters until housing becomes available. You're tired and eager to get settled. I'll do what I can to make the transition as easy as possible." *And this is the last time I extend the olive branch to you.* I slowly looked down at my hand and then slipped it into my pocket.

"Let me know what I can do," I said, turning to leave.

"How do I get help moving in?" she asked. The room temperature had chilled to sub-arctic.

"No problem, Commander," I said. "The guys on the dock have a hand cart you can borrow, and the gray building across the pad from the dock is the maintenance shop. They have some extra paint you can requisition. I think there is some gray and possibly institutional green or blue."

"And what am I supposed to do with that?"

I gave her my blank, surprised look—one more from the vast repertoire. "They'll also have paint brushes and rollers. You can paint your office to match Tufts' morgue."

"Am I expected to paint my own office? I'm a physician and naval officer. I don't have time for this nonsense."

"Oh, I'm sorry. I thought you knew I'd scheduled you off today to get moved in," I answered innocently. "I don't expect you to start seeing patients until tomorrow." *Normally I'd give you a week to settle in, but not now. Keep it up and I'll find an old guy to cough up a gob of lung on you this afternoon.*

"Or you can hire an independent contractor but be sure and turn in form 3462 Alpha in triplicate. I'll personally push it through the committee; will take a couple weeks, but I doubt the command will authorize payment. You might be able to get a local painter for a couple hundred dollars." There is no form 3462 Alpha or a committee. I'd have been willing to get one of the enlisted guys to help paint, heck—I would have pitched in, but the refused handshake still tingled in my pocket.

As I turned to leave, I heard one of the chairs bounce against a wall accompanied by a decidedly un-ladylike epitaph.

At first, I was only a little concerned with her attitude and wrote it off to a new command and new staff. We all get jittery in new situations, and some of us react differently.

Her second week, she called our general surgeon to the OR for a consultation in the middle of a procedure. She had problems assembling the endoscopic equipment needed to look into a patient's lung and obtain biopsy specimens. Okay, so maybe she was unfamiliar with our specific equipment, but any reputable surgeon knows his tools and assembly before the patient is under anesthesia on the table.

Shortly after this incident, I had an emergency tubal pregnancy roll in at midnight. A patient presented to the ER with abdominal pain, a positive pregnancy test, and a mass in the pelvis. Her embryo was stuck in the fallopian tube threatening to rupture. This is a life-threatening emergency that requires immediate surgery. I didn't have time to wait for back up and called Hawknose to assist. I figured that since she lived in the BOQ a hundred yards away, it would be an opportune moment to try again to establish a working relationship. I'd also have a chance to assess her skills. Pulmonary specialist or not, she was trained as a surgeon and could assist with a straightforward abdominal surgery.

"Why are you calling me?" she snarled. I had obviously woken her up in a foul mood. "I'm not on call, and this is an OB problem, not a pulmonary case."

"Birdina," this was last time I ever referred to her by her first name. "I need your help in the OR, you're five minutes away, and I have a patient who can't wait for one of the other OBs to get here. Please," I pleaded nicely.

"Shit." She hung up.

Forty minutes later, the swollen ectopic pregnancy was in a jar on its way to pathology, and I was closing the incision when she pushed her way into the OR.

"Do you still need me?" She was dressed in sweatpants, a sweatshirt and entering my sterile suite. She leaned against the wall and swayed. She was close enough for me to smell her sweat, body odor, and something else. *Wine?*

"My patient needed you thirty minutes ago. Where the hell have you been? And get the hell out of my operating room in those clothes." She stood there a moment looking surprised at not receiving accolades for her appearance to save the day, and then turned to leave.

At the door, she turned again. "I don't appreciate your attitude one bit, Dr. Matthews. You called me, remember? In the middle of the night, after a long day, when I wasn't feeling well, to come help you. If this is how you treat your staff, don't ever bother calling me again." She tried to slam the swinging door to the OR as she stormed out. The rebound smacked her in the ass. I heard her stumble and cuss.

Dr. Como looked up from his side of 'the blood-brain barrier', as he referred to the curtain between his anesthesia area and my surgical field. "Well, that was certainly pleasant."

He fiddled with some knobs on his machinery and then said, "You should see her when she's in a really good mood—like every time she's in here with us." The rest of the team concentrated on the job at hand, but most heads nodded in agreement.

The next morning, the Skipper summoned me to his office. He was standing with his back to the door, arms clasped behind him, staring at the wall. "Commander Hawke was here and filed a complaint that you insulted her in front of other officers last night." He turned to me, then continued, "I spoke with Dr. Como before rounds and got the story. So what the hell happened?"

"I really don't know, Skipper. I called her to help me with an emergency surgery because she was close and she went off on me for waking her up, and then showed up forty minutes late in street clothes in my OR. I made her leave the sterile area. She was clearly pissed off about something. I think she has a personality disorder or some type of chemical imbalance."

"Okay, don't worry about it, but we'll keep an eye on her. Let me know if anything else occurs."

Part of my job involves reporting problems with surgical staff to the Skipper or the Staff Practice Committee if there are ethical violations of medical practice.

As certain as the sun rises in the East, Hawknose and I crossed paths that very afternoon.

It started as a routine dental procedure—the placement of a simple gold crown in an elderly woman. No problem until the crown slipped and dropped onto the back of her tongue. The dentist reached for it with a small forceps, which caused the patient to gag and inhale the crown into her upper airway. As she gasped, wheezed, and coughed, the dentist wisely summoned an ambulance.

A corpsman had wheeled the marginally breathing patient into the operating room where a bronchoscope would visualize the crown and remove it. This is a delicate procedure since the surgeon must visually observe the trachea and bronchi while the patient breathes through the same tube. I practiced this several times during my training, as have most surgical residents, regardless of their specialty. Not a huge deal, but it does require concentration and some skill.

"Bones," Fred Bird called into the delivery room where I was calmly waiting for my patient to make progress toward delivery. "Skipper called and wants you in the operating room, STAT."

"Huh? Why's the Skipper calling, rather than the charge nurse in the OR? What the hell is going on?"

"I know nothing, I see nothing, I hear nothing, and I say nothing." He looked at my patient. "I'll keep an eye on Mrs. Goody for you, while you save the world. Oh, and I put your lead-lined jock strap by the door." He gave me a knowing look.

"Oh, no. It's not . . ."

"Yep."

"Oh shucks," I said. Mrs. Goody was the President of the Conservative Coalition for Decency and Do-Goodery and on most church committees. If I dared say, "Oh shit." I was in big doo-doo.

I changed to clean scrubs, a fresh surgical cap, and a mask. Then, I pushed through the doors of hell. Despite continual scrubbing, the walls exuded a musky odor of mildew. A sweet overlay let me know that the anesthesia machine was leaking again.

"Oh shit," I muttered as I did a quick survey. Chaos would be a mild description of the room. Beyond the usual controlled clutter and activity of any surgery, there was an overturned tray of surgical instruments littering the floor, and a patient bucking on the table.

Hmm . . . are we in Dante's fifth or sixth circle?

Dr. Como glanced up, took a deep breath of relief, looked at Hawknose, and rolled his eyes skyward. He finished injecting something into the patient's IV, and she started to relax.

"Gimme a damn scope that works, for Christ's sake." Hawknose turned to confront the scrub tech.

"Yes, Sir. Uhh, I mean Commander, uhh, Doctor. . ." he stuttered.

"Hi. We having fun yet?" I asked. I looked at the video monitor above the operating table and could see the view down the patient's trachea to the bifurcation of the two primary bronchi. A gold nugget shone in the light of the endoscopic camera.

"What are you doing here?" Hawknose demanded. "I didn't call you for help." She turned back to what she was trying to do.

"Give me the medium loop again," she commanded. The scrub tech handed her a long slender rod with a small wire loop attached to one end. The other end had a finger grip that allowed it to retract. Similar to the one the guy on the Discovery Channel would use to lasso a snake—only smaller—and sterile *I hoped*, looking at the tools on the floor.

I looked to Como and arched my eyebrows in question.

"Got us a chunk lodged in the right mainstem bronchia. Started out a little higher, but we've had some 'equipment'," eye roll again, "problems that have pushed it deeper."

"Shut up while I'm trying to do this," snapped Hawknose at Como. "Everybody *just shut up while I do this.*"

Her shaking hand tried to guide the retrieval loop down the bronchoscope but missed several times.

The circulating nurse nudged me gently and pointed to a tray with a sterile gown and a pair of surgical gloves. She raised her eyebrows in inquiry.

"Nudge me like that again and I'll either have to report you to my wife or meet you at midnight on Lovers Beach." I whispered in her ear. My mouth was on auto-flirt, my brain was scrambling.

"Shut the fuck up, I said." Hawknose didn't bother to look up as she snarled.

I slipped into the gown and gloves while Hawknose continued to try to lasso the golden treasure.

"Would you like me to try?" I asked, moving next to her at the table.

"You're so damn smart, why don't you do this," she snarled, shoving the loop into my hands. Then she stormed out of the OR for the second time in 12 hours.

I stood there a moment and looked at Como. *I don't believe this.*

"Am I imagining this, or did the operating surgeon just abandon her patient in the middle of an operation?" I was trying to make sense of what had just happened. You never walk out of the OR with your patient on the table. The only acceptable reason for a surgeon to abandon a surgery is death—the surgeon's.

At least she'd learned not to slam a swinging door.

"Yep," he concurred, "and I don't think that was Chanel No. 5 she was wearing." He looked at me knowingly.

"I thought it was Eau de Jack Daniels," whispered the circulating nurse. Dr. Como heard the comment, and he looked me directly in the eye, unflinching.

Commander Hawke was missing the next two days, claiming that she was ill. She had not heard anyone at her door or the telephone ring. The Skipper ordered a 'random' drug and alcohol screen on all hospital personnel that afternoon, but when Hawknose finally reported to duty, her system was clean.

The Staff Performance Committee met the following day and placed Dr. Hawke on administrative probation. All clinical and surgical duties were suspended. There was even discussion of bringing up charges of criminal abandonment. I had the dubious pleasure of informing her of the committee's decision.

"We'll just see about this." She slammed her door in my face. I felt no guilt.

Two weeks later, orders arrived at the command promoting her to the position of Executive Officer and replacing the outgoing XO. Although I outranked her by a couple weeks, she was now my boss and answered only to the Skipper or the Admiral. The Skipper wouldn't discuss this with me. The rest of the staff was shocked senseless. Politics suck and something was seriously wrong. I didn't like this a bit, not one teeny, weenie bit.

Busted

Three weeks after the quake, Charlie, TJ, and I made our last dive on Kelly's Reef. We just didn't know it at the time. We'd retrieved Hanna's gear and Charlie's camera two days after the quake; now we were taking our first days off to assess the damage. A chill, unrelated to temperature, gripped my spine as I looked at the collapsed roof of Auraka's cave. Hanna survived the quake, but Auraka was missing and that worried me. She always showed up whenever we came near. Not today.

Today felt different. Fish were more abundant than I had ever seen, and the coral was spectacular. The reef vibrated with life. The water was translucent with a hint of that unusual blue tint. I floated weightlessly, observing the miracle of creation and feeling an overwhelming sense of awe.

I wondered about the blue globes I'd found. In the aftermath of the quake, the emergency surgery on Isa, a letter from a whacko, and another battle with Hawknose, I had almost forgotten them. The night of the quake, when I finally got home, I moved them from the glove compartment of my truck to the safety of my salt-water aquarium. Once before, I'd found a shark egg—an opalescent fluid filled sack with a small embryo. Maybe the blue globes were Auraka's eggs. I couldn't remember if eels laid eggs or bore live young.

I remembered similar blue globes I had glimpsed on the *Swordfish*. That was too large a coincidence, and I don't believe in coincidences. They would be safe in the aquarium until I could sort this out and get them checked out.

Charlie was filming the damage at the entrance to the cave; a few yards off TJ was engrossed with coral research— his private passion. I descended to where I'd first noticed the globes, hoping to find more. The crack uncovered by the earthquake beckoned, but held no globes, only globs of a blue leathery substance I assumed were remnants. I probed one with the tip of my dive knife and released a swirl of blue. Immediately, small zebra fish swarmed, nipping and fighting over the fluid. *These things must be good eatin'. Here, try some of this.* I lifted the remains of a casing for them to eat, but had no takers. As quickly as they appeared, they disappeared. Zip. Vanished. *Aha, Auraka must have arrived. I'd be spooked too if I were a small fish.*

I turned to greet her. Even though she knew me and I could safely feed her, I wasn't comfortable with her sneaking up behind me. "Never trust a near sighted eel, even when she smiles," my Pappy would say. Sure enough—there she was.

Wait a minute, that's not Auraka.

I cleared my mask and tilted my head to get a better view. My custom dive mask with built-in bifocal prescription sometimes distorts my vision. *I need one of those mirror decals that say 'Caution, objects are closer than they appear'.* It wasn't my mask, however. It was a miniature Auraka, both heads bright green, and all four eyes coal black. It was all of six inches long and in my face. So were the brothers, sisters, cousins, uncles, and extended family.

Holy conglomeration, Batman—what is this? Let's see, it's a herd of cows, a flock of ducks, a gaggle of geese, a murder of crows, a squirm of worms, and what, a nightmare of eels? I'm losing it here.

There were hundreds of them, all staring at me. I looked toward Charlie to see if maybe I had bad gas in my tank and was hallucinating, but he was pointing wildly at me while filming. TJ was pointing excitedly as well, but at the reef he was examining.

Now what? I'm in a nightmare of eels and TJ's found something more appealing?

I inhaled, producing increased buoyancy to lift me away from my newfound friends. They didn't seem to be anything but curious, but not enough to follow. Charlie moved closer, filming the Aurakettes as I moved out of range. TJ banged on his tank with his knife hilt to get my attention. He pointed at the reef again. *What the hell is happening here?* I did a quick double check of my air, depth, and time down. They were normal. Nothing else was.

I joined TJ and saw that he was pointing with his knife at debris and broken coral pieces, illuminating the area with his dive light. All I saw was a smooth black surface where coral had broken off the substrata. I looked at him and shook my head. I shrugged with incomprehension, putting my hands out, palms up. Again, he poked it with his knife and rapped on it with the handle. I heard a dull echo and shook my head again. He took a deep breath and exhaled forcefully, clearly exasperated with my stupidity. He took the knife and scraped the surface, pointing. I got it. There was something metallic under the coral.

So what? Big deal. Probably some chunk of iron from a wreck, or garbage, or WWII salvage overgrown by the reef.

Many reefs begin life as simple junk on the sea floor. Maybe that was Kelly's genesis. I shrugged at TJ, losing interest and wanting to get back to Auraka's family. He vigorously shook his head and again scraped with his knife. It was just a shiny, black, metallic surface.

Wait a minute. Black? Shiny? No rust? Covered in what appears to be a hundred year growth of coral? Hollow sounding?

That's when I felt the thrumming in my chest. *Oh fudge, not again? Not another earthquake?*

I looked toward Charlie who had abandoned filming and was giving me a thumbs-up 'let's get out of here' signal. I turned back to TJ, who also recognized something was amiss and had started his ascent. I was awaiting the inevitable crush of water, wondering how it was that I was so lucky to be underwater during not one, but two earthquakes. And I waited . . . and waited. Nothing. The thrumming increased, and I knew this would be a killer—literally.

I looked up to locate TJ and saw the wake of a large, twin prop keel in the distance racing toward the *Chipmunk.*

Hey asshole, don't you see I'm flying a 'diver down' flag?

The ship cut power, and the thrumming ceased immediately. It floated next to the *Chipmunk* on a calm sea. My heart rate didn't slow. From below, its enormous keel sitting next to the small keel of the *Chipmunk* seemed ominous.

We floated at 15 feet for the next five minutes off-gassing. The mystery craft loomed next to the *Chipmunk,* engine sputtering, props still.

'PIRATES?' I wrote on my slate. I was kidding, but surfacing next to an unknown boat, without defenses might not be the wisest thing to do. A couple of times a year a small fishing boat or personal pleasure craft is lost, and rumors of pirates circulate.

Regardless of the risk, I knew we had to either surface or grow gills. Charlie secured his camera to the 15-foot line we use for our safety stop. He signaled that he would surface, look around, and for TJ and me to stay put. A few minutes later, he leaned over the gunnel and signaled for us to surface. I pulled myself onto the *Chipmunk* and turned to face a USN service boat tied off to us.

Marines with automatic weapons greeted me.

Lieutenant Moron

"Who's the fuckin' moron that doesn't know what a diver down flag means?" I screamed. "Somebody's ass is going to wish it was stationed on another planet when I'm through frying it." I was steaming when TJ nudged me and pointed his chin toward the service boat.

Forty feet long and dull gray, she rode several feet higher than the *Chipmunk*. At the stern, a USNS number covered the original YB number identifying her as a navy yard boat. The United States Nautical Service is a civilian branch of the Navy tasked with a variety of nautical and oceanographic assignments. *Who the hell is this? And why is there an armed Marine?*

"It's Lieutenant Moran, to you, and you're hereby ordered to cease all activities. You are in a restricted zone and ordered to leave this area immediately." As I finished pulling myself over the gunnels of the *Chipmunk*, I looked up into the baby faced, khaki-clad lieutenant staring down at me. As he spoke, two more armed marines moved into view, weapons visible. "I also need to search your vessel and confiscate any contraband and photographic equipment."

"Bullshit, moron—uh, I mean Moran. You could have killed us with this stunt and you have no authority here. I am a US Navy Commander, and I'm ordering you to cast off and leave the area immediately." My bluff probably wouldn't work, but there was no way they would shoot us. "Only the US Coast Guard has interdiction authority." He unsnapped the flap on his sidearm and rested his hand on the grip as one of his marines came to alert. Now he had my attention.

"Easy son," TJ calmly said, holding his hands in full view and outstretched. He'd managed to find a cigar that he was chewing furiously. "I'm Lieutenant Commander Justis, and you're about to shoot two unarmed officers, and a dangerous, renegade Master Chief. Not a smart move on your part—the paperwork alone will take you all the way through adolescence." He spit a gob of tobacco overboard.

Facing down a boatload of armed marines is not something I do every day, but I somehow knew they wouldn't harm us. Marines receive extensive training in fire discipline. I knew they would not shoot indiscriminately. It was a Mexican standoff. I looked at TJ, who winked. He wasn't going to let this youngster hijack us without teaching him a lesson. I relaxed a little.

Charlie broke into a huge grin, showing more teeth than seemed possible in the human mouth. His head twitched twice on his bull neck, and he said so softly I caught the Lieutenant leaning in to hear. "Lieutenant, be extremely careful. Dr. Matthews here," twitching his head in my direction, "has to keep me heavily medicated so I can dive without killing things." His voice took on a agitated tone. He giggled. Then, he picked his nose and examined the find. That even spooked me. I'd seen Charlie back down three drunken bikers with this same routine. The marines just looked at each other.

Trying to keep his eye on all three of us, the Lieutenant's gaze settled back on me. He hadn't blinked or flinched yet but was sweating from more than the sun.

"Lieutenant Commander Justis, did you personally witness the Master Chief taking his meds this morning?" I asked, not taking my eyes off Moran. I stood at parade rest with my hands clasped behind my back to hide their shaking.

"That's a negative, Commander Matthews."

Charlie started laughing manically and crab-walking sideways toward the cooler. The other two Marines came to a higher state of alert, glancing at 'the Khaki Kid' for guidance.

"It's okay Master Chief, they're new here and don't understand. Please try not to hurt them. They're on our side, I think." I could see confusion in the eyes of the Lieutenant and uncertainty in the Marines who waited for his leadership.

"Son," I spoke directly and softly to the kid, "I can probably forgive and forget that you flagrantly ignored my diver down flag, are illegally tied off to my vessel, are gesturing at us with weapons and are severely annoying my master chief. However, if he hurts you and I have to fill out all those damned forms, I'm going to be seriously pissed." I started toward the bow to pull the anchor rope. "I suggest you let go your line, move back, and stand down."

"No can do, Sir. I have strict orders to remove all personnel within three miles of Old Wives Beach. There is a potentially hazardous spill in this region, and you will leave immediately after we search your vessel." He sounded serious, but didn't make a move to board us.

"You have no authority to board; I'm in United States coastal waters and have not violated any laws. Corporal," I said, pointing at the most nervous looking Marine, "stand down. I am identifying myself as the senior officer present, and ordering you to put down that weapon." His eyes twitched toward the Khaki Kid. "And a safety notification of a hazardous spill does not require an armed threat."

"Bones," Charlie had become deadpan. "What if they find all that C-4 we're smuggling? I'm not going back to Leavenworth, again. I'll blow us all into another time zone first." His right hand started to twitch, and he kept looking at the cooler and then at the Lieutenant.

Okay pal—don't overdo it. A nervous Marine with an automatic weapon is not the same as a drunken biker in a bar. Easy now, Charlie.

TJ pulled the soggy cheroot out of his mouth and pointed it at the Lieutenant, who jumped and started to remove his sidearm from its holster. "If your men do not stand down, someone will get hurt. You don't want that, now do you?"

"I have strict orders from Captain LaRouche, that—"

"The Djibouti Cutie! You work for LaRouche?" Charlie broke the spell and launched into a huge laugh. "That son of a sea hag owes me big time for what he did to me in Somalia. Why didn't you say so in the first place?" The tension shattered. TJ and I looked at each other and joined Charlie in laughter.

"LaRouche?" I echoed. "Where the hell is he? I need to collect on an old poker wager. Isn't he still cleaning up sewage or something off the coast of Somalia?"

Lieutenant Moran was now thoroughly befuddled; his blouse heavily stained with perspiration. His hand remained near his sidearm, but he didn't make further aggressive moves. He looked over his shoulder at the horizon, and I shifted position enough to see a pristine white ship sitting off my bow.

Well, I'll be damned. It's the USNS Swordfish, LaRouche's 'research' ship. The Djibouti Cutie has come back to haunt me.

I said, "Lieutenant Moron, uh . . . sorry, Moran. Here's what we do. You get on your radio and call the good Captain. Tell him you have Dr. Matthews, Master Chief Albright, and Lieutenant Commander Justis in custody and he damn well better have an admiral's welcome for us when we come aboard. Mention Djibouti. He'll understand."

Three minutes later, the frazzled Lieutenant was apologizing and extending an invitation to lunch aboard the *Swordfish*. The Marines were smoking cigarettes and shaking their heads.

"That's more like it," I said as we clambered aboard their boat and headed toward the *Swordfish*. An afternoon squall drenched us as we proceeded to a highly unusual and unexpected reunion.

Lunch with the Djibouti Cutie

"Permission to come aboard?" I asked as I turned toward the ensign. Since hastily thrown together uniform consisted of ragged cutoffs, a Hawaiian shirt, and sandals, I didn't think throwing a snappy salute was in order. Besides, in the Medical Corps we salute with an exaggerated shrug.

The *Swordfish* hadn't changed since I was last onboard her. Maintained in immaculate condition, there wasn't a spot of rust. She smelled of diesel fuel and mystery. I often wondered what happened to her crew, especially the chief in charge of medical and the boson's mate both of whom were pregnant and couldn't be.

And what about that camera case of blue marbles? Like the ones I found directly under us.

Now Captain LaRouche was shanghaiing me and my warning sensors were flashing. There was no activity topside. The good Lieutenant Moran had dismissed his goons, but kept his nervous eyes on the three of us as we headed toward the chow hall. Sweating more than the climate demanded, he looked confused about what just went down on his watch.

"Dr. Matthews. What a fantastic surprise to find you here. I never quite got to say good bye and thank you for all you did for us in Djibouti." I turned and almost ran into LaRouche ducking through a hatchway. He nodded curtly at TJ and Charlie while he shook my hand so vigorously I wondered if my arm might come loose from my shoulder. "When my lieutenant radioed that you were coming aboard, I couldn't believe my luck. Come, come—join me for lunch and let's revisit old times." Other than an increase in the tonsure, he hadn't changed a bit.

"Old times? What old times? I've never met you, I've never been on your ship, I was never in Djibouti, and I don't want to share a cell with a guy named Bubba at Leavenworth." I shuddered as the Djibouti nightmare rushed through my memory. "Surprised to see me, huh? Gimme a break, Captain. With all due respect, I doubt this was an accidental meeting. Last time we met I was damn near killed during a boondoggle that never happened, remember?"

"Why Commander, I have no idea what you mean." He smiled innocently, frowned and hitched his head toward the lieutenant—a warning not to say more. "We noticed a dive boat and thought the occupants might be thirsty and hungry, so I determined that a luncheon invitation was in order." I reminded myself not to play cards with this shark—he cleaned my clock last time. Moran just stood there looking back and forth at us.

"Well, in that case, we accept," TJ said, "but perhaps we should return later when we've had a chance to put on our dress white uniforms? And leave word with our next of kin."

LaRouche's uniform, as always, was crisp—the gig line straight and the creases perfect. Charlie hadn't bothered to put on a shirt and his skin foretold of serious sunburn. At least he had flip-flops on his feet. TJ wore a brilliant white Hawaiian shirt festooned with surfer dudes—as usual, the fashion plate of our group. I wore a shirt with hula girls, the same shirt I wore the night we blew up Kelly's Bar and Grill.

"Don't bother; we'll be quite informal today. You're fine," said LaRouche.

"Lieutenant, Sir." Charlie piped in, again flashing enormous teeth at Moran, "Could I borrow a uniform shirt, just for lunch. Feeling a little naked here." The kid clearly had no idea what to do and looked toward his captain for help.

"Sir?" he bleated.

"Lieutenant, why don't you go down to medical and see if we have a pajama top for the Master Chief? Would that be okay, Master Chief?" LaRouche raised his eyebrows in Charlie's direction.

"Thank you, Sir. That is very thoughtful of you." He turned to the Lieutenant. "See if there are any with those little bunnies on them—they're my favorite."

Lunch was sliders, the naval version of bad burgers, baked beans, wilted salad, and Kool-Aid. At least the chow hall was deserted. Despite air conditioning, the kitchen exuded a rancid butter smell.

Sparkling inane conversation about the weather (hot), the water (clear and warm), the hospital (busy), recent vacations (wonderful), etc., filled the gap between mouthfuls of slop. I cleaned my plate because my mom always reminded me of the starving children in Africa, to whom I would have gladly sent my slider. I rinsed my last bite down with some green bug juice and looked directly at LaRouche.

"Permission to speak freely?" I asked.

"Of course, Doctor. I would expect nothing less from you."

"What the fuck are you up to, Sir?" I paused. "You sent an armed guard to my dive boat with some friggin' story about pollution and demanding not only that we leave, but to search my craft. And, while I'm thinking about it, Lieutenant Moron needs to learn what a diver down flag means. If he'd killed me, I'd be seriously pissed. So give." I sat back and crossed my arms.

"First, I apologize for my lieutenant. He's new and a little zealous. Information on the Djibouti mission is above his pay grade. I'll personally speak to him about his boat handling. However, I won't apologize for the subterfuge getting you here. You know this isn't an accidental encounter." He waited.

"Of course not. What do you want and why am I here?" I asked

"It is no coincidence that we stationed the three of you together on Guam. We felt it was better than risk individual exposure." LaRouche looked around to be sure we were alone.

"What do you mean exposure?" I asked. He ignored my question. My stomach clenched. One of the florescent lights blinked and sputtered. At the same moment, someone dropped a pot in the kitchen and we all startled.

"Obviously I knew you three were diving today and took the opportunity to arrange this meeting. And I also took the liberty of checking your craft to be sure she is seaworthy."

"So, you illegally searched the *Chipmunk*? That tuna I caught had better be in my cooler when we get back."

I'm glad Charlie left his camera hanging under the Chipmunk. I don't trust this guy with a film of what we found today.

"Nothing illegal, just a courtesy safety inspection." LaRouche smiled.

"Okay, why?" I asked. "What do you mean about the three of us being deliberately stationed together here?" *Coincidence again? I thought it was unusual that Charlie and TJ got orders here. None of us thought it was more than just luck that we were stationed together again.*

"The *four* of you that were involved with the Djibouti mission were sent on special assignments long enough for the Pentagon to sort things out. Now three of you are here, together again. You truly didn't think that was a coincidence, did you?"

"Four?" Charlie asked. "Why isn't Vignalli here, then?"

"I'll get to that. But first I need to warn you and ask a favor."

"Warn us of what?" I asked. My suspicion meter pegged the danger range. "And the last favor you asked ended up with my getting shot at, almost blown up, kidnapped, and nearly an aircraft crash statistic. Your track record for favors leaves a lot to be desired, Sir."

"Sir," Charlie broke in, his voice serious even if the yellow Easter bunny pajama top wasn't. "What does this have to do with the Djibouti mission? I thought we'd completed that."

"Master Chief, I know you are sworn to secrecy and can't reveal the details, but it looks like the mission was only partially successful. All three of you know that we were successful in capturing Alzera, but lost him en route to the carrier." He looked at me, and I suddenly felt guilty, then angry. LaRouche, sensing my reaction, raised a palm in surrender.

"We know nothing could have been done; he was fatally wounded long before you ever got to him," he said to mollify me, "but we didn't get all the information he could have supplied."

"And that information was?" I asked.

"Where he found the Blue Death." LaRouche waited for that to register. I remembered Alzera's last words—something about Blue Death—and his sick smile just before he died. "And where the rest of his terrorist cells are located."

TJ sat up, stogie firmly ensconced, and asked, "So what is this Blue Death? Was it those blue marble things we carried back in the sealed camera case with us? My understanding is that it is some kind of terrorist weapon they were planning to release on L.A. Wasn't getting that info and samples to the proper authorities the whole purpose of our mission?"

And unless Charlie told you about the blue globes we found the night of the quake . . .

LaRouche sat back, idly scratched his ear, and sighed. "We lost them."

"Lost them? Lost what? Where the hell is this going?" I asked.

"The samples never got to the eggheads at the Pentagon. They never left Okinawa. The courier never made the connection."

"Do you mean that spook who took the case from us after we landed on the carrier? What happened to him?" I asked.

"We still don't know. He arrived on Okinawa, scheduled to fly out two hours later, but was a no show. He disappeared along with the sample case—gone with no trace. At first, we thought he might have defected and tried to sell the samples, but that made no sense. Very few people even knew what was in the case and whether it had any value. He was just a courier and didn't know what he carried. A few months later, we identified a body as his. We thought it was a mugging at first, but the investigation revealed that he had been severely beaten, and several of his fingers cut off before he died." LaRouche stopped, took a drink of coffee, and waited for the questions.

"Who else knew?" Charlie had begun to pace the small space, rubbing his hand across his flattop. "Kelly ran the operation. Sultani and I were the point men on the ground, but neither of us knew exactly what it was—just that the threat was real. Your lab crew," Charlie said, looking toward the wall that separated us from the lab facilities, "had samples, but most of them weren't cleared for the eyes only nature of the mission." He pointed at LaRouche. "So who knew . . . and who leaked?"

This was not the happy-go-lucky, goofy Charlie I knew. *What is going on here? What is Charlie's role in this drama? What is it he's not telling me?*

"The spooks at the top knew," LaRouche answered. "But even they didn't know what we were dealing with at that time, or at least I've always assumed that. So there was no reason for the courier to be a target. Then . . ." He paused.

"What changed?" asked Charlie. A volcano was rumbling just below the surface of his sunburn.

"Vignalli." Again, LaRouche paused and took a deep breath. "He's dead; was found beaten to death outside a gay nightclub in Boston about a year ago. Boston PD writes it off as a mugging or hate crime. No witnesses, no suspects, no information, but his fiancée and classmates are convinced he wasn't gay, so this wasn't random violence. He was also miles away from home and was supposed to be in a class at Tufts University that evening. According to everyone who knew him, he was an honor student, never missed a class, and scheduled to be married at the end of the term. His apartment had been professionally tossed, so whoever killed him was searching for something."

"It's connected, isn't it?" asked Charlie. He stopped pacing and placed both hands on the table facing LaRouche. "Someone's trying to get info on the Djibouti mission, and they've taken out the courier and Vignalli. Who else?"

"Ambassador Dweck is missing, and I have to presume the worst. He went to a desk job for State in D.C shortly after the operation shut down. He disappeared about eight months ago; took a trip to Boston to visit family and simply vanished. His sister alerted the authorities, who notified State, but again—nothing." He stopped to let the impact of this news settle.

"What about Sultani?" asked Charlie.

LaRouche shook his head. "Missing in action. Sorry."

"And Kelly?"

"I can't say."

I asked, "So you think someone is after information about this Blue Death stuff, and they may attack us?" He nodded.

"But we don't know anything, so why would anyone come after us?"

Wonderful. I thought I left the James Bond games behind in Djibouti. Was finding those globes on Kelly's Reef a coincidence?

149

"Doesn't matter. Whoever is doing this doesn't care whether you know anything or not. That's why I need to warn you. Kelly and I initially mounted a major investigation, but when nothing turned up, the CIA reassigned her. Until I find out who's doing this, you need to be careful. I figure you're isolated here, and someone unknown to you would have difficulty getting by your radar, but you do need to be cautious."

"Is that why we all ended up here together?" asked TJ. "So big brother can keep an eye on us?"

"And why wasn't anyone watching Vignalli?" asked Charlie.

LaRouche looked at him and said, "TJ was also in the Boston area until he finished his program and we transferred him here. We didn't think there was a problem, and besides, Vignalli didn't know anything, so why would someone come after him? As soon as we learned the samples were missing, we had people in the area."

"Well, they certainly screwed up that assignment," said TJ. "I was studying at M.I.T and he was at Tufts. Yeah, they're both in the Boston area, but we had no reason to keep in contact. Now you're telling me he's dead, and I was sent here deliberately?"

I turned to TJ. "Did you know about any of this?" Before he could answer, the ship's bell rang four times—two o'clock.

"Of course not," TJ answered. He was studiously chewing his cigar and staring at the fluorescent light. "This is fucked up. I asked for assignment and came here to be with you and Charlie. I didn't know Vignalli was killed until just now."

Changing tact I said, "Captain, I received a threatening letter. I don't think it has anything to do with this, but. . ."

"I know about the letter—that was the trigger for me coming here now to warn you. However, I still think your risk is minimal."

"And how did you know about the letter?" I asked.

"A little bird told me." He wasn't revealing his sources—need to know and all that.

"This is my wife and children you're playing games with. Minimal risk my ass. You have no right . . ."

"I know, but they are safer here than anywhere else. Where would you send them? To your parents' house in Mexico? Don't look at me like that. If I know, then anybody who wants to hurt you can find out too."

He was rubbing his index finger against his thumb. "You're on an island with restricted access, and they are safer here with the three of you than anywhere else. Besides, none of you actually knows anything."

"Neither did Vignalli," I reminded him. I stopped as what he said registered. "And now half the people involved with this Blue Death stuff are dead? What does that mean?"

TJ spoke, "It means that you're bait, Bones—we all are. The alphabet guys want to stake us out and see what crawls out of the dark." He rolled the cheroot from one side of his mouth to the other as he summarized the situation. "That's the favor you need, isn't it?"

LaRouche nodded. "That and to keep your eyes open for anything unusual in the area. Strangers, unusual events, unexplained deaths—that sort of thing."

"You're not going to tell them the rest of it, are you?" asked Charlie, sitting back down and staring directly at LaRouche. "Need to know? Not directly related? That it?"

"Tell us what?" I looked from Charlie to LaRouche. The mental arm wrestling continued between them.

"You know what Blue Death really is, don't you, Captain?" Charlie finally looked at TJ and me, but not until LaRouche flinched and broke eye contact. "Somebody else knows, and that secret has killed three or more already. The killer wants the information, and it's valuable enough to put us at risk to find who that is." He looked back at LaRouche. "Are you going to tell them, or do I?"

In the silence that followed, Lieutenant Moran stuck his head through the door, thought better of entering, and just as quickly disappeared. I got up and filled my glass with more bug juice—red this time.

"They both have the necessary clearance and deserve the truth," Charlie prompted.

LaRouche thought a moment, absently fingering the gold eagles on his collars. Shaking his head he said, "Blue Death? I actually know a lot less than you think, Master Chief, but you're right, the good doctor and TJ deserve to know what's at stake here." He walked to the counter and got more coffee. "Where to begin?"

Then he told us. He lied.

Blue Death

LaRouche walked to the door and summoned Lieutenant Moran. "Make sure no one disturbs us," was all he said.

He sighed and turned to us. "The first indication of a problem was a year before what you refer to as the great Djibouti boondoggle. Kelly and her crew started hearing about problems in the villages along the coast and in the mountains. Women were having difficult births, goats and cattle were dying during the birthing process, and rumors of a toxic attack were popping up. Our local resources confirmed that there was an increase in fetal anomalies and stillbirths."

"And?" I prompted.

"The U.N. offered assistance, but the local warlords refused, as usual. A team of researchers from USAMRID arrived at the Somali border where rebel troops fired on them. The world was left wondering and soon lost interest. No headlines, no film at eleven, no blood, no guts. In America, the prevailing attitude continued that they were only Africans."

Charlie, who had begun pacing again, took up the story. "The rumors continued, and Kelly began to feel the tickle on her antennae that something wasn't kosher in Jerusalem. The Virgins' clients were bragging about how many children they fathered. One went so far as to claim his wife had three babies in the last year. Praise be onto Allah. But alas, none survived. Allah must be wise. After all, hadn't He sent Alzera throughout the land promising many new warriors to wage a Jihad?" Charlie's voice oozed cynicism. I suspected that killing fundamentalists who wanted to rule civilization, was part of his secret job he enjoyed.

LaRouche continued, "Alzera was showing Allah's miracle and sharing the Blue Wonder with the faithful, so they could multiply and go forth, but something wasn't right. The women and children were dying."

"And that's where you came in?"

LaRouche nodded. "We anchored off the coasts of Somalia and Djibouti, pretending to do legitimate oceanographic work. In reality, I was there to find out what was actually going on."

The troubled fluorescent light decided to die. LaRouche climbed onto the table and smacked it back to life with his palm. Then he continued his story. "Kelly blackmailed a client into an introduction. Sultani met with a mid-level member of Alzera's tribe and was passed off as a willing jihadist."

"He was CIA and worked for Kelly?" I was beginning to see the connections.

Charlie quickly said, "Doesn't matter, and you don't need to know. He, Kelly, and I go back a long way; I was his back up. He'd managed to infiltrate Alzera's tribe and the information faucet began to flow. The urgency of the situation became apparent, so we developed a plan of action."

Between LaRouche and Charlie, I pieced together the rest of the story.

Alzera had obtained something from a village located on the Somali coast. That something was a chemical compound found in the sea that would magically cause a woman to have children. What he quickly realized was that most of the pregnancies ended in stillbirth or fatal complications to the mother. He tested this conclusion in several villages, slipping a small quantity into the water supply causing female mammals and offspring to die off. Women died. Goats died. Chickens laid defective eggs. Men were unaffected and began to believe they could impregnate a woman just by looking at her. Village elders, impotent for years, bragged about creating harems to rival Ali Baba.

LaRouche continued, "Alzera, however, had other plans. Those plans included poisoning the water supply for L.A. Blue Death was a real threat. His Jihad was starting."

Charlie said, "That's where you came in, Bones. Kelly arranged to kidnap Alzera and get a sample. Before that happened, the word got out, his people turned on him, and well . . ."

LaRouche concluded, "We don't know what this stuff is and now our only sample has been lost or stolen. And somebody else discovered the weapon potential, and wants it. That's why we need your help. If they come looking for you, we'll be there. In the meantime, we wait and continue to hunt for the source."

"You going to tell them the rest?" Charlie again confronted LaRouche.

"No, and neither can you. You know that, and you know it is all conjecture anyway. We may have confirmation soon, and then the world will know." LaRouche stared at Charlie, silently daring him to say something.

"Ah, the little green men theory, again?" I finally asked. Silence. Charlie and LaRouche exchanged a look.

"What we *do* know is that whatever this is, we have another chance to find more," said LaRouche. The pesky fluorescent light blinked off and back on as soon as he stood up. He just scowled at it.

"How's that?" asked TJ. He picked a piece of tobacco off his shirt. "I thought we had it all in that camera case. It was those blue marble things, right?"

"Believe it or not, the *Swordfish* is an authentic research vessel. We were off the coast of Somalia doing sea floor exploration at the time of the initial discovery of this Blue Death stuff. We were surveying a lateral slippage of the upper, soft seafloor crust over underlying bedrock. Could have been an avalanche, minor earthquake, or who knows what, that caused it. There was no seismic data, but a low flying military surveillance aircraft noted a spike in radioactivity in the area. Not enough to suggest a weapons threat, but a concerning spike nonetheless. It eventually faded after a couple weeks."

"So? Blue Death is a dirty bomb or something?" I asked. "Doesn't fit with what you told us about it, and I can't believe you didn't test it before sending it to Washington."

Lieutenant Moran opened the door and this time had the courage to enter. He stood at attention. "We will be ready to get underway with the tide in about six hours, Sir." Charlie grinned at him and fingered the Easter bunny pajama top.

"Thank you—that will be all, Lieutenant," said LaRouche. Moran turned and left.

LaRouche straightened his gig line and sat back down. "You're right about Blue Death. It's not a radioactive weapon. I think the radioactivity was from low-level natural sources that the quake uncovered. More intriguing were the water samples we obtained. They contained unusually high levels of selenium, gold, and germanium. Added to that, the ratios of potassium, sodium, and calcium were all out of kilter. We also found high levels of long chain hydrocarbons, nucleic acids, and amino acids—all outside the range of normal seawater."

I looked at TJ. After we left Djibouti, he finished a PhD program at M.I.T. I knew he'd defended his dissertation on the evolutionary implication of ocean chemistry in the development of complex life on this planet. I didn't understand why someone with degrees in biochemistry and English ended up on an isolated island running a medical service. I wrote it off to military planning at its finest, but now we knew it was intentional. He had removed his cigar and was frowning. Despite the air-conditioning in the mess hall, his scalp was damp. I realized I was sweating too, and not from the temperature.

"What?" TJ focused on LaRouche. "That's very strange. What did your science guys think and how long did the anomaly last?"

"Things were back to normal within a month," LaRouche answered. "The geologists think the slide uncovered a pocket of rare trace metals that diluted and washed away. The biologists believe there may have been a resultant population die-off with the breakdown of nucleic acids and proteins. Frankly, we don't know what it was, but there is no evidence of anything similar in worldwide historical oceanographic data."

"Know what I think, Captain?" TJ leaned his chair back and stuck the cigar back into his mouth. "I think radioactivity, and I think energy and power. I think long chain hydrocarbons, and I think fatty acids that make up cell membranes. I think nucleic and amino acids, and I think DNA and proteins. I would hazard a guess that the ratios of salts are more similar to plasma than seawater. Right?"

LaRouche nodded.

"The rare metals are intriguing though. I'm not an engineer, but I seem to remember selenium, gold, and germanium are found in high levels in materials used on electronics and aircraft." LaRouche nodded again.

"And?" I asked. I was struggling to make a connection.

TJ said, "Don't know, but seems to me that there was an incident with both a mechanical component and a biologic component. But I fail to see how that helps figure out what Blue Death is or how to find more to test?" We all looked at LaRouche.

"The same configuration of findings has repeated itself off Wollei, a small inhabited atoll in the southern Micronesia chain. It's about three days steaming from here. Seems a local weather station was testing ocean salinity, found an increase in radioactivity, and similar trace metals. I'm heading there to research the area. We'll be back here in a month to finish." He looked at Charlie. "I might need your help with this."

"Do we even know what this stuff looks like? Is it a liquid, solid, what?" asked TJ.

Charlie answered him. "We have no idea. The box Sultani recovered contained an animal skin with a couple lumps in it. Because we thought it might be a bio hazard, we immediately put it in a camera case and shipped it."

I thought of my glimpse into the *Swordfish*'s lab and a technician placing blue globes into a camera case. Blue globes similar to those I found during the earthquake. Then I remembered the medical chief and bosons mate who tested pregnant and claimed they weren't. Then I thought about Auraka's two heads and her two-headed offspring.

"We considered examining it, but the *Swordfish* has no biologic containment facilities, so . . ." LaRouche made his reluctance to risk his crew obvious. It was also clear he was lying to me. His thumb was receiving a vigorous rubbing.

But you'd let me carry it back to an aircraft carrier with 6000 men without knowing the risk? Brilliant move, Jerk.

"So, let me see if I understand this," I said. "We are dealing with something we know nothing about, but might be a serious biological weapon. Someone wants it, has probably killed three people associated with it, and we're supposed to sit tight and act like goats tied to a stake? Am I getting this correct? In the meantime, you're going hunting for weird shit in the ocean, which may or may not have anything to do with this, right?"

Toto—this ain't Kansas. It's an asylum.

"That about sums it up, Commander." LaRouche rose and extended his hand, signaling lunch was over. He escorted us back to the gangplank where the yard boat waited to ferry us back to the *Chipmunk*.

"Oh. One more issue, Dr. Matthews. You shouldn't be diving anywhere near Old Wives Beach for a few weeks."

"And why is that?" I really did not trust this man. Something wasn't right.

"It seems there actually has been some kind of toxic spill in the area. Radioactivity levels are up slightly in the water."

Family Barbeque

"How do you want your steak?" I asked, flipping over slabs of beef on the barbeque grill. The portable generator we shared with two neighbors rumbled beside the house, spewing oily exhaust. At least our three houses had one working refrigerator we shared, a couple of lights during the night, and of course a TV—but no stations to watch. Drinking water was bottled. Toilet flushing required a bucket of collected rainwater. Aftershocks occurred daily. We all took it in stride.

There were five of us—TJ, Charlie, Hanna, Emily, and me. The kids were sleeping over with friends. We were the only ones who knew of Kelly's Reef, had enjoyed her hospitality, and had experienced her beauty. Three of us had known her power. All of us knew of Auraka. I was eager to tell the girls about the Aurakettes. Dinner first, then afterward we'd look at Charlie's film of our dive. I needed some time to consider how to break the news from LaRouche.

We sat around on what I generously called the back patio of my assigned housing. The naval housing department had thoughtfully added a concrete slab on the backside of the concrete block boxes that housed officers. The Corps of Engineers built every identical house to last, efficiently fashioned from a single blueprint, painted with a choice of gray, off white, dull green or dingy blue. Windows had a coconut 100 rating, to reassure the residents that they could withstand the impact of a coconut thrown by a wind gust at 100 mph. The walls might blow over, but the windows would not shatter.

Over time, the concrete block concept had proven itself. Casa Matthews had survived several typhoons and the 'big shake and bake' as we now called the earthquake. The patio concept, however, was an abject failure.

The original idea of a patio to enjoy lasted about one week after the arrival of the first Turner Road inhabitants. The enemy followed, arriving by the millions. Step outside, they waited. Leave a door or window open, they invaded—buzzing around in mindless figure-of-eights. Dare go outdoors wearing shorts, and they cut you off at the knees. Knee-high white stockings soaked in insecticide, or a grass skirt were the only defense from the onslaught. The worst were the terrorists who would attack and consume a piece of meat or fruit in seconds if left unguarded. They'd dive bomb a forkful and be halfway down your throat before you closed your lips. The housefly is the national bird of Guam.

"Want me to do something about the flies?" asked TJ. Showered, shaved, and in a clean, pressed uniform, the flies surrounded him. The rest of us must have had a repellent cloud of body odor—or they just liked his aftershave.

I said, "Just stand over there so they don't get near the food and we'll be fine."

"At least you got the upgraded patio this summer, with screens. Your neighbor," said Charlie pointing to the house north of ours, "still has his patio boarded up."

"The genius in housing who came up with the idea of boarding up the patios to keep the flies out and then handing out scenic beach posters to provide ambiance—remember him?" Charlie nodded.

"Well, he seems to have developed a problem that required a urology consult. Dr. Peters, the urologist, who just happens to live there," I said, pointing to another block building with a screened in patio to the south, "explained that if his patio didn't get the boards removed and screens installed, all the Viagra in China wouldn't help him."

"And now all the patio caves are being converted into screened porches," Emily finished.

"Take my steak off the coals when it quits mooing and moving," Charlie said. *Slap!* "But let's make this one well done." He tossed a fly onto the charcoal.

We finished the barbeque, and Emily surprised us with strawberries and ice cream. She and Hanna had spent most of the afternoon in line at the commissary waiting for their share of berries, milk, and other rare imports. Being at the end of the supply line has challenges, but that made the fruit all the more succulent.

We settled into our lawn chairs and watched a family of wild pigs rooting in the back yard at the edge of the jungle. TJ and Charlie both looked at me, waiting to begin our tale.

"We had an interesting dive today," I said. "Kelly's Reef is filled with miniature two-headed eels, and the coral seems to have re-grown just since the damage from the quake."

"I've got some film we need to look at this evening," said Charlie. "I'm sure glad I tied the camera under the *Chipmunk* before LaRouche searched the boat."

"LaRouche? As in the Djibouti Cutie?" asked Emily. Although she knew we'd been to Djibouti, she didn't know the classified story. Moreover, she certainly wasn't aware of my alter ego—the mild mannered gynecological killing machine. However, whatever Emily knew, Hanna also knew. It had nothing to do with telepathy or twin empathy; they just loved to gossip.

"Well, yeah. He kinda invited us to have lunch with him and reminisce."

"Sent his marines to kidnap us at gunpoint is more like it," said Charlie, starting to get into the story.

"Thanks pal, but maybe we should downplay some of the drama." I looked into Emily's alarmed eyes. "It wasn't a big deal," I said to reassure her. *Wait 'till you find out we're being used as bait.*

Charlie became quiet and serious. His expression said 'Yeah, right.' "He searched the *Chipmunk* and would have confiscated my video files if he'd found it. And he had that moron lieutenant follow us all the way to the boat landing. Tomorrow I'm putting the disc in a safe deposit box."

"So what the hell do you think LaRouche was really up to?" I asked. I smeared catsup over my steak and opened a Nehi. Room temperature grape soda tasted worse than wine in a square bottle and paper bag. I poured it down the drain in exchange for a glass of water.

Charlie got up and looked out the screen at the boonie pigs rooting for fruit from the date palms. "He's up to something and knows far more than he's telling us." Charlie turned toward me and became more serious than I'd ever seen him. "I know what he's up to, but . . ." He looked at the twins and TJ. "Need to know and all that." He nodded toward the back yard and stepped out of the patio. I followed him.

When we were out of earshot he said, "Those blue globes you found the night of the earthquake?"

"Yeah?"

"Does TJ know about them?"

"No, I don't think so. Unless you told him."

"Good. You know what they are, don't you?"

I had my suspicions, but waited for Charlie to confirm them. He just looked at me. Mommy pig and the piglets looked up from their hunt and grunted at us.

"They are the same thing LaRouche found in Djibouti, right?" I finally said. "What he calls Blue Death?"

"And by not telling him about our find, we might be committing treason. You understand that we're withholding information LaRouche is seeking?" Ninety degrees, ninety percent humidity outdoors, and I still felt a cold chill.

What the hell is going on here? I know these things are the same globes we found in Djibouti. Only Charlie and Hanna know about the find, and we're keeping it a secret. I'm withholding information from my government and TJ. Why?

My gut instinct told me there was something I didn't trust about LaRouche. Charlie confirmed that. A tacit agreement passed between us.

Back indoors, I looked at the girls. "LaRouche said he's just doing some research on the water around Old Wives Beach and told me there might be a toxic spill. He claims that he noticed us diving from the *Chipmunk* and invited us to have lunch with him."

"And?" Emily and Hanna asked simultaneously.

"He said the water is radioactive," I continued, "and ordered us to curtail all diving."

"Dangerous?" Again, they spoke in two-part harmony.

TJ said, "I checked when we got back, and there is no spill warning I can find, but there are now warning signs posted on the beach. And," he added, "there is a Coast Guard cruiser anchored about a mile off the reef. It took station as soon as the *Swordfish* weighed anchor for Wollei. Not only is it unusual for it to be there, rather than anchored in the harbor, but nobody seems to know anything about it— or isn't speaking."

If anyone can find out what's up, it's TJ, and if his sources were dry, that spoke volumes. He said, "I asked Angel and Ramón to find a boat and make a run out past Kelly's Reef to see what's happening. I figure they owe me that much."

At that moment, the phone burbled. The phone system doesn't ring, it just, well . . . burbles. Sometimes I can actually hear someone on the other end; sometimes it's just static. Occasionally I speak to spirits in the other world, but it's tough to distinguish that from talking to the Skipper. Emily answered and looked at me. She frowned as she handed the phone to TJ. He listened, grunted, and hung up.

"They tried to arrest Angel and Ramón twenty minutes ago. Seems they were trespassing in a secured area and chased ashore." TJ took the cigar out of his mouth, scratched his scalp, smiled, and shook his head. "But a few hundred family members and close friends were on the beach and convinced the Coast Guard not to continue the pursuit." He paused.

161

"But that's good news. Now I get to go to bat for them again with the Skipper, and they'll owe me even more. I do loves da politics, boss. Thinks me outta run for office, Mon?"

"Your jive talk is horrid, your Ebonics is worse, and the Rastafarian dialect is pathetic. I seriously need to work on my Tennessee redneck accent to keep up with you, TJ," I wisecracked. There was no Black or White between us; we both bled the same color. TJ, Charlie, and I share a disdain for bigotry or racism. We make fun of those who don't with our banter; the more racist, sexist, or bigoted we are, the closer we become.

Charlie, never one to pass up a straight line, said, "They already have a dog catcher, and you're too dark brown to convince anyone you're related to the governor, so that just leaves Congressional Representative; but you're not stupid or corrupt enough."

Emily piped in, "I think we should start a campaign to get you elected as the Commissioner of Public Works. Then, as soon as you're elected, you announce that Charlie has invented a shovel that will stand up all by itself and you fire the governor's five hundred cousins who work there."

TJ gave a condescending smile to the ribbing he was getting. "Well, regardless, we do know that someone doesn't want anyone around Old Wives Beach or Kelly's Reef. Until LaRouche gets back from Wollei, we need to be cautious, and continue to keep Kelly's existence to ourselves. If anyone hears anything, I want to know immediately. Okay?" TJ finished off his warm beer with a grimace.

"What is our risk?" asked Hanna and Emily. They often ask the same question at the same time and complete each other's sentences without a pause. What is distressing to the listener is that they both switch topics in the middle of a thought without warning. Charlie and I have learned to nod our head and grunt as if we understand when they are using twin think.

Charlie, TJ, and I looked at each other and had our own group think moment. Time to tell the twins what was actually going on. We did. TJ and Charlie told the Djibouti story, of the unexplained pregnancies, and of the attack on Kelly's Bar and Grill, downplaying the carnage. They also told of Alzera and Blue Death.

I fixed coffee and challenged my pancreas with a second helping of strawberries. Then I took up my part of the narrative and told them what LaRouche knew about Blue Death possibly being a bio-weapon, about Petty Officer Vignalli being murdered, Ambassador Dweck going missing, the agent assigned to deliver the sample being murdered, and how LaRouche wanted to use us as bait.

As I finished relating LaRouche's tale of intrigue, Emily gave me 'the look'. It is the look of a mother bear when she finds you holding her cub. "The kids go stateside to stay with your folks in Mexico. I mean it, damn it. It's almost Christmas, and they won't miss much school. Besides, Jenny will spend the time to get ahead on her studies, and Benjamin can practice his guitar and go snorkeling with Grandpa. They're *not* staying here if there is any risk."

"Oh, I agree entirely," I said. "I already have tickets for the three of you and Hanna on the evening flight to Honolulu tomorrow." *Despite what LaRouche said about knowing my parents live in Mexico, they will be safer there.*

"We," started Emily.

"Are not leaving," finished Hanna.

"The children go," continued Emily.

"And we stay," finished Hanna. That was the obvious end of discussion. Charlie and I nodded and grunted.

Charlie put his arms around Hanna, pulled her close, and kissed her. "They'll have to get through me to get to you," was all he said. I knew that promise extended to all of us.

Emily wrapped her arms around me and said, "I'm not leaving you, and I'm not putting the children on a plane by themselves all the way to Mexico if they are in danger. What do I do?" She looked up at me her eyes mixed with fear and tears.

"I call my parents to fly over and pick them up. Would that be okay?"

"As long as they get off island safely, that's okay."

TJ said, "Do you think the women are safe here? What if someone uses them as a lever to get to one of us? There was that letter and whoever wrote it knows about your family."

"All the better to get our children out of here as soon as possible," I said.

"So what do we do now?" Hanna asked.

Charlie walked over to the television and popped a DVD into the player. "First, I want you to see the raw footage from today's dive and what we found. Something fascinating I want you to look at. LaRouche knows more than he's telling you, and this is the proof." He pressed the play button. "What you are about to see should be considered classified on a need to know basis." TJ and Hanna nodded. They were military officers. Emily, the wife of a doctor and military officer understood that we were breaking the rules. Nobody disagreed with that decision.

"No. First we bring the children home," said Emily. Her hands trembled as she picked up the phone and dialed. "I need for you to send them home now. No, wait. I'll walk over and get them." She turned to me. The fear in her eyes was gone; they had turned to obsidian. I sure as hell wouldn't want to be threatening one of her cubs at that moment.

TJ said, "I'll walk over with you. Let me get a fresh shirt out of the trunk of my car."

He had removed his uniform blouse and his khaki t-shirt molded to his torso. Changing shirts meant he was getting firearms from his car, and a shirt he could conceal them under. I hoped they were something big and deadly—just in case.

Emily and TJ hurried off next door to collect the children. Tripod hobbled to the door on his three sturdy legs and sang the beagle version of a Puccini opera. His humans were going on an adventure without him, and he wanted the world to mourn. I opened the door and told him, "Protect."

Yeah right. Took me a year to housebreak you and another year to teach you sit and stay. Fat chance you'll be beneficial in a gunfight, but at least you'll caterwaul if something happens to your humans.

Five minutes later, Emily, TJ and the kids walked in the front door. Tripod hobbled in behind them and immediately came front and center to see if he'd receive a dog biscuit for heroism. TJ sported a large lump under a brilliant flower on his gaudy shirt.

"Dad," my daughter Jenny said, making eye contact. "What's wrong? Why can't Becky and I have our sleepover? I didn't do anything." She looked at her brother. "What did you do?" she accused him. "I told Mom I didn't want you to sleep over at Tommy's the same night as Becky and me. I'm gonna kick . . ." She paused before the butt word slipped out.

"Suck Granola." Benjamin, our son, actually thumbed his nose at her. Ever since my twelve-year-old daughter decided not to eat anything with a face, her eight-year-old brother made a point of ridiculing her vegetarian ideals at every opportunity. As an only child, I missed all this Machiavellian sibling rivalry.

"Hey, young man," said Emily.

"Watch the mouth or you'll be," continued Hanna.

"Eating a bar of soap," finished Emily.

Facing a team approach to discipline, all he could mutter was "Sorry." He started toward his room, stopped, and looked back. "It's not fair, Dad. She always blames me for everything. Tommy and I weren't going to look at her stupid magazine anyway; *Seventeen* is about girly stuff and we could get cooties from it."

"Hey, you two," I said wrapping them both in my arms. "You didn't do anything wrong, but something has come up and I need for you to be here tonight where you're safe."

"Dad . . ." Jenny whined.

TJ growled, "Knock it off, both of you, or I'll have you thrown in the stockades together to live on bread and water for a month. You know I hate children unless they are marinated and cooked to a crisp." TJ to the rescue, scowling his best. As soon as he wiggled his eyebrows and rolled the stogie, both the children broke into giggles. He squatted down and looked directly at Jenny, suddenly serious. "Someone dangerous may be coming to talk to your dad, and we just need for you to be extra careful and let us know if anything unusual happens. Okay?"

Jenny looked at the ground and said, "I forgot. I'm sorry, Dad. I was thinking about Becky and our sleep-over and . . ."

"What?"

"Somebody left you a letter in my locker at school today." She un-slung her backpack, rummaged around and produced a wrinkled white envelope. The room was silent as a tomb.

Second Letter

The address read: Dr. Matthews. No return address; no stamp.

Doctor M-

Been here a cuple weeks and this place is really getting to me. What a bunch of ashole there are on this stinking ~~iland,~~ **island. Some old man was tailgating me and had the balls to flash his lights so I'd pull over. I showed him. I slowed down real slow until he almost hit me, then hit the brakes real fast and jumped out and pulled his fat ass out of his stupid car and beat the shit out of him. I should have runn over him when I got done.**

Saw you daughter coming out of that fancy private school toady. Don't you have time to pick her up? She is such a pretty girl and it can be dangerous out there. How's you boy doing? He still at that school for those monkey that live here.

My daughter would have been almost that old if you hadn't killed her that night.

See you real soon.

A old friend.

Off to Cozumel

The vagus nerve snakes its way from the deep core of the brain, through the neck, into the chest, and past the heart, on its journey to the abdominal organs. It's the master control nerve. Fear triggers a release of adrenaline from those pesky adrenal glands atop the kidneys. Immediately, the fight or flight survival instructions are activated. Vision sharpens, heart rate rampages, lungs open to oxygen flow, the bowel shuts down, and blood vessels to the muscles open. The vagus nerve counteracts these effects. Vagal stimulus slows the heart, lowers blood pressure, and increases peristalsis to the bowel for digestion. The vagus is S.L.U.D.—salivation, lacrimation, urination, and defecation.

The moment Jenny handed me the envelope I knew its content, and my vagus nerve fired—big time. I became short of breath and faint from bradycardia. My bowels turned to undigested, semi-solid Jell-O. If there had been a nickel in my sphincter, the squeeze necessary to prevent toxic spillage would have made the buffalo cough and Jefferson squint. I sat down abruptly, thankful there was a lawn chair under my butt.

Okay. Breathe in, breathe out, don't panic. Repeat.

"Here, you need to read this." I looked into Emily's eyes; her fear mirrored mine. I handed her the letter. She slowly read it and passed it to TJ.

He read and handed the letter to Charlie. "Do you have the other one?" he asked me.

"I'll get it." At the time, the first letter struck me as unusual—a little weird and threatening. With the recent information from LaRouche, it took on a new aura. I had assumed that someone who knew me during my residency was on Guam and planned to make contact. Now I was trying to remember exactly what it said as I struggled to get my heart rate back to normal. Jefferson and the buffalo died of asphyxiation.

Charlie read, re-read the letter, then handed it to Hanna and picked up the telephone. His skin flushed deep red; a single vein on his forehead throbbed. In the years I'd known him, he had hidden his true emotions beneath a veneer of comedic goofiness. A dark, dangerous river of focused energy now flooded across his face.

"It's Charlie." Pause. "I need your team and gear." Another pause. "That's right. On me—and I need you five minutes ago." He hung up and sat down, then stood back up and began to pace.

"What's that about?" I asked. I looked over at Hanna. She didn't have the momma bear look. She had the sister bear, and I'm extremely dangerous look. Nobody would ever threaten the Sisters, or what they loved.

"I've got us back-up," was all he said. He looked out the front window, fidgeting. I watched him flex and relax his fists. Hanna stood and took his hand; a signal passed between them. The overloaded generator kicked in, and the noise of a solitary fan rattled all three of us. I smelled testosterone and estrogen in the swelter—a lethal combo.

Charlie left his vigil at the window and nodded at TJ. "Security's set."

"Do you think these letters have anything to do with the Alzera thing?" asked Hanna. She had finished the first letter and passed it to the others.

"I don't know," I said frowning, "but it doesn't feel right. I mean, if someone wants info about Alzera, he'll come straight at me, or ambush one of us without notice, not send love notes like these. This is something else. This is personal."

Emily interrupted, "These seem like they were written by different people. I mean, the grammar and style are different, there are two different fonts, and the second one seems . . . I don't know, almost artificially threatening. There are a lot of misspellings and poor English, but when he talks about Jenny, it changes. He spells couple as cuple, but he can spell private and dangerous correctly. Something's not right about this."

Charlie took both letters back and studied them.

"Doesn't matter, he's clearly looking at Jenny and Benjamin. He knows you well enough to find them." Charlie looked at Jenny, who had figured out something was wrong. This week her hair was dyed Atomic Purple or something equally gauche. Her gray eyes didn't leave mine. She trusted me to tell her the truth. She was old enough to warrant no less. "Did you see who left the letter in your locker, or anyone hanging around school?" he asked.

"Dad," she looked at me for support, "I really didn't see anyone, honest. That envelope was stuffed under my locker door when I got my bag after class. It said it was for you, so I just stuck it in my bag and brought it home. And no, there wasn't any scummy creep drooling by the bus stop offering candy."

"Nah, that guy is standing in line outside the sperm bank, but I'm glad you're being careful and observant," I said. Emily cleared her throat and gave me the 'watch your mouth around the children' look.

"It's okay, Sweetie," I said, "but someone is playing a very bad joke on us." I thought about what to say next, balancing honesty with protection. "So we need to be very careful for a little while. I want to make sure you and your brother are safe."

Benjamin said, "Can Uncle Charlie teach me how to shoot a gun? I could put a tent in the yard, and stand guard, and Tommy could come over, and . . ." Benjamin lost interest in *Seventeen*, his thoughts overtaken by guns and mayhem.

"Tell you what; you and Jenny are going to visit Grandma and Grandpa in Mexico. Maybe Grandma will teach you how to shoot. She almost shot Grandpa once. She blew a hole in the dining room floor the one time Grandpa tried to show her how to load the .22."

The children looked at each other, did a high five, and ran off to their rooms to pack. At least I knew they would be safe.

We settled down to the background sounds of youthful excitement as they prepared for their big adventure. Tripod hobbled from body to body seeking the comfort of a good crotch sniffing. He knew the score.

"What does the letter mean about a daughter that you killed?" TJ asked as he shooed Tripod away from his leg.

"I have no idea," I lied. I knew who wrote the letters, but I paused, pretending to search my memory. I tried to look blank.

TJ looked at me and raised his eyebrows—he knew I was lying. "Whoever wrote this seems to have accomplished at least one thing."

"What's that?" I asked.

"He managed to get your kids off Guam and safely out of the way. Don't know if that's what he planned, but that's what's happening." He thought a moment. "If your parents can't get here to accompany them, I'll arrange for security to fly with them."

As soon as he said it, I knew TJ was right.

Emily stood on tiptoes and gave him a peck on the cheek.

"But why?" I asked. "Why would he want to get my children away? He must know I'll hide them where they'll be safe; somewhere nobody without intimate knowledge of my family can find. If he is after me, why not use my children as a direct threat? Makes no sense."

"Doesn't need to make sense," said Charlie. "The kids are leaving because of the info we learned from LaRouche. If this character is trying to find out about Djibouti, he's too late to use the kids as hostages. If he's just a nutbag, he's not going to be able to harm them. But how does a letter about a daughter dying have anything to do with Djibouti?"

Why would a drug dealer come after me now—all these years later? Mother and baby are dead. He should still be in prison. He's not subtle enough to send threatening letters—he'd just fire bomb my house. Why?

Party Time with Angel

There was a pounding on the door, and I jumped. I saw TJ reach under his shirt and massage the lump. Charlie peered out the window, then walked over, and opened the door.

"Let's party. Show me your tits. Gimme a beer," Lucy cackled from Angel's shoulder. He stood backlit by headlights in my doorway, with Ramón right behind him. I looked past them and saw a small caravan of low-riders filled with locals. An empty beer can sailed across the front yard as a rowdy group climbed out the backs and cabs of the fleet. The moonless night provided cover as they vanished into the jungle darkness.

Before I could react, Angel said, "Charlie called and said you was having a fiesta and we should come by and get some free food and beer. So here we are. The party at the beach was getting boring, especially when the Coast Guard arrived, so we decided to join ya up here. Hey," he paused looking around, "this is some pretty fancy place you got, Doc. Bet it even has running water. Do I smell steak? Where's the beer?" He and Ramón pushed past me into the living room. Ramón was carrying another shotgun.

"All I smell is you and your brother," said Hanna.

"What . . ." was the best I could come up with. In the meantime, Tripod joined Lucy in the *Bugle and Obscenity Symphony*. Tripod clearly wanted to sniff Lucy, and she clearly wanted to kill any beagle that came close. Benjamin had returned and was admiring Ramón's shotgun with bright-eyed enthusiasm.

"I invited some friends to come over and spend the night. Thought it might be fun," Charlie said, lifting his chin toward the children. "The brats might enjoy the company for a change. Whadda ya think? Anybody up for more strawberries and ice cream?" He pulled a bowl out of the cupboard and began dishing up.

"This is your security patrol?" TJ asked Charlie. "Tripod, quiet! Zip it, Lucy." There was an immediate end to the cacophony. Lucy tucked her head under her wing. Tripod rolled onto his back. Everyone was surprised—except TJ, who expected this as his due.

Charlie grinned. "Yeah, I was going to get a .50 caliber and some ninjas, but the paperwork was too much. Besides, the Sanchez family works cheap, and the others don't mind sleeping out there in the boonies. They might even get lucky and shoot a wild pig tonight." I thought back to the evening he had calmly walked up to Ramón in the bed of Angel's lowrider and taken the shotgun away. I had been amazed at Charlie's cool under fire, but now I wondered if there wasn't a prior history I didn't know about.

"Hey Doc, these steaks in the icebox are gonna go bad if they don't get used up real soon. I'll stick them on the grill for you. Got anything better than sissy pop in here?" Angel was removing food and beverages, stacking his treasures on the countertop. Lucy perched just out of Tripod's reach and looked like she was saving up expletives. Tripod was volunteering to help with the steaks. Benjamin was considering becoming Ramón's new best friend. I was going crazy.

Charlie took me aside and whispered, "It's okay, Bones. Angel and Ramón have worked for me several times before. That's why I recommended them to TJ to check out what's going on at Kelly's Reef, and that's why I called them to keep watch here tonight. As long as you don't sleepwalk in the jungle you'll be safe, and nobody can get near this place until the kids are safely on the flight to Mexico."

"Does that mean?" I asked, "that they work for the agency?"

"What agency would that be?" Charlie asked, poker faced. Then he gave me a long, dead stare warning me not to pursue that line of inquiry further. "They're just a couple good ol' boys who'll work for a six pack."

"But, is this necessary? Is a group of terrorists likely to invade Casa Matthews tonight? Come on."

"Three dead or missing? You willing to take the risk?"

"Hey, Doc," Angel called from the patio. "Got any boonie peppers?"

"Sorry, Angel," I answered, "best I can do is a bottle of Tabasco Sauce."

"Gimme a Tasco," Lucy crowed, ending her brief silence. Tripod looked up at TJ to see if he could join the conversation, but apparently thought better of it and rolled back over. TJ glared at Lucy who indignantly stuck her head back under her wing.

"So what about that video from today?" I asked Charlie. "Hope you got some good shots of Auraka's relatives?"

"Video will have to wait until tomorrow," Charlie whispered, nodding toward the Sanchez brothers, who were busy cooking up enough food to feed the troops bivouacked in my back yard. "Best wait. The fewer who know about our find, the better." His paranoia was beginning to infect me.

The phone rang again, and Benjamin arm-wrestled it away from Jenny. "Hello, Matthews' residence. This is Benjamin speaking." Perfect phone manners. Jenny would have answered with, "Ah, yeah, whadda ya want?"

"Yes, my father is home, may I tell him who's calling?" Benjamin paused and handed the phone to me. "It's an old friend." Every adult eye in the room stared at the hand piece.

"Good evening, this is Dr. Matthews. May I help you?" The tremor in my hand increased the longer the silence on the other end lasted. "Hello? Hello?" Without air conditioning, the room sweltered, but ice water beaded up on my forehead and neck. I looked up and noticed Charlie's usual Tequila Sunset skin had faded to a milky Peña Colada. He took the phone from my hand and listened for a moment. Then he clicked the cutoff switch and looked up.

"It's dead."

"Let me," TJ said holding his hand out for the phone. He listened for a dial tone and punched in a number.

"Sparks, this is TJ. Need an urgent favor. No . . . now. I know, I know. Tag this number and run a trace on the last call, then set a trap on it." He paused, listening. "I don't care, put down Admiral Arlie Burke on the request chit." Another pause. "I *know* he's dead. He won't be able to say it wasn't him that ordered it, will he?" TJ rolled his eyes and shook his head at the heavens. "Okay, get back to me."

Emily put her hand on my arm. "That's the third call today where there was no one on the other end. I thought it was the phone system being screwy since the earthquake, so I didn't think much about it. Do you think it's the same person?"

The phone chirped and gurgled. TJ snatched it before it finished signaling. He listened. Then he did the impossible. He went from ebony to mocha to cream. "Thanks Sparks, I owe ya."

"Didn't know you could get a phone call traced after the fact. And that fast," said Charlie.

"Sparks works for a special intelligence agency. He has some unique toys at his disposal. But he doesn't exist, right?" His expression made it clear that there was no Sparks, there was no special intelligence branch, that TJ was just a supply officer, and Charlie was just a boson's mate.

"So what did he say? Who called?" I asked.

"We don't know who called, but the call originated from the hospital." He waited for that to sink in before dropping the other boot. "It came from your office, Bones."

Charlie reached out and snatched the receiver from TJ. He dialed.

"Get someone up to Dr. Matthews' office, NOW. There's an intruder. Hold anyone in the area. I'll wait." He put his hand over the receiver and asked if I usually keep my office locked. I nodded. We waited.

"Okay, thanks for trying." Charlie shook his head. "Too late."

"Now what?" I asked. Someone writing threatening letters was calling my home from my office. I was suddenly grateful for the Sanchez family camped outside.

"Tomorrow we get the kids off island." said Charlie. "Arrange to have your folks meet them in Honolulu or here. Otherwise, TJ will get an escort. Meanwhile, you talk to NIS. We also need to look at the video from today, but that can wait." He nodded at TJ and the Sanchez brothers. "In the meantime you're all safe here."

Hanna took my arm and pulled me aside. "I need to see you in clinic first thing tomorrow morning." I must have frowned because she said, "Please. It's urgent."

<u>Joyous News</u>

Dawn arrived at 6:04 AM, within 10 minutes of dawn all year 'round. Living near the equator provides 12 hours daylight, 12 hours night, a dry season, and a rainy season. Boring. I sat in my office swirling the sludge in my coffee cup.

"Are donuts one of the FDA food groups? Should be." Hanna set a box of Chamorro Nuts on my desk next to my stack of morning paperwork. Even hot out of the oven, they tasted like stale gym socks. The frosting smelled of mildew. If Guam ever froze, we would have pucks for the hockey team. Nuts come in three flavors—somewhat chocolate, not chocolate, and mystery.

I was looking for anything amiss that would tell me who the caller the previous evening had been. Everything was in the same state of disarray I left the day before.

The hospital was running on its emergency generator; indications were that local power would be down for several more weeks. The morning shower had blown through, and Turtledove had paraded her generous flesh around her backyard doing ablutions. I chose to use the shower at the hospital, provided by emergency generator pumps. There are limits to what I'll suffer through.

"I assume Charlie got you home okay and stood guard last night?" I asked Hanna. "You look lovely this morning. What's up? Why the donut bribe?" As usual, she was crisp in her white uniform. Her ankle was healing nicely. There hadn't been a fracture, the laceration and abrasions hadn't become infected, and my stitches had dissolved, leaving a clean, invisible scar.

"I feel pretty good, considering." She sighed and sat down. "Actually I came to see if I could sign up for your research project." She was referring to a study of the effects of scuba diving during the first three months of gestation. Nobody knew if depth, pressure, or gas combinations would harm a fetus, and I was in a perfect place to find out. Many of the people stationed on Guam take up scuba diving; there isn't much else to do. Many females continue to dive during the first two months of pregnancy, often unaware they are even pregnant. I was studying the long-term effects of diving on the newborns of those mothers. Once it was determined a woman was pregnant she wasn't allowed to dive, but we had a growing sample of those who logged a number of sport dives before they found out they were pregnant.

"Great, I could actually use help with the statistics. Emily's planning to edit the files once we have the data analyzed."

"No. I mean as a research subject." She let that sink in. "I'm HCG positive." She waited for my reaction.

"I've got a bun in the oven, in the family way, eating for two, preggers, knocked up, dead bunny rabbit." She stuck her head further forward with each pronouncement, waiting for me to get it.

Years of experience taught me, often painfully, not to ask the obvious male chauvinistic question of who the lucky man was. So I put on my 'how terrific for you' smile and waited. Hanna waited; the standoff ended when she couldn't hold back the tears.

"That's okay. Everything's going to be okay. Being pregnant makes some women emotional because of all those raging hormones. It's okay, really." I tried my benign 'I'm just one of the girlfriends you can talk to' looks.

She sniffed. "You can be *such* a pig sometimes."

I switched to my 'Huh, what did I do?' look.

"I can't be pregnant. This is wrong. You prescribed the pill, and I haven't missed one in a year. My periods are like clockwork and Charlie and I only had that once . . . the night of the quake."

Whew, at least I don't have to ask who the father is, not that there was any doubt.

"But there is something wrong, I know it. I'm not supposed to be pregnant; this doesn't feel right."

I moved my chair closer, then, as an afterthought, I got up and closed the office door. I sat back down and took Hanna's hand in mine. I knew this was her first pregnancy and that a nulliparous female can be hypersensitive, hormonal, and scared. The biggest part of my job as an obstetrician is to provide the reassurance that a normally progressing pregnancy is just that. I also knew Hanna. I trusted her instincts as much as my own.

"What's wrong? Help me sort this out," I said. Animals can smell fear; humans empathize—same thing. I could feel the boa constrictor squeezing my heart as I looked into the azure rims of her irises. I waited for her to put her fear into a package she could deliver.

"My last period, on the pill, started exactly fourteen days before the quake. If I hadn't been on the pill, I would have been ovulating that night. I'm now a week late, and the urine test this morning was positive."

"Well, sometimes, even when used perfectly, the pill fails. This isn't the first time a woman got pregnant on the pill." I wouldn't question her compliance; that would be a wrong turn down a dangerous, pot-holed, dead-end road.

"But Charlie used a condom too. With a spermicidal lubricant. So, you tell me, what are the chances all three methods failed? I looked up the failure rates and did the math. O.J. Simpson having an identical DNA doppelganger is more likely than me being pregnant."

She took a deep breath and said, "And I think I felt movement today. I know that's not possible, so don't give me that look."

"Okay, then the test is wrong. False positives happen all the time. Home pregnancy tests are set up so that if they fail, it is as a false positive. Drug companies can't take a risk missing a pregnancy and facing a lawsuit. Let's double check it."

"I already did. I had the lab run the HCG levels, estrogen levels, and progesterone levels this morning. I told them you ordered it, and they'll call you with the results." Of course, the phone buried under the clutter on my desk chose that precise moment to intrude. Lab was calling with rush results.

The lab tech gave me the data and then said, "By the way, we had an identical request from Hilltop Hospital this morning. You'll be interested in that patient as well,"

"Yeah? Okay. Get back to you later on that."

I sat a moment looking at the lab values I'd written on a notepad. I shuffled through a stack of texts and found the reference I was looking for. It confirmed my suspicions.

"Well, according to these hormone levels, you are about 18 weeks along. And nothing is out of the normal levels for that stage of pregnancy, so I think you're going to be fine." I tried to be reassuring, knowing that nothing in this scenario fit.

"The night I met your two-headed eel, did I look like I was 4 months or more pregnant? I know both you and Charlie were paying attention to my bikini." She stood up, pulled the shirttails of her blouse out of her skirt, and lifted them, revealing her abdomen from the pubic ridge to the lower ribs. "Do I look like I'm 18 weeks pregnant? *Well? Do I?*" She started to cry again and sat back down. I believed my eyes and her assertion. Every red flag in the back of my medulla was waving frantically at me.

Houston, we have another problem . . . and it's a doozy.

"Well . . ." I began, stalling to have time to make sense of this.

Then, she inserted the secret code into the launcher and ignited a surgical nuclear strike.

"I haven't had sex in the years I've been stationed here until that night. Charlie is the first man I've had intercourse with in years and that was three weeks ago. *I am not, repeat not, eighteen weeks pregnant.*"

If it were anyone but Hanna, I wouldn't believe it. The number of times I've had women swear they couldn't possibly be six weeks pregnant because their partner's deployment began three months ago, makes me a doubting Thomas. This equaled the number of times a woman claimed her term infant must have arrived prematurely with exact dates to match the father's deployment. These were situations where I'd put on my 'wise old physician' look, stroke my clean-shaven chin, and nod sagely. A shrug helps. I'm a doctor, not a judge.

"Does Charlie know?" I asked the obvious question, having settled the parentage issue.

"Know what? That I'm pregnant with his child, and there is something seriously wrong? No, not yet. That's why I'm here—first to find out what's going on. And don't you dare . . ." I held up my hand signally my complacency.

"Let's go take a look with the ultrasound and see what's what, shall we." Her relief was palpable as we walked down the hall to the delivery ward. We had to step over a large crack in the floor and skirt around puddles of rainwater that leaked through the quake-damaged roof. I had other considerations, including an obscure list of complications that could present as an 18-week pregnancy.

In my department, most of the obstetricians do their own ultrasound exams; it's personal preference based on training and experience. Other facilities have the radiologists perform it, but I was glad I was the one doing this exam. I waited outside the exam room while Hanna changed into a patient gown, then one of my female technicians acted as a chaperone while I looked. I usually have a female standby when I'm examining a patient, and with Hawknose on the warpath, I didn't want to give her any ammunition by being alone in a room with any disrobed patient, let alone a relative.

As I applied the blue conduction jelly for the ultrasound to her abdomen, I palpated a protrusion consistent with an early pregnancy. A woman doesn't 'show' for many weeks, but with Hanna's thin build, I could feel an enlarged uterus, however, not 18 weeks' worth. The last time I had been aware of her abdomen was three weeks ago—on the night dive. I would have noticed. Pieces of this mystery simply weren't falling into place. She looked like she had advanced six to eight weeks in a three-week period.

Wrong. Maybe she has an ovarian tumor? Or . . .

As I scanned, an image appeared in shades of gray on the monitor. The uterus was obvious and centered. Enlarged, consistent with 12 weeks gestation, it had smooth walls, no growths, or tumors. A quick look at the rest of the abdomen failed to find any indication of a cancerous growth.

Breathe in. Good. Breathe out. Good. Doesn't look like one of the rare ovarian cancers that can mimic pregnancy. Very good.

179

"Have your breasts been tender?" Under any other circumstance, she would have run with that query and found a double entendre. Not today.

"Hurt like mothers to be. And my bra was tight." She gently pressed one breast under the gown and winced. Another positive sign of advancing pregnancy.

"What do you see?" Hanna has helped me with many ultrasound exams. To the uninitiated, most of the images are fuzzy goops. I explained the findings of normal ovaries and showed her the enlarged uterus.

"Is that what I think it is?" she asked, pointing at a pulsating point on the screen.

No doubt about that one, bucko. You're preggers.

"Yep. That's a heartbeat alright." I silently counted the rate at about 150 beats per minute. I knew that meant this pregnancy had to be at least six or seven weeks along, the earliest an ultrasound detects a heartbeat. Hanna knew that too and just looked at me, daring me to contradict her dating. *What do I believe? The science, technology, or Hanna's integrity? There is a disconnect here. Something is wrong.*

Then I saw it. So did Hanna.

"There's another one," we said simultaneously. I maneuvered the wand around to get a cleaner look. There was a second heartbeat. I swung back toward where I'd found the first.

There it is. Or is that it? Wait a minute. What's that one? Where is the first one? Okay—there's one, and there's two. And—there's number three. I'll be damned, she has triplets. No, wait. One, two, three, and way over there. Is that four? Can't be. Wrong location. Check again. Four, I see four heartbeats. Wrong, wrong, wrong.

Hanna looked at me and then at the screen. Ice water flowed through my sweat glands, and a wet-footed possum crawled across my grave. I tried not to let my hand shake as I continued to scan. The quaking on the monitor wasn't from aftershocks. Hanna's anxiety and awe reflected in her eyes, but she lacked my experience to know what this was.

"How many babies she got in there, Doc?" I had completely forgotten there was a tech in the room with us. Her question broke the spell.

"Four," Hanna answered before I could. "Right? I counted four separate heartbeats. Right?" Her eyes implored me to put everything into perspective. She needed an explanation.

"Page Dr. Zebo," I calmly told the tech. "I want him to confirm what we're seeing." She scurried out the door on her assigned task. I held Hanna's eyes awaiting her reaction and awareness. Those eyes fluttered nervously around the room as the mental cogs turned. I watched reality register in her expression.

"Quadruplets would explain the elevated hormone levels, but not the timing. There is something wrong because I can't be that far along." There was no hesitancy or denial. I believed her. If she ovulated three weeks ago, there was no possibility she was carrying quads at six to seven weeks gestation.

She wasn't aware of the other finding, and I wasn't ready to break it to her until I had confirmation.

Dr. Ralph Zebo tapped softly on the exam room door and entered. He smiled at Hanna and looked inquiringly at me. Two thick, rebellious eyebrows lifted. "Howdy. What are we up to in here today?" He leaned down from his towering six foot, eight inch height and laid a gentle hand on Hanna's arm. He waited, looking to me for directions.

"Need for you to take a look at something and let me know what you think. Lieutenant Sanders," I started, referring to her professionally rather than familiarly, "had her last period five weeks ago, on oral contraceptives and condom protected intercourse at the time of ovulation. Hormone levels are consistent with 18 weeks. I need for you to look at the ultrasound and tell me what you see."

Ralph didn't question my request, took the wand from me, and proceeded to do his own exam. The rogue eyebrows continued to rise as he looked. Twice he turned slightly away from Hanna and looked at me. All I could do was nod in agreement.

"Wow. This is fantastic." He looked at Hanna; joy intermixed with concern. "Four? I think that might be a record for this place. I assume that congratulations are in order?" He tried to hide the secret he and I now shared, but failed.

181

Hanna *knew* something was wrong. She could read it in our faces.

"I'll be right back. Ralph and I need to step out and check on some things. Okay?"

"Bullshit! There's something wrong, and you two stay right here and tell me. We all know it, so tell me. Please." She started to cry. My heart ached for her. I wanted desperately for this to be a bad dream, and that I would wake up in bed with Tripod blowing dog breath in my face. No such luck.

"I saw it too," was all Ralph had to say. He looked at Hanna with undisguised compassion and squeezed her hand. "You'll be okay, kiddo." He calls everyone he likes kiddo. "I have a patient prepping in the OR. She's losing an early fetus, and I need to be there to help her. I'll check back on you in an hour." He squeezed my arm and left. Hanna looked at me, waiting.

"Let me show you something," I said and put the wand back on her belly. "Here's the uterus and here is the first embryo. Here's the second, and the third. See?" I was orienting the wand so they could be distinguished. "But we don't see fluid filled sacks around them, and there should be at least some fluid by now. And look here. There's number four. And here's the wall of the uterus." I moved back and forth to make my point, waiting. Fresh tears splashed forth when the reality hit.

"It's not in the uterus, is it?" She knew the answer already. I shook my head, and breathed shallowly to gain control over the tide of emotions flooding me. Mouth breathing also kept my fear-generated nausea at bay.

"No, it appears that it has attached to the outer wall of the uterus, or maybe to bowel." I paused to let this register, and then continued, "And that's not good."

An embryo is like an aggressive, invasive tumor in many ways. Normally the trophoblastic tissue, which becomes the placenta, invades the lining of the uterus and leaches from the mother. Now this invasive tissue was outside the uterus where it could cause serious damage.

I could see her absorbing this, using her education and training in obstetrics to push ahead mentally. To her credit, she just nodded. Pragmatist to the end, she *knew*, and was evaluating her options even before I gave them to her. Then she looked puzzled.

"I'm not the only one, am I?" She looked at me, and I must have been wearing the 'Huh?' look again.

"Think about it. I can't be as far along as the tests indicate. I have multiple pregnancies, one of which managed to plant outside the uterus and the other three don't look normal—there are no amniotic sacks." She paused as I considered this. "Are you aware of how many spontaneous abortions we've seen here since the earthquake? And the number of pregnancies we diagnosed this week alone?" I knew that Hanna was involved with keeping statistical data for the department. She would know the pregnancy statistics; I was clueless.

"What do you mean?" I was having trouble switching gears from telling someone they had a potentially fatal complication, to sorting out statistical reports I consider busy work. Hanna had stepped off the oblivion train at the last station and was strapped into a rocket headed another direction.

"Did you know we've had an average of one spontaneous abortion a day at less than eight weeks gestation since the quake? Did you know we've diagnosed two new sets of twins this week alone and have seen an increase in pregnancy of forty percent over the normal expectation for this time of the year and deployment schedules? Did you also know we have sent three severely premature labors off island for care? The average gestation at delivery the past three weeks has only been thirty five weeks?" She stopped expectantly.

I am supposed to know this stuff, but I have other, more urgent reports to evaluate. The Vice President of the United States was due to visit next week, for cripe's sake. We had to make sure the command had her correct insulin and asthma inhalers in stock, just in case. Moreover, the locals were selling snake oil . . . again.

Oh, so many weighty problems and so little give-a-shit attitude. How can I expect to know things that might actually be relevant to my job? This is the military, after all.

"No, I didn't," I answered truthfully. "What are you suggesting; that there is a statistically significant blimp in abnormal OB data since the quake?" She let me ponder that a moment. "You're suggesting that we are seeing too many pregnancies, too many spontaneous abortions and premature deliveries?" I thought about it.

Screw the VP's asthma and departmental budgets; this is something important. Blue Death?

"If what you're suggesting is real, and I don't doubt your work at all, I don't know what it means or what we need to do next." I was considering all the implications when Hanna changed the thought train at the crossing, leaving me to grunt and nod.

"Well, the first thing is that you need to get me in the OR and fix this. Are you going to do a laparoscope to find critter number four and try to take it out that way?" She was referring to placing an endoscope into the abdomen through a tiny hole to see if I could surgically remove this abnormal pregnancy without cutting her open. Gynecologists joke that this is like rebuilding the engine on a '54 Chevy through the tailpipe with chopsticks. My concern was whether the other three embryos could or should survive. I was not the one to make those decisions or do the surgery. She trusted me to amputate her leg when trapped by the quake on Kelly's Reef. As family, she trusted me now to do whatever I needed, but I couldn't, legally or ethically. Besides, I was so upset that I would have dripped tears into the surgical field—a no-no in sterile technique.

"Better call Charlie," she said.

Ralph chose that moment to stick his head in the room. "Did you tell her?" I was surprised to see him return so soon. "My patient had already aborted by the time we got her to the OR," he said, explaining his quick return. "Third one I've seen in two days. That's unusual." He had just confirmed Hanna's hypothesis.

Hanna said, "Yes, he did, and tag, you're it. Jake won't do the surgery, even if I bribe him. So you need to get me prepped and pop a scope in there and fix things." Hanna, to her credit, was not only up to speed, but also ahead of Ralph and me. The no nonsense woman we all loved was back; off the pity pot and onward ho. "And Jakey will be there to protect my virtue while you've got your hands on me."

184

"Jakey?" Ralph's caterpillar brows reached new heights. "Kiddo, you're in good hands," Ralph nodded toward me, "if I do say so myself. I'll go get things set-up while Jakey here," a chuckle mixed with a snort, "does the paperwork."

"Oh, and did you hear the latest juicy gossip?" He waited. "The lab leaked that an OB in town sent in blood work. Hawknose is pregnant. TJ's already started a pool on who the lucky turkey baster is."

Post-Op

Charlie and I waited by a hallway window next to the OR for information on Hanna's surgery. Brilliant flowers of a flame tree outside the windows made me squint. Midwinter and Guam was alive with color. Daily squalls carried fresh air from offshore. The leaking anesthesia machine filled the hall with an antiseptic odor. My mood was black and tasted foul. I wanted to be in there looking over Ralph's shoulder, but knew better; he didn't need a looky-lu breathing down his neck.

"How is she doing, Bones?" Charlie's face was pale. He was pacing from the windowsill to the OR door like a caged panther. We waited. For Charlie and me, time moved like poured molasses. For Ralph, it was warp speed—all a matter of perspective.

"So far she's fine," I replied. I had explained the pregnancy to Charlie, and at first, he beamed with joy. Then I watched him fall apart as the reality sank in. He is a best friend and I could do nothing to shield him from this pain; nor help him make sense of a personal tragedy that lacked reason.

"Ralph is doing miracles in there. Remember I told you he was going to put a tiny telescope through her belly button and see if he could remove the embryo that is attached outside the uterus?" He nodded, but I could tell from his face that his mind was elsewhere. "Well, he was successful and didn't have to open her up, as we initially feared. Her uterus will heal just fine, and you'll be able to have children next time you're ready."

"But?" He looked directly at me; his face a mask of expectation glazed with fear.

"But . . ." I hesitated. "But the other embryos were lost. I'm so sorry. I don't know what else to say." I put my hand on his shoulder. *My patients lose pregnancies all the time, but this time it's family.*

The hospital chaplain turned the far corner of the hallway and looked at me. I waved him off. "He," I said pointing, "would tell you that god works in mysterious ways. Bullshit." I felt my chest tighten as my eyes fogged. I took a couple deep breaths through my mouth to quell my tears.

"I'd tell you that you can try again later, but that would be like telling Jenny she can get a new puppy if Tripod walks across the street and under a car." I had no other words, so I kept quiet.

"But why?" I could feel his confusion, denial, and pain, but couldn't take that away. The anger would soon arrive, then the acceptance. I could only wait and be there for him. "Why were the other babies bad?" Like most parents suffering this loss, he thought in terms of his baby, his son, his daughter; a life unfulfilled. He couldn't conceive of this being abnormal tissue and Hanna's survival at risk. I am in awe at the complexity of a developing human and still wonder how it is even possible. How an embryo manages to complete the perilous journey to birth is incomprehensible to me, and I'm supposed to be an expert. To Charlie it was incomprehensible that this didn't happen.

"Charlie. You know I love Hanna as much as I love you. If I had the answers, the logic, or even the reason why, I'd tell you. I don't." I took a deep breath and waited. He only shook his head. If he was capable of tears, this was his moment. A deep sniff was as close as he came.

"I do know this," I continued. "There was something wrong from the very beginning of her pregnancy. She told me the first time you two had sex was the night of the quake." He looked up, his face flushed. I couldn't determine if it was shame, anger, denial, or just Charlie blushing. "Everything I know puts her months further into this pregnancy than is possible. All the lab data points at the wrong dates; the heartbeats we saw were all wrong. And even though we saw heartbeats, we didn't see babies." I watched for him to consider that and ask the obvious question.

"But if they weren't babies, what were they? Little green aliens?" I felt a dark storm pass. The hair on my back rubbed against my blouse.

"Remember when we talked about why Auraka has two heads and how many millions of things have to happen in exactly the correct sequence at the exact right time for a fetus to develop? The only miracle I believe in is that this can happen at all. Think about it—millions of signals from DNA happening precisely to make a baby. The odds are so against that, it is mind-boggling that it ever occurs."

Charlie nodded. "I get the biology 101 lesson, but I don't get why this pregnancy is different?"

"I don't know how Hanna got pregnant." I saw him lift his eyebrows. "Okay, that didn't come out quite right. I assume you two did it the normal way, without being abducted into the mother ship." His eyebrows dropped, and a darker storm passed across his expression. I flashed back to the silence around a table at Kelly's Bar and Grill when I joked about little green men.

"Regardless, what I'm trying to tell you is that something happened the night of the quake when Hanna got pregnant and whatever it was threw everything out of sync. Some of the steps were missing, or out of sequence, and I don't know why. I promise you I'll do everything I can to find out."

"Pinky Swear?" He held up his pinky to me; I took it in mine. Charlie, TJ and I did this when we kidded each other— a bonding symbol we shared when we wanted to be silly. This gesture was flat, lacking kidding and joy. This was a solemn pledge.

"Thanks, Bones." Then he pulled me forward and wrapped his massive arms around me. I was shocked, then asphyxiated. First, by the emotion from someone who grimaces watching football players pat each other on the ass, and secondly from the smell of kimchee, ginger, and spiced vegetables. That meant he was heading out for fieldwork. He told me once that whenever he went 'in country', he ate enough noxious food to blend his sweat into the exotic odors of the local environment.

"So, who are you invading this week?" I asked, moving back and wrinkling my nose.

"I'm going undercover at Gold's Gym in Manila." He said this without even blinking.

"Seriously?" I asked.

"No, but I just got orders and have to leave in an hour. I can't wait for her to recover to say goodbye, but she'll understand. You keep an eye on her for me while I'm gone. Please." He stopped, and I saw his eyes water. "Don't lose her. I . . . I . . ." His shoulders slumped. I'd never seen Charlie this distressed.

"When will you be back?"

"When the problem is fixed." He took a deep breath. "In the meantime I've arranged for Angel and Ramón to keep an eye on you. They're also taking the kids to the airport because I know you'll want to stay here until Ralph is finished operating. And when I get back, we need to talk about Djibouti."

"Okay?"

"I mean seriously talk. Don't trust LaRouche if you see him again; he's not telling you everything. For that matter, don't trust anyone. You and TJ look at the video I took of Kelly's Reef. Then we talk."

"How do I get in touch with you?"

"You don't. I'll let you know where I am as soon as possible."

Before Charlie could leave, Ralph pushed through the OR doors and told us that Hanna was stable. The surgery was successful, and she'd go home in a day or two.

Charlie reached to give Ralph a hug.

"Sterile," he said backing into the OR, his arms raised defensively. "Oh, man. Is that Mama Kreech's kimchee you've been eating?" With that Ralph went back to finish up with Hanna's surgery.

Charlie took a last look at the door to the OR and was gone. I wondered what I'd tell Hanna if he didn't return this time.

The Summons

```
Orders
To:  CDR J. Matthews, MD, USNMC
Dtd:  1 DEC 1400.
Re: Command inquiry into
circumstances    of Sanchez birth
dtd: 10 NOV 2100.
Encl: Command Directive 3744A, JAG
   Manual Sec8:para6
CC:  Commanding Officer, Naval
Hospital
     LCDR R. Zebo, MD. Head: Medical
Practices Review Committee (acting)
CDR Matthews:
You are hereby directed to:
```

1. Present at 0800 to room 101, 2 DEC,
   without delay.

2. Bring all medical records, charts,
   notes, video or audio tapes, staff
   statements, and papers related to the
   surgery performed on subject Isa
   Sanchez on the above noted date.

3. Immediately cease all medical care
   for all active patients and transfer
   said care to appropriate staff.
   You are hereby further informed that
   all medical and surgical privileges
   are in abeyance pending the outcome
   of this hearing. This is a medical
   practice hearing, protected by due
   confidentiality, and not reported to
   licensing authorities unless
   otherwise directed by the findings of
   the Board.
   You are hereby notified that you are
   removed as chairman of the Medical

Practice Committee. LCDR R. Zebo
replaces you as acting Chairman.

Failure to present will be a direct
violation of UCMJ ART 16 and result
in immediate imprisonment pending
court-martial.

Signed this date:
CDR B. Hawke, Executive Officer,
Naval Hospital.

"So, what does this mean?" I asked. I was in the Skipper's office, grinding my teeth, barely able to talk.

A dingy window lit the office, and a huge 'I love me' wall of photos, degrees, and minor achievements. His favorite was a photo of the mayor of Lake Comatose, Kansas pinning a Boy Scout badge on his shirt. A patina of dust covered everything. Although he ran the largest medical facility in this part of the world, the office lacked the matching panache. I'd spent many hours in here with him planning, cajoling, arguing, and then going along with whatever he decided to do. He was a shoot, point, and aim type of leader.

He lowered his substantial bulk into his creaking desk chair. I secretly hoped to be there when it collapsed under him, but that was not to be today. His uniform, sporting yellow stained armpits, looked like he'd slept in it. He probably had. Breakfast remains adorned the pocket like a medal, The Magnificent Order of the Bacon and the Egg. Deep bags under rheumy eyes and a bulbous nose accented his jowls. At times, I visualized him as a hung-over bloodhound, but I never forget he is The Skipper.

"What it means, Commander," he responded, "is that you finally managed to pee in Commander Hawke's oatmeal. She has been gunning for you since she arrived; especially after you had her license removed and then embarrassed her at morning report last week."

"So now she's trying to get *my* license pulled? How can she possibly think she'll get away with that?" I started feeling the old anger boiling under my tectonic plates, ready to erupt.

The Skipper held up both palms. "You know she has the authority to ask the committee to investigate, I can't stop that." He shrugged. "But we both know this probably won't go anywhere, so I wouldn't worry about it if I were you."

"It's not your medical license at stake." I knew it was time to get an answer to the real question.

"Skipper, it's more than this, and you know it. How did she manage to remain on Guam after having her privileges to practice revoked, and then reassigned as your Executive Officer? That's unheard of, Skipper. No one in the command believes you actually asked her to replace the old XO. Every day she remains here, morale festers. The other physicians can't stand her. The medics are going out of their way to be passive-aggressive toward her. Rumor has it that they were going to send her a bottle of scotch laced with laxatives. And don't get me started on what the nursing staff is saying." I took a shaky breath and tried to lower my blood pressure below stoke level. "She's the poster child for fragging." I caught the Skipper smirking despite himself. Nobody liked her.

"I'm as aware as anyone how disruptive she can be—."

I cut him off. "If you don't do something about her, something terrible will happen. I think TJ even has a pool going on how long she'll survive. I'm serious Skipper, she's dangerous, and someone's going to get hurt if you don't muzzle her."

The Skipper cleared his throat and shuffled some papers on his desk. "It's out of my hands."

I was incensed. "When the staff finds out she's bringing me up on charges because I took care of Isa Sanchez, all hell's going to break loose. Can you imagine tomorrow's headline in the *Chamorro Times*—HERO DOCTOR WHO SAVED ISA CHARGED WITH MALPRACTICE BY CRAZED BITCH AT THE NAVAL HOSPITAL."

"This is a matter for the Practice Committee, and I've already ordered all members not to discuss this." I could see him spinning the politics. He thought a moment. "And that includes you. This remains within the walls of the committee room." He nodded, satisfied that all his bases were covered. I popped his bubble.

"What about the petty officer who handed Ralph and me our orders? And the one who typed them? And there is no way my wife isn't going to hear about this, which means Lieutenant Sanders will know which means the nursing staff will know and . . . see what I mean? This worm is already out of the bag." I watched him deflate as he idly scratched at his dandruff.

"What, I don't understand," I continued, "is why she's out to create so much hate and discontent. That's not the function of an Executive Officer. So again Skipper, why is she even here? What is her agenda and why is she targeting me?" I waited.

"Jake," he began, "her orders came directly from Pacific Fleet Command. I've been pushing for her transfer ever since I got those orders, but it's apparently valuable to someone very high up that she stays here. Someone with enough pull made sure she rotated here after her residency, and made her the XO, so I'm stuck with her for now." He looked at me. "You just have to get along with her."

"Get along with her?" I was shocked. "That would earn me the Nobel Peace Prize. I'm more likely to get life without parole when I strangle her." I just shook my head. I was disgusted with all the bullshit Hawknose generated. I had a killer looking for Blue Death or something equally insane, an 'old friend' threatening my family, Hanna recovering from surgery for what she thought was just one more abnormal pregnancy on Guam, Angel camped out at my house, and now this crap.

"Jake," the Skipper said, continuing to use the familiar, "I'm on your side. We both know you did the right thing that night, and I support you entirely, but she *is* dangerous. I don't want to lose you, so take this seriously. I think Commander Hawke is just marking her territory and getting even, but . . ." I had a vision of her standing beside the corner of the hospital and lifting her leg . . . I hoped he was right, but the hair standing up on my neck told me otherwise.

Ambushed

"This command meeting of the Medical Practice Committee will now come to order. We are video-recording this meeting. Note: present are Commander Hawke, Executive Officer, Dr. Zebo, acting chair, Doctors Como, Heard, and Winters. Also present is Dr. Matthews, Department Head for Obstetrics and Gynecology, Chief of Surgical Services, and Chairman of this Committee for Medical Practice." Ralph winked at me, letting me know he added all the titles just to irritate Hawknose. He would have added 'walks on water' if he could have.

"For the record," Hawknose shot to her feet, "Matthews is not the chairman of this committee; he is the reason this committee has convened."

"For the record," Ralph cut her off, "*Doctor* Matthews remains the chair of this committee until such time as members of the committee vote otherwise. I am simply acting chair for this one meeting. And I would also request, *Commander* Hawke that you refer to the members of this committee by either their rank or the title Doctor."

"I am the Executive Officer," she screeched, and then glanced at the camera in the corner. She straightened her posture and uniform.

"Yes ma'am," Ralph answered quietly, smiling. "*You* are the XO, and *we* are physicians. Everyone present will show due respect and appropriate protocol during these proceedings. I would also remind you that Commander Matthews, although of the same rank, has more time in service than you. This is a medical issue and your function as Executive Officer does not allow rude or inappropriate behavior toward a superior officer." He paused, having set the rules of engagement, and raised his eyebrows. "Let's proceed, shall we?" He shuffled the papers in front of him. "Since you ordered this committee meeting rather than the normal procedure of a privileged physician member requesting committee support, I would ask that you begin."

"Point of order." Dr. Como raised his hand. Ralph nodded his consent.

"Let the record show that the normal dress for a formal meeting of this committee is whites." Dr. Como sat up straighter in his crisp white uniform. He had visited the barber last night, as did the rest of us. A tiny swab of toilet paper stuck to a shaving nick under his ear marred his otherwise immaculate appearance.

My committee always convenes in our best, inspection grade white uniform. Crisp white blouse, trousers, stockings, shoes, and cover are the usual expectation. Medals and command insignias are included. I had taken particular care with my uniform to iron creases midline on my pockets, polish the brass, and square up my medals. I had even added my 'command designator'.

When a naval officer takes command of a unit, he wears an indicator of that command just above the flap of the left blouse pocket. This is usually a small gold emblem recognized as authority. Today, by conspiracy and unsaid consent of the others, I added my command insignia to my uniform—a tiny red button. Reading it requires getting within six inches. Printed in micro-font it proudly proclaims, "Pardon me. You're standing on my penis."

Hawknose was dressed in working khaki: dull brown, stabilized with unpolished black shoes, no medals, or insignias.

"I *am* in the appropriate uniform of the day," she said. She didn't forget to wear whites; she was wearing her arrogance.

"Yes Ma'am, but as you are certainly aware, formal meetings of Dr. Matthews' committee are always attended in white." The corner of Ralph's mouth lifted slightly.

Hawknose began to look more like a cornered rat than a raptor. I knew she expected the committee to roll over upon her arrival. She turned her malevolent gaze on me. I smiled my best beatific smile.

"And," Dr. Como said, "I would also like the record to reflect that the Executive Officer is wearing the insignia of the Naval Medical Corps, on the left collar of her *khaki* working uniform. It was my understanding that this committee had removed all medical privileges from *Commander* Hawke. I would therefore move that this committee request clarification of *Commander* Hawke's rank and service unit, specifically whether the XO of this hospital is currently a medical or line officer."

"So moved. Second. In favor. The aye's carry." I love it when a well-oiled group of devious individuals on a common mission comes together.

"I will now turn over the floor to the Executive Officer." Ralph extended his arm to Hawknose. Then he rolled his wrist looking at his watch. "And since most of us in this room have real work to be done, I ask that all comments and discussions be brief and to the point."

Hawknose sputtered, tried to regain composure, then stood up and walked around the committee table to face my inquisitors. Sitting in the hot seat, I was behind her, facing the committee table. Looking at the backside of her skinny frame, I briefly wondered how she would look in Hanna's thong bikini.

I considered sneaking up behind her and holding up rabbit ears behind her head, but I held my arrested development in check. I could lose my medical license. I could lose my commission. My life balanced on the edge of this woman's vendetta. But, I still wanted to shoot a spit wad at her.

"Gentlemen," Hawknose began, taking the safe road on the proper title issue, "as you are aware, on the night in question, Matthews," she paused to make sure we caught her lack of respect. Then, she looked into the camera. "Excuse me, *Doctor* Matthews, did willfully, and knowingly disregard my direct orders by permitting an armed civilian to physically force his way onto the grounds and demand medical care." She turned to glare at me with bloodshot eyes.

"Point of order." Dr. Henry broke in. Ralph recognized him with a nod.

"I am not finished," said Hawknose.

"Point of order has precedence. Please precede *Doctor* Henry."

"Thank you, *Doctor* Zebo. My point is that access through the gate and events at the gate that night are not within the purview of this committee. That's a security issue, not medical care. Move to discontinue all further discussion of security events for the night in question."

"Second. In favor. Ayes carry."

"Did you have anything else, Ma'am?" and, before she could respond, "Motion to adjourn."

"Stand Down! We are *not* finished here." Her look dared anyone in the room to cross her.

Dr. Heard, our audiologist, had been probing his ear with a pencil and now examined his wax treasure with more interest than he showed the proceedings. He looked up and sighed. Then he looked past Hawknose at me and winked.

"Dr. Matthews," Hawknose continued, dropping all pretense of snubbing me further, "do you have the records I requested?" She turned to face me and held out her hand.

"*Doctor* Zebo has your copy. I made copies for everyone on the committee. And, oh yeah, the Skipper and the JAG office." The committee had already reviewed the details at a 5 AM breakfast meeting.

She grinned maliciously at me. "Excellent. Then I would ask the committee to open the records to the surgical consent form?" I could tell she wanted to throw a fist in the air and scream 'Gottcha.' I wanted to throw a fist into her face and yell 'Gottcha.'

"As you know, Birdina," the second time I had ever referred to her in the familiar, "excuse me, *Commander* Hawke, there is no surgical consent form in the file. I documented an emergency surgery, and there wasn't time to get the patient's signature. Mrs. Sanchez was barely conscious."

"So you claim. However, there are no witnesses, so it appears that you operated on a civilian without permission. That constitutes assault, conduct unbecoming an officer, and willful disregard for the safety of your patient. And, after this committee removes your medical privileges, rest assured that I plan to press criminal charges as well." She glowed with smugness. The room was muggy and silent. My white uniform was beginning to stick to me. My gut squeezed acid into my throat as I realized how much I hated this woman.

"Petty Officer Rush, who assisted me with the surgery, was a witness," I corrected.

"Petty Officer Rush is not a physician, nor is he qualified to perform surgery. His actions have resulted in his transfer stateside. I have arranged for a disciplinary board to investigate his actions and dishonorably discharge him from the service. Doesn't look like he'll be going to medical school after all." She was bursting at the seams. I was nauseated. I forced myself not to visibly shake.

"How can you be so petty and vindictive? You do that to Petty Officer Rush, and I'll get you." I stood and approached her. Ralph cleared his throat and shook his head.

Oh, fuck. I just threatened the XO and had it recorded on film. Shit. I caught my breath and sat back down, shaking with rage.

"Thank you, Doctor. I'll make sure the Admiral sees this video." She bounced on her toes and grinned at me.

"Master Chief Albright—," I began.

"Is on unspecified duty and cannot be reached for comment," she countered.

Ah Ha. That explains why Charlie had to leave before Hanna was out of surgery. Calling you a bitch is an insult to canines.

"Lieutenant Sanders was present and will confirm verbal consent was obtained," I said. *Can't deny that, can you? Come on dawg, let's tangle.* My hands ached from squeezing them into fists.

Her grin broadened into a smile, satisfaction lighting her cadaverous face. "I'm afraid not. Your sister-in-law just had an abortion at this facility," She looked at Ralph with an undisguised threat, "and even if she was available, her statement can't help you. It seems she was under the influence of drugs during the Sanchez surgery. I'm charging her with dereliction of duty and drug abuse." Every eye in the room was on her. A cloud of shock and disgust descended upon every face.

"I don't believe that." Ralph stood up, and his chair clattered to the floor behind him. It had the effect of cymbals in vespers. "I don't know what you're thinking, or how you can make such an unfounded accusation."

Smiling, Hawknose handed him a lab report. Ralph read it, looking at me and passed it to the other members.

"The morning after the quake, I ordered a command-wide urinalysis. It seems that Lieutenant Sanders' came back positive for opiates." She let that percolate. "So, *Doctor*, you performed unauthorized surgery, using an untrained and unqualified assistant as well as a nurse who was under the influence." She pointed a claw at me. "And you prescribed her the drugs." She placed her fists on bony hips and turned back to face the committee.

"You're right," I said. "I did prescribe Tylenol with codeine for her that night. She had an injury to her leg that I was treating. It's all documented in her medical records. She wasn't intoxicated when she helped with the surgery . . . and she has never had a positive drug screen."

"So you *do* admit to prescribing controlled substances to a family member?" She gloated.

"Commander," Dr. Heard broke in, addressing Hawknose, "this report is only qualitative, not quantitative. All this tells me is that some time before the urinalysis she took codeine. Without a level, there is no way to know when Lieutenant Sanders ingested the codeine. I believe it is more likely that she took some before bed that evening, don't you? I don't see any problem with any of us prescribing appropriate medications for a family member in an emergency. And I personally examined her the following morning and found her prescription bottle still had three of the four tablets present, hardly a conspiracy or evidence of drug abuse. That's less than a shot of Jack Daniels." He let that accusation lay. "Moreover, because of your surprise screening, she notified me, as per protocol that she had taken one tablet the evening before, after she was off duty. I had her submit a quantitative blood sample and those levels confirm her story."

He removed a similar lab slip from his briefcase, handed it to Ralph, and raised thin eyebrows in her direction. I had expected an ambush the morning after the quake, when the XO ordered everyone to provide a urinalysis. I'd arranged for Hanna to see Dr. Heard, just in case Hawknose tried something.

"That won't matter. Her statement about whether you obtained informed consent or not has no bearing on this inquiry. She was in no condition to make that judgment. And without verification Dr. Matthews is still guilty of operating without permission." She paused to look triumphant. "So it is the duty of this committee to bring findings against Dr. Matthews. I demand that his medical privileges be removed." She pointed her finger at me.

That your best shot, Birdina? Nice try. Now, watch this, birdbrain.

"But we *do* have a qualified witness at the time of surgery." Dr. Heard had lost interest in his earwax and sat forward, both elbows on the table.

He looked at the other members. Clearly, he was up to something spectacular. I could sense that the rat had just nibbled on the stinky cheese, and the trap spring was primed. Ralph nodded permission and Dr. Heard went to the committee room door. "Come on in," he said.

Ramón was wearing cut off Levis, a grimy t-shirt proclaiming 'Freedom for Guam Nation', and flip-flops. He looked around the room and fixed on me.

"Hey Doc. Thanks for the steaks and beer. They was great. And Sammy caught a pig out back a' your place. We'll party next week and you're invited." He stopped and remembered his manners. "And all you guys can come too, she was a really big pig." He had finally turned to look at Hawknose and the timing of his look, and big pig comment wasn't lost on anyone. He grinned.

"Who is this?" Hawknose demanded. "And what is he doing here? What does this have to do with these proceedings?" She was starting to look almost as yellow as Ramón's teeth as the trap snapped shut.

"This is Mr. Sanchez, Isa Sanchez' husband," Dr. Heard informed her. "He was the armed civilian you didn't want to allow through the gate the night of the earthquake. His wife would be dead if Dr. Matthews hadn't intervened."

"This is the man who stormed the gate that night, and threatened the staff with a rifle? Why isn't he in custody?" The yellow pallor had become butter cream.

How's that stinky cheese taste, Birdina?

"Ain't no rifle, it was a shotgun, a 12 gauge, and the big guy in that fancy office at the front of this place said it was okay for me to be here. He and I decided to be friends ever since you guys saved Isa." His smile conveyed trust and good will to all those foreign devils he used to hate. "And Eight Ball said I owed him, and if I didn't come, he was gonna kick my ass. Like him and what army I asked? But he says I owe him, so . . ."

"Eight Ball?" Hawknose looked confused. Sweat stains were forming on her khakis that her emaciated arms couldn't hide.

"You know," said Ramón. "That humongous black dude downstairs with the shiny head who eats cigars. That guy."

"The Skipper approved Mr. Sanchez to be here after he heard about this committee meeting." Dr. Heard was playing the straight man, hoping Ramón got his lines right. He turned to Ramón and started to place a hand on his shoulder then stopped. "Mr. Sanchez, would you tell this committee what happened that night?"

"Oh yeah, sure. There was this really big earthquake and everything fell off the walls at Momma Rosa's place, and Angel, he's my brother, came by to see if we was okay and everything, and we was, so he left, and then Isa, she's my woman, she started complaining about the baby, but I told her the baby was just shook up 'cause of everything, and . . ." He paused to take a breath.

Before he could ramble forth, Dr. Zebo interrupted. "Ramón, we just need to know why you're here today." Dr. Zebo waited while Ramón thought about this. "We already know about Isa and what happened at the gate and all about her surgery." He made a 'come on' gesture with his hand. The 'ah ha' bulb lit Ramón's otherwise dim chandelier.

"Oh yeah, I was supposed to give you guys this paper." He pulled a crumpled paper out of his hip pocket, unfolded it, and smoothed the wrinkles before handing it to Dr. Zebo.

"It appears this is a surgical consent form. Looks like he signed it as Mrs. Sanchez' husband giving consent for Dr. Matthews to do a C-Section on her. And it's witnessed by Lieutenant Commander Justis." Dr. Zebo paused and smiled at Hawknose before proceeding. "How did you come to have this, Mr. Sanchez?"

"The night Isa had her baby, see, these marine guys was holding me in a room downstairs and I thought we'd be getting it on, and all, and Eight Ball comes in and says Isa and the baby was real sick and might die if the doc here," nodding in my direction, "didn't do some emergency surgery. He wanted to know if it was okay with me, 'cause Isa was out of it and all, and so I says you bet, and he let me come up afterward to see my son and all, so I'd know everything was okay. But he was talkin' to the marines about not shooting me, you know, and he forgot to take it with him, so's I grabbed it and stuck it in my pocket and all, and well, there it is." He looked incredibly proud—because he hadn't killed a marine, had a new son, remembered his lines, or saved my bacon. It didn't matter. He'd dealt Hawknose a fatal blow, and we all felt it. I wondered how much of his story was true.

"Move to dismiss the abeyance and restore Dr. Matthew to full staff status." Dr. Zebo said. "Second. In favor. Ayes carry, meeting adjourned." With that, *The Stinky Cheese Caper* failed.

As we filed past a stricken looking Hawknose, I heard Dr. Winters whisper to her loudly enough for all to overhear, "Is it true you're pregnant? How could that possibly be?" Her color faded to white ash as she tried to open her mouth.

Hawknose rolled her eyes as she collapsed, hitting the corner of the committee table on her way down. The dull thunk and pooling of blood around her head as she landed on the floor told me she'd split her scalp. We all stood there looking, waiting to see who would assist her.

"You guys gonna do nothin'?" asked Ramón. He nodded in approval. The rest of us waited to see who would be first to offer aid.

"Oh hell," I said. "Help me get her on a gurney."

Hawknose Down

"Bones, you need to see this." TJ was on the phone to my office an hour after we carted Hawknose to the ER to have her scalp sutured. "And bring Ralph with you."

I knew the committee members had mixed feelings when Hawknose hit the deck. Nobody liked her; most ignored her; a few hated her. We'd sprung the trap on her, but none of us wanted her physically hurt. Nobody goes into medicine to cause harm.

Ralph and I met TJ at the triage station of the ER. I saw Hawknose sitting on a gurney, her skin the color of soured goat milk. Squared off against a corpsman valiantly trying to apply a head dressing, she was demanding a mirror. Patients in the waiting area cringed as she shrieked.

"Check it out," I said to the others. "She's got half a high an' tight." The corpsman assisting with her suturing had taken a razor and shaved half her scalp to expose the laceration. The other half looked like a Brillo pad.

"Yeah, she's this week's pin-up model," said TJ, "but we have a greater concern than hair style." He paused to get our attention. "She's pregnant."

"We know that," I said. "The lab let that little surprise out of the bag yesterday. Maybe you didn't get the memo. So what?"

"So what? So, she doesn't have a uterus, is so what." He let Ralph and me ponder that a moment and continued, "I pulled her medical records when she arrived in the ER." He handed me a brown record folder. "While she was stationed in Boston, she underwent a hysterectomy." He waited while I weighed that bit of information and searched through her records. I stopped at the summary of her admission to Boston Hospital and skimmed the findings. A giant *Whiskey Tango* did a *Foxtrot* with my head. I thought about Hanna's research and wondered if this was another storm brewing.

I read from her records. "She had a molar pregnancy at the age of 28 and underwent a hysterectomy. Looks like they tried a couple rounds of chemotherapy without effect before resorting to surgery."

"What does that mean?" asked TJ, "and how does a woman get pregnant without a uterus? What the hell is going on here?" He looked at us, waiting.

Ralph explained, "During her residency she became pregnant, but the embryo never developed. In her case, what arrived at the uterus was trophoblastic tissue—an abnormal placental. We call that trophoblastic disease, molar pregnancy, hyditaform mole; it all means the same thing. Her pregnancy resulted in an extremely rare cancer of the uterus."

"I've never heard of such a thing." TJ, despite his education, was lost in this morass. "And why is it called a mole?"

"I'm only guessing," I said, "but mole is a fitting description of how these things burrow into the uterus and take up residence. The problem is that they are incredibly invasive and have the advantage of turning off the mother's normal immune protection, the same way a normal pregnancy does. Most people don't realize that a fetus is an invasive parasite, and able to suppress the mother's normal protection to foreign tissue invasion."

TJ nodded. "So . . . she had this mole-like invasive tumor that was treated with chemotherapy." A corpsman approached with a report. TJ perused it and signed off.

Ralph said, "Yeah, lucky for her they caught it early, but these things can metastasize to lungs, brain, and who knows where else. Nasty disease—I'm not surprised that she lost her uterus. But she's fortunate that follow-up labs have all been negative—until now."

"Ah, of course," I said. "That's why she got a pregnancy test at an outside lab. She was checking herself and didn't want anyone to know."

"What do you mean? Is this pregnancy a recurrence of her mole thing?" TJ continued to struggle with this.

I had only seen one case of molar pregnancy during my training and had spent months reading about it before I understood the ramifications. There were too many variations on this theme to make sense.

"I don't know. This many years out from her first occurrence, it's unlikely this is a recurrence, but we need to be sure. If it's not another molar pregnancy, we're left with the problem of how a woman without a uterus gets pregnant." I looked at TJ. "And don't start with the jokes." I felt the three of us mentally take a step back and consider the problem.

"Does she know?" Ralph asked.

"Not yet," said TJ. "I still don't get this. If it's not molar cancer and she doesn't have a uterus, how does the sperm get to the egg in the first place? It doesn't seem like that can happen, can it?" He squeezed his eyebrows in consternation.

Ralph asked the obvious questions. "Has anyone looked with ultrasound to see if there is a mass in the abdomen? We also need to get a CAT scan to rule out metastatic disease in her lungs or brain."

"The ER doc ran those tests." TJ read from a pile of reports. "Ultrasound is negative; slight swelling of her remaining ovaries, but no masses or unusual findings. He ran a quantitative HCG test that puts her at about eight weeks, so if there's an embryo, we should be able to see it, don't you think?" TJ handed me the lab reports.

"Eight week levels don't indicate a mole; they're usually sky high." I looked at Ralph, my mind spinning through all the possibilities.

Lab error? Recurrence of the mole? No, unlikely this far out. Pregnancy by way of a fistula or hole in the vagina allowing sperm to get to an ovary? Nah, who in their right mind would ever consider having sex with her?

I looked at Ralph and saw him going through the same process and arriving at the same conclusion. "Parthenogenesis?" we said simultaneously.

"What's parthenogenesis?" asked TJ, switching to a deep English accent. "You chaps are using those big words again that the brother doesn't understand."

A young man walked through the ER door and approached the triage area. He was holding a bloody bandage to his face. TJ signaled for a corpsman and helped get the patient on a gurney and into a treatment room. He returned shaking his head and grinning.

"What's that all about?" I asked.

"Teaching his son to play catch. Caught a hardball to the nose." He chuckled. "So what's this partheno-something?"

"There are life forms that can self-fertilize," I said. "There's a red lizard species capable of combining the DNA from two of her eggs to create an offspring; a male is not required. Same with the Komodo dragon, and several sexually reproducing single cell bacteria. In humans, it's only been hinted at." I looked back toward Hawknose as she continued to fuss at the corpsman bandaging her scalp. *Is she actually human?*

Ralph continued, "Parthenogenesis is the basis of the Amazon women myth; a race of women who don't need men to reproduce."

"I almost married one a few years ago," TJ said deadpan. "So what do we do with Hawknose?"

"Well, bottom line is we're going to need to follow her labs and get that CAT scan," I said. "Ralph, you'll have to follow her care since there is no way I can get directly involved."

"Okay, but you owe me big time for this one." Ralph looked toward his newest patient and snorted. "Remind me to personally thank the corpsman responsible for the hairstyling. Hope someone got photos."

Two corpsmen rolled a gurney with a patient into the triage area. To me, the patient looked pregnant under the blanket. Everyone looked pregnant to me. Then I saw his beard.

In the last three days, I'd been shanghaied by LaRouche and told about Blue Death, threatened by a whacko letter writer, helped Hanna with abnormal quadruplets, fought Hawknose, who now might have a molar pregnancy, and only slept a few hours. I was one pair short of a full house.

Hanna's data on atypical pregnancies; how many others are there? I've been preoccupied, exhausted, and haven't paid attention. Now it's time to find out what's going on.

"Jake. You okay?" asked TJ. I snapped back, and we stepped away from the counter.

"I don't know," I answered. "Have either of you been aware of an increase in obstetric problems lately? Hanna told me she thinks there's significant bump in our numbers."

"Ya know, now that you mention it, we have seen a lot of new pregnancies as well as spontaneous abortions lately." Ralph paused to consider this. "And I've seen two new patients this week who claim they can't be pregnant. I wrote that off as the usual denial, but . . ."

"And Hanna was on the pill when she got pregnant with quadruplets," I said. "Now Hawknose. Have you been aware of anything weird, TJ?" He frowned, eyebrows meeting above his nose. He took the cigar out of his mouth. "And," I continued, "the night of the quake, Isa went into labor a month early. Something is going on."

TJ rubbed his thumb across his nose. "We ran out of home pregnancy tests given out in the ER, and I order them by the gross. That would be over a hundred tests since the quake."

"Hold that thought a minute. I gotta hit the head." Ralph shuffled down the hallway. There was a brief aftershock and the fluorescent lights blinked. The emergency doors automatically closed and I heard a muffled scream emanating from the waiting room.

"You don't suppose . . ." TJ stopped, shifting his eyes toward Ralph, making sure he was out of hearing range. I caught the signal and shook my head. "I mean, all that stuff LaRouche told us about Blue Death, and now this? Do you think we are dealing with this Blue Death stuff and how would it get here?"

TJ hadn't been diving the night of the quake, the night I found the blue globes, the night Hanna became pregnant, the night Isa delivered. He didn't know about the globes I found unless someone told him.

I continued, "Don't know what it is, but I'm going to do some records research on my own. Why don't you come by tonight? Charlie wanted us to view the video of Kelly's Reef and all the little two headed eels before he gets back. I'll let you know what I find out from the records."

I went to medical records where more evidence of Blue Death loomed its ugly head.

The Third Letter

The envelope was plain and addressed to Matthews. No return address. It was sitting on the desk in my office when I returned from medical records. Only someone with access to my office could have done that. I called Lieutenant Frisk, the investigator from Naval Investigative Services. My hands were shaking so hard I dropped the phone. The sunshine yellow paint on my office walls was painfully bright, the heat oppressive. My vision dimmed. My head began to throb.

"I'll be right there. Don't handle it, I'll want fingerprints." I sat motionless for what felt like hours before he arrived.

"That it?" he asked, pointing at the envelope. I nodded in the affirmative. "See anyone around your office?"

"No. I was in medical records, and it was on my desk when I opened the door."

"Office door locked?"

"Umm . . . yeah, I had to unlock it to get in, and dropping my keys when I saw the letter."

"Okay, let's see what we've got here." He pulled on latex gloves and using tweezers and an X-Acto knife carefully slit the envelope and removed the latest letter. There was no salutation:

I heard that that nasty bitch was trying to get you fucked up. Don't worry my freind, I make sure she wont create you problems. I got plans and she aint going to fuck them.

Whre did your kids go? I was really hopping to meet them. Do you remembr my daughter? I don't understand why she died. I hope you can explain when we get together. You got sumthing I want. Be cautious. your friend

I stepped into the bathroom and threw up.

Frisk Points a Finger

The rain stopped after two hours. I had spent that time on the porch watching, and thinking; thinking of who wanted to harm my family. The overcast sky matched my mood. The roof, the grass, and my uniform all steamed after the afternoon deluge ended and the heat returned. Turtledove finished her joyous flaunting of flesh, scrubbing in the rain while the neighborhood cringed at that monumental event. Tripod wandered out, tried to lift a leg, tipped over, bugled once, and beat a hasty retreat back indoors. The air conditioner was out, and the geckos were multiplying on the green slime growing on the concrete block walls. The house smelled closed-in. The undertone aroma I recognized as Angel Sanchez.

TJ was flipping burgers when a knock on my door sounded.

"Please don't let that be Turtledove needing a towel," he muttered. Before he could answer the door, Lieutenant Frisk walked in without invitation and walked past TJ to the patio. He stood with his nose inches from mine.

Tripod went nuts, bugling a high-pitched alarm at the intruder.

"Hey Lieutenant, how ya doin'?" I reached down to pet Tripod. "It's okay fella, he doesn't know we have a trained attack dog in the house." Frisk ignored Tripod.

"Can you explain why your prints were all over this letter? You said you hadn't touched it, and I personally opened the envelope." Frisk handed me a plastic sleeved letter. Splotchy magenta fingerprints dotted the document. He tapped his foot, waiting.

"You opened it, so how could my prints be on it? That's not possible, so obviously someone in your lab screwed up." At that, he snorted. Tripod sat in front of him and snorted too.

"What else did you find?" I asked.

"The lab matched the paper to a ream in your desk."

"So what? It's Government Issue paper you'll find in every office in the hospital. What are you implying?"

"And," he continued, pointing to a faint smudge and crease line in the upper corner, "see this crease and ink spot?" He threw the letter on the table and opened his briefcase. He pulled out the second letter, handing it to me. "And here and here?" he said, pointing out identical smudges and a crease on that page. He stopped, awaiting my response. When I had none, he dropped the bomb.

"The toner matches your Hewlett Packard laser printer, at least on the second and third letters. And yours is the only one of that type in the building." He eyed me sharply. "When I ran a test sheet through it, the crease and smudge matched exactly." He turned both palms up. "So?"

Tripod looked up at me and nodded with another snort as if to say, "So?"

"Well, duh. The cheapskates in accounting wouldn't give me a printer, so I had to buy my own."

TJ, having abandoned the burgers, wedged himself between us and got nose to nose with the Lieutenant. "What you're suggesting is that Dr. Matthews created those letters himself, for whatever reason? Is that what you're saying?" Cigar debris crumbled to the floor as he clenched his fists. Frisk flinched and took a step back.

"No, Sir," Frisk answered, straightening up, "but it is mighty suspicious. I'm just here to give Dr. Matthews this information." He paused and took a deep breath. "Listen. If I thought you were up to something, we'd be having this discussion in my office, not your home. I'm not making any accusations, but you have to admit that it looks suspicious. Either you or someone with access to your computer printed the letters. Who or how that happened I don't know. Maybe your prints are from handling the ream in your desk. My job is to figure this out." He looked at me with a mixture of resignation and determination. "I'm trying to be on your side, so help me out here." He paused. "You told me that you got a phone call from this person. Tell me more about that."

I took a deep breath and forced myself to calm down. No sense pissing the guy off. I needed his help, not his interference. "My son answered the call, and when I picked it up, there was a dial tone. Benjamin said it was from 'an old friend', the same way the letters are signed."

"Is your son here? Can I talk to him?"

"I sent both my children off island. This asshole is threatening them, and I made sure they were safe. So, no, you can't talk to him. Besides, why would Benjamin tell me 'an old friend' was calling if he didn't hear that?" Despite my efforts to remain objective, I was getting pissed off with his attitude that I had done something wrong. I took another breath and shook it off. "He's only eight years old, so I don't know what he could tell you."

"Anyone else 'talk' to this 'friend'?" Frisk used finger quotes to emphasize his question.

Wiggle those quote signs at me again, buster, and a proctologist will need to be involved with their removal.

"The line was dead when Benjamin handed it to me," I said, exasperated. "So nobody else actually talked to this creep."

"Lieutenant," TJ interrupted, still only a cigar distance from his face, "I can verify the line was dead. And I know without a doubt that call came from Dr. Matthew's office— while he was here." TJ poked him in the chest. "And before you ask how I know that, you'll need to speak with your commanding officer. That information is classified and," he poked him again, "you don't have the clearance or need to know. Clear about that?" He calmly unwrapped a fresh cigar, stuck it in his mouth, flipped the stale one across the room into the trashcan, and glared.

"Yes, Sir. As I've said, I'm not here to make accusations, only to try to sort this out."

I said, "Yeah well, fuck you. You walk into my house and accuse me of writing threatening letters to myself. I'm going to . . ." TJ turned around and stopped me with a look that said stand down.

Frisk held up his palms in surrender. "Obviously the phone call is concerning, but I need to understand how two letters and this phone call *all* came from your locked office." He looked at me with an apology. "I've checked your movements over the last week."

"You what?" I stepped forward and only TJ's bulk prevented me from punching him.

"And the timing doesn't work," he continued. "My tech people checked your printer log against where you were at those times, and it doesn't look like you could have written those letters. So, who else had access to your office and would be threatening you?"

"If you already knew I wasn't in my office to write those letters, why did you ask?"

"I wouldn't be doing my job if I didn't at least ask. So who else would do this?"

I realized that maybe he was trying to be helpful, and I calmed down. "I keep my office locked, but there are any number of others who can get access. I have no idea who this is or why he's writing these letters." Deep in the recesses, I was asking that same question; the caution flag was fluttering. I had a good idea who wrote the letters, but that was impossible.

"Well." He turned to the door. "Thank you for your time and information. I'll get back to you if we learn anything else." He shook my hand, nodded to TJ, and opened the door. He turned at the last minute to face me, "And we've sent DNA from whoever licked the envelope to the FBI lab." He turned and left.

"Burgers are burning." TJ returned to the porch and his grill. He flipped the meat and turned to look at me.

"What?" I tried my innocent look of surprise on him. It failed.

"You and I both know who's writing these letters. It sure sounds like that scumbag during your last year of residency has returned." TJ and I swapped war stories and skeletons when we bunked together on the aircraft carrier. He knew.

"But how could he be involved?" I asked, "and why is he coming after me here and now?" I sat down in resignation, then jumped up, got a bottle of water, and sat again. History repeats itself. My history had come back to haunt me.

Perfect Medicine

I had known Erin since medical school. Hers was the first baby I helped into the world when I was a lowly medical student. That baby spent months in an incubator fighting for life with the crack addiction he received as a birthday gift. The State took that one and Erin's next two infants, placing them with non-addicted families. Three babies in three years and I had delivered all three of them. The fourth was a stillborn home delivery with no one in attendance.

TJ finished decorating our burgers with catsup, mayo, mustard, onions, pickles, and boonie sauce. The potato chips were limp with humidity. The house reeked of wet, sweat, and pet.

"Remind me," he said. "She was a drug addict who died of an overdose near the end of your residency? Then her boyfriend tried to kill you?"

I took a bite of my burger, squeezing grease, goop, and sauce onto my lap. Tripod circled my legs to help clean up.

"Not quite. She arrived on the doorstep of the ER that night, in labor and overdosed on crank, crack, or some other noseshit. Her boyfriend was some gangbanger who was too busy to be bothered with her. I was sure she was going to die on my watch."

My chest tightened as the suppressed memories gripped me; this time in daylight. I relived the fatigue of that night again, just as I did during my recurrent night terrors.

Pregnancy number five ended with Erin on the steps of the ER in the middle of the night—in labor. I'd seen her twice that pregnancy; both times blitzed on booze, on crack, or on crank; I didn't care. This baby was lost. She was lost, and I was tired of trying to find her. I was tired of being 48 hours on call, responsible for everything, and forced to practice defensive medicine. I was tired of an insurance dweeb with a three ring binder telling me what I could or couldn't do for my patients. I was tired of my taxes taking care of Erin's lifestyle mistakes. I was just plain tired.

I jerked back to the here and now as Tripod stole the remains of my burger from my hand. TJ sat unmoving; watching me; giving me the opportunity to unload on a friend.

"I hated her, TJ. I honestly did. I hated me for hating her. I hated medicine. Years of sleep deprivation, and being the butt of the Socratic Method—keep asking me a question until I don't have an answer, then piling on the ridicule . . ." I paused, not wanting to go there. I could feel a shaky pressure in my chest that would explode into a scream of frustration or tears.

"That sucks." With those two words, TJ expressed understanding of what medical practice was like, empathized, and gave me permission to let go.

"Her blood pressure was 220 over 130. She looked like a bloated whale grounded on a gurney; dying from her drug of choice that week. So was her baby. Neither could survive the hours ahead. I was just three weeks from completing my chief residency and escaping the insanity. I just wanted to survive, and she threatened that survival. She was the enemy. Learning medicine had gone from altruism to combat." Pain from all the unfulfilled promises and dreams, buried for years, surfaced, and I knew I could finally let go.

I remembered looking at her face, a deep purple bruise surrounding one eye.

"Doctor, I'm so sorry. I don't know what happened." I tuned out her whimpering. "The baby is not due yet, and I was supposed to see you in the clinic tomorrow. But . . ."

I couldn't dredge up any sympathy, then or now. "Damn it Erin—you're pre-eclamptic, your blood pressure is so high you're about to have a stroke, and you're probably overdosed on crystal or some other shit you shove up your nose. So don't give me that I'm sorry crap. Your baby's gonna die if I don't deliver it right now. And you'll die too." I remembered thinking that would be no significant loss to society. I remembered this was where I lost my humanity.

"Will I get to keep this one?" Her look pleaded with me.

"Not up to me to decide," I said. "Right now I'm more concerned that you and the baby remain alive." I wanted to

213

tell her that I was more concerned that if she didn't, I'd somehow be blamed.

"That's right," said TJ, pushing Tripod away from his burger. "The baby died from the drugs she took; she lived. I remember now. And you got blamed for it."

Before I could deliver her baby, Erin had a massive eclamptic seizure. She survived; the baby didn't. I handed a limp newborn from the surgical incision to waiting neonatal specialists. An hour later, after heroic efforts, the baby died. An autopsy documented lethal levels of methamphetamine.

I nodded. "It was horrible. Dead baby; mother overdosed on meth. The DA tried to charge her, but I fucked up because there was no written permission before the surgery to test her for drugs. So she walked." The anger at this woman and the legal system that allowed her to murder a baby swelled in my gut and threatened to unleash the single bite of burger in my stomach.

"But I thought you told me she died? So she can't be involved with writing the letters." TJ took a bite of his meal, not a single dollop falling onto his immaculate uniform.

"A couple weeks after she left the hospital, she returned DOA. Meth overdose mixed with heroin." I didn't feel happy about that; maybe I could have prevented it? I didn't hate her anymore. I was just sad.

"She sued you for malpractice before she died, didn't she? She and the scumbag boyfriend?"

I just nodded. Apparently, I was somehow responsible for her overdose and the death of her baby. Within a week, my malpractice insurance carrier bought her off for less than the cost of defending me. The hospital needed a scapegoat and threw me under a bus full of lawyers.

Two days after receiving an obscene amount of cash to settle the case out of court, Erin died of an overdose. The boyfriend disappeared but was arrested a month later and jailed for 'unrelated' drug charges. He should still be there.

TJ continued to stare at me. "So, do you think these letters have anything to do with that guy? The second letter said something about the daughter you killed. Do you think he's out of prison and coming after you now?"

"Someone is sure trying to make me believe that, but think about it. That guy, if he even survived prison, doesn't have it together to come here and write threatening letters, on my computer, in my locked office. Doesn't fit."

I mentally reviewed the letters. "These were written by someone pretending to be un-educated. Typos and misspellings filled the last one. However, whoever wrote it could spell cautious. Erin's boyfriend had the IQ of a turnip—he couldn't write a letter like that, and he's probably dead by now. Someone wants me to think these letters are about the past, but I don't believe that."

"Who else would have access to this information to be able to threaten you?" TJ looked at me carefully. Tripod eyed him, waiting for a scrap to fall off his plate.

"Well, the lawsuit was a matter of public record, and the deaths were investigated. The records show I was not at fault. Peer review confidentiality is supposed to protect that information from the public, but my service records would contain summaries in it. I would guess that anyone who could get to my file would have the information. Still, something's not right." I considered my options. "Maybe I should call Lieutenant Frisk and let him know?"

"He knows."

"Who, Frisk? Knows what?"

"No, the letter writer knows about Blue Death. He said he wants something from you. What else could that mean? He thinks it's here on Guam and wants it. You're right; the scumbag didn't show up and write threatening letters. Whoever is writing this wants you to believe that."

"And thinks I'm stupid enough to fall for it?" The insult burned me.

"Unless Frisk is right, and you wrote them." As soon as he said it, TJ looked stricken. "Oh shit, I didn't . . ."

"I know, I don't think it was you either, but if Frisk thinks I did, it's only a matter of time before the entire command starts looking at me funny."

TJ gave Tripod a soggy chip, which he promptly spit out. "No, the writer knows we'll figure this out. The typos and lousy grammar are just there to create confusion. He wants to scare you into getting your family off the island so he can get to you alone?"

"Shit. That would also explain why he wants to know where the kids are. If he has access to my records, he might already know. I have to call my folks and warn them."

"Before you panic, let me look into it," TJ said. "In the meantime, I know Charlie has Ramón and Angel keeping an eye on you, Emily, and Hanna, just in case."

The idea of Shotgun Sanchez running amok, protecting me, was not reassuring. There was nothing I could do until tomorrow. I'd call my folks and arrange protection for them.

"Go cook a couple more burgers," I said, "and I'll stick Charlie's DVD of our last dive in the player. I'm curious to see what he found and take another look at all those two-headed Auraka family members. Ralph is coming by later, and I want to let you both know what I discovered in the medical records today. There is a link to everything going on."

Discovery

There they were, hundreds of the little monsters. All exact miniatures of Auraka, all with two heads, all curious. I don't know the gestation period for an eel, or if they are live bearing or egg layers. I do know there were too many to be normal. Besides having two heads, that is.

We watched Charlie's video of our last dive on Kelly's Reef. Had it only been two days ago? The sheer abundance of marine life struck me. Kelly had always been exceptional in that regard—healthy plant, animal, and coral life. Many of the reefs surrounding Guam were dead from pollution and climate change. Kelly was the exception. The reef was growing and reproducing before our eyes at an impressive rate, and she wasn't even on the nautical charts. A vibrant, uncharted reef, this close to Guam made no sense, but I was beginning to understand why.

"What do you think?" I asked TJ. He wiped the sweat from his forehead with a napkin and took a bite of burger.

"Do you see this growth around the entrance to Auraka's cave?" He pointed at a patch of staghorn coral. "That wasn't there the last time I dove the reef, and that was just a week before the earthquake."

The earth and my house shook briefly at that moment; another aftershock. I still tensed every time it happened. TJ grabbed his glass of warm iced tea to prevent it from bouncing off the table. Tripod bugled once and hid behind my legs, quivering.

I know exactly how you feel, little buddy.

When things settled down, TJ took a swallow of tea and continued. "Staghorn coral grows about twenty to thirty centimeters a year. That much growth should take years, yet it appeared literally overnight. Doesn't make sense." He pointed again. "Look here—see the notching at the junctions of the coral arms? There are nine and eleven branches on many of them. Staghorn usually has three, sometimes five branches. That's not normal. Neither are all those tiny two-headed eels." On the video, Charlie swam the camera toward the spot where TJ had been prodding the coral. He hit the pause button.

"We need to get back down there to study this area some more," TJ said. "We've found something that affects growth and reproduction."

"It's more than that," I said. "The timing is just too weird. I mean, LaRouche arrives the same day to tell us about Blue Death. And then chases everybody away from the reef."

"So, you think those blue globes that you found in Djibouti are Blue Death? And now it's here; sixty eight hundred miles away, years later?"

I thought about the blue globes we found the night of the quake, and the blue globes packed into the camera case on LaRouche's ship. Charlie and Hanna were aware of my find during the quake. TJ wasn't.

"How do you know I found more globes?"

He looked startled at my question. "You told me, didn't you? Maybe it was Charlie. I don't know. I'm just assuming this Blue Death thing has arrived on the island."

I let it go. Maybe I did mention it, or maybe Charlie said something.

"Regardless," TJ said, changing the subject, "fat chance finding out if there is something going on at Kelly's Reef with the Coast Guard chasing everyone away."

"What do you suppose that's all about?" I asked. "And that fairy tale LaRouche is peddling about radioactivity and pollutants in the area? I think LaRouche is lying like a coonhound on an Alabama porch."

"Coonhound? Where do you get this stuff?" He shook his head. "But yeah, he's lying. Even Charlie knows more about this than he's saying. Remember he pushed LaRouche about info he wasn't telling us?"

"Not only that, but look at this." He reset the DVD to the scene where he was probing the coral with his dive knife. "There's something under the reef, and I want to find out what it is. Look."

"Is that what you were trying to show me when we were interrupted? What is it?"

"I don't know. That's why I want to get back there. Something is under the coral—right there." He poked his cigar at the TV screen. "A section of coral split off during the quake and uncovered a shiny black surface. There's nothing found in the ocean, under coral, that appears smooth and rust-free that looks like that. I was tapping it with the handle of my knife, and it sounded vaguely metallic, but felt more like plastic when I touched it. What actually interested me is that it felt warmer than the surrounding water." He paused and we both watched the last few moments of the film as Charlie aimed his camera toward the surface and the mighty *Chipmunk*, the wake of lieutenant Moran's yard boat approaching.

"Do you suppose it is some wreck or junk that the coral has used as a growth base? We have wrecks and debris from World War II scattered all around the area. Most of it's encrusted with coral."

"No, I doubt that's it. We've been diving on most of the local wrecks, and you can usually tell they are manmade— they're rusted and flaking but aren't entirely overgrown. This is too shiny and new for me to believe it's an old wreck."

The DVD ended, and I turned it off.

"What do you think is going on?" I asked.

"Beats me, but I think there is something under Kelly's Reef that is causing sea life to multiply at an abnormal rate, and reproduce weirdly. Think about it. First there's an earthquake, Kelly's Reef goes nuts, and then LaRouche shows up?"

"So you didn't believe his cockamamie story either?" I asked.

"I checked today and what he said about Vignalli, Dweck, Sultani, and the courier all being missing or dead is true. I'm not worried about the threat of some mysterious bogeyman coming after us because of whatever went down in Djibouti," he looked directly at me, "because officially we were never there and only a few people even knew about the mission."

"Except that Petty Officer Vignalli is dead, and that's not a coincidence. Somebody had to know. I did my own checking this morning. I called and spoke with his fiancée to offer my condolences. She confirmed that he was murdered, and the police think robbery was the motive. Seems one of his fingers was cut off, and his class ring was missing. LaRouche told us the courier had his fingers cut off. That's no coincidence. I convinced that LaRouche is looking for Blue Death, and we may very well be in danger. And I'm just not sure whose side LaRouche is on or where the threat is coming from."

"You're right," said TJ.

"About?"

"LaRouche or someone connected to Djibouti thinks there is something here and that you know about it. They want what you found."

"But all we found was Auraka and an unusual reef. And nobody else even knows about that, do they?" I glanced toward the blue globes that were hidden on the bottom of my aquarium.

"You're a pretty good poker player, Bones." His unexpected change of topic caught me off guard. "Stay with me now. Do you know what your poker tell is?" He brought his thumb up under his chin. "Whenever you bluff, you rest your chin on your thumb and look down and left. What do I do?"

219

"You roll that dog turd in your mouth to the other side." He looked surprised that I had figured that one out.

"What about LaRouche?" TJ asked. "We played poker with him on the *Swordfish* en route to Djibouti. Did you pick up his tell?"

"No, and I lost a hundred bucks to him that night."

"He scratches his right thumb with his right index finger when he's lying. Dead giveaway." He let that sink in. "He was doing that the whole time he was spinning the yarn about Cozumel and finding something in the water similar to what he found in Somalia. He was lying to us."

Cozumel? The kids are in Cozumel with my parents. Wait a minute; I thought LaRouche said he was going to Wollei. TJ must have been thinking about where we sent the kids. Still, the closely clipped hairs on my neck stood at attention.

"Where do you think Charlie is? Taking off before Hanna was out of surgery was unusual, even for Charlie. And he warned me not to trust LaRouche just before he left."

"He knows something about this that he's not saying . . . or can't say," TJ said.

I thought about that. At lunch on the *Swordfish*, Charlie and LaRouche seemed to be hiding something about the origin of Blue Death. Charlie had been there when LaRouche made the original discovery; he knew the real Kelly, and he had been actively involved with getting whatever Blue Death was to the courier. Now Charlie was missing, too. Would he be the next body?

I continued, "I know that Charlie does something for the government. He's gone on missions for weeks at times that he won't, or can't, talk about when he returns. So I didn't think too much of him being ordered somewhere without notice yesterday. But, I found out that Hawknose sent him away so he couldn't testify in my defense at her kangaroo court."

"Hawknose had nothing to do with Charlie's disappearance. He received classified orders from D.C.—destination and duration unknown," said TJ. "I checked as soon as I discovered he was gone. Probably LaRouche's doing. LaRouche did say he might need his help."

"Then, it's even more troubling that he leaves now"

"I hope he gets back," TJ said. "Last time he was involved with LaRouche he got shot." He let that thought fester in my imagination.

Just then, Tripod announced Ralph's arrival and waited for his treat. Ralph always carries a dog biscuit for Tripod and chocolate for the kids whenever he visits. Tripod also took the opportunity to see if he could snatch my second burger while I answered the door. I heard TJ clear his throat and knew he gave him 'the look'. Tripod abandoned his idea of burger burglary.

The Wading Hippo Club

"No thanks, I've already had dinner," Ralph answered when I offered him a burger. "But ice water would be great."

"Hope you brought your own ice, 'cause we've been on intermittent generator power here ever since the quake." A rare lightning bolt exploded and unleashed a downpour. Palm fronds lashed wildly, cascading coconuts onto the roof as the evening winds blew through.

"No ice? Darn. Hawknose was demanding ice this afternoon. I was hoping I could send her up here for some."

"I've killed better men for less." I grinned at him.

"So how is our favorite Executive Officer doing this afternoon?" I asked, not caring at all about the answer.

Ralph said. "She was her usual intolerable self until she saw the 'Wanted by the Fashion Police' poster of her haircut in the doctor's lounge." TJ choked on his tea.

"But, on a more serious note, her scans were all clear and I can't find any evidence of a recurrence of her trophoblastic tumor. Lungs are clear, brain has no evidence of evil spirits, liver shows damage from a different kind of spirits, but otherwise nothing. I placed a call to the oncology department stateside for their advice. Maybe we can ship her off island for a long course of chemotherapy?"

"Oh be still my aching heart."

"So, what the hell is going on around here?" asked Ralph. "Before her surgery, Hanna was jabbering about too many pregnancies, and abortions, and two headed eels. I figured it was the pre-op meds talking, but then, this morning you were asking if I noticed anything unusual. What gives?"

I looked first at TJ then at Ralph. "Hanna told me the same thing. So this afternoon I searched our records and called our colleagues at Hilltop to confirm. Pregnancy rates are up 1000 percent since the earthquake. And those are just the ones that have been reported."

"Yeah," said Ralph, "it's been busy in clinic lately. That fits."

"Not only that, but the number of early spontaneous abortions tripled."

I watch him stroke the bridge of his nose as this sank in.

"Have you had a term delivery recently?" he asked.

Ever since Isa showed up the night of the quake, I couldn't remember delivering a single infant near its due date. But, I had a more ominous statistic to confirm this finding.

"Every woman we've been following in the clinic that is beyond 28 weeks gestation has delivered since the quake. And every one of my mothers in the Wading Hippos Club has delivered."

"Wading hippos?" TJ interrupted.

"One of my pregnant patients once told me she felt like a hippopotamus and found relief wading in chest deep ocean water. The pressure three feet deep on their ankles is greater than at their waist. The result is that excess fluid is squeezed into the lymphatic canals. The kidneys then kick into action, eliminating it. The hippos reduce swelling, take the weight stress off their back and pelvis, and generally feel better after 20 to 30 minutes," I explained. "Hence, the Wading Hippos Club. They meet several times a week at Old Wives Beach to wallow in the lagoon near the parking lot."

"We've also seen an unusual number of multiple gestations lately if my sense is correct," Ralph said.

"You're right, almost two sets of twins a week. We only had four sets of twins all last year. We've seen one triplet, plus Hanna and her quadruplets. And all just since the earthquake."

"So, what do you think it is? And what do we need to do?" Ralph sounded alarmed.

"I don't know, but I sent a request to the National Institute of Health for advice. In the meantime, we need to have a department meeting and invite the Hilltop group to join us. We all need to be up to speed until we sort this out."

"I'll get on top of that right away." He placed his hand behind his ear. "Wait, I think I can hear the screech of a blood sucking raptor calling me." With that, Ralph departed, hopefully to transfer Hawknose to some unsuspecting fool stateside.

Tripod waited to see if he was going to get another treat before Ralph left. Failing that mission, he begrudgingly limped back inside and snatched the remains of my second burger. TJ looked at me with his brows arched in question.

"You were resting your chin on your thumb and looking down," was all he said.

"I think we're dealing with Blue Death. Until I know what's going on, I'm not going to create a panic."

Blue Globes

The evening downpour ended as dramatically as it started, the air crisp with the scent of plumaria blossoms. Light from the outdoor security system scattered through a cloud of flies. It was that magical moment when the world took a breath and sighed.

"What do you notice about the water?" I asked. TJ leaned forward and looked at the TV screen. I had restarted Charlie's DVD, and we were looking at the area around Auraka's cave. To my eye, the water still held the faint blue glow I'd seen the night of the quake. I pointed that out to TJ, but he wasn't impressed.

"I guess it's a little blue, but maybe that's just the video." He shrugged.

I thought back to the *Swordfish* and seeing blue globes. TJ hadn't seen them, so I told him about the lab on the *Swordfish* and my suspicions.

"So you think that what you saw in Djibouti and the globes are causing the problems here? How did they get here?" He got up and walked out the back door to the patio. I followed him, disrupting a cloud of flies.

The sky had cleared and stars coated the sky like glitter. The moon was approaching full again and illuminating a wild boar that grunted from the edge of the jungle.

"How did it get here?" I repeated. "I have no friggin' idea. I just know something's wrong and I'm worried."

"What do you think this means?"

"What do I think? I think there was something that was released during the earthquake; something that creates havoc with reproduction—maybe some type of pollutant, or who knows what. LaRouche told us about Blue Death—all those rumors about pregnancy and old men becoming virile again. Maybe we have what Alzera found. Maybe that something is responsible for what's been going on since the quake. I do think we're dealing with Blue Death, whatever that means."

"The Wading Hippos." The light bulb went on over TJ. "They all wallow within sight of Kelly's Reef, and you think they were all exposed? And all delivered early because of that?"

"That's *exactly* what I think. I also think that Hanna received a massive dose of Blue Death while diving during the quake. We discovered some globes similar to those we saw in Djibouti that were uncovered. The water had a deeper blue tint than you see in the film. Hanna swam in whatever that was. I believe her when she tells me that night was her only opportunity to get pregnant. She and Charlie used double protection. She was exposed, she impregnated despite protection, and she had multiple abnormal embryos. It fits, and I don't like what I'm seeing."

Somehow, sensing I needed a distraction before my thoughts spiraled away, Tripod sidled up to give me the 'beagle-dying-of-hunger' look while holding the remains of my stolen burger in his jaw. I gave in and removed the pickle for him.

"So, if we're dealing with what Alzera called Blue Death," TJ said, "let me have the globes, and I'll get them analyzed." TJ shifted the cigar to the side of his mouth and back.

"Too late, I already did that. Packed and sent them this morning to a friend who runs a research lab at U.C. Berkeley. I should hear back in a few days."

"Maybe I should put the others in a safe place? If someone is after them and willing to kill for them, you need to be careful."

"There are no others. I sent all of them to the lab." I resisted resting my chin on my thumb and made sure I was looking directly at him. I stole a glance at Leo, a large lionfish in my aquarium. He was faithfully guarding the remaining three globes hidden among the coral on the bottom.

I don't want you or anyone else to know about them. If you don't know, you can't tell. Look what happened to Vignalli and the courier. They knew, and someone cut off their fingers.

I don't know why I didn't tell TJ. He was a shipmate and trusted friend, but the prickly feeling remained. How did he know about finding the globes? Why did he think LaRouche was in Cozumel where I'd sent the kids? Wollei was LaRouche's supposed destination.

"Which lab did you use? I can contact them and help with the analysis," he said.

"I don't know specifically what lab is involved. I sent them to a friend from medical school who teaches pathology, so he'll know what to do with them."

TJ looked disappointed but gave an accepting shrug. "Do you think we should contact LaRouche about this?" I could tell from his manner that his suggestion was just that—he didn't want anyone else to know either.

"Nah, let's wait to see what Charlie has to say when he gets back. He may be with LaRouche, whom I don't trust. They have secrets. In the meantime, we need to be cautious. If what I suspect is correct, this thing has potential that we don't understand. I'm worried this stuff is affecting our patients, and I can't tell if the problem is escalating or not. What if this is just the beginning?"

"What do you mean?" asked TJ.

"What if a woman gets pregnant just by exposure? What if that pregnancy aborts? Or worse, grows into something?" I let that linger. "And what if she dies? What if it affects all mammals? LaRouche told us that Alzera's Blue Death affected more than just humans? What if . . .?"

The front door opened. Tripod gave an enthusiastic woof to Emily as she entered, then hobbled over to her, his wagging tail offsetting his gait. She had been at the hospital all day with Hanna. Her eyes were bloodshot and her face was bloated from crying. She set down her packages and rushed to have me hold her. She was quivering. I caught the lingering antiseptic smell of the hospital on her clothing.

TJ discretely departed. "I'll catch you in the morning."

"What's wrong?" I asked, holding her away from me so I could see her eyes. "Did something happen to Hanna?" She shook her head and buried it in my chest, then began to cry again.

"I'm pregnant," she sobbed.

More Joyous News

In a microsecond, I went through all stages of death—shock, denial, bartering, anger, and acceptance. I settled on abject fear. When Emily announced both her previous pregnancies, I was overjoyed. Two amazing children kept that joy alive. This announcement left me with a sense of dread.

I had a vasectomy after the birth of our son, so there was no need for birth control. My growing awareness of Blue Death ratcheted the fear. Emily was the water aerobics instructor for the Wading Hippos. Ralph had suggested that Hawknose had become pregnant by parthenogenesis. We both came to that conclusion as an insult to her. *After all, who in their right mind would have sex with that shrew?* Now that joke became a terrifying reality—pregnancy without egg and sperm.

"It's going to be okay," was all I could manage.

"But I can't be pregnant. This has to be a mistake. You know I'd never . . ." and she started crying again. I held her closer, hoping to absorb her anguish.

"Shhh. I know that. But you need to know what's been happening on Guam since the earthquake."

I fixed her a cup of tea and told her of my suspicious findings—the blue globes, the abnormal pregnancies, the miscarriages, Hawknose and her molar pregnancy, the Wading Hippos, and why I thought Hanna got a super dose of Blue Death. Her face moved through disbelief, comprehension, and finally to fear. She held my hand in a death grip.

"So? I'm not pregnant? I don't understand. You're saying there might be something in the water near Old Wives Beach that made me pregnant and also caused Hanna's problem?"

"I don't know if you are really pregnant. You either are, or you aren't—can't be just a little bit pregnant." That got a small smile out of her. "We'll find out, and I promise, I won't let anything in the world harm you. I'll have Ralph get some blood tests and an ultrasound in the morning. We'll start with that, then wait and see."

Do I keep you on Guam where I can protect you? Or get you stateside? Are you destined to lose this pregnancy? If it's a keeper, what do we do?

"I'm going to lose this baby, aren't I?" She was already identifying with whatever was happening as a baby.

"Let's figure out what's going on first, and then we'll cross that bridge when we get there." She stretched out on the couch, put her head in my lap, and closed her eyes. I gently brushed her golden hair. "Hang on, Sweetheart. We'll get through this together."

The Fourth Letter

I let Ralph believe I was the father of Emily's conception. I wasn't willing to share my fears with anyone else just yet. Emily understood and became my accomplice. I knew I had to tell Hanna of my suspicions. If I didn't, Emily would, or their twin telepathy would kick in. Later that afternoon Ralph would discharge Hanna, and I planned to bring her to our home to finish her recovery. She'd be safe there with Charlie gone.

The blood tests confirmed Emily's pregnancy. The ultrasound didn't see anything, but it was too early to visualize a heartbeat. We had to wait. Emily, without room for debate, declared she was staying on Guam, period.

Emily went home to restock food and be sure Angel was still on guard duty. I went back to work. After my usual patient rounds, I checked out and spent the rest of the day at Hilltop Hospital reviewing medical records and confirming my suspicions.

When I returned from medical records at Hilltop after lunch, I checked my mail. Then, I called Lieutenant Frisk to report the letter awaiting me.

Just wanted to let you know that I got your problem solved. She not going to bothr you anymore. I've make sure of that. And where did your kids go? Are you trying to secrete them. it won't work.

Not you freind

Frisk

"So, this was in your box this morning?" asked Frisk after he carefully opened it and put it in an evidence bag. It was a statement, not a question. He was sitting in my patient chair, rubbing facial stubble. He looked up at me, concerned.

"You know what I need to ask, don't you?" he continued.

"Of course. I'm not stupid, nor blind. That letter has the same smudge and crease as the others. It likely came from my computer in my office. And you'll probably find my fingerprints on the paper because it came from the ream I'm using." He nodded, acknowledging me.

I continued. "And you were in my office the day before yesterday when we found the last one. Therefore, the writer produced this since then. And I've been in here since then, so I have no alibi." He nodded again. I waited him out.

"So what I don't understand is why you would write letters like this to yourself?"

The good ol' boy façade was gone. He stood up, straightened his uniform, and leaned over the desk.

"Think about that, Sir. I don't know what's going on, but I don't see any other explanation for this." He waved the letter at me and then put it in his brief case. "So, Doctor, I need to ask you to—"

"Give you a DNA sample to see if I sealed the envelopes," I finished. "No problem, let's go down to the lab right now and take care of that." *There is no way my saliva was on those envelopes.*

"Thank you, Sir. I know this is difficult, and I just want to say . . ." He paused looking for words. I could tell he had mixed feelings.

"Look, Lieutenant. I could say that you're just doing your job or some other happy horseshit to make you feel better, but the fact is . . . you're seriously pissing me off. I don't appreciate what you're implying, at all. But. . ."

He cut me off. "Sir, I mean no disrespect, and I honestly am just doing my job. I know that sounds phony, but—" He stopped and looked quizzically at me. "You really don't remember who I am, do you?"

You got me there, bucky. You're just some minor flunky who is pissing me off. He must have read that in my face.

He cocked his head and said, "Last year you took care of my wife. She went into labor two months before my son was due. You figured out what was happening and kept her from delivering. You also flew with her to Okinawa where they have the specialists to take care of the baby. Remember?"

The whole incident flooded back to me. The premature labor, the work to prevent it, the emergency flight to Okinawa—it all came back. She held off another month before finally delivering a healthy near-term baby boy. A good outcome.

"Of course. Now I remember." I smiled. "How's your son doing?"

"He's great. We are grateful to you for that, so believe me when I tell you that having to investigate this is extremely difficult for me. I know you're too smart to do something this dumb. I can't believe you would write those letters on your own computer and leave your fingerprints all over the paper.

There is no reason. Whoever is doing this is trying to act dumb and puts in typos, but uses a word like 'secretes'. He's trying to frame you for something. I can't figure it out, so I need your help." He held up his hand in surrender and then held it out to me. "Please?"

I relented. He was trying to do his job and using the good cop, bad cop routine single-handedly without success. "Okay, I understand." I took his hand and that simple gesture cemented a bond between us. "Frankly, I need your help too. I know I had nothing to do with this and I hope you believe that." Then I lied to him. "I don't even know why someone is writing them or what they mean."

"Yeah, I wondered about that too. Kind of a weird threat."

"So, if you need information, just ask, and I'll do whatever is necessary to help you, but you have to keep me up to speed too. Okay? No games, no innuendo, no bad cop, good cop shit. Deal?"

"Deal, but I still need your DNA." He pulled a swab from his pocket and took his sample. Then he shook my hand again and departed.

Before the door could close, Ralph walked in. He watched the lieutenant walk down the hall and turned back to me. "That the guy investigating those letters?"

How did you know about the letters? I didn't tell you. So, I asked him how he knew.

"Oh, grapevine rumor is that there's some crackpot sending you threats. We're all wondering what's going on." He waited, hoping I'd give him a firsthand report for the gossip mill. I out-waited him.

"So, what's up?" I asked. My office was an oven, so I opened the window to receive a blast from the outdoor furnace. I had commandeered a small fan, but it only pushed hot air around. The emergency generator coughed and sputtered in the background.

"Hawknose is missing in action. She checked herself out this morning and disappeared." He was smiling, and despite the heat, his uniform was dry, unstained, and hung perfectly on his lank frame. I was wearing sweat soaked surgical scrubs and couldn't imagine a t-shirt and rayon blouse in this heat. Ralph was always cool—in dress, manner, and actions.

"I'd check the Hideaway Bar first, then behind the Booze-R-Us store. Maybe look in the dumpsters by the officers club. I don't know anyone who likes her well enough to keep her as a house guest, so . . ."

"I've notified security to keep an eye out for her. Eventually, she'll show up." Unfortunately she did.

Missing, Presumed Dead

The following week we diagnosed and lost more pregnancies; two more sets of twins failed to survive; even the brown snake population seemed to decline. Hawknose remained missing; Charlie remained unavailable; Emily remained pregnant. The NIH said they would look into 'the issue'. The Skipper's chair finally collapsed, but nobody was there to see it. A letter arrived from Cassidy, my friend and colleague at U.C. Berkeley.

```
Jake-
Good to hear from you after all these
years. Hope all is well with your family. I
received the samples you sent. Attached is
my preliminary report. I am running all the
tests again because they make no sense.
What are these things and where in the
world did you get them? I've never seen
anything like them.
    You are dealing with a virus encased in
a semi-impermeable shell. Your blue globe
has a virus with DNA necessary for protein
production. They are highly contagious.
    I infected E. coli and they immediately
began producing human-like reproductive
hormones. Same thing with mouse stem cells.
This virus uses cells to produce these
```

hormones, and that's all it does. It doesn't kill the host cell.

I exposed mice to the virus and had a tripling of fecundity, but they all aborted or died. We even had female mice become pregnant without male involvement. Males were entirely unaffected except for a few that showed slight feminization. What concerns me—and the reason I am running the entire series a second time—is that the DNA translates errors into the proteins they code. I've identified six separate codons that consistently translate <u>for the wrong amino acid</u> in the sequence. That can't be.

If what I suspect is true, we're dealing with an evolutionary event that didn't happen; at least, not on this planet.

I know you asked me to keep this secret. I will. As promised, I ran the tests myself.

Two days ago, I received an unexpected phone call. Someone who said they were from your hospital called to see if we received a package you shipped. I happened to be available to answer the phone. The person insisted that chemical samples sent for analysis were an error, and they needed to get them back immediately. The caller sounded desperate. When I asked who was calling, the line went dead.

What is going on? I've got some vacation time saved up and want to suck compressed air underwater. I'd like to fly out and discuss this with you. Call me.

Cassidy

I set the letter down on the dining room table and stared out the window. My watch said 0700, the middle of the night in California. I'd wait to call. A knot of fear tightened in my gut. I hoped he was wrong.

Translation

Emily had brought Hanna home from the hospital to recover from her surgery. I insisted she stay with us until Charlie returned. The three of us were having dinner discussing Cassidy's letter. I washed down a bite of salad while Tripod stationed himself under the table.

"You know what this letter means don't you?" I asked them. They both shook their beautiful heads in perfect synchrony.

"It means we have found the answer to Blue Death and what the hell is going on around here," I answered.

If Cassidy is correct, this means—Lima Golf Mike—little green men.

Tripod crawled from person to person, rolled over and drooled, expecting a food treat. He got his reward.

"You also know that this must not leave this room under any circumstances," I said to the girls.

Hanna rewarded Tripod with a pat. He snorted and moved on to Emily, who said, "I don't understand what it means. It's a virus and causes pregnancy?"

I wonder if TJ should be here for this? After all, he has the advanced degree in this stuff. I haven't made him aware of Cassidy's letter yet—he isn't answering his pager.

"Bad Ju-Ju, boss lady," I said. "We're dealing with something mankind has never seen. Something deadly."

Emily shook her head, her blonde hair seeming to float on an invisible current. "English, please. My Swahili is a little rusty."

"Okay, Evolution 101. We know that 3.5 billion years ago the first cell appeared. We also know that every cell, bacteria, plant, and animal on this planet evolved from that first cell. God—if you choose to believe in an anthropomorphic creator or intelligent designer—didn't create man. It created a bacterium."

Hanna has a few hot topic buttons, and I had just pressed hers. "That's not what the wackos from the Non-Intelligent Church of Design think."

Before she could get a full head of steam about creationists, Emily stopped her. "There ain't no atheists in this foxhole, Sister. So, can it. Go on."

"The reason we know there was only one original cell that evolved into all life forms on this planet is in the way DNA codes for amino acids. DNA is that double helix that we think carries a code for all proteins. You know—that A-G, C-T base pairing stuff you heard about in school?" I waited for them to nod. "When the helix unwinds it's like reading a program on a computer." I was using hand gestures to help the explanation, wishing I had a chalkboard.

Hanna, always the nurse, said, "And those amino acids get linked together into proteins. And proteins are what life is all about."

"Right. DNA carries the code to produce chains of amino acids that become proteins. Every set of three base pairs, called a codon, translates into a single amino acid. The reproductive mechanism within all cells uses the same translation table," I said. "That means that three DNA pairs in a bacterium and the same three pairs in a human will stick the same amino acid into a protein chain. As an example, GGT translates to the amino acid Glycine in all species on this planet, whether it's a bacteria or a human. All life uses the same translation table to decode DNA into the same protein." I got up to allow Tripod out to scout the area while this sank in.

"So this virus is using a different translation table and creating abnormal proteins?" she asked. I saw dawning comprehension in her eyes.

"*Bingo*, you've got it. This virus translates the code differently. It's programming proteins that are almost, but not quite human. In this case, the proteins are human reproductive hormones with some translation errors."

Hanna leaned forward and finished the thought. "And those funky hormones are causing all the abnormal pregnancies?" She looked at Emily and took her hand, the concern, and love unmistakable.

I nodded. "That's what I think." I waited a moment and continued. "Do you understand the significance of this virus using a different translation table?"

I knew what it meant, but did the Sisters? It only took a moment for the real implication to register with Emily. She blanched and looked stricken. Then she got up, walked into the bathroom, and closed the door. I heard her retching.

"Do you mean—" Hanna started to say, and then looked at the bathroom door.

"This virus didn't originate on this planet. There is no possible way it would have a different translation table if it originated here. There is no way to manufacture this in a laboratory. It's alien." I turned my palms up. "Bad Ju-Ju."

She nodded. "We, I mean you, I mean . . ." Hanna paused. "We just proved there is life outside this planet. Do you know what this means?"

"It means we can't say anything to anyone about this."

"This is the most historic moment in human history. If this proves true, we need to—"

"We need to keep our mouths shut and try to stay alive long enough to prove it," I said. "Three people have already been killed for this secret, and we might be next. Someone knows I sent the globes to Cassidy for testing. That same someone is trying to find them and is only one step behind me. This was part of a terrorist plot to destroy the US. The commercial potential is worth billions, and the weapons potential is unthinkable. This is the most dangerous find in history. Nobody can know about this."

"But . . ." she started to say.

"But nothing. Everyone who knows about this is dead. We're not joining that list."

Emily returned from the bathroom, looking pale; her face was wet and her hair was limp. Then she surprised me. She cursed; she never curses.

"I've got a goddamn alien in me—like in that Sigourney Weaver movie, and some asshole wants to kill or torture us because you found this shit? What the hell happened to living in paradise, practicing medicine, and raising our children in safety? This ends right now." She clenched her fists and sought something to pound them on. Then she dry-retched. I grabbed her in my arms, and she pounded her fear into my chest until the storm subsided. I knew this was serious—she never curses.

She looked up at me with dilated pupils. Tears escaped her control and crept down her cheek. I could feel her anguish.

"Tomorrow, Ralph is going to terminate this abomination. Then we get to the bottom of this . . . this . . ." she looked for a word, "mess." As soon as she made this decision, a storm of frustration and fear passed. In its wake remained determination. I wouldn't want to get in her way.

"What do you suggest we do now?" I asked. I knew what we needed to do, but she needed to feel some sense of control over this situation.

"As soon as possible, we get off this damn island and join the children. I don't feel safe here anymore. We need to get away from here, and then you need to go somewhere to get help. No more cloak and dagger stuff. We have friends who can help, and you're going to enlist them."

She sagged against me. "Where is Charlie when we need him?" she asked. Then she broke free and ran to the bedroom, slamming the door. Hanna followed her, leaving me to wonder about creation and evolution.

Cassidy Warned Off

"Cassidy, my friend. It's Jake." I had waited until 0200 to be sure I'd catch Cassidy at work. There is an 18-hour time difference to the West Coast. The house was silent except for the scrabble of Tripod's nails as he joined me in the kitchen. Even at this hour, it was 80 degrees and sticky.

Without opening pleasantries or small talk, he said, "What the hell are you up to out there? If this is some kind of a joke, I'm not laughing." I could feel his heat through the receiver.

"No joke. You know me well enough. Those samples are real, and I'm scared. That's why I called." I caught a movement in the front window out of the corner of my eye. My chest squeezed. "Hold on a minute—someone's outside." I set down the receiver, crossed the darkened room, and peered out the window. *Oh, shit. Angel?* I caught sight of him heading into the boonies. I picked the phone back up. "Sorry, a friend's out in the yard guarding us. It's the middle of the night here, and he just scared the hell out of me. So, did you get a chance to re-run the tests?"

I looked at Tripod and wondered why he hadn't bugled a warning about Angel.

"Yeah, I did, and I got the same results." I heard Cassidy shuffle papers.

I waited. "So? What do you think?"

"I think this is an incredibly elaborate hoax and I want to know how it was accomplished."

"Or?"

"You've found proof of an extra-terrestrial life-form."

"I don't know what the globes are or where they came from, but I found them buried in a decidedly unusual reef. Nobody planted them there, that's for sure. And I can't imagine how someone could create a phony virus with an altered translation table."

"Hold on." I opened the front door and looked out again. Angel was nowhere near. Tripod hobbled out and sniffed the air. He looked at me quizzically.

"Who's out there?" I asked him. He had recently developed a distinctive bugle for Angel, alerting me whenever he was around. This morning he just growled before coming back indoors. I shrugged. Tripod looked back at me, sniffed the air, and lay down by the door. He was uncomfortable. Both our hackles stood at attention, but I didn't see or hear anyone.

Angel must have spooked you too, huh?

I picked up the phone. "I'm back. Sorry, I'm a little jumpy with all that's going on here."

"What *is* going on out there?" he asked. "If this isn't a hoax, it's epic. Whatever else happens, I want to be included in the credits on the research papers." I could hear undertones of Nobel hopes in his voice.

"Absolutely. However, the reason I called is to make sure nobody learns about this until it's safe. I want for you to shut down everything, erase your data, and lock everything in a vault away from your lab."

"Whoa. Seriously? Why?"

I explained about the unexpected and abnormal pregnancies on Guam and about my suspicions that Blue Death was involved.

"Blue Death is what you're calling these globes?"

"Yeah, but listen," I said, "there are some things I can't tell you about yet, but you are in danger. People have disappeared and been killed over this. So, please be careful and destroy all evidence that you've been involved. Okay?"

The refrigerator came alive, and I heard the generator start in the back yard. I startled, and Tripod yelped.

"Of course, but how 'bout if I come out and help you?"

"No. Don't even consider that. Someone here knows these things exist and is killing to get them. Everyone near me is in danger. You already got a call from someone who somehow knows you're involved. I'm getting threatening letters and have already sent the kids away."

"Oh my God, are you serious?"

"Deadly. So what I need is for you to stay alive and dumb. I'm going to get my family off island as soon as possible. You need to get your family somewhere safe."

"You're scaring me here."

"Good, you need to be scared. And figure out a way to kill this stuff. If it gets into the water supply . . ."

"Okay. How do I contact you?"

"I'll contact you again when I can. In the meantime, stay low."

"Okay, but one more thing you need to know." At that moment, a huge aftershock hit, knocking several framed prints off the walls and the remaining glassware off the shelves. The phone went dead.

The Morning Of

The following morning arrived a soggy mess; humidity hung like a shroud over everything. The sun barely penetrated the haze. With an emergency generator shared by three neighbors, there was not enough power for continuous air conditioning. Mold and mildew were recapturing the concrete block walls. My mood matched the environment.

The lights blinked briefly, went out, and back on. A moment later, the air conditioner rumbled to life, and the refrigerator compressor began to hum.

Hanna awoke, shuffled into the kitchen, and plugged in the coffee pot. "I hope this lasts long enough to make a pot of coffee. I'm tired of driving to the hospital to drink caffeinated bilge water."

"Hot damn," I said. "We got power, we got light, and we have hope for a hot shower. Is that real coffee? Be still my un-caffeinated heart."

"Do you think they've been able get power to the water pumps yet?" She turned on the kitchen faucet. It sputtered and coughed to life, spewing rusty slime into the sink. Something dead in the pipe resurrected to haunt my sense of smell. Suddenly, the stink of mildew didn't seem so bad.

Emily joined us, looking brave-faced despite the physical weight of the humidity. The discovery that she and her sister became pregnant because of an alien virus was like a monster in the closet waiting to catch us if we opened that door. She received a long hug from Hanna. I wrapped her in my arms, rubbing my hand along her back, and then kissed her good morning.

Tripod bugled Angel's arrival at the same moment a loud banging assaulted the front door. As usual, he just walked in. "That real coffee I smell?"

"Touch my coffee and Tripod won't be the only male in this room missing something," Hanna warned, then gave him a peck on the cheek. The lights blinked out again, the air-conditioner quit, and the faucet puked a final wad of sludge.

"Shit," we said in four-part harmony.

I eyed the inch of ultra-test the percolator managed to produce before we lost power, then stepped onto the back porch, lit the Coleman stove and set water to boil. Breakfast would be instant coffee and something dehydrated—just add hot water and pretend.

"Angel," I asked him, "what were you doing sneaking around here last night? I might have shot you."

"Sorry, Doc, but I thought I saw someone trying to get in, and I was checkin' it out. It gets kinda boring on guard duty, and I thought I'd catch me a bad guy." His gold tooth emphasized his proud smile.

"You saw someone sneaking around?" My shiver was not entirely from the trickle of sweat that drizzled down my back.

"Yeah, a really big guy all dressed in black." He held a hand above his head. At a little over five foot, everybody seemed big to Angel. "He was looking in the kitchen window, and he tried the door handle on the porch. Then he saw me and took off into the boonies. Made more noise than a scared hog stomping through there. I followed him until he was down in the hollow, then he quit running and disappeared in the dark. Sorry."

"Oh yeah, he dropped this." He handed me a small white disposable penlight, identical to the ones used in every hospital and clinic worldwide.

"Did you see anything else? His face? Clothes?"

"Nah, he was just big, and everything was black."

"Well, thanks for trying. I appreciate your help. But you need to be careful yourself." I paused. "Would you be willing to talk to Lieutenant Frisk, the cop who is investigating this thing and tell him what you saw?"

"But I didn't see nothin' and don't want to talk to no cop." I could tell there was no use arguing the point and he was right—he had little evidence to provide. "I gotta go, Doc. Just wanted to let ya know my cousin Carlos will keep an eye on things tonight—so don't worry 'bout nothin'."

Half an hour later we were washing down that world famous culinary delight, reconstituted chipped beef on stale bread, with bitter pond scum that passed for instant coffee. Emily wasn't eating in anticipation of her surgery later in the morning. Hanna pushed the goop around her plate; her fork never reached her mouth. I created art deco with my gravy. Tripod whimpered until he received our uneaten plates.

"So are you going to tell us what went on last night, or do we continue to pretend everything's okay?" Emily asked me.

I related Cassidy's phone call. "So someone knows about the globes and is trying to find them. And, someone was sneaking around the house last night. I was going to notify base security this morning, but with Angel and his family guarding us, I feel safer than if security patrols the neighborhood. I'd hate to have a patrol officer shot by Ramón in a fit of protective zeal. I wish Charlie were here. Any word?"

Hanna shook her head. "You know how he can just disappear for days and weeks and then show up again. I checked with his command, but they can't give out any information. You know how that goes."

"Well, if you do hear from him . . . ," I stopped.

I don't know what we could tell him that would make a bit of difference. I just feel safer when he's around.

It was time to open that door and deal with the monster. I reached across the table and squeezed Emily's hand.

"You sure?" was all I needed to ask. She nodded.

Emily and Hanna, raised in a strong Catholic family, went to parochial schools and practiced their faith. The conflict about terminating a pregnancy was real. We'd had many discussions about it in the past. As part of my training, I learned to do terminations, but chose not to.

Emily was pregnant because of an alien virus invading her body. I considered this abomination as nothing more than a wart to remove. If ever there was justification, this was it, but I could see in the red rims of her eyes the stress and conflict this decision created. I hoped she didn't read the fear in my eyes. I wasn't afraid of the surgical risks. I feared the emotional healing to follow.

Ralph would list Emily's procedure as an endometrial biopsy and only the immediate staff involved would know what was actually happening.

Except for the writer of the letter that appeared on my desk later that morning.

You killed my baby, now you goin to kill yours two. Maybe I kill you.

Not you friend any more.

Called Away

Surgery went without a hitch and the 'biopsy' eliminated the alien invader. Dinner was tea, toast, and rice. If Emily had to eat it for her meal post-op, we all would.

"Get that stuff away from me. I want a McDonalds and fries, not that crud," she said.

"Now Sister, you know Mickey D's has been shut down ever since the earthquake." The mention of earthquake, of course caused a minor aftershock and yelp from Tripod.

"Fine, then barbeque me a slab of flesh from a four legged beast." We all looked at Tripod, who grinned and twitched his stump.

Hanna force fed another spoonful of broth into Emily and handed her a piece of toast. "Shut up and eat." End of discussion.

Clouds rolled in just before we settled down for bed. We hadn't talked about Emily's procedure. I knew she would talk through it when she was ready. Hanna had already crashed, and Emily was starting to breathe heavily when the phone rang.

Good. That's working again. Maybe we'll get the lights soon.

TJ's gravelly voice was unmistakable. "Bones, they need you in OB," was all he said.

"What's up?"

"Not sure. I'm at the warehouse at the far end of the island swapping supplies and received a call from the hospital front desk that OB is swamped, and you're needed right away."

"Why didn't they call me directly?"

"No idea. They disconnected before I could get more info."

"Okay, I'm on my way." In all that had happened in the last 24 hours, I'd forgotten that I was the on-call OB physician for the evening.

But, if the phones are working, my pager should be working, so why am I getting this call from TJ?

TJ said, "I'll be back in a couple hours, then we need to catch up. I heard about the prowler last night. Everything okay?"

"Yeah. Angel scared him off, but you're right—we need to talk."

I opened the door to our bedroom. "Hey, sorry," I whispered. Emily groaned and pulled the sheet over her head. "I just got called back to work; should be home in a couple hours. You two will be okay 'til I get back. Carlos is guarding the place."

Just then, Hanna staggered past me. "We'll be fine. I'm going to sleep in here with Sister. You use the couch when you get home." They had shared a bed growing up. It continued to be safe and comforting for them.

The clouds emptied a late evening shower as I drove down the hill to the hospital. The typical island background noises were missing. No crickets, birds, or traffic sounds, only the heavy splatter of rain on the roof of my truck. The roadway was dark, as were the houses I passed.

The sergeant at the gate passed me through with a crisp salute. A gas lantern lit his post with a jaundiced glow. In the distance, I could see the hospital lit at half capacity. Emergency generators were supplying power to the main buildings. Several outbuildings were dark, including Hawknose's quarters. Security had searched her usual haunts, but still hadn't turned up anything. She was MIA, and I hoped she would remain so.

I parked, entered through the loading dock, and climbed the stairs to the OB ward. As I passed my office, I checked the lock on the door—secured. Whoever wrote the letters had a key—a large list of suspects at this command.

I took a deep breath as I entered the ward. I expected pandemonium, or at least chaos, a few laboring women, or some action. A nurse sat behind the counter with her feet propped up, snoring. The lights in all but one area were off. The delivery suite was empty.

"Oh, good evening, Dr. Matthews," the nurse startled awake and lowered her feet to the floor. She looked sheepish at being caught napping. "Is there something I can do for you?"

"I got called in to help. What's going on?" I must have looked as confused as I sounded. My subconscious waved a red flag.

"Well, Dr. Zebo has a patient in early labor, but other than that nothing. Who called you?"

"Lieutenant Commander Justis got a call that I was needed and passed it on to me. I don't understand. Did anyone here call for me?"

"No, Sir. I've been the only one here for the last three hours." She notched her eyebrows into a V. "Is everything okay?"

"I don't know. Maybe it was a mistake," I said. "If Dr. Zebo needs me I'll be at home."

"Thank you, Sir." She sat back down and propped her feet back on the desk. The hair on my back was standing at full attention.

"Did TJ call in?"

"Who?"

"Sorry, did Lieutenant Commander Justis call in?"

She shook her head. "No, Sir. Not that I'm aware of."

"I need to use the phone," I said and reached over the counter for the receiver. I dialed the ER. "This is Dr. Mathews. Has anyone been looking for me in the last 30 minutes?" The corpsman at the other end checked and said no. I dialed home. The line was dead. My finger had trouble finding the buttons to dial base security.

"This is Dr. Matthews. I need a security team to check out my house immediately." I tried to keep my voice calm.

"Yes, Sir. What seems to be the problem?" the petty officer taking the call asked.

"I'm not sure, but I was called to the hospital on an emergency that doesn't exist and my wife and Lieutenant Sanders are at my home alone. We had a prowler last night, and I'm concerned for their safety."

"Yes, Sir. I'll get someone there as soon as possible. Be about an hour before we have a unit free though." He waited.

"That's no good—they could be in danger right now, not an hour from now. Why the delay?" Panic reverberated from my vocal cords into his ears.

"Sorry, Sir. We've had four calls in the last ten minutes for fights, domestic violence, a car wreck at the pier, and a body that washed ashore. Every unit we have is out, but hang on." The phone line went silent. The nurse walked from behind the counter and asked if everything was okay. I couldn't answer her. The phone line clicked, and the petty officer was back.

"Sir, I have a unit responding code three from the Air Force base. They will be there in about 20 minutes. Best I can do at the moment, Sir. Sorry."

"Well, thanks for that at least. Let them know I'm headed home and will meet them. Also, tell them to proceed with caution—there is an armed civilian guarding the house. I don't want anyone hurt." I put down the receiver and had another thought. I dialed the front desk. "Please see if you can find Lieutenant Commander Justis and inform him that I need his help as soon as possible. Thanks." I hung up, and before the nurse could ask, I was gone.

I ran down the stairs, through the ER, to my truck, and roared toward home. I almost took out the guard at the gate. He waved for me to slow down, and managed to jump out of the way just in time. A few minutes later, near the top of the hill, I skidded on the rain slickened road, missed a turn, and hit a palm tree. Toyota built my rust bucket before airbags, so my face connected directly with the steering wheel. As I climbed out of the wreck, my tongue found a missing tooth and a split lip. I spit into the dirt as blood ran down my chin. That was the least of my concerns. I ran the last mile through the rain to my house, arriving winded, and soaking wet. The rainsquall had turned into a downpour. Wind whipped the palm trees. No moonlight made it through the clouds.

The concrete blocks I call home sat squat, ugly, and dark. The front door was open. I couldn't catch my breath and felt a squeezing pain in my left shoulder. My legs gave out and I dropped to one knee, gasping in the front yard. I began to see floaters flash across my vision.

The ringing in my ears drowned the scream of a distant siren. I tried to focus, leaning forward on my palms as I sucked in air. As my vision cleared, I registered a burst of light behind the building. An explosive *BOOOOOM* left no doubt to the origin of that flash; someone had discharged a shotgun. That got me to my feet, looking for a weapon. The chest pressure eased as I picked up a coconut from the grass. I moved cautiously through the front door. I called out. Nothing. I called again and heard a soft moan from the rear bedroom. Without thinking, I rushed in, brandishing my coconut.

I grabbed a flashlight near the bed and turned it on. Emily was on her side next to the bed, holding her head. Blood oozed through her fingers onto the carpet. She was struggling to sit up. My olfactory nerve registered a faint, sickly-sweet aroma mixed with the coppery smell of blood.

"Oh my god, what happened?" I kneeled down and took her in my arms, carefully prying her fingers apart to look at her scalp. The flashlight held awkwardly in my mouth revealed a large scalp laceration. Tripod crawled out from under the bed and whimpered.

"Get that dang thing out of my eyes," she said, holding her hand up to protect her vision.

"That's the nicest thing I've ever heard you say," I said. I pressed my handkerchief against the wound to staunch the bleeding.

"FREEZE! GET YOUR HANDS WHERE WE CAN SEE THEM! DO IT! DO IT NOW!" A giant beacon blinded me, and I instinctively raised a hand to block the light.

"DON'T MOVE! DON'T MOVE!" A pair of hands grabbed me and threw me backward against a wall. A boot pressed against my neck cutting off my airway. Someone yanked my arms roughly behind me. Handcuffs clamped my wrists.

"Wait a minute. What—," I tried to say.

"JUST SHUT UP AND DON'T MOVE."

The Mistake

"Commander, again, my apologies for this incident." A baby-faced Air Force security officer looked sheepishly at the floor. "We got a call on a break-in and well, obviously we thought . . ."

I was sitting on my couch in the living room, rubbing my chafed wrists where the handcuffs had cut off circulation. I took a drink of water using two hands to control the shaking. The chest pain was gone, but the ringing in my ears remained. I tasted copper and my lip throbbed mercilessly, but the bleeding had stopped.

An ambulance had already taken Emily to the hospital for evaluation. She alternated between hysterics and incoherence. She couldn't tell me what had happened, but I knew. Someone had kidnapped Hanna and had tried to kill my wife. Denial and bargaining disappeared—unmitigated rage reigned.

I stormed around the room, alternately shoving my hands into my pockets and removing them, cracking my knuckles. I hunted for a reason for this insanity until Lieutenant Frisk arrived and took charge of the investigation. His assignment apparently was anything that involved me. "How are you feeling, Sir?" he asked. I think he was feigning concern.

"I'll be okay, but we need to start looking for Lieutenant Sanders. She's been kidnapped."

"We don't know that for sure, but I'm getting back-up to search the area as soon as possible. Was your wife able to tell you what happened?"

"No. She's in shock and only told me they took Lieutenant Sanders—that's her twin sister."

"Did she get a look at who did this?" He wandered around, rummaging through papers on my desk and looking around the room.

"No, but it could be the same guy who was seen prowling around here last night."

He dropped the papers he was examining and looked at me. "Tell me about that. You saw someone here last night? Why didn't you call and let me know?" He opened his notebook and shook his head as he made a note.

I told him about Angel standing guard, and how he'd spotted someone trying to break in. I also explained that Angel wasn't likely to co-operate with authorities. Frisk frowned and made another note.

"How did you get that?" he asked, pointing at my lip. "Looks nasty." His gaze dropped to the blood on my uniform.

"Looks worse than it is. Hit my face on the steering wheel when I went off the road getting here. It's nothing." I touched my wound and it reminded me that even nothing could hurt like a hornet in the outhouse.

"I saw a little blue pick-up in the ditch a mile or so down the hill. That yours?"

"Yeah. The coral they use in the asphalt is slippery as cat snot in the rain."

"Hmm . . . didn't see much blood. You say that's how you got hurt?" He waited; I waited. He wrote another line and flipped the notebook closed.

One of the security guards stuck his head in the front door, looking pale. "Lieutenant, you better come out here and look at this."

On TV, the hero takes a blast in the shoulder from a shotgun and continues on his journey. Angel's cousin Carlos didn't have a shoulder, or most of a face. What pellets missed him took the bark off a palm tree behind his body. He would not be continuing any journey, ever. Nearby I heard grunting of the wild boars that populate the neighborhood. Had we not discovered Carlos' body, he would be a feast for them before the morning light.

I've dealt with enough blood, guts, and gore not to be squeamish, but it was all I could do to look. The lieutenant wasn't as strong. The stench of his regurgitated dinner mixed with Carlos' blood was too much for the patrol officer who also rushed for cover. I gagged and swallowed. The rain and wind continued unabated, uncaring.

"Secure the scene until forensics can get here," the Lieutenant commanded after he gained his composure. He wiped his mouth with a handkerchief, and then turned to me. "What happened here?"

"I have no idea," I answered, "but I thought I'd heard a gunshot just as I arrived."

"See anything?"

"Not a thing. My home was dark, and the front door was open. I was kinda preoccupied worrying about my wife. Some of the locals have been hunting wild pigs out back here, and I guess I thought that's what it was." I looked at the remains again. "I had no idea . . ."

"Do you know who this is?" he asked. Carlos' corpse let loose a wet death rattle—trapped gas escaping from the gut—and tipped sideways. The security guard who had found the body jumped back and crossed himself.

I shook my head. Not enough remained of the face, even if I did know him. "Never saw him before, but I'm pretty sure this is, or *was*, Angel Sanchez's Cousin Carlos. Angel told me he would be guarding the area tonight."

"Why was that?"

"Because someone has been threatening me and Angel owes me a favor. Remember all those letters?" I turned to go back inside out of the weather.

"You should have notified me of those plans." He reached out and grabbed my shoulder, turning me toward him.

I reacted instinctively and had him in an arm lock before I realized it. The security officer unsnapped his holster, pulled his sidearm, and aimed it at me. I released Lieutenant Frisk and stepped back, holding my hands up in surrender.

"Sorry, Lieutenant." I dusted off his arm. "I know you're trying to help, and I should have notified you that Angel spotted someone creeping around last night. His family is providing 24-hour protection, which is something you can't do. Carlos was tonight's watch; that's all there is to it."

"Did you know it's illegal for a civilian, or anyone for that matter, to hunt on a federal reserve? Why would you assume the gunshot you heard was someone hunting?" He rubbed his shoulder.

"Did you know Lieutenant Sanders has been kidnapped, my wife mugged, a dead body in my backyard, and I don't give a shit about your hunting regulations? Hunting regulations? Get with the program."

"How do you know she was kidnapped? Maybe she saw someone break in and just took off? Or maybe she and her sister had a fight and . . ." He paused. I took a deep breath and stretched my neck. I looked once more at Carlos' remains and walked to the house. Frisk followed.

As I entered, the baby-faced officer stepped out of the bedroom holding an envelope with a pair of tweezers. There was a large bloodstain on the envelope; an envelope identical to those I'd already received.

"Lieutenant, I found this next to the pillow."

"Hold on, let me put on some gloves," the lieutenant said.

You no what I want. When I get them you get your kidnapped wife back. Shes alive and Ok for now. But if I dont get them she won't be. I'll be in contact with you soon.
Your old friend

Frisk and I both looked at the smudge and crease on the computer printed note. He arched his eyebrow.

"What do you think?" he asked.

"What do I think?" I got so close to his face, our nose hairs needed a referee. "I think Lieutenant Sanders has been abducted. She didn't have a fight with my wife. She didn't get scared and run off. Someone took her, thinking she is my wife, and I think you need to find her, *now*."

"So, for the record—you didn't write this? This isn't your blood on the envelope?" He stared at me, unblinking. "Sorry, you know I have to ask."

"Fuck you. Someone is trying to extort me, or has a personal grudge he is trying to settle. He misuses and misspells words, and yet uses words like 'kidnapped' and 'contact' correctly? He wants us to think he's illiterate, but he's smart enough to get into my office and use my computer."

"What do you think he wants?" Frisk asked me. "This says he knows you have something he wants. What's that all about?"

"I have no idea," I lied, "but he thinks he has my wife, and is holding her for ransom. That means she's in danger when he finds out he grabbed her twin sister. I want to go to the hospital right now, and you need to get a guard on her. The rest of this," I said, waving my arm around the area, "can wait."

"Why would he take the wrong one?" he called after me as I started for the door.

"He screwed up. Other than for a small, private tattoo, they are truly identical. And, tonight they were in the same room, so I'm guessing whoever it was made a crucial mistake. Now, if it's okay Lieutenant, I'm going to the hospital to make sure my wife is safe."

"Yes, Sir, of course. I'll get one of my men to drive you. I have to stay here, but I'll post someone at the hospital to protect your wife. We'll do everything we can to find Lieutenant Sanders, I promise." He picked up his radio and began to issue orders.

Before I could thank him, the baby-faced one stepped out of the bedroom again. "Found this on the floor." He held up a rag and walked over to us. When he was within two feet, I knew what it was. Frisk sniffed.

"Chloroform, right? That explains some of the how. He hit your wife and drugged your sister-in-law, but where would someone get their hands on chloroform?"

"Hospital supply would stock it; requires a prescription," I answered.

"That reduces the suspects significantly, wouldn't you think? Someone connected to the hospital, or a pharmacist, *or a doctor?*" He let that hang.

"You still think I had something to do with this, don't you?" *One minute you want to help, the next minute you think I'm somehow involved. Well, fuck you and stay out of my way.*

He shrugged, and then gave instructions for one of the enlisted men to drive me to the hospital.

As we drove off, I saw a sow and group of piglets crossing the road.

Spinelli

The hospital ER was eerie; soundless as the OB ward had been two hours earlier. A musk of antiseptic filled the air. Nothing happening—except Emily. I spotted an exam area with the curtain pulled and walked past the nursing staff directly through the curtains.

Emily was sitting up in bed. She squinted as Dr. Spinelli, our neurosurgeon, waved a penlight across her pupil. A bulky bandage wrapped her head. The other eye was swollen shut. My heart seized, and I couldn't get my mind around the idea that someone had tried to kill her.

This is no longer an abstract philosophical discussion about good and evil, god and the devil, yin and yang, or other bullshit. I am going to kill you when I find you.

I wanted to hit something, to break something, to make somebody pay for this, but there was nobody. The frustration boiled inside me.

Dr. Spinelli looked up at my intrusion. "Ah, Jake, good to see you. I'm just finishing my examination of your lovely wife." He stepped around the other side of the bed and tapped her knees and elbows with a small rubber hammer. She jerked appropriately and looked at me with her good eye.

"What happened?" she asked. Her speech was slurred and hesitant.

I pulled up a stool and sat next to her. "I don't know yet. I'm hoping you can tell me." I turned to Dr. Spinelli. "How is she?"

"Hold on, one thing at a time." Dr. Spinelli went patiently about the rest of his exam while I kissed her forehead through the bandage. I caught the harsh smell of her blood.

Mild shock painted her pale face with a faint sheen of perspiration.

Dr. Spinelli put away his instruments and stepped back. He glanced from me to Emily. "You're fine, my dear. A pretty good bump on the noggin' that will require some stitches, but overall I think you'll survive just dandy. I do want to keep you here to get a CAT scan to rule out anything more serious. You've had a concussion and memory loss of the last few hours, but I don't expect any long-term problems."

I exhaled.

"You, however, look like, well . . ." Spinelli said pointing at my busted lip.

"Where the hell is Dr. Matthews?" I heard TJ's booming voice. I opened the curtain and our eyes met. I couldn't read them. There was no emotion in the deep black pools.

<u>Emily's Night in the Hospital</u>

In all the years I've known TJ, I've never seen him in anything but crisp uniforms, and polished shoes, except when we went diving. On dive days, he steps out of the mold into a matched set of sweats and spotless tennis shoes. Tonight he was in Levis and a sleeveless sweatshirt advertising the USS Constitution. On the back, it read "Antique Ships Have Full Masts" above a Viagra logo. He was sweating, and his cigar had an ash. He never actually smokes or lights one of those foul things.

"Is Em okay?" He looked at the curtains and raised his eyebrows. I ushered him in.

"She'll be fine. Dr. Spinelli looked her over and said she's had a concussion, but will be okay."

TJ moved next to the gurney and reached for Emily's hand. She reacted by taking mine in both of hers. She seemed confused as if he were a stranger.

"It's okay," I said. "It's TJ. Do you recognize him?" I worried that her memory loss might be more severe than expected.

She stared at him for a moment and then frowned. "Sorry, I am a little confused." She turned worried eyes back at me.

TJ said, "I heard about the attack and just want you to know I'm doing everything I can to find out what happened and make sure Hanna is returned safely." He turned to Emily. "Do you remember anything?"

Emily shook her head and flinched with the motion. She spoke directly to me. "It's all a blur. Hanna and I went to bed after you called Jake back to the hospital." She looked at TJ quizzically. "Then there was someone in the room, and everything went black. Then I was here in the emergency room."

"Did you see him?" TJ asked.

Emily continued speaking to me, not looking at TJ. "No, just a sense of someone there. Really big. Really dark. Maybe black." She snuck a glance at TJ. "I just don't remember anything else."

"A black man, or dressed in black?" TJ asked her. He leaned in closer to her.

She flinched and closed her eyes. I could tell she was exhausted. "I don't know. I have a headache and need to sleep." I leaned over and kissed her as she drifted off.

"You get some sleep. The nurses will be waking you hourly to check on you. I'll be here all night. Okay?" She didn't hear me. I heard the soft night music of her snoring. I renewed my vow to kill her attacker—slowly. TJ and I went out to the main area.

"So what happened?" he asked.

"You called and said I was needed here, so I came in. This place was like a morgue. Nobody on OB, or in the OR, or here in the ER." I looked at him. "So, who called you and said I was needed? I think someone used you to set me up. I was to be away so whoever did this didn't have to deal with me."

"I don't have any idea who called. I got a page when I was at the Air Force base supply warehouse. I called into the front desk, and there was a message that OB needed you. They couldn't page you, so they asked if I could help find you.

"But who called the front desk?" I asked.

"Let's find out." We walked around the corner of the ER to the front reception area. The corpsman operating the phone was animatedly waving his arms while he talked to someone, so we waited until he was finished.

"Tell me about that call you received asking Dr. Matthews to come in for an emergency." The corpsman jumped to attention and reached for his logbook.

"Yes, Sir." He thumbed back a page and looked up. "I received a call from an in-house extension at 21:13 hours. The caller stated there was an emergency on the obstetrics ward; Dr. Matthews was to report, STAT. I tried calling his, I mean your home, Sir," he looked at me, "but there was no response. I also tried paging you." His eyes shifted between us. "I hope I did the right thing by calling Lieutenant Commander Justis. I thought he might know how to reach you in an emergency. I'm sorry, Sir. I know I should have called my chief first, but—"

"You did the right thing, son. Thank you for showing initiative under fire, but tell me," I asked, "did you recognize the voice or where it originated?"

The corpsman let out a deep breath and answered, "No, Sir. I didn't recognize the voice, but the phone system automatically logs where all incoming calls originate, both in-house and off-base. I'm sure it was 361."

TJ and I looked at each other. *Extension 361 is my office.*

"Regardless, someone managed to get me out of the house, attack Emily, and kidnap Hanna."

TJ and I had checked my office—locked as expected—and had returned to the ER.

"What?" He grabbed both of my arms and turned me to face him. "Hanna's been kidnapped? How'd that happen? I mean, security called and said you needed me at your house. When I got there, they told me Emily had been attacked and taken to the hospital."

Wait a minute. I thought you knew about the kidnapping? Why else are you here?

"Whoever broke in hit Emily, and we think used chloroform on Hanna. She's gone, and there doesn't appear to have been much of a struggle. MPs are looking for her right now." The stress over the last few hours had left me exhausted; a giant knot in my stomach secreted acid. I wanted to scream in frustration at my helplessness.

"But why would someone take Hanna? What possible reason could there be? She doesn't have any money, and there is no way someone can get her off this island without me finding out." TJ looked at the burnt offering he was chewing.

"They want the Blue Death."

"But I still don't understand why? You told me you don't have any, and Hanna can't help them, even if you do. Just doesn't make sense."

"They weren't after Hanna," I said. I saw realization light up his eyes, and he looked toward the curtains surrounding Emily. The same security officer who had tackled me and then driven me to the hospital had quietly set a chair next to the cubicle and was watching us, his sidearm in plain view. He looked at me and nodded. I suspected having handcuffed me by mistake embarrassed him enough that he wouldn't let anyone near her. I felt a small wave of relief knowing no one would get to Emily tonight.

"Let me get some others to help keep an eye on things." TJ reached across the counter for a phone. I put my hand on his before he grabbed the receiver.

"If you mean Angel's family—forget it. Someone blew off most of Cousin Carlos' head tonight outside my house. I don't know if anyone has notified Angel or Ramón yet, but when they find out, all hell is going to break loose. Maybe we can get their family to help us hunt for Hanna rather than guard Emily."

"Carlos was murdered?" TJ looked shocked at this news.

"Sorry, I thought you knew what had happened. Isn't that why you're here? You didn't know about Hanna's kidnapping or Carlos' murder?"

"No, when I saw Frisk at your place, he just said Emily had been injured and taken to the hospital. I had no idea." He rolled the soggy, burnt cigar across his mouth. "Wait a minute. He did say something about Hanna being missing. Yeah, that was it."

Then I told him about the ransom note found on the bed.

"Let me guess," he said. "It was written on your office computer." It was a statement rather than a question.

"Probably the same time the call was made from my office."

He thought a moment and said, "But you told me that there aren't any globes left; you sent them all to a lab for analysis? You don't still have any, do you?"

"Of course not, but someone thinks I do, and is holding who he thinks is my wife for them. This isn't about some druggie getting even; this is about getting Blue Death."

TJ said, "Charlie needs to be here, not MIA. He needs to know that Hanna is missing. He has resources we need right now."

He stopped, took the cigar out of his mouth, and angrily threw it into a trashcan. "Son of a bitch—of course. I know who's behind all this. Come on." He bolted out of the ER.

The Break-In

"What the hell are you doing?" I asked TJ. We were in the main lobby of the dark, empty entrance to the hospital. TJ bent over the door of the Executive Officer's suite, fiddling with the lock.

He shushed me. Then, looking around, he removed a key from his pocket and opened the door. "Nice to have a passkey to this place." He grinned. If anyone would have the master key to any door in the command, it would be TJ. *Interesting.* For a moment, I wondered if he had Hanna stashed in a closet in the hospital. Then I dismissed the idea. He wouldn't. He couldn't.

The storm had abated. Moonlight filtered through a window into the office waiting room providing enough illumination. The yeoman, functioning as assistant to

Hawknose, had left her desk spotless. TJ and I bypassed the outer office and crept into the inner sanctum. Shutting the door, I flipped the switch.

"Nice digs," I whispered admiring the expensive rosewood furniture, artwork, and oriental rugs. "Certainly not within my pay grade." There was a faint jasmine scent in the air. A gecko scurried across the desk and up a wall.

"Nor Hawknose's pay grade either," said TJ. He opened several desk drawers looking for something. "Wonder if this is the substitute sperm donor," he said, holding up a moderate sized vibrator. "Think I should leave it on the desk for someone to find?"

"Don't even think about that," I said. He smiled evilly but put the toy away.

"I shared a room on the aircraft carrier with you. I don't wish to share a cell in Leavenworth. What the hell are we doing here?"

Cripes, I'm breaking into the Executive Officer's office. Not even TJ has enough juice to get us out of this one.

I picked up the only framed picture in the office. It showed Hawknose standing at attention in front of a nondescript building. There were no other photos, no family, no friends, no vacations, nothing.

"Got a paperclip?" TJ asked. He rummaged through the desk again and found one. Unfolding it, he attacked the lock on the single file cabinet in the office. A moment later, his fingers flipped through file folders. He extracted one and spread it out on the desk.

"Damn, I knew it. Look at this. Son of a bitch." He poked at the papers with a cigar he had unwrapped. I made sure he didn't leave the wrapper lying around as evidence of our misadventure.

"What?" I scanned the folder over his shoulder. He was reading a document on letterhead from a company called GFI—Genetic Frontiers InterNational. Under the heading was the Boston address of the corporate headquarters. A premonition crawled on centipede legs down my spine.

"Look at the date." TJ pointed. "Two months after we left Djibouti. That would have put her what, about the end of her residency? Just about the time she arrived here?"

"Damn," I said as the timing hit home. "That's not a coincidence."

Dr. Hawke:

Per previous communications, our company remains committed to further research and development of your findings. Enclosed you will find your copies of the contract and a retainer in the amount of $500,000.

We both understand the immense commercial potential this represents and the need for absolute confidentiality.

The head of R&D needs more of the product. You provided only the single sample with your initial inquiry. It is imperative that we obtain additional samples to complete the testing.

The letter continued with contact information and another plea for speed.

TJ shuffled through the file and pulled out another letter from GFI dated two months later.

Dr. Hawke:

Congratulations on your orders to Naval Hospital Guam. As you requested, GFI used our influence to ensure your assignment there.

It is imperative that you acquire more of the samples you

indicated are there. We have reached a critical threshold with your original. Without additional globes, we cannot complete the project. I do not need to remind you of the financial implications of such failure.

Good luck with your search. We will continue to provide whatever aid you require.

Again, there was contact information and the same vice president in charge of research signed the letter. Further search through the file uncovered lab results, DNA analyses, and miscellaneous notes. A folded scrap fell to the floor. TJ picked it up and flattened it on the desk. It was a hand-drawn map of the coast of North Africa.

Just then, the antechamber door rattled. My heart jerked from the adrenaline rush. Before I could react, TJ grabbed me and doused the lights. He pulled me behind the desk.

Oh shit, we left the file cabinet open and the file on the desk.

"It's the security fire watch making their rounds," whispered TJ.

"Hey, check it out," an excited young voice said. "This is the desk of that hottie who works for the XO. What do you think? Is she doin' the hag?" Another exclamation and laughter from the anteroom followed.

TJ put a finger to his lips. He picked up the desk phone and dialed. A moment later, I heard a radio in the anteroom. "Security alert, security alert. There is an intruder in the XO's office. Security personnel report immediately."

"What the hell?" the young voice asked. "That three legged cowboy at the front desk thinks we're breaking in." Radio static. "This is Rover One. We're doing security rounds on the XO's office, and all is clear. Please cancel the alert."

"10-4 Rover One. Copy that the office is secured," responded the front desk.

"Copy this, numb nuts." I assumed Rover One didn't have his finger on the microphone key—it would be making an obscene gesture. "Come on, the game starts in a minute. Let's get outta here. I don't want to miss the kickoff." I heard the door close and realized I'd forgotten the first rule of scuba and clandestine operations: *Breathe in, breathe out. Don't lose your cool.*

Twenty minutes later TJ and I were sitting in the cafeteria. I was using two hands to steady my shaking cup as I drank coffee. "What the hell was that all about?" I thought I knew, but I still wanted TJ's confirmation.

"Hawknose is the one," TJ said. "Everything fits." He ticked off the points.

"That map was the coastline of Djibouti, so she knew, or found out. Somehow, she got her hands on a globe of Blue Death and made a deal with this GFI Corporation to get rich from it. Maybe she's the one who got to Petty Officer Vignalli and cut off his finger? Tufts Medical School, where she trained, and GFI are both in Boston, and that was his duty station after Djibouti. Then she shows up at the same command as you, Charlie, and me. That's no coincidence."

"Sounds like she had help getting here," I threw in.

"And—"

"And that's why she got promoted instead of busted when she was sanctioned for being drunk in the operating room. I knew there had to be something or someone pulling strings to keep her around. Even the Skipper had no clue why he got stuck with her."

"Of course," TJ said, "she also has access to your office, your personnel file, and could have written the letters. And she went out of her way to bring you up on charges. And I'll bet she had something to do with getting Charlie out of the way during that kangaroo court. If she wrote the letters that got your kids off island, she'd have a clear field to attack you."

"But, you said that she hadn't written Charlie's orders. Besides, there is nothing to connect her to Blue Death. We're assuming whoever killed the courier stole the globes, right? So if she had one to sell to GFI, whoever they are, where did she get it?"

TJ said, "I don't know. But if she did . . ."

I thought about those letters from GFI we just uncovered. "This is too pat. Why would a global business write incriminating letters like that? And even Hawknose isn't stupid enough to keep them. Doesn't add up."

"You're allowed to use Hawknose and stupid in the same sentence, but you forget to add arrogant," was all he said.

"Do you think Hawknose took Hanna?" I asked. "Is she capable?" As much as I hated her, I couldn't imagine her breaking into my house, braining my wife, drugging my sister-in-law, and then holding her for ransom. *But, what if?* The premonition evolved into a certainty.

"Think about it," TJ said. "She has motive; getting more of those blue globes would make her rich. She has opportunity; access to your computer and medical supplies for chloroform. And she's been missing in action for a week; plenty of time to find a way to get to you."

"But it didn't sound like who Angel saw last night or who attacked Emily."

"It was dark. Some padding, dark clothes, face paint and . . . and she always has one of those little penlights in her pocket."

"TJ," I looked him directly in the eye. "How did you know about the penlight? How did you know where to look in Hawknose's office for those letters? And how did you know Hawknose didn't send Charlie on his current assignment?"

He held my stare. "It's my job to know things. Frisk told me about the light when I was at your house this evening, I checked with Charlie's command who deny all knowledge of where he is. They may just be covering, or Hawknose is somehow involved. Besides, who else but her has motive, means, and the opportunity?"

I guess it fits. Revenge and money are great motivators, especially for someone like her. She has been out to get me ever since I had her license to practice revoked. And then she ends up as the second in command here—my boss? GFI must have some mighty powerful connections. I must remember to ask Charlie about them.

A mess crank gathered our dishes and took them to the hopper. "Ya finished with that, Sir?" he asked too late for me to object.

"We need to find Charlie," I said to TJ.

"I'll make some calls in the morning." I knew TJ had the contacts to find our friend. I didn't know what I would tell him when he did. Charlie's life revolved around Hanna. I wouldn't want to be the focus of his attention when he went after whomever took her.

A corpsman approached the table and cleared his throat. "Sir, there is a Mr. Angel Sanchez at the front gate asking to see you and Dr. Matthews. Can we let him on base?"

"Granted. Have him join us in the ER."

"Oh shit, what do I tell Angel?" I asked. "He may not know about Cousin Carlos yet." TJ shrugged.

"I'm gonna kill that bitch when I catch her." Angel spoke softly with a voice that carried more threat than a drill sergeant screaming in your face. "See this?" he asked pointing at a small teardrop tattoo under his right eye. He waited.

"You had a friend in prison that was killed?" I asked. "Isn't that what it usually means?"

"Yeah, I did a nickel for aggravated assault when I was a kid. Me and Ramón both. This dude I didn't even know shanked my friend over a pack of cigarettes. The tear is for him."

"I don't understand."

"Me and Ramón, see. We took the dude out. I filled a light bulb with kerosene and replaced it with the one in the ceiling of his cell. Night comes, and the guards turn on the lights. He burned for a long time before they could get him outta that cell. Lived almost two days."

The coldness in his voice and eyes terrified me. This wasn't the Angel who sold bait from a shack and took care of my dive gear. This was death on a grim mission.

"That bitch killed Carlos. Now she pays."

Thirty minutes later, we had enlisted Angel's help to search for Hanna. With his extended family and their intimate knowledge of the surrounding jungle, I felt confident that we would find her. I hoped it wasn't too late. I knew that if Hawknose figured out she grabbed the wrong twin, Hanna's life was forfeit. So was Emily's.

No News is Bad News

I spent the balance of a restless night in a chair at the nursing station. Hourly I checked on Emily, awakening her gently to be sure there was no swelling of the brain. As a weak sun tried to escape the morning haze, she threatened my manhood if I woke her up one more time. I took the coward's walk to the chow hall for breakfast. My favorite chipped beef on toast, smelling of comfort and Momma's hug, congealed when I put it on hold to answer a call from Frick.

"I just wanted you to know that every able-body we can find is searching for Lieutenant Sanders," he said.

"And?"

"And nothing so far. My forensic techs are completing their work and running fingerprints. I'm tracking down the chloroform. I've also confirmed that it *was* Carlos Sanchez murdered in your back yard. We're doing an autopsy on him this morning, but clearly the cause of death was a shotgun."

"I spoke with Angel last night and his family is also looking for Hanna. I'll let you know if they find anything."

"One more thing, Sir."

"Let me guess. The ransom note came from my office and has my fingerprints on it. Right?"

"Yes, Sir."

He didn't seem to have anything else to say, and I was about to hang up when he asked if I knew where Hawknose might be.

"Not a clue, and frankly, I don't give a damn, Scarlett." He was too young to have ever seen *Gone With the Wind.*

"Everybody at this command is better off without her," I said, considering whether to tell him what she was up to and why I thought she was responsible. I reconsidered and decided to wait until I had proof. Admitting to breaking and entering the Executive Officer's lair was not a bright idea. TJ and I would have to figure out some other way to get her files into the proper hands.

"Sounds like you have a problem with your Commander Hawke. I understand you brought her up on charges and had her privileges revoked. And she tried to return the favor? There's even a rumor that you threatened to kill her during a committee meeting last week." He waited. I let him wait.

So much for privacy and security during confidential committee meetings.

"Anything else you need, Lieutenant?" I asked.

"Just one more thing, Sir. Do you own a firearm?"

Wow. Where is this leading, bucko?

"I have an antique .22 target pistol locked up at home somewhere. Why? Do you think I should get a permit and start packing?"

"Just checking out a few things is all. I'll talk with you later this afternoon." With that he hung-up, leaving me feeling queasy.

Needs

I avoided morning report. By then, everyone in the hospital knew about the attack and I wasn't up to playing 20 questions or pretending I cared about their sympathy. I needed space. I needed to find Charlie and Hanna. I needed to protect Emily. I needed to find and kill Hawknose. I needed so much it ached. I needed a drink and the oblivion alcohol promised. What I got was a box and a handwritten note.

A Letter Home

YOU'LL NEED THESE. DO WHATEVER IS NECESSARY TO GET HANNA AND EMILY OFF GUAM. YOUR CHILDREN AND PARENTS ARE SAFE. I HAVE SOMEONE HERE WATCHING THEM FOR YOU.

BE CAREFUL AND DON'T TRUST ANYONE. GET RID OF ANY GLOBES YOU STILL HAVE. THEY ARE MORE DEADLY THAN YOU CAN IMAGINE. I'LL EXPLAIN WHEN I GET BACK. IN THE MEANTIME, PLEASE BE CAREFUL AND TAKE CARE OF OUR WOMEN.

CHARLES

The note was inside a plain box sent first class from Cozumel, Mexico four days previously. The return address was general delivery. I thumbed through a US Passport with a name for someone from Kansas that I didn't recognize. I recognized the photo. It was Emily; it was Hanna. Charlie didn't know about Hanna when he sent this.

It looked real; it was embossed and stamped. The immigration stamps included a recent arrival on Guam and many years of travel throughout the world. Smudged and dog-eared, it rang true of a seasoned traveler. In the same envelope was a clone—almost. Different name of a woman from South Dakota, similar stamps including island entry the same day, but a different profile of world travel. The photo was Hanna, or Emily. The enclosed bundle of US currency and Mexican pesos would justify a mugging.

I checked my phone and found I had a dial tone. "I need two confirmed first-class seats as soon as possible, one-way to Honolulu, connecting to Cozumel, Mexico." I read the names and pertinent info from the open-ended tickets I'd found banded to the cash.

I need to get the girls safely on that plane. I need to talk to Charlie. Why would he sign the letter Charles? Who the hell is Charles?

I reached into the carton and removed the remaining two items. The large caliber semi-automatic handgun didn't surprise me. It smelled of Hoppes gun oil. It felt coldly lethal; it felt right. Charlie knew I didn't have a personal arsenal other than my dad's target pistol.

The other item in the bottom of the box was a surprise.

Ransom

"How was lunch?"

I waited while the nurse finished taking vital signs and cleaned up the remains of Emily's meal. She sat up in bed, her skin color as pale as the bandage on her head. The room sweltered from the lack of air-conditioning, and no one opened windows because of a fly infestation. Nobody had ever thought of installing screens—except in the operating room, where no one could open windows. Go figure.

"The mess cranks can do wonders with Jell-O. Eight colors that all taste the same—yummy, gummy water. Now, are you going to ask if the bed is comfortable, or if I have enough magazines to read?" She glared at me.

Wow, am I in trouble or what?

"No," I said sheepishly as I sat on the edge of her bed. I took her hand in mine. "I came to tell you I love you and that we haven't found Hanna yet. They're turning this island upside down, and we'll find her. Angel, Ramón, and most of the Guam Nation are looking. In the meantime, there is a guard posted outside your door, so you'll be safe until I can get you to Mexico with the kids."

"What are you talking about? A guard? Leave Guam? I'm not leaving. Especially with Sister missing." I realized she didn't know about the latest letter.

"Sweetheart . . . there was another letter left on our bed last night." Her skin blanched whiter than her bandage. The tremble of her lip released the tear she was holding back.

I told her, "Whoever did this thought they took you. They got the wrong twin by mistake. If they figure that out, they'll come after you. That's why I'm getting you and Hanna off island tomorrow afternoon." I left no room in my tone, attitude, or posture to brook an argument.

"But why? Why do they want me? I don't understand." She squeezed my hand in a death grip.

"Whoever is doing this will use you to get to me. That's why."

"But—"

"They want the remaining Blue Death globes. That's what this is about. They're worth a fortune to someone, and they'll kill to get them. They've already killed, and I think Hawknose is behind this somehow."

"Are those the little blue globes in the aquarium with Leo?" I startled, and looked at the closed door. Nobody could overhear us.

"How do you know about that?" I asked. "Nobody knows they exist and that I'm hiding them in the aquarium."

"I noticed them yesterday when I fed him, and realized they were new. They seem to glow and change color as I watched them. I figured that's what they were when I heard you explaining what Cassidy said about an alien virus."

"Did you tell anyone about them? Did Hanna know?" My reaction surprised her. "That information is dangerous."

She thought a minute and shook her head, then winced from the pain. "No, I'm sure I didn't. I had too many other things on my mind the last couple of days. They didn't seem important. Now you need to get rid of them."

"Hanna? Are you sure she doesn't know? It's important. Her life could depend on whether she knows or not."

"She's been killed, hasn't she?" With that, the last remnant of composure dissolved, and she started to sob, her body trembling.

I pulled her into my arms and let the tears run their course. "Shh," I whispered, "we don't know that at all. We'll find her, and she'll be on the plane with you tomorrow, I promise. Charlie sent new passports and plane tickets for both of you."

She pulled away. "Charlie's back? Did you tell him?"

"No, he just sent a package. I have no way to contact him to let him know about Hanna. TJ's working on that right now, but it looks like he was in Mexico a few days ago." I told her about the package he sent, but not everything it contained. Then I slid next to her on the bed, held her in my arms, and quietly told her about Hawknose.

"I'm going to kill that hag," she said. Two days ago, my wife cursed, now she was threatening to kill someone. Both events were real, and our universe shifted as a result. I felt like we were on the horizon of a black hole—forces conspiring that I couldn't control.

<u>Report to the CO</u>

"Dr. Matthews, please report to the Commanding Officer." The hospital loudspeaker distracted me from Emily's discharge paperwork. The Skipper never summons me to his office over the hospital speaker system. Usually an enlisted person tracks me down, or the Skipper just buzzes my pager. I had slept a few hours, caught up on my patient rounds, and showered with tepid water in the locker room. Coffee completed my punch list. A summons to the CO was not on that list.

The conference room contained all the department heads. I was the last to arrive. All eyes turned toward me.

"Thank you for joining us, Dr. Matthews," the Skipper said. His tone let all of us know he was not pleased. If he aimed his displeasure at me, I didn't care.

"I have some sad news to share this morning. That's why I asked all of you here." He looked directly at me. "Be seated, please."

There was a loud bang and shutter through the building as an aftershock hit. The lights flickered as the air-conditioning coughed and choked to life. Nobody in the room dared breathe for fear of jinxing the return of island power. A few moments later, we all cheered and clapped.

The Skipper cleared his throat. "A body washed ashore last night; it was Commander Hawke." Nobody moved. I glanced around the room; they all looked back at me. The lights flickered and went out. The air conditioner gave a death rattle. Someone groaned, breaking the spell.

I was too stunned to care if we had power or not. My mind refused to hear what the Skipper said; Hawknose was dead. I should feel something; I didn't. I finally realized that, for a moment, I was sure he was going to tell us that Hanna was dead. This wasn't about Hanna.

I found my voice. "What happened, Skipper?"

"NIS is investigating, but it appears she was murdered. Someone shot her in the back of the head, execution style, and then dumped her in the ocean. The autopsy will tell us more. In the meantime, the investigators will need to talk to each of you. You know the drill; cooperation is mandatory. They promised not to disrupt your schedules, but when they call—you report. Got it?" We all nodded. "Dismissed. Jake, stick around a minute, would you?"

Jake, not Doctor, or Commander. This is serious.

I hung back as the room emptied, and then we proceeded toward his office. I asked, "Do you know why Commander Hawke cut orders for Master Chief Albright the day Hanna had her surgery?"

"Commander Hawke?" He stopped, looking puzzled. "She had nothing to do with his orders; they came directly from his command. Commander Hawke wasn't in his chain of command. Why do you think she wrote orders for him? Do you know something about her death?"

"No, Sir. No particular reason. Thought I'd heard that she had something to do with sending Charlie away is all. And it was strange that Charlie got orders the same day she summoned me to her kangaroo court."

That's right, first TJ tells me that Charlie's command wrote his orders. Then he said Hawknose sent him away? Now the Skipper confirms that she had nothing to do with it.

"Do we know when she was killed?" I asked.

"Have to wait for the final report, but it looks like a week ago, maybe the same day she disappeared."

So she couldn't have been involved with abducting Hanna. She's involved somehow though. I just know it.

I halted half way through the office door when I spotted a chaplain sitting in a chair, waiting, his hands clasped. He stood up as I entered and slithered toward me, sadness painted on his cadaverous face. He sucked all the available oxygen from the room as he put his hand on my shoulder.

"I am so sorry, Commander," was all he said.

"I don't understand, I'm not related to Hawknose, excuse me Commander Hawke." I looked to the Skipper.

He looked at his shoes. "I am so sorry." The Skipper paused. "Hanna is dead."

My vision went gray as I collapsed against the wall. I couldn't feel my face; couldn't feel my legs either. I could see their lips moving, but the buzz in my ears prevented hearing. I knew the universe would never be the same.

". . . in a few days," said a voice in the chaos.

"Excuse me?"

"I said that we've located Master Chief Albright, and he'll be here in a few days."

"Huh?"

"The Master Chief—Charlie has been notified and will be here in a couple days. You with us, Jake?"

"Huh, with you?"

I'm not with anything. Hanna is dead. How can I make sense of anything else?

"Does Charlie know?"

"Not yet. I know how important Lieutenant Sanders was to him, but he's not family, so . . ."

"He *is* family, Skipper. He's *my* family. Emily and I want to be available when he arrives. I . . . we owe him that much . . . I need to . . ." I was numb to the freight train hurtling down the tracks at me. "What happened? I . . . I mean, how . . . Are you sure?"

Elizabeth Kübler-Ross presented the original research on dying and the psychological stages we encounter. I had reached Stage 1—Denial. This can't possibly be happening.

The Skipper and the chaplain helped me up and into a chair. The light in the room was flat and colorless. I couldn't feel anything. I gripped the arm of the chair and willed myself to deal with this—willed myself to breathe.

"I'm afraid we don't have much information yet. Apparently, searchers found her body in the jungle near your home. I made the identification early this morning. I hope you don't mind—you had enough on your plate, what with your wife being admitted and all." The Skipper had stepped out of his command disguise, and I saw a compassionate, caring person previously unknown to me. He sat next to me while the chaplain fidgeted in the corner.

"You'll let me know if you hear anything else?" I asked, responding on autopilot. My mind refused to function, grasping at mental quicksand as I tried to crawl to the shores of sanity.

"Of course. In the meantime, get your wife home. You're on bereavement leave until further orders. Do you want me to call anyone for you?"

"No, thank you, Sir." I wasn't hearing, just responding; going through the motions. This just wasn't happening. "I'll take care of the necessary calls later." A nagging thought tugged at the edges. Hawknose was dead; I didn't care. She, somehow, murdered Hanna.

"She did it, Skipper. I don't know how, but I know she did it."

"What are you talking about? Who did what?"

"Hawknose killed her. I know it."

My rage boiled the fog clear, and I shifted into hyper-drive. The CPU in my brain processed information faster than I could collate it. Hawknose hadn't sent Charlie away, but she had somehow killed Hanna, and now had a bullet in her own head. Hawknose was dead. I secretly hoped she suffered before dying.

But the bitch was killed a week before someone got to Hanna, and she doesn't have anything to do with Charlie leaving. So she couldn't have written that last ransom note or killed Hanna. How does her involvement with GFI and Blue Death fit in with this? Shit. Nothing made sense; I was too angry to think.

"You'll be okay," said the preacher. He approached, thumbing a bible to a ribbon-marked passage.

I turned all my anger, fear, and rage on him. Stage 2—the Anger, had arrived. "Don't you dare tell me your god works in mysterious ways." The threat in my voice made it clear his services weren't required. "Please leave." As he started toward the door, he held up his Bible, as if to ward me off.

I knew Stage 3—Bargaining, would arrive soon. I had no one to deal with; no chip I could barter in exchange for turning the clock back to a different reality. There was no god, only a black hole left after Hanna's supernova.

"What can I do?" asked the Skipper.

"Take me to her. I want to see for myself."

"Are you sure that's a good idea?"

Hell no—it's a terrible idea, but she can't be dead. This is a mistake, and it's not her body in the morgue.

Thirty minutes later, I knew it was true. When the body rolled out of the cooler, all I saw was my wife, gray and cold. I had to check for the butterfly tattoo that adorned Hanna to be certain it was Hanna and not my wife.

The shock of seeing Emily on the table and her twin sister, at the same time passed. I just shook my head and began the emotional preparations to tell Emily her sister was murdered. There was no easy way. The demon in the bottle was telling me otherwise—a couple drinks, and it would be easier. The hole in my being was screaming for liquid filler, even after all the years of abstinence.

Avoiding Ghosts

The ghost wasted no time taking up residence. Emily and I encountered Hanna in every doorway, sitting at the table, and unloading equipment from the *Chipmunk*. I heard her laughing over my shoulder and smelled her perfume. Even the coffee pot cried for her missing touch. The hole she left would be around forever with no hope of healing. Her spirit was not a terrifying ghost, but a shadow in the limbo of denial.

I spent hours holding my wife and at the same time, Hanna's spirit. Identical, yet unique, they always blurred to me. Both were an integral part of my life. Half that life was gone. As reality solidified, my frustration grew. Somehow, Hawknose was responsible, even from the grave, and I wanted to hurt her. She took my cold plate of revenge and dumped it down the drain. I wanted to scream.

Tripod lumbered up onto the couch between us and put his head in Emily's lap

"I can't stand it here," Emily said rubbing Tripod's head. "Hanna's everywhere I look." She wiped tears off her chapped cheeks. Her voice was hollow, echoing the emptiness of her heart; her eyes were vacant, staring into a vacuum.

"We'll be on a plane tomorrow. I changed reservations, and we'll be off to Cozumel to see the kids by this time tomorrow."

"I don't mean that. I mean right now. I have to get out of here. I'll go crazy if I stay in this house one more minute." She curled into a ball and put her head on my lap. "Please."

"Pack a bag; we're going to the Royal Pagoda Hotel for the night. I need to get out of here too." The Royal Pagoda is our secret get-away on Guam. Built to wine and dine Japanese tourists, it is an oasis in the madness of everyday life for Emily and me. A pool, spa, in-room massage, and a world-class seafood restaurant were part of the attraction; English as a second language insured privacy.

Tripod stood by the door looking out, then back at me. A single howl made it clear that he wanted to find Hanna and the kids. He begged to go with us.

"I'm sorry, you have to stay home," I told him. He responded by lying down and rolling on his side, face tucked under a paw. "But I have some hamburger you can have for dinner." Hamburger was the magic word. He was up, on his way to the refrigerator, and wagging his tail in anticipation; the ghost vanquished. If only it was that simple

An hour later we were in our suite with the do not disturb sign on the door. The illusion of security and peace was just that—an illusion.

"Why?" Emily finally asked the question that hung like a shroud over us. She was still in denial.

"It's pretty clear from that last letter that the attack is an attempt to force me to give them the remaining samples."

"You and those goddamn blue balls. It's all your fault. If you hadn't found them, this would never have happened." She slapped me and pulled her hand back for a second strike. I grabbed her and pulled her struggling into my arms. "I hate you. I hate Hawknose. This isn't fair." Gradually the fight left her, and she put her arms around my neck and cried.

"I sorry, I didn't mean that. I just . . ."

"Shh. I love you too. We'll get through this. I promise." Then I started to cry too. Kübler-Ross Stage 4—Depression came crushing in.

Room service knocked, announcing dinner—fish something, with other stuff. Emily fled to the bathroom. I mumbled something about allergies to explain my red eyes to the bellhop as I over-tipped him.

Emily emerged a few minutes later. She had scrubbed the tears off her face and replaced them with a look of determination. Kübler-Ross Stage 5 of the dying process— Acceptance. For Hanna's death, Stage 5 would be Revenge.

We stepped onto the deck overlooking the pool. I couldn't understand how all those people could be having fun. Even the sun and dazzling aqua sky felt dull and lifeless. *What do you have to laugh about? Don't you see the world is ending?* I picked at a piece of non-descript fish on my plate. My stomach wasn't interested, but my hands needed activity. I

275

knew Emily and I were discussing events and plans in monotones as a way to fend off the depression neither of us was equipped to handle at that moment.

Emily broke the spell. "What are we going to do?" A quiver of fear emphasized the emptiness of her voice.

"You are getting on a plane to Mexico tomorrow morning. You'll be safe with my parents and the kids. Charlie said he has security set up, so I know you'll be safe there. I'll be right behind you. There's a later flight out, and we'll meet in Honolulu." I saw her lip quiver and knew she was going to try to change my mind.

"You know I have to," I said. "I need to get the globes out of the aquarium, pack clothes for us, and figure out how to get Tripod on the plane with me. Besides, I need to contact Charlie as soon as TJ locates him. What if the wrong person gets the globes? What if our government, or *any* government for that matter, gets them? Would you give that kind of power to incompetents? I can't."

"I don't care about those damn globes. I lost Sister because of them. I can't lose you too. Can't you just get rid of them somehow? Or give them to someone?"

"There's nobody I trust, and I have no idea how to destroy them; I need Cassidy's help with that. I don't want to take a chance. Even hiding them with Leo in the aquarium is risky."

From our balcony, beyond the pool, the bay was calm, and the crystalline blue invited me to suck compressed air. The honor bar invited me to say fuck it, let's suck down a drink or three. Emily returned to the room and opened the mini-bar. Popping the tab on a soda, she poured it into two glasses and returned. It seared like battery acid in my stomach.

There was a knock at the door, and I jumped. I thought about the gun Charlie sent. It was in a case in my overnight bag. *Nice place to hide a weapon, genius.* I peeped through the hole in the door and saw a petite Asian woman in a hotel uniform.

"Yes. What is it?" I called.

"I have a gift basket for Dr. Matthews." I unlocked the door, and she handed me a large basket of fruit, candy, and champagne.

"What's this for?"

"I don't know, Sir. There's a card." She pointed, accepted a tip, and left. Emily looked at me questioningly. I shrugged and opened the card.

Meet me in the bar. Urgent I talk to you, alone. - Kelly

"Who's it from?"

"Kelly, and she wants to meet me downstairs." I turned the card over to see if there was anything else. There wasn't.

"Djibouti Kelly? Kelly's Reef Kelly? What's she doing here?" Emily was as confounded as I was.

"Don't know. I should go meet her and find out. Will you be okay?"

"I can't take this anymore. Do whatever the fuck you need to do; I'm going to bed." With that, she threw herself onto the bed and buried her head under a pillow.

Kelly

Cigarette smoke wafted through the dark hotel lounge. Although not politically correct, Guam still allowed smoking in bars. The lighting suggested seduction. Banging a shin on furniture in the darkness was not my idea of seduction.

Emily and I would meet here occasionally and pretend we were strangers. Decked out in a killer dress and heels, she would fend off suitors at the bar. I would stumble in looking like I'd crawled out from under a bridge. One of us would make a pass at the other, and we would play at picking each other up, loudly, and rudely. Then we would rush to a room, leaving the tourists aghast.

Not tonight— this wasn't a time for games.

I spotted Kelly seated at a booth in the back facing the door. Even in the dark, her flowing red hair and abundant curves drew my attention. She was just as I remembered her. She smelled of trouble and exotic adventure.

"I see that your eyebrows grew back." I slid onto the pale leather bench across from her.

I rewound my memory of Djibouti at high speed as she pushed a beer across the table at me. Foam sloshed over the rim and ran down the side of the glass, mesmerizing me. Too tired and stressed to deal with it; I just looked away.

"Here, look like we're old friends just meeting for a drink after work." She reached across the table to take my hand. "Rough week, huh? Thought you could use a break."

"Cut the crap, what are you doing here?" I asked, leaning back, distancing myself.

She leaned forward, glanced over my shoulder, and scanned the otherwise empty room. "Who else knows you're here?"

"Nobody. So again, why are you here?"

Her face softened. "I have a message and couldn't just ring you up, now could I?"

"And?"

"And I know about Hanna and Commander Hawke, too. And the fellow killed guarding you—Carlos, wasn't it?" She signaled the bartender to refill her wine. "You're not drinking?"

"If you know what's happened here in the last two days, surely your CIA dossier on me shows that I can't drink."

I continued, "So you know about Hanna, Hawknose, and Carlos. What else do you know?" The bartender brought Kelly's wine, and I ordered a Coke. "Really. Why are you here?"

She paused, and I could tell she was deciding what to reveal. "Okay . . . I've been in contact with Charlie, and we need your help. What do you know about Commander Hawke and her disappearance?"

"Charlie? Where is he? What's he going to do?" I felt a loss at not being with my close friend when he learned of Hanna's murder. I wouldn't want to be alone if it were Emily; I didn't want him to be alone either.

"He found out as soon as I did. He's pretty broken up as you can imagine. He'll be back soon to help take care of Hanna's memorial, but for now, he's staying in Mexico. There are things he needs to finish. That's part of what he wants me to talk to you about."

"He's not on his way back? Hanna's dead and he's in Mexico on one of his undercover assignments? That's not right."

"I know it, and you know it. So does Charlie. What he's doing is critical and will help him find her murderer." She paused. "Trust him, okay? I need to know about Commander Hawke."

Charlie I trust. I don't trust you.

"Uh uh. You tell me what you know first," I said.

"I know Hawke was involved with Hanna's murder somehow, but she had someone else working with her."

"You think Hawknose had something to do with murdering Hanna? That she mixed up the twins and kidnapped the wrong one?"

"I did, but that doesn't work," she said. "Hawke was killed a week ago, so she couldn't have been involved with the kidnapping."

"Okay, Hawknose didn't snatch Hanna. Who did?"

Kelly quickly changed subject. "Who else even knows you have the globes?"

I was stunned. "How is it that you know about them?"

She shook her head. "Come on, Doc. I found them in Djibouti, remember. With Charlie. He told me as soon as he suspected you found another source. That's why I'm here." She tilted her head, and curls ran across her shoulder. "So who else knows?"

Good question.

"A lot of people know they exist," I said. "Alzera and his cell knew about it. Somebody in the intelligence service knew, because a spook arrived to pick them up on the aircraft carrier. Now he's dead. I assumed you notified Washington. Vignalli might have known, and he's dead too." I paused for a breath. "And then there are you, Ambassador Dweck, who's dead, and Hawknose, who's dead. She somehow had a sample."

279

"I agree completely, but the sixty-four thousand dollar question is how did Hawknose get it, and why?" Kelly asked the question that plagued me.

I had my own theories, but wanted to know what Kelly knew. If I was to trust her, I needed to know that she wasn't just playing me.

"I have an idea," she said. "We know that Alzera was the first to discover Blue Death in North Africa. He wouldn't have been a source, and Hawknose had no way to get to Djibouti when she was a resident in training. The sample I sent back with you is the only thing I can think of. Again, how would she know? Moreover, how would she have had contact with the courier? Doesn't work."

I nodded and said, "And she had a sample before I even found it on the reef, so it must have been what was in that camera case we took from Djibouti, or there is another source out there we don't know about," I said.

She took a sip of white wine and pushed the beer back across the table at me. It sat there beckoning.

"So, Hawke somehow got her hands on the sample shortly after it left Djibouti. Maybe your petty officer, Vignalli wasn't it? Wasn't he stationed near her?" Kelly asked, her brow knotted.

"Don't play me for an idiot," I said. "You know more than you're telling me, and if you want my help, you need to level with me. Vignalli had nothing to do with this. He was just 'collateral damage'. I have a right to know what's going on."

She took a deep breath and slumped. "You're right. I know all about Vignalli and that he was taking classes at Tufts University, where Hawke did her residency. That connects them. But, he wouldn't have had access to Blue Death, so Hawknose couldn't have obtained it from him."

"So Vignalli wasn't the source of the sample Hawknose had." I scratched my head.

Kelly said, "I think maybe he found out about it and was killed because he knew too much. He was in Djibouti, flew home with Alzera, and knew about the camera case with the globes you were transporting. That was enough to get him killed. Hawknose might not have pulled the trigger, but she had her ugly nose in his death, somehow."

There are too many loose ends.

I said, "She was working for some multi-national research company who got her stationed here long before I even found what she wanted. I found letters indicating they were paying her a fortune for a globe, and that was before I'd found the others on the reef. I'm missing something."

"Same conclusion I came to," Kelly said. "So we're back to who else knows about your find."

"Charlie and Hanna were there when I found the globes." Just saying her name gave my heart a stab. "I sent everything I had to a lab for analysis, but they didn't get my samples until after all this began, so . . ."

She nodded. "But you said she had letters from some company that was paying her for the globes? Tell me about that."

I thought about it a bit and decided that if she didn't know, she would find out eventually.

"We found letters in her office from an international genetics firm offering her money for the globes. They also used their influence to help her find more of them. It looks like she knew I found a local source. But, she already had a sample and received orders here before I ever found them on the reef. How do you explain that?"

"She was working with someone who had inside knowledge. Maybe that's why she's dead," Kelly said.

I nodded. That made sense.

Kelly asked, "Who actually found the letters from GFI and where were they?"

"Why?"

"Jake, it's vital. This is all connected with Hanna's murder, and if it's what Charlie and I think, it may be evidence."

I relented. "TJ and I found them in Hawknose's filing cabinet."

"That fits too. You know they're fakes don't you?"

"What?"

"The company, the research director—all faked. She was set up to take the fall. Think about it. If she had a partner, he planted them to make you think she was responsible, and then killed her."

Of course. Nobody would write those letters and then leave them to be so easily found. Not even Hawknose.

"Too bad the body washed ashore so soon." Kelly raised her eyebrows. "Otherwise Hawke would have been the perfect patsy."

I stared at my Coke, absorbing all this.

She's not the only chump. What about all those letters?

"Someone's been writing threatening letters," I started to say.

"Yeah, from that guy during your residency who was released from Folsom and is stalking you?"

"But how?"

"They're fakes too. There is nothing in your file about that person so Hawknose couldn't have written them. Somebody who knows about that part of your history was trying to distract you. If you were worried about your family, you wouldn't be paying attention to anything else. That opens the door for someone to take the globes from you."

Before I could respond, she changed course. "Did you call this place to make a reservation?"

"Uh?" I thought a moment. "No. We just showed up." Then it hit me. "How the hell did you find me?"

"You'd make a lousy criminal, Doctor." She made a finger gun, pointed at me, and fired the thumb. "You checked in with your real name and a credit card. Anyone who wants to find you can—would take about five minutes. That's why you're moving to a different hotel under a different name." She looked at her watch, and I realized I had been away from Emily way too long.

She continued, "Tomorrow we get your wife out of here. Emily will use one of the passports Charlie sent. The one you made her airline reservation with."

"But . . . how did . . ."

"Here is yours." She handed me a US Passport, with a surname to match one of those Charlie sent. A younger me stared back. "Don't fly under your name or military ID."

She continued, "You'll be safer somewhere else until I get your wife on that plane tomorrow. You'll need this passport to get out of here later. I know you plan to leave with your wife tomorrow, but that can't happen," she looked at me, "in the meantime, you need to stay under cover. I'll have people on the plane with Emily to protect her."

"Why? All this cloak and dagger stuff is scaring me."

"Because you have Blue Death, Jake, and someone will kill you to get it. If I found you, they will. They might be on their way here as we speak."

"What makes you think I still have any?"

She stared at me with a 'get real' expression. "First of all, Charlie told me about your find. Secondly I don't believe you sent it all to your friend Cassidy in Oakland." She saw my reaction. "Don't look so surprised—I know about that too, and even if you did send all of it, whoever is after it doesn't care. He'll kill you if you have some stashed away and he finds it, and he *will* find it. On the other hand, he'll kill you if you don't have any because then you'll no longer matter. Either way, until we catch him, you're as good as dead. If you have any hidden at home or the hospital, you need to get them to me so I can protect them . . . and you."

I had been staring at the beer. Suddenly, drinking it seemed like a great idea. I changed subject. "You said you had a message from Charlie. Where is he?"

"He's in Cozumel with LaRouche. They're after the remainder of Blue Death, and he can't leave until they locate it." She took a pretzel stick from the bowl on the table and nibbled at it.

"Wait a minute." I shook my head. "Isn't LaRouche supposed to be in Wollei? What's he doing in Mexico?"

"Wollei was the cover story. I mean, whoever heard of Wollei? Or cares? There are too many ears and eyes to let slip his real destination and purpose. He *is* in Mexico and Charlie is there, working with him."

"I'm confused." I certainly must have looked confused. "Why are they in Mexico and what do you mean—the remainder? There's more Blue Death somewhere?"

I looked around; her paranoia was infectious. "Is that how Hawknose got some?"

"Who knows? Alzera found some off the coast of Djibouti; you found some off Guam. Hawknose had some." She didn't appear concerned.

<u>Roswell</u>

A man in a dark suit entered the lounge, looked around, and spotted us. He approached and said, "Ma'am, the cars are ready for the transfer whenever you are." Kelly nodded and waved him off.

"You're not hearing this." I nodded. She scanned the room again then drained the rest of her wine. Leaning in she said, "We think there are four potential sites for Blue Death. One was off the coast of Djibouti; Alzera found that one. Another is the one you found offshore here." She ticked them off on her fingers.

"Oh, by the way, it was really sweet of you guys to name your secret reef after me."

"How—"

She explained, "Charlie told me. Don't worry; your secret is safe with me. LaRouche is the only other person who knows about my reef and what you found."

"You said four sites?"

"There's a source somewhere near Cozumel." She put her hand up. "And it has nothing to do with your parents or children. It's pure coincidence. Luckily, Charlie can keep an eye on them while he's working."

"What, exactly, is Charlie doing there?"

"Hunting Blue Death, of course."

I sighed, resigned. "And that's more important than Hanna's death?" The bartender lit a cigarette and the acrid aroma wafted past my nose. Two Japanese tourists entered the bar and Kelly tensed. They walked through the bar, through the patio doors and into the pool area.

"It's okay," Kelly said. "They are part of my team just checking on our safety"

I asked, "Four? You said there were four sites."

"Right. The first site we knew about was in New Mexico." She smiled as the cartoon light bulb lit above my head.

"Roswell, right? You're going to tell me this is part of the Roswell UFO alien myth, aren't you?" I sat back and crossed my arms. "Yeah right. Gimme a break."

She crooked her finger to coax me back within whisper range. "Nah, Roswell is exactly what most intelligent people believe it to be—just a hoax. The Air Force came up with that one in 1947 and keeps the myth alive today. Best PR job the military ever invented. Those who want to believe in a government conspiracy have something to believe in. The doubters can believe it's a hoax. Meanwhile, real investigation into extraterrestrial phenomena can go quietly forth."

I looked at the beer. *Fuck it,—down the hatch. Here's to little green men.* I picked up the Coke instead.

"You do know what is inside the globes you found, don't you?" She waited for me to answer.

"It's an alien virus according to what I've figured out. Correct? We're talking about an extraterrestrial life form. Right? The real Roswell aliens."

"Very good." She sounded like a favorite teacher rewarding a bright pupil. "But it didn't start with Roswell. Roswell was a smoke screen. The real impact occurred fifty miles north of Roswell. The stuff found at Roswell was a plant. The government needed to keep the curious away from the real site."

"Wait a minute—there was something found outside Roswell?" I thought about Area 51, conspiracy theorists, and just plain kooks who *knew* the government was hiding an alien in a warehouse somewhere.

Kelly said, "There were a few remnants of unusual metallic pieces. And a single blue globe."

Whoa. Didn't TJ find something metallic under the coral on the reef?

"Wait a minute," I said. "What are you talking about?"

The bartender dumped a bucket of ice into his hopper, and the noise made me jump. I was starting to look around the room to see who might be listening.

"In 1947 we had an extraterrestrial strike. Something—maybe a meteorite, or something else, hit the atmosphere and broke up. The Air Force tracked it, but the technology at that time was primitive. All we knew is that there were four pieces. One landed outside Roswell, one somewhere near Northern Africa, one in this general area, and one in the Gulf of Mexico. That's where things sat until Alzera showed up."

Kelly continued, "As soon as we knew there was something unusual happening in North Africa, I was alerted."

"So the government has known about Blue Death since 1947, and kept it secret?"

"Pretty much," she agreed. She signaled the bartender. "It wasn't until a few years ago that anyone was able to thoroughly examine the globe. That's when we found out about the altered translation table for DNA. But, nobody had any idea what it would do until we started hearing about Alzera. That's when we put things together and figured out that he found the same thing we did at Roswell."

She got up and went to the bar. The bartender poured her another white wine, pulled a beer out of the cooler, and held it up to me. I held up my Coke and pointed at the glass. She slid back into the booth, took a delicate sip, and placed the Coke and an iced glass in front of me.

Refocusing, I asked, "I'm still missing something here. You're saying Charlie found another site in Mexico?"

"Not yet, but he's close. After we found one of the pieces from the original strike near Djibouti, we started plotting the others. As soon as Charlie realized what you found, he notified LaRouche and me of the co-ordinates. We suspected there was something near here. That's why we had you and Charlie and TJ assigned to Guam."

"You had us assigned here?" I started to ask.

Before I could finish, she continued, "Then, we had the entry point into the atmosphere and three solid strike co-ordinates. The rest was just computer muscle to locate the fourth site."

I got up and went to the bar. I grabbed a bowl of peanuts. It wasn't what I wanted, but I needed some time to assimilate. The beer continued to sit on the table, seducing me.

"So, how does all this connect Hawknose to Hanna's murder?" I asked as I sat back down.

"Well," she said, raising a fingertip to her lips and nodding, "what you told me about TJ finding those letters from GFI explains a lot. I hadn't been able to figure out that connection until now. This finally makes sense."

"So?" I asked.

"It means, Doctor, that Charlie and I know who killed Hanna and is behind all this, but right now I need to get you moved somewhere safe."

"Who killed her? How do you know?" I asked. She didn't answer.

Before she left the bar, she gave me the rest of Charlie's message and his plan to take down the murderer. Anger and dread swept over me. Everything I knew and believed, everyone I loved and cared about, was funneling into a path I couldn't envision. I wanted off this funhouse ride. Instead, I signaled the bartender. Then, I signaled him again.

Here's to little green men.

Arrest

"What do you mean you're not going to Cozumel with me? You promised." Emily stormed into the bathroom and slammed the door.

"That was before I talked to Kelly," I said through the door. "She and Charlie need my help to catch whoever killed Hanna," I said. I was nauseated, nursing a killer hangover, and feeling demoralized. Emily emerged from the bathroom, pushed past me, grabbed a bagel, and ignored her tea. She was pissed at me. I was pissed at me. The sunlight hurt my eyes and the room stank of used towels. The room service breakfast sat congealing—a puddle of poached eggs and burnt oatmeal. Kelly and two SUV's full of men in dark, double-breasted suits moved us to the Pacific Island Club. Despite the luxury accommodations, neither of us could enjoy the surroundings. I told Emily Kelly's story; she was not mollified.

"This is the same CIA bitch that got Charlie shot, and you almost killed in Djibouti. And now you trust her?" Emily shook her head.

Bitch? Whoa, you really are pissed.

"No. I think she's lying, but I trust Charlie. I have to do whatever I can to help him catch Hanna's killer," I said. "It'll only be a day." I continued to gather my clothing and stuff my overnight bag. "I'll meet you and the kids day after tomorrow in Mexico. You'll stay with my folks where you'll be safe while I finish this." I hugged her. "You'll be fine. There's a guard right across the hall, and I've arranged for Angel to fly with you to Mexico. You can't be safer than that."

"It's not me I'm worried about." She pulled me closer.

"Kelly has people watching me, and I've got extra protection." I stepped back and patted the shoulder holster with the gun Charlie had sent. She flinched. I hoped I wouldn't need to use it—I'd never fired an automatic. On TV, the actor pulls the top and starts shooting. I doubted it was that easy. Despite the anticipated heat, I pulled a light windbreaker over my T-shirt and firearm. I'd finish getting ready later.

"Do you have to go in? You're supposed to be on leave. Please," she pleaded, "I need you. I'm afraid to stay here without you." She reached out and took my hand. "I couldn't live if something happened to you. Not after losing Sister."

I couldn't tell her everything; what I held back hurt more than any lie I could have ever told her. What I was going to do was cruel, but I loved her too much; I had no choice. Neither Christian nor religious, I felt like Jesus heading for Gethsemane—knowing the future.

At morning report, the Skipper sat at the head of the table, waiting. The others nodded in my direction as I entered. The mood was somber. "I didn't expect to see you today. You don't need to be here." I poured a cup of coffee and took my usual seat. I was surprised to see TJ sitting in Hawknose's seat.

"So," I asked him, "are you our next executive officer, now that Hawknose has—"

"It's just temporary." I noticed he was drinking coffee from a new mug with 'XO' printed on the side.

The weight of my sidearm made me feel lopsided. I hoped nobody would see that I was packing, but morning report continued as if nothing had happened. Patient statistics, operations scheduled, supply, and budget issues all blended.

"Commander Matthews," said the Skipper. "Do you concur?"

"Sure. I mean yes, Sir. Whatever you say, Sir."

Whatever. By now, Kelly has Emily safely on a plane to Honolulu. I just want to get this over with.

As things wound down, a corpsman knocked and entered. The Skipper frowned and furrowed his eyebrows as he read the note. I began to sweat and wished I could shed my windbreaker.

"Dr. Matthews, Lieutenant Frisk needs to talk to you. He's at your house." He made a dismissed motion. "Come back and see me when you're done, please." He stopped and looked at me. "Jake . . . I," he looked around uncomfortably, and then turned back to his agenda. TJ followed me out the door.

"What's this all about?" TJ asked as we pulled into the driveway of my house.

"I don't know. But you didn't need to come. I can take care of this."

But TJ *did* need to come; I needed him here. I would have skipped morning report, but I knew TJ would be there.

Three military police cars sat at the street. I could see MPs scouring the edge of the jungle behind my yard. The front door gaped open. Frisk walked out to meet me.

"What's he doing here?" Frisk pointed his chin at TJ.

"I'm here to be his witness," was TJ's response. He popped the cigar out of his mouth and invaded Frisk's personal space. His posture was a clear message that Frisk would not dismiss him. Frisk held his stare.

"Well, that's fine, I suppose." Frisk, scowling, turned toward me. "I need Dr. Matthews to look around inside and tell me if anything is missing." He started toward the front door.

"What do you mean missing?" I asked.

"Your house was broken into last night. Someone was looking for something. I need for you to see if they found it." I wondered what he meant—did *he* actually know about Blue Death, or just following the script?

"What do you think they were looking for?" TJ asked Frisk as he tried to push his way past the Lieutenant into my house.

Frisk held his hand up, not touching TJ, but clearly barring the way. "Why do you think there was more than one person?" Frisk was standing his ground with TJ.

"They? He? She? I'm just guessing. Who do *you* think is responsible?" asked TJ.

Frisk ignored him and stood aside just enough to let me enter first.

The night of the earthquake, I had come home to chaos, but today the effects were more subtle, more personally violating. Furniture moved out of place, doors and drawers opened, not fully closed. Papers and files on my desk rearranged. Books stacked wrong in the bookshelves. In the middle of the floor was Tripod's collar. That's when it hit me.

"Where's my dog? Did you let him out?" I picked up the collar and imagined the grime on the inside of the leather to be blood.

"No, Sir. The door was open, and I didn't see a dog when I arrived." Frisk turned to his crew. "Anybody see a dog?" He turned back to me. "What kind of dog do you have, Sir?"

"A three legged beagle," I answered as I ran out the door whistling and calling for him. As I approached the edge of the jungle, an MP stopped me. "Sorry Sir. You can't go in there. This is a crime scene." He placed himself in front of me.

"I need to find my dog. He's loose."

His perfect military posture slumped, and he looked down. "Was it a beagle, Sir?"

I looked over his shoulder into the jungle to a mound of brown, white, and black fur. And blood.

"Noooooooooo . . ." I picked up a coconut and threw it at the jungle. "No, please. Not Tripod. *Fuck you, god.*" TJ's iron grip on my arm brought me back to reality. He didn't say a thing as he led me indoors.

Back in the living room, I slumped onto the couch and stole a glance at my aquarium. Leo the lionfish was looking back at me as he continued his guard duty. The remaining blue globes were well hidden in the sand and coral decorations. Whoever had ransacked my place hadn't thought to search the aquarium. Or stick his hand into the water with a poisonous fish.

Good boy. I'll feed you an extra goldfish for doing such a terrific job.

"I need to know what's missing," said Frisk.

"My dog is dead, and my sister-in-law is dead, isn't that enough?" I asked Frisk.

"Anything else?"

"Huh? No . . . I just don't know."

"Do you have any firearms, Doctor?" Suddenly the gun in my armpit felt like it would drag me to the ground. I wanted to pull it out and shoot something—anything. Instead, I froze and wondered if he could see what must have been a bulge as big as Brooklyn.

"I have my father's old .22 target pistol, but that's all. I already told you about that."

"Check and see if it's here, please." He followed me into the bedroom, where I opened the closet door. I took down the case where I kept the pistol and could feel that it was empty. "It appears to be missing," I said.

"When was the last time you saw your gun?" Frisk opened and examined the empty container.

"Let's see. I killed some tin cans about two months ago. Three or four times a year, I shoot off a box of rounds. Otherwise, I keep it here with the chamber removed. I don't carry it, so I don't have a permit."

"I know. I already checked. Any ammunition?"

"In my desk." I went over to my desk and found a partial box of shells on in the bottom drawer. "Here."

"Don't touch them," he yelled. I jerked back. He took a handkerchief from his pocket, carefully picked up the box, and placed it in a plastic bag.

"Do you have any other weapons? Any rifles or a shotgun?"

"I don't hunt." I considered telling him about Charlie's gun, but I didn't have a permit to carry. All I needed now was a weapons problem when I was trying to get out of here. As uncomfortable as the idea of carrying a gun made me; its physical presence remained comforting.

"What is this all about, Lieutenant?" TJ was standing next to me at parade rest. My friend was trying to provide protection in the way he understood best—intimidation. It wasn't working.

"What is this about?" The Lieutenant pointed at me. "It's about time the good doctor here quits lying to me."

"What are you talking about?" I asked. My mind remained on Tripod—dead in the jungle.

"Where were you the morning Commander Hawke checked out of the hospital and disappeared? The morning she was killed."

I pulled myself back and thought about it for a heartbeat. "I was at the hospital. I did rounds. I went to Hilltop Hospital to do some research."

"Can anybody verify you were at Hilltop that morning?"

"Probably not. Maybe the medical records clerk? Why, do I need an alibi?" I took a deep breath.

"Where were *you* that morning, Lieutenant?" TJ asked. Frisk glared at him. "Or that guy pawing through the underwear drawer?" An enlisted MP looked up from his search and blushed.

"I don't care about him. I want to know where Dr. Matthews was the morning Commander Hawke died."

"I told you where I was," I said.

"So, you really can't verify your whereabouts that morning, and you still can't explain why a letter threatening Commander Hawke came from your office and had only *your* fingerprints on it." He waited.

TJ moved in closer. "He explained that already. Clearly, someone with access to his office broke in and used his computer. Maybe Commander Hawke broke into his office and wrote them herself."

Frisk nodded and then said, "Okay. Then how do you explain your DNA on the seals of all the envelopes?" The world stopped, and in that moment I knew it was true. Kelly was right. I knew who killed Hanna and the others.

"My DNA? I can't explain that. I just know I didn't lick those envelopes, so the lab must be wrong. I had no reason to write those letters to myself."

"Can you explain how your fingerprints are all over a shotgun we found thrown in the jungle near the body of Carlos Santos? You told me you didn't own a shotgun."

Oh, shit. I forgot all about Ramón's gun in the closet.

TJ hadn't. "It belongs to Ramón Sanchez. Master Chief Albright confiscated it from him the night of the earthquake and stored it here."

"Lieutenant Commander Justis is right. I just forgot all about that. It should be in the front hall closet where he left it."

"It's not, I already checked," said Frisk.

TJ said, "So someone took it too? So what? What are you suggesting? Do you really think Dr. Matthews killed Carlos? That's crazy. He had no reason."

"Unless he saw something he shouldn't have?" Frisk turned to me. "Like you with Mrs. Matthews and Lieutenant Sanders that night, and you killed him to shut him up? Kinda cozy, with the three of you living together. What's it like to do twins, Doc?" He smirked just before I slammed him against the wall.

"That's enough!" TJ bellowed, stepping between us. "If you think Dr. Matthews is responsible for killing Carlos, you'd better arrest him. But I'll tell you this," he almost poked Frisk in the eye with the cigar, "you'd better be damn sure, or I'll make it my mission in life to ensure that you regret that decision."

Frisk stood his ground. "Not only do I have evidence that Carlos Santos was killed by a shotgun in Dr. Matthew's possession, with his fingerprints all over it, I also know that both Commander Hawke and Lieutenant Sanders were killed with a .22 caliber handgun we've recovered. Fingerprints and ballistics will prove it to be your gun, Sir."

That's when I knew what I had to do. I had been set-up by a master.

Do I trust Charlie? More importantly, do I trust Kelly? Do I even have a choice anymore?

"You have the right to remain silent . . ." Frisk was reaching behind his back for handcuffs. I looked at TJ and wondered what he would do in the next five seconds.

You're a key player right now, even though you don't know it. Don't be a fucking hero—please.

I backed away from Frisk. "If you arrest me, my wife will be dead before anyone can stop it. I can't let that happen." Surprise registered in Frisk's eyes when he saw the automatic pointed at his head. He blinked. He blinked again.

"Bones? What the hell are you doing? Where did you get that?" TJ backed away from both the door and me.

Good boy. Don't get dumb now.

I waved the gun at him. "I didn't kill anybody. You know it and so does he. I've been set up, and if I'm locked up until this is sorted out, someone will get . . ." I stopped myself before revealing that I knew someone tossed the place to find the Blue Death. I shook my head. "Can't allow that to happen."

Frisk slowly raised his hands and held them palms out in front of him. "Don't do this, Sir."

I turned and ran out the door. My life and all my choices had funneled to this one desperate act. If I was wrong, everything precious to me was lost. I ran blindly, not certain where I was going. I had no options left.

"He's running!" "Halt!" "Look out!" "Don't!" "Watch it, he's armed!" "Freeze!" "On the ground—do it now!" The cacophony closed in from all sides. My vision tunneled.

I felt the thud at the same moment I heard the shot. A second explosion of pain and sound occurred moments before the ground came up to meet my face. I couldn't breathe, and I felt a dull ache between my shoulder blades. I rolled onto my back but couldn't get up.

"I got him. I got him." The voice came to me from a great distance.

"Bones? Bones? You're okay. You're going to be fine. I'm right here."

I strained to see who was talking. The blue sky was now gray and overcast. *Funny, I don't remember them saying it was going to rain? TJ? You look funny. Your face is all bent and melting. What are you doing here? It's getting dark. I'm cold.*

Headline News

The Pacific Daily News—Special Addition
Multiple Murder Suspect Killed in Police Shootout
By Anne Reyes, Staff Reporter
Police and military sources confirmed the death of Dr. Jake Matthews, following a shootout at Matthews' home on Turner Road. Police arrived to serve an arrest warrant and shot Matthews as he attempted to flee. Matthews was a person of interest in the death of three local residents.
Naval Investigator, Lieutenant Mark Frisk said: "We are still looking into the connection between Commander Matthews and the shooting victims."
See related stories of the murders in the local event section.

PART 3- COZUMEL

<u>The Set-Up</u>

"Hey sailor, buy a lassie a beer?" Kelly's auburn curls glowed in the Caribbean sunset. She eased into a chair at a patio table and gazed north across the bay toward Playa Del Carmen. The main plaza in San Juan, Cozumel was quiet this evening, the last cruise ship preparing to depart. The waiter was busy turning over the beer for cheap prices signs. He came over and explained that the higher price was only for tourists from the cruise ships.

"That was an impressive memorial service they held for Dr. Matthews. Most of the command, the entire Island League, and hundreds of locals all attended. Both Charlie and TJ gave stirring eulogies—not a dry eye in the crowd. It was too bad Emily and the children couldn't be there—they would have appreciated it."

Her dinner companion turned to watch the sunset. "They are safe until this affair is resolved."

Kelly threw down a shot of José Cuervo tequila. She washed it down with a beer and looked for the waiter to refill both. The scent of fried fish wafted in from a local street vendor pushing his cart through the plaza.

The sun blinked below the horizon as streetlights encroached on the evening darkness. Most of the local shops were reopening for the evening. Siesta complete, it was time to wheel and deal, or drink tequila—depending on how many tourists wandered past.

Kelly arched her back, stretching stiff muscles and said, "I spoke with the owner of Dive Paradise today, and she has an available boat. We'll use the *Atlantis*, which at forty foot is large enough for what we need to do. Charlie located the site. He has GPS co-ordinates, so we should be ready. LaRouche met with TJ back on Guam two days ago, and brought him up to speed about finding the fourth Roswell site."

"So he knows about the alien DNA and the four crash sites?" The companion broke the seal on a bottle of water and drank. Kelly nodded.

A young couple at the next table quit talking and pretended not to eavesdrop. They both glanced at Kelly, and then quickly looked away.

"Excuse me a moment," Kelly said. Outfitted in a pale gray tailored pantsuit, a low-cut cream silk blouse with a single strand of pearls, and stilettos, she stood out from the throngs of tourists in shorts and flip-flops. She smelled of vanilla. She walked to the young couple's table and leaned over to whisper to them. They looked at each other and left without finishing their dinner. Kelly threw some pesos on their table.

"Told them there are two-for-one margaritas at Señor Frog's, and that was a better deal than getting a bullet in a kneecap," she said with a poker face.

She sat back down and looked across the plaza. A four-story white cruise ship pulled anchor and carried thousands of tourists into sunset travel oblivion. She signaled for the local cigar merchant and lit up a Cuban Cohiba.

She continued, "TJ's terribly excited to be part of the group making what he thinks will be a historic dive. He's even promising to give the Dr. Matthews foundation all the credit for finding the first evidence of extra-terrestrial life. He even went so far as to suggest creating a memorial fund for pregnancy research." She smiled. "I think that's sweet." She blew three smoke rings. "Too bad he won't be around to enjoy it."

The waiter returned with another round of Cuervo and bowls of Sopa de Tortilla, the restaurant's world famous dish. The steam carried an exotic aroma of chilies and spice. He waited to see if anything else was required. Kelly dismissed him with a dazzling smile that hinted at unimagined pleasures. Her cell phone rang, interrupting the quiet.

"Yes. Yes. Tomorrow before dawn, latest. You have the special gear I requested? Okay, the tank will have a new label on it. Good. Thank you. See you in the morning then." Kelly smiled as she hung up.

"It's all set," she said. "LaRouche destroyed the Djibouti site just after Alzera died, and I'm sad to say my namesake reef is no more. A few hundred pounds of thermite will do a phenomenal job of vaporizing coral. Good news though—they were able to catch Auraka and several Aurakettes and transplant them to a new place where they will be protected. Tomorrow a meteor fragment several kilometers from here will cease to exist. Maybe then, we will end this nightmare." She finished her meal in silence and rose to leave.

"What if blowing up the reef spreads the virus?" The guest tasted the Sopa.

"Seems to have a limited life span and the further from the source the more dilute it is. Both Djibouti and Guam were within a mile or two of the actual source. This site is farther out with currents running away from the shore, so we should be okay," answered Kelly.

Kelly threw down the last of her tequila and said, "Be on the boat before dawn; the lower berth is secured. I'll meet you there. He can't know we're on board." She blew an air kiss and disappeared into the Cuban cigar shop, where she began arguing with the merchant and pointing at his wares. The waiter collected the tab and a generous tip. "Muchas Gracias, Señor."

Last Dive

Dawn was an hour distant when the *Atlantis*, pride of the Dive Paradise fleet, arrived at the Hotel Barracuda. She rocked gently against her boat fenders; exhaust gas bubbling into the turquoise ocean. A seagull landed on the sundeck and poked about for a morsel of fish. The chill air smelled of dead fish and ocean.

A dark skinned man, decorated in tattoos, and clad only in cut-offs, loaded scuba tanks with lime green labels. The labels indicated $HelOx_2$, a particular gas mixture of helium and oxygen that allows dives at greater depths for longer times with fewer decompression problems. One tank was newer, its label lacking wear and tear. More gear and coolers followed. The last items loaded were a large Plexiglas aquarium and some plastic gallon jugs. After a final check of the equipment, Angel Sanchez moved onto the flying bridge and prepared the *Atlantis* to depart.

The *Atlantis*, accommodates ten to fifteen scuba divers. The aft deck was wide and featured a row of seats on each gunnel. A flat dive platform extended off the aft rail. A small cabin and storage locker below decks and a flying bridge equipped with the latest navigational and safety gear completed her appointments. Twin diesel engines gave her the ability to navigate tricky currents off the shore of Cozumel.

Slowly, the small fishing village began to awaken. At dawn, the Mexican naval base next door raised the national flag to the strains of their anthem played by a mediocre brass band. Pale sunlight lit the pink stucco of the Hotel Barracuda. As the closing off-key notes died, Charlie and TJ crossed the gangplank and loaded their personal dive gear aboard.

"Thanks for bringing Angel with you to help. He can certainly handle the boat and equipment for our dive," Charlie said as he moved aft to release the lines.

TJ said, "After LaRouche told me what you found and asked for my help, I figured we would like to keep this secret. Angel can be trusted. Besides, he works cheap." TJ laughed. "Nice boat Kelly found for us." He looked around the craft, noting the diving platform, safety equipment, and accommodations.

"Kelly said she'll see us back at the hotel when we return. She'll do the debriefing herself." Charlie cast off the bowline. "Okay, Angel, let's move out."

The twin engines rumbled to life, and the *Atlantis* moved away from the dock and into the channel. TJ poured a cup of coffee for himself and settled onto a bench. His sea-salt encrusted cigar alternated with his coffee cup for attention from his lips. Charlie completed his inspection and began setting up the gear.

"How deep did you say we're going?" TJ asked him. "And what did you find down there?"

Below deck, a speaker relayed their conversation.

"The site's about 150 feet deep, so we'll be breathing mixed gases. I tagged the site with a float, but it's the only thing around, so it will be easy to find. And we have GPS to within a few feet." He continued to attach a regulator to one of the lime labeled tanks.

"And you're sure there are Blue Death globes on site?" asked TJ. "Did you find any?"

"I saw some buried under a ledge, but couldn't get to them. Doesn't matter though—our job is just to document and then set the thermite charges."

TJ fixed his gaze on a distant point of the horizon. The early light ignited the gold flecks in his otherwise obsidian eyes. "I know it has to be done," he said, shaking his head in resignation, "but it seems a shame to destroy proof of life from another world. What if we can reach those globes? Shouldn't we keep them for research?"

"I'll gather a few just to test Dr. Cassidy's formula for destruction," said Charlie.

"You'd destroy them?" asked TJ.

"That's the idea, isn't it? We all agreed that this has too great a potential for a disaster in the wrong hands. Alzera wanted to terrorize the US, Hawknose wanted to get rich, and good people have died for it. Jake and Hanna would want it. We owe them that," Charlie said. A silence descended as they realized their loss.

"I know, but it just doesn't seem right somehow."

"We all know what we've found," said Charlie, "and that counts for something. Jake and Cassidy documented the data. We won't lose the knowledge, just the threat. Every person who has knowledge of Blue Death agrees it's too dangerous to keep—or is dead."

"But . . ."

"But nothing. Humans thought they had eradicated smallpox, but scientific curiosity and political demands kept that demon in a freezer for "future study." Charlie made the quote signs. "Now smallpox is a weapon of mass destruction. Imagine something this deadly getting in the hands of a modern day Josef Mengele? Or some fundamentalist asshole? That knowledge dies here, and the world will be that much better for it. That's it. End of discussion."

TJ sighed in resignation. "I know you're right, but I wonder if we'll regret this."

Angel called down from the flying loft. "Twenty minutes to the site. Nobody anywhere around us."

The surrounding sea was empty. To the southwest was the tip of Cozumel—flat, dry, and brown in the distance. The Mexican coastline was beyond the horizon. As the *Atlantis* moved, the glassy calm began to break up into mild chop. By midday, the solar heated winds and currents would make the area impassable to a boat the size of the *Atlantis*. Divers could only venture underwater during a narrow time window.

Charlie and TJ completed their pre-dive check. The twenty minutes to the dive site went quickly while both divers drank coffee and discussed their dive plan.

Charlie said, "The site is a flat, sandy field that extends several hundred yards in all directions, so we'll see it as soon as we enter the water. There is one large object. Looks like a Volkswagen bus sitting there, covered in sand and silt. Nothing is growing on or around it. Under the silt, you'll see the same shiny substance you found at Kelly's Reef."

"So the site is barren? I would have expected incredible life similar to Kelly's Reef. Why the difference?" asked TJ.

"I have no idea, but LaRouche and Cassidy think that Kelly's Reef was exposed to Blue Death for a year or two before the quake on Guam. Something leaked during that period, and Kelly's Reef grew exponentially. That's why she wasn't on any charts when we found her."

TJ considered this information. "That makes sense, I guess, and why this site is barren, but is this a meteorite or something else?"

"You tell me. I've never heard of a shiny meteor, have you? Especially if it's been here since 1947," said Charlie.

"We're there," shouted Angel. "I'll set up so you can drift onto the site. Then, I'll be down current to pick you up. Okay?" He raised a Corona beer in salute, and took a deep swallow.

Charlie gave him a thumbs-up and looked at TJ. "Once we're down, we'll have about 20 minutes to film the area and set the thermite charges. I've tested the timed igniters at this depth, and they work. We'll have about thirty minutes to ascend and leave the area. Okay, ready?" Thumbs-up.

The channel between Isla Cozumel and the mainland is a world class, sport diving destination. Pristine reefs draw thousands of tourists each year drift with the currents that run from south to north. Beyond Punta Sur, the southernmost point, tides and currents become unpredictable. Angel maneuvered the *Atlantis* sideways against an increasingly strong current. Charlie and TJ broke the silence as they rolled into the water.

The two descended through crystal water and current to the bottom. Charlie checked his depth gauge and GPS. He pointed toward an indistinct lump a few yards distant. A stingray lifted off the bottom as they approached.

Right on time, a fluorescent orange float appeared twenty yards off the starboard bow. Angel circled the *Atlantis* and the divers came aboard. Charlie toweled off and then chugged water from a jug. He threw a red nylon catch bag onto the deck, opened it, and pulled out three bright blue, marble sized globes.

TJ had trouble climbing up from the dive platform. He stumbled to a bench and sat awkwardly. "Did you see that? That wasn't some meteor fragment, for cripes sake. That was . . . that was . . ." He paused and looked at Charlie. "That was . . . not natural. A meteor doesn't have hard smooth edges that are shiny like that. And when . . . when we lifted the side to get the globes it was only paper thin."

Charlie just nodded in acknowledgement, and proceeded to put the globes into the Plexiglas tank sitting on the bench opposite TJ. He reached over the gunnels with a bucket and added some seawater.

"We found a damn flying saucer. Can you believe it? A flying saucer? Do you know what this means?" TJ started to rise, but sat down heavily, his legs unable to contain his bulk upright. He fumbled with the straps on his BCD. "Hey, Angel," he shouted, "can you help me with my gear, please? What the hell is wrong with this latch?"

"You okay?" asked Charlie.

TJ took a swallow from a small brown medicine bottle he retrieved from his dive bag. "I don't know. Maybe I was a little too deep, a little too long. Feel kinda off, ya know." TJ continued to fumble with his straps as Charlie added bleach from one of the plastic jugs into the Plexiglas tank holding the globes.

Angel came down from the loft, looked at Charlie who nodded, and helped TJ out of his dive gear.

"Well, this is the end of it. Cassidy figured out that simple bleach and potassium chloride somehow opens the globes and destroys the virus. So here we go." Charlie opened another plastic jug and tilted the lip over the tank.

"*Don't!*" TJ stood up on shaky legs and backhanded the jug into the ocean. "I can't let you do that." He leaned back and grabbed the rail with his hand. The other hand reached into his dive bag and pulled out an automatic pistol. He pointed it at Charlie's head. "Stop," he whispered. Then he vomited onto the deck.

<u>Revealed</u>

One hundred yards off the stern of the *Atlantis*, the turquoise ocean boiled and spewed a column of seawater into the sky. The thermite Charlie set on the site had ignited; the final lost chunk of the 1947 Roswell spacecraft vaporized.

Charlie placidly looked at the gun TJ pointed at him. "You don't want to do this," was all he said.

"I can't let you destroy them. Proof of extraterrestrial life is too valuable to lose. Give them to me." TJ held out his hand.

"Take it easy. I'd tell you not to do something foolish, but it's too late for that." Charlie slowly reached into the tank and withdrew the blue globes. He looked over the railing at the surrounding ocean.

"Don't even think about it." TJ stuck out his hand. Charlie carefully placed them into TJ's palm and backed away. He kept his hands in clear sight, but his eyes never wavered.

TJ turned them over and held one up to the sunlight. "Amazing," he said. "They look just like the old cat's-eye marbles I played with as a kid. Is the blue streak the virus?"

Charlie continued to stare deadpan. "No, that's blue glass."

"What do you mean?"

"Just that, the blue tint is glass inside a cat's-eye marble."

"Bullshit. I saw you remove them from the spacecraft myself. Same as Jake found on Guam." Somehow, he had managed to find a cigar to chew.

"Okay, you got me. Those are real Blue Death globes, and the space ship isn't an old Volkswagen LaRouche and I painted black and planted there last week. You're too smart to fall for such an obvious scam." Charlie remained still, but a slight smile formed on his lips.

TJ put the blue globes in his dive bag and sat back down on the bench. He groaned and rubbed his temple with the butt of the gun. "I think you screwed up the HelOx$_2$ mix, and I'm getting a headache from it. Give me that emergency oxygen bottle. And don't get any ideas." He pointed to a dark green cylinder attached to the bulkhead—emergency O$_2$.

Charlie handed him the canister and TJ took several deep breaths through a clear plastic mask.

"So? What do we do now?" asked Charlie. "Are you going to kill me too?"

"Kill you? What are you talking about? I just can't let you destroy this— don't you see that? It's not about the money— GFI could make us rich enough to fund research in Jake's name if we wanted that. We could be world famous—the first humans to discover alien life on earth. It can't die here."

"And that's what was worth killing over? What about the others you killed to get this? Don't they count for anything?" Charlie hadn't moved, but the air around him was charged; his every muscle tensed and ready.

"I didn't kill anyone," said TJ.

"Bullshit, you killed Hawknose and dumped her in the ocean, so you'd get the discovery all to yourself." Charlie let his up-raised arms relax as TJ's aim wavered.

"But I'm the one who discovered she sold out to that genetics company. I know she'd been threatening Jake and his family ever since she arrived," TJ said.

Charlie backed against the gunnel and sat on one of the coolers. "So, you're telling me that Jake killed her? Why—because the psychopath threatened his family, so he shot her with his own gun?"

TJ groaned and pressed his palms into his eyes, then refocused the gun on Charlie. "He set her up. He wrote those letters to give himself an alibi. They had his fingerprints all over them and his DNA on the envelopes. Who else could have done that?"

"I can't believe Jake was behind all this." Charlie paused. "Water?" Charlie took a drink from the water jug and handed it to TJ.

"Set it down there, carefully," TJ said, pointing. He took two swallows and gagged, never taking his eyes off Charlie.

Charlie said, "You're lying. *You* set her up. You were close enough to Jake to get his DNA from his toothbrush or maybe his scuba mouthpiece. You had access to his office and printer. His fingerprints would have been all over his printer paper."

"And?" asked TJ.

"And, there was no way Hawknose could get that close to him. Someone closer had that access. You."

TJ took another drink of water and several breaths of the oxygen. He shook his head and groaned, then regained his composure enough to focus the weapon back at Charlie.

"You were close enough to pull this off too," TJ said.

Charlie lifted his hands again, in mock surrender. "Is that what you'll tell everyone when we get back? That I masterminded a plot to steal a bio-weapon, framed Jake for it, and killed a bunch of people to hide it? I suppose that might work, but you'd be better off just killing me." Charlie stretched his legs onto a cooler, leaned back, and interlaced his fingers behind his head.

Below deck, the two who had been watching and listening looked at each other and nodded in understanding.

TJ licked his lips and took another deep draft of water. Before he could lean over the rail, he vomited a second time onto his feet. "Oh shit, I'm bent." He sucked more oxygen, and wiped his face with his towel. He said, "We need to head in. I need to see a doctor and get to the decompression chamber. I'm sick."

Charlie looked up at him. "You killed the courier to get the samples. Only the five of us on the plane to Okinawa knew about Blue Death. You took out the courier."

TJ stared back at Charlie. "You're full of shit. Dweck and Kelly knew about the mission. LaRouche knew, and even told us someone was after us to get them. So did someone in the spook house. Somebody else obviously knew and took those samples."

"Full of shit. Full of shit," a parrot cackled. Both Charlie and TJ looked up to the flying bridge and saw Lucy perched on a railing. Angel looked down and grinned. Then he took another pull on his beer. "Sorry," he said. "Ramón wouldn't feed her while I was gone, so . . ." With a shrug, he turned back to the controls.

"I guess there were a lot of people who might have known about Blue Death—you, me, Kelly, Jake, Dweck, Vignalli," said Charlie. "Anyone could have arranged to kill the courier and snatch the sample. But tell me this—why was Vignalli killed? He didn't even know what Blue Death was. Tell me, why did Vignalli have to die?"

"I have no idea." TJ sank lower against the bulkhead. His usual ebony was a dusty gray. "We really need to quit trying to figure out this whole thing and get me ashore."

Charlie called up to the flying nest. "Hey Angel, take us out to point Bravo, okay?"

"Bravo," brayed Lucy. "Gimme a bravo and a beer, motherfucker."

Angel backhanded her off the rail onto the deck with a "Shut the fuck up, birdbrain."

The motors rumbled to life, and the *Atlantis* turned into the midmorning sun.

Charlie continued. "You had to kill him because he was the only connection between you, Hawknose, and the globes. You were all in the Boston area, and somehow he found out what you and Hawknose were up to. You killed him. Right?"

TJ raised his head and coughed. He wiped nasal mucus on the back of his hand and said. "So you think Hawke and the people from GFI killed Vignalli?"

"No, you killed him, or Hawknose killed him. Doesn't matter. You were working together." Charlie didn't move but looked directly into TJ's eyes.

"Fuck you. So what? Because I was in the area, you think I was somehow part of some great plot with Hawknose to kill Vignalli because he knew something? That is total bullshit, and you know it."

The two below deck continued to listen.

Charlie got up, poured coffee into a cup. He took a mouthful and spit it over the rail. "That's cold." He looked back at TJ, and it was clear he wasn't talking about the coffee temperature.

"You got this all wrong," TJ said, his voice cracking, shoulders sagging.

The *Atlantis* plowed through increasing chop as she headed away from the tip of Cozumel. The clear turquoise sea became angry gray. Gulls chasing the boat gave up their hope of cast-off scraps and headed back to shore. Contrails marked an otherwise clear sky.

Charlie stood, walked to TJ, and took the gun from his hand, setting it on the bench out of reach.

"I can understand," he said. "why Blue Death is so important and valuable. I can understand why someone would kill for it. I can understand that, I actually can. What I can't understand, is why you would kill my Hanna?" He waited. "I get that you fucked up and grabbed the wrong twin in the dark, but . . ."

"I . . ." Then TJ vomited for the third time. He crumpled to the deck and pulled his knees into a fetal position.

"Why did you kill her? That's all I want to know," Charlie said. "She was my life, the mother of my child, my soul— everything important to me. And you killed her. Why? Because you thought you were taking Emily and took Hanna by mistake? Then you killed her when you found out? Was that it?" Charlie grabbed TJ by his wetsuit. He hauled him onto the railing in a chokehold.

"You're crazy. I had nothing to do with that. I was at the other side of Guam that night. I couldn't have killed her. Please, Charlie. You have to trust me. I don't know where you're getting all this, but it's not true. Please, just get me to the chamber and we'll sort it all out."

I had been dead long enough. "But you *were* at my house that night," I said as I came up the steps from the below deck cabin.

TJ looked at me as if he'd seen a ghost, which he had. His gray went to chalk and his mouth opened, gasping for air.

Charlie released him, and he scrambled across the bench. He grabbed the gun and fired at me. The firing pin clicked. He tried again with the same result. He looked at the gun, then back at me, and screamed.

You're Dead

"You're dead. I saw Frisk shoot you. I saw them load you into an ambulance. I was at your funeral. You can't be . . ."

"You saw slugs hitting a bullet proof vest Charlie sent me. What you saw was a set-up, plus a little Hollywood magic blood. We had to get Emily safely off Guam, and I needed to die. That gave us time to set up this trip and get you here. I knew that dangling Blue Death would be bait you couldn't pass up."

"You set me up? Frisk didn't shoot you?" TJ looked shocked and confused. He looked at the weapon, opened the magazine and found it unloaded. He was drooling and gasping for breath. His eyes had a yellow cast.

"Of course not. Frisk never fell for your act, and he never believed I was a killer. Kelly contacted him with what she knew, and he went along with our plan. Gotta tell you though, even a wad-cutter fired at that range into a vest hurts like hell."

"I can't believe you're alive. Thank God," TJ said, trying to look relieved.

I shook my head and watched Lucy try to climb onto the railing. I put out my arm, and she climbed onto my shoulder and rubbed her beak against my ear. "Fuck you," she screeched, then made a loud fart noise. *My sentiments exactly, birdbrain.*

"You don't look like you feel well, my friend," I said to TJ. I looked into his clouded irises, and in that moment, I felt all the deaths at Kelly's World Famous Bar and Grill. I hurt for both Men in Black, Tony Vignalli, a nameless spook on a plane, and Ambassador Dweck. I even finally felt a modicum of regret for Alzera and his brood. I saw Hawknose in my face on all those occasions we battled, and almost mourned her too. I looked deeper into TJ's depthless black eyes and understood hate.

I understood the mindless hate Alzera had for the world. I understood road rage. I finally understood what it meant to hate without redemption.

"Why Hanna?" was all I could ask. I felt like my very being was sucking against the dry mouthpiece of an empty tank. I was drowning in a sea of hatred. I wasn't speaking to TJ—I was railing against god and his minions.

"Bones," TJ began.

"*DON'T*," I stopped him. "*EVER* call me that again. You will address me as Dr. Matthews or Sir, understand?" I walked up to him and slapped the cigar out of his mouth. "I hate those fucking things."

TJ tried to rise, but only succeeded in getting to his hands and knees. He looked up at me. "I don't know what you're thinking, but you're wrong."

"I'm bent." He had a wracking spasm of dry heaves. "I thought you were dead. I didn't know what I was doing. I'm dying; get me to the decompression chamber. We can resolve this." He rolled onto his side and held his head in both hands.

I felt the sympathy I would for a slug I caught nibbling my vegetable garden.

"I didn't kill anybody. Commander Hawke must have. You saw her letters. It was all about money to her. She hated you. She was the one." TJ was sweating profusely. He wiped his head with his towel.

The last listener made her move.

"Nice try, but that doesn't fly." We all turned to watch as Kelly came up the steps onto the deck. "Commander Hawke worked for me, asshole. She knew what you were up to all along."

Secret Agent Hawk

The chop increased as the *Atlantis* moved farther south. Spray misted over the rails as the mid-morning temperature rose. A swarm of flying fish broke the surface and coasted across the bow, the sun reflecting off pearlescent wings. Kelly pointed to them and said, "Wish I could fly like that, don't you?" She directed the comment to no one specific.

TJ looked stunned. "Kelly? Why are you here? We're supposed to meet at the hotel this afternoon. I was going to bring you the globes. Tell them." He looked expectant.

"Tell them what?" asked Kelly. "That I suspected you would do whatever you could to get your hands on the prize? That I suspected you were behind the missing samples? That you killed Vignalli, Dweck, and set up Commander Hawke to take the fall? That you killed Hanna because you thought she was her sister?"

"What are you saying? We needed to protect the globes. That was your goal, wasn't it? You said I couldn't let Charlie destroy them. You said we'd make sure they get into the right hands where they'd be safe."

Charlie stared at him. "It almost worked, TJ. You had me believing that Hawknose knew about the virus and killed to get rich from it. The letters in her file cabinet, which by the way, I confiscated, were a nice touch."

TJ pulled his knees into his chest and groaned. He was panting.

I looked at him and said, "Too bad you assumed I wouldn't check on them. Kelly told me they were fakes. I tried to contact their researcher. Seems he is still the VP by title, but has been in a nursing home with Alzheimer's for several years. He couldn't have written those letters."

"You went directly to the third file drawer the night we broke into Hawknose's office. You wouldn't have known about them unless you planted them. You almost had me fooled. I genuinely thought Hawknose was behind this whole thing until I discovered she was dead before you kidnapped Hanna. You didn't expect her body to wash ashore and be discovered so quickly, did you? A fickle tide screwed you, didn't it?" I stared into his eyes as they flicked from face to face, trying to find help, trying to find a lie that would work. There was none. Even Lucy stared back, silent for a change.

"You hated her more than anybody did. You were gone the morning she disappeared," TJ pleaded. "Your gun killed her—your fingerprints were all over it. Maybe you killed her—I didn't." TJ pointed his finger at me. I saw the tremor.

"You're right," I countered. "I had every reason to hate the bitch—she made all our lives miserable. Frankly, I'm not sorry she's gone. But she didn't kill Hanna—Hawknose was already dead when you killed Hanna." I looked at Kelly and gave her the cue.

Kelly leaned toward TJ and gave him her lethal smile. "As I said, she worked for me, not GFI. I recruited her while she was at Tufts; as soon as Alzera's original samples went missing. I figured they would show up somewhere in the MIT system and needed someone in the Boston area to be on the lookout." Kelly had moved to the stern and leaned onto the rail next to TJ.

Charlie, who had been watching TJ, asked Kelly, "Why Boston?" He was playing the shill in this drama.

"Matter of elimination. The courier I figured for dead because he was in possession of Blue Death. Dweck was still in Djibouti, so it wasn't likely that he took them. You had a serious gunshot wound to your leg. Dr. Matthews was involved in your care right up to the minute he flew to his training program in California." Kelly looked at TJ, but continued to talk to Charlie. "That only left Petty Officer Vignalli and TJ who knew. Both had the opportunity. Either could have taken out the courier and stolen the samples."

Charlie completed the thought, "And they were both heading to the Boston area for their training after Djibouti. Right?"

"Exactly." Kelly looked up as a persistent seagull coasted by, considered landing, and then changed its mind; a feces bomb missed by a good foot.

Kelly continued, "I recruited Commander Hawke specifically to watch for Blue Death in the area and then to monitor TJ when he transferred to Guam. I knew there was more near Guam." She paused and shook her head.

She said to TJ, "Boy, did I ever pick the wrong person. Stupid cunt couldn't do anything right. She knew you were somehow involved. The stupid shit actually told you about it, didn't she?"

"Fuck you—I don't have any idea what you're talking about."

"Tell me?" she asked, her hand caressing his ear. "Did you kill Vignalli to shut him up or was he just a loose end that would screw up your partnership with Hawknose?"

"This is insane," said TJ. He was rubbing his elbows and knees. "I've got the bends. I need to get to a chamber." We ignored his plea.

Kelly continued, "Commander Hawke contacted me after Vignalli was killed and said you'd been asking questions about him and the samples."

"You have that all wrong," TJ said to Kelly. "She came to me when she arrived on Guam and said she was working for you as a consultant to the CIA. I believed her. I'd never set eyes on her before she arrived, I swear. I didn't even know Vignalli was dead until Captain LaRouche told us."

"Right," I said.

"Kelly, please tell him the truth," TJ pleaded.

Kelly shook her head. "The truth? The truth is you've known all along about Blue Death, worked with Hawke until she became a liability and killed her, and everyone who stood in your way. Truth?"

Charlie stood up and brought the scuba tank TJ had been using to him. The new lime-green label distinguished it. "You're not bent. I mixed this tank myself. It has the same mixture of oxygen and helium I was breathing." He grinned. "And enough carbon monoxide to make sure you'll be dead in about two hours."

"What? Why?"

"For Hanna, you filthy piece of shit. I'm going to make sure you suffer before you die," said Charlie. "And when your body washes ashore, you'll just be another diving statistic, if that shark doesn't get you first." A dorsal fin cut the surface off the bow. I figured it was a dolphin looking for a playmate, but the drama—ah, the drama.

"I didn't kill her." TJ's head sank onto his chest, and he shuttered.

I said, "You fucked up, TJ. I could almost believe the rest of this crap, but you made one fatal error."

"What?" he asked.

"The night Hanna was killed. Remember? You were at the Air Force warehouse and received an emergency call to find me. That call came from my office."

"I couldn't have called you, I wasn't there."

"No, but you pre-programmed a recorded call to the house and the front desk of the hospital. I don't know how you did it, but you've got the resources to make that happen."

TJ held his head in both hands. "I didn't," was all he could say. Then he looked up. "Where are we going? The harbor is the other direction. Angel," he shouted, "turn us around—you're going the wrong direction!"

Kelly said, "We can't do that. There isn't time to get you to a decompression chamber in an oxygen environment to offset the carbon monoxide. You're a dead man." She smiled, but now the smile was evil. I remembered that look just before she shot a terrorist in the forehead.

313

Charlie said, "I'll give you a chance, which is more than you gave anyone else. I'm going to throw you overboard; you manage to swim the two miles ashore and you might just make it. Fifty-fifty chance. Best you're going to get, I'm afraid."

"Charlie, I *didn't* kill Hanna. This is all wrong." He began to weep.

"I can't let you do this." TJ picked up his gun again and pointed it at me. "*Angel.* Turn us around now and get me ashore." The gun shook in his hand. He sagged as he realized it was still empty.

I held out my hand and showed him the bullets. "Kelly warned me that you'd be armed, so I took the trouble of searching your dive bag and emptying that thing while you were diving." He squeezed the trigger with a dull click just to make sure, and then threw it at me.

I picked up the weapon, reloaded it, jacked a round in the chamber, and stowed it in the waistband of my cut-offs.

"*Angel. Now!*" TJ shouted. "Hurry up, do what I told you."

Angel appeared behind us brandishing a lethal looking automatic rifle. I was impressed enough with his attitude and steady aim to raise my hands. So did Charlie and Kelly.

TJ managed a grin. "Thank you, Angel. The rest of your money is waiting at the hotel when we get back." TJ looked back at me. "Always keep an ace up your sleeve, right Ace? You knew Angel worked for me. Did you think his being here was an accident?"

Angel looked at me with flat, dark eyes. There was no emotion showing.

"Fuck this shit," squawked Lucy and flew to the top of the mast.

"Angel, whatever you're thinking we can work this out," I said.

"Shoot them. Do it. Do it now," screamed TJ

"Like you shot Carlos?" Angel turned and fired at TJ. A red spray splattered the wetsuit at his thigh, and he crumpled forward with a yelp. "He didn't get no chance. These haoles want to give you a chance to swim and possibly live. I give you a chance, just like you give Carlos."

Angel set down the gun, grabbed TJ, and pushed him over the railing. "Suck on this," he said and flipped TJ the bird. TJ thrashed in the water as the current pulled him away.

"Thank you, Mr. Sanchez. Well done," said Kelly. "I knew I could count on you. I'll make sure Washington knows."

"Thank you, Ma'am," he said. All pretense of an island dialect vanished.

I looked at Kelly and asked, "Do you mean he was part of this set-up too?"

"Of course, I always keep an ace up my sleeve and a hit-man in hiding." She looked up at Lucy on the mast and wiggled her finger. Lucy immediately flew down and perched on her shoulder, cooing. She rocked from foot to foot and said, "Kelly is beautiful." Angel looked embarrassed and just shrugged.

"Let's head in." Kelly looked at Charlie. "That was remarkably smooth, the way you looked like you were actually destroying them. We knew that would make TJ do something desperate, and it worked. He couldn't stand the idea we might actually destroy the greatest discovery in history. Where did he put them?"

Charlie reached into TJ's bag and pulled the globes out. He handed them to Kelly. She rolled them in her hand and frowned.

"I thought they would be soft somehow. These look like ordinary glass marbles."

"They are," said Charlie, and shrugged. "I wasn't lying to TJ about that. And that flying saucer we found? That really was an old VW we painted black and sank out here. All just smoke and mirrors to deceive him."

"Well, you fooled me too. Good work." She smiled. "I assume you have the real thing with you? I need to get them back." She held out her hand. The expectation in her eyes faded to confusion when Charlie reached into his dive bag and pulled out his gun.

"Sorry, Sweetheart. They belong to Jake and me. You didn't really think *you'd* ever get them, did you?

Cozumel

Beyond the leeward end of Cozumel, the morning breeze became wind. The *Atlantis* rocked with the waves. I felt the sun beating on my shirtless back as I watched Kelly. Despite the heat, I could smell a hint of Irish Spring soap on her. I looked over her shoulder and spotted TJ. He was floating about 50 yards off the port bow, a large orange diver's sausage visible in the water next to him.

"What are you talking about?" she asked Charlie and me. "We agreed that once we took care of Lieutenant Commander Justis, you would turn over the last of Blue Death to the government for study."

"Sorry," I said, "but I don't trust the government with this and I don't trust you to get it to them."

"That's ridiculous. If you'd feel better, let me get them to Cassidy. You trust him don't you?" An explosion of sea mist erupted over the bow as the *Atlantis* slammed into a wave. Angel had returned to the wheelhouse and worked to keep the craft on station and into the wind.

"Oh, I trust Cassidy alright," I said. "I trust he destroyed all the samples I sent him."

Charlie said, "And the last of the globes I brought up from the real site were destroyed. I tested Cassidy's formula for doing just that, and it works. There is no Blue Death anymore. This site is a phony LaRouche and I rigged."

Kelly frowned. She turned to me and said, "But you have the other samples from your find on Guam. I know you do."

"And that's your problem isn't it. You *know* I have some stashed away, and you can't find them. That's why you ransacked my home—you were looking for them. That's why you took Hanna—you thought you had my wife, and she'd know where I hid them. You figured she'd talk, or I'd turn them over to you to get her back. Then, when you discovered that you snatched the wrong twin, you had an even bigger

316

problem. You had to get me away from the house, so you could search it. Breaking into my office to use my computer would have been simple for you. So was calling TJ the night of the kidnapping to convince me to come to the hospital."

"We both know you killed my Hanna," Charlie said as he flipped the safety off his gun. "You're the one who set TJ up. You arranged for all of this. You went along with me about using carbon monoxide to poison him. Easier to explain than a bullet, wasn't it?"

I looked at Charlie, who just nodded. I looked back at Kelly. Her green eyes flared.

"How did you find Emily and me at the Royal Pagoda Hotel, before you moved us to the Pacific Island Club?" I asked

Kelly shook her head with a dismissive look. "I explained that to you. You used your credit card when you checked in. Did you think the CIA couldn't find you?"

"You fucked up. I paid *cash* for the room that day. Small detail I didn't think about at the time."

"So what? Cash . . . credit card? I was able to find you, wasn't I? What—you think I wasn't watching you? That's why I hired Hawke and Angel."

Before Charlie or I could react, Kelly stepped behind me, grabbing TJ's gun from my waistband. My temple exploded in pain as she pressed the muzzle into my ear. She was off balance, holding me over my shoulder and across my chest. A quick step to the side, a hip, an arm lock, and she would be on the deck, disarmed. It was all I could do not to allow my martial arts training to kick in.

"Give me my samples," was all she said. I saw her lock Charlie with a death stare. "And drop that gun."

Charlie stood carefully and held his arms out, dropping his gun overboard. "After all we meant to each other; all the happy times in Pakistan and China? That weekend in Dublin? The pubic crabs in London? We've come to this?" His head bowed and shook. "Why Hanna? At least tell me that." He raised his head and stared into her eyes.

"The doc here was right. I missed the Intel that he was married to a twin, and I got the wrong one. When I realized she was the sister and that she didn't know where the other globes were, I had no options. She fought me and tried to get away."

Kelly's eyes glazed as she looked into history. "She didn't suffer. One quick shot to the back of her head. I truly am sorry, Charlie. If that means much." Kelly shrugged. The nonchalance of that shrug made me want to kill her.

"It means that you are dead." He spoke in a whisper wrapped with rage.

Kelly's smile was brilliant. "You first," she said, and shot him in the chest as she knocked me to the deck. Charlie fell backward against the stern, a large red blossom on the front of his wetsuit. He coughed once and collapsed onto the deck.

She pushed away from me, and then returned her aim. "Sorry doc. This is too valuable. *Now*, where are they?"

"They're gone. The three I had left I destroyed. I couldn't let this continue."

"Bullshit. You're a lousy liar." She aimed what looked like a cannon at my leg. "Do you have any idea how painful a bullet through the kneecap is?"

I cowered, pulling my knees against my chest. "Please don't. They're gone, honest." *Come on, come on, come on. Do it, bitch.*

She put both hands on her gun and took a perfect shooter stance. "You can tell me now, or when I'm done, I'll find the twin that knows. Think about your children. They're next."

"Kelly, please don't. I swear they're gone."

"Too bad then." She aimed at my kneecap and pulled the trigger.

Betrayal

The ringing in my ears was because of the silence. The wind had stilled. The seas had calmed. In the distant sky, a jet left a single contrail; it's roar too far away to hear. The empty click of Kelly's firing pin broke the silence. She looked at the gun in confusion.

"TJ's gun was loaded with blanks. You didn't think that I'd put live ammo in a gun that I let you take from me, did you? You weren't paying attention." I stepped toward her, my hand out. She stepped back and pulled the trigger on another empty round.

"But?" she said looking at Charlie as he stood up. He smiled at her and unzipped his wetsuit. Then he pulled the squib off and dangled it in front of her to see. It dripped fake blood on the deck.

"Hollywood magic. Same thing you had Jake use when Frisk shot him." He wiped the red stain off his chest and tasted it. "Strawberry, I think."

She turned to me and grinned. "Very good, Doctor. I'm impressed. You're not quite the fool I took you for, after all."

She tossed TJ's gun overboard and sat down on the bench. "Got a cigarette?" She arched her eyebrows.

"So what do we do now?" I asked. "Blue Death is gone . . ."

"We? We do nothing. You can't prove a thing, and The Company will never acknowledge this happened. So, I'm back to my ace in the hole." She looked behind her and called, "Angel. *Now.*"

Angel appeared with the same weapon I'd seen him use to shoot TJ. He pointed it at me and winked.

Kelly said, "Sorry, guys. It's been fun." She turned to Angel and nodded. He pulled the trigger.

Double Cross

Lucy probably had the last laugh. She paraded about the deck next to Kelly saying, "Shit. Shit. Gimme a beer, bitch." Then she climbed onto Kelly's lap as she slumped against the bulkhead. Her shoulder bled profusely. She was sinking into shock, not so much from blood loss as realization. I went below and grabbed the first aid kit.

I really shouldn't do this. You deserve to die for what you've done. But as much hate as you generated, I am not an Alzera, or a mindless killer. I won't sink to your level.

The shoulder had a clean through and through wound that missed the lung and major arteries. I applied a bulky pressure bandage and secured it with duct tape. As an afterthought, I secured her wrists and ankles with more tape.

"Thank you, Angel. We would never have been able to pull this off without your help. Now we need to go pick up TJ before he drifts all the way to Cuba."

"This was for saving Isa and her baby the night of the quake. Ramón and me, we still owe you." He turned to Kelly. "And this is for Carlos." He shot her in the knee. This time there was no squib as her leg exploded into a cloud of blood and bone fragments. She screamed and passed out.

"Damn it, Angel. I want her alive when we get back, and I'm low on bandages as it is. You gotta stop shooting her. Okay?"

"Sure Doc, whatever you say," he said, and shrugged.

"Well, let's consider that one pay back for tripod."

"Gimme a beer," screeched Lucy, her feathers ruffled by the noise of the gunshots.

Closure

The same waiter that had served Kelly and me looked expectant. He remembered the tip I left last time. He wiped his hands on his apron and fidgeted with his order book.

"May I?" I asked my best friends. Charlie, TJ, and Angel shared my table. My family would meet me tomorrow in Cancun. Lucy was doing her version of the Macarena on the table next to us, to the delight of some tourists. Menus were stowed, and our waiter turned his attention to me.

"Bring everybody what they want to drink, water bottles with the seals intact, shrimp and calamari appetizers for starters." I saw nods of appreciation. "And make sure everyone has your Sopa de Tortilla."

"Then," I continued, "several plates of rock lobster with your salsa, ceviche, fruit platters, and for dessert, orange slices with lemon ice."

TJ, who had his leg elevated on a bar stool, said in his usual gravelly voice, "And tell Pedro over there at the Cuban cigar store to bring me a box of his best." He paused. "Oh, and a bottle of the best blue agave tequila you carry." Another pause. "And bring the good doctor here a grape NeHi."

"Fuck you," I said and laughed. "I'm a pure root beer man these days." We all laughed. I looked at TJ. "How's the leg, pal?"

TJ rubbed the dark purple, angry lump below his baggy gym shorts. "Hurts like a blind date with a maiden aunt. Thanks for loading a blank instead of a wad cutter. Just firing that squib under my wetsuit with the fake blood surprised me."

"Tell me about it," said Charlie rubbing a similar bruise under his Hawaiian shirt. "This wasn't the Purple Heart I expected."

"How did you manage to catch two slugs the day Frisk 'killed' you?" asked TJ, making finger quotes.

"I've got the bruises despite the flak jacket Charlie sent me, but I thought I'd actually been shot, just before I passed out." I looked at him. "Thanks, by the way."

"Don't thank me, it was Kelly's idea." Charlie took a long swallow of Corona and shook his head. "I was so friggin' blind to what she was up to that I bought her lies—hook, line, and sinker. Killing you to set up TJ seemed so convincing at the time. She even had me send you the package with the passports and equipment, so you'd buy into it as well."

I said, "Luckily, I finally figured out that she was behind all this and decided to turn the tables on her, with her own idea. Using the fake blood was brilliant. She actually believed Angel shot you and TJ. I thought she was going to dance a jig when she saw Angel throw TJ over the side."

TJ looked at Angel and said, "Thanks for shooting me, I think. She had to believe you would actually kill me as she planned. Otherwise, she wouldn't have believed you would take out Charlie and Jake when she needed you. I was worried we'd lose count of the shells—a blank in your rifle for me, then real loads." He looked at me. "And the blank you loaded in my gun that she shot Charlie with. Brilliant."

The gold tooth glinted in the sunlight as Angel smiled. "No problem. After you told me what she'd done and Ramón and I knew she had killed Carlos, I just wanted to put her down. I wish Ramón was there to help, but he'd have killed her as soon as he saw her, so…"

Charlie set his Corona on the table and said, "Angel, I'm curious. When did she contact you and try to hire you?"

"Ramón and me, we've been on The Company payroll for years, but I guess this will blow our cover. Getting an envelope of cash each month just to call someone if there is anything weird going on sure beats the FEMA typhoon scam we do."

I was shocked. "You've been working for the CIA all this time?"

"Yup, and we even got Lucy on the payroll as a consultant." His pride reflected in his grin. "Oh and that thing about killing a guy in prison? Just part of my cover story." I just shook my head.

He continued, "So when she approached me to join her and track you, I knew something wasn't right. My controller knew who she was, but couldn't tell me why she broke my cover. He gave me some bullshit story about the need to know and interdepartmental cooperation. Never did trust her, but the evidence against TJ was remarkably convincing. She almost convinced me." He whistled softly for Lucy, who turned her head in his direction then went back to her dance.

"Well I, for one, am glad you're not as stupid as you seem sometimes," I said.

"Stupid is. Stupid does," squawked Lucy.

Where the hell does she get this stuff?

"What almost got me," I said, "were the letters with my fingerprints and DNA. I knew I didn't write them, but couldn't figure out how they came from my printer unless someone broke in. I decided at first that it had to be Hawknose, but then she turned up dead before writing the ransom note." I raised my water glass in a good riddance salute. Others followed the gesture.

Charlie asked, "Does everyone know what Frisk found when his forensic team examined your office and the letters?" A couple heads shook. "The fingerprints were altered. The top ten sheets of the ream in the office had imprints of your index finger, but they were the exact same. Apparently, a laser copy of a partial fingerprint imprinted onto the paper using oil and sweat based inks that will show up when examined in the usual manner by a fingerprint expert. But when Frisk had the FBI lab look at the originals, they were *too* perfect."

I continued, "They were high quality fakes. I *should* have realized that the CIA was the only one who could do that, but I assumed TJ was the source." I shrugged at TJ. "I thought the only person who had access, technical ability, and motive was you, TJ. Sorry. Fortunately, Frisk realized I'd been set up at that point. It had to be Kelly who was writing those letters."

"I appreciate your misplaced faith in this poor humble person." TJ smirked. He opened a fresh Cuban and nodded. "Apology accepted. It was brilliant the way she set everyone up."

"What I didn't get," I continued, "was the references in those letters to that incident during my residency. Kelly tried to use TJ to convince me Hawknose was the author, but then she turned up dead before she could have written the ransom note." I looked at TJ and shrugged again.

I said, "If Hawknose had just been missing, we would have continued to think she was the one trying to get the Blue Death and responsible for the killings. But her body surfacing too soon ruined that. Kelly changed plans and used that to convince me that TJ was the one and he'd set up Hawknose to take the fall. It almost worked."

TJ said, "But you figured it out? What gave her away?"

Charlie answered, "You were, shall we say, adrift when she said she found Jake at the Royal Pagoda Hotel through his credit card. But he used cash. That was her big mistake. She had to be following Jake to know where he was."

A blast from the horn of a departing cruise ship caused everyone in the café to turn toward the dock.

I set my American Express card on the table. "But I did use a credit card. I never carry that much cash on me." All heads at the table turned toward me. I could see the surprise and confusion in the faces.

"But you said . . ."

"I know," I said raising my hands in surrender. "I lied to her." I took a bite of the lobster dipped in butter and salsa. *Cheese and crackers. How much jalapeno do they put in this salsa?* I took several breaths to cool my mouth while they all waited.

TJ broke the silence. "So? How *did* you know she was behind all this?"

"I didn't."

"But how?"

"She has a poker tell. When she met me in the bar at the Royal Pagoda Hotel, I picked up on it. Unfortunately, I slipped and had a beer, then several more and almost forgot about it." I waited.

"Ok, I'll bite. What's her tell?" asked Charlie.

"Remember when we were in Djibouti? She told one of the terrorists that Alzera had left the country and was telling all to the authorities. She made a finger gun and pointed at him. I knew she was bluffing, and the finger gun was her tell." Charlie and TJ thought a minute and nodded. "She was trying to bluff him into telling her something."

"And?"

"And at the Royal Pagoda, when she was explaining how TJ was setting up Hawknose, had killed Hanna, and was going to kill me for Blue Death, she pointed that same gun finger at me and said 'and that's the truth'."

Charlie said, "And that's when you knew?"

"Nah. I never knew for sure she was behind everything, but when it all boiled down, there was nobody else. Angel and Ramón had no clue. LaRouche has been out to sea since Djibouti—I checked. Hawknose was a perfect candidate, but I couldn't believe she was ever sober enough to pull something off like this." I took another bite of lobster. I tried to remember if I had any antacid in my room.

Lucy continued to entertain the table next to us, dipping her beak into their beer and belching. The tourists laughed and applauded her antics. I threw her a bit of lobster that she sniffed and kicked off the table. I could see a 'fuck you' building in her birdbrain until TJ raised his finger at her. She bobbed and nobbed and went back to her dancing.

I said, "That only left Charlie and TJ. I've seen Charlie limp around like a three-legged cowboy whenever he was near Hanna, and I couldn't believe he had anything to do with this. So that left just you, TJ." I looked directly into his eyes.

"And . . ." he said.

"And we've been friends, colleagues, and shipmates for too many years. My trust runs too deep for me to believe you would do me harm. Kelly spun a compelling tale, and you certainly had the ability and access to pull this off. But, I just didn't believe it."

TJ handed me one of the Cubans from his box and raised his tequila in salute. Nobody spoke. I returned the salute with my root beer, wishing it *were* tequila.

Charlie said, "So, by process of elimination you figured out it was Kelly all along?"

"No, but I was willing to bluff her. She was so convinced that she had the winning hand, that when I told her I paid cash, she folded her cards. She didn't need to check my credit card because she had been following me around Guam for weeks. She thought I'd believe that she tracked me through that card. She had no idea if I used a credit card or not. She bought my bluff and then tried to intimidate me with force. I didn't leave her an out, so she essentially confessed and then tried to kill us."

Charlie said, "So this whole elaborate charade with TJ drinking Ipecac to force puking and pretending to be bent—"

TJ interrupted, "You should have warned me to take a swallow instead of the whole bottle I had stashed. By the time I was 'shot' I was ready to die—for real."

I said, "Sorry. I'll put you up for an Oscar for that performance. You too, Charlie. It was brilliant. She believed we all thought TJ was the killer."

Charlie continued, "So this was all based on a hunch? What if she hadn't fallen for the credit card, cash ploy?"

"I guess we'd move to plan B."

"And that was?"

"Angel shoots her anyway."

TJ said, "And if she hadn't confessed, we wouldn't be able to turn her over to the authorities for trial. What do you think are the chances that she'll be convicted?"

"She'll never be convicted because she'll never go to trial," said Charlie. "The CIA will never allow that. If they have their way, she'll vanish and show up somewhere else with a new identity."

"You sure?" I asked.

"I'd have to kill you if I told you how I know." He smiled.

Angel said, "He's right. She'll never make it to trial. The Agency can't allow that."

I realized Charlie was Agency also, and they were right— Kelly would get away with it after all. "I should have let you shoot her some more, Angel. Sorry 'bout that."

"Don't worry; I didn't want Ramón to miss all the fun."

"Huh?"

"He was driving the ambulance when we returned to the dock. He has some Mayan blood and had planned to take her to one of the sacrificial temples inland." He left the specifics to my imagination.

Epilogue

Benjamin and Jenny were quiet as the *Atlantis* rocked gently on the calm sea. Unlike the stench blowing off Guam, the breeze off Cozumel was clean and crisp. The sun setting against a perfect sky was subtle. A simple quieting of the day and soft prelude into the tomorrows we would have.

It was over; Charlie and Angel reported that officially this never happened. I was sure that there were no records. Kelly didn't exist in either form—reef or human. Roswell continues to be a conspiracy joke.

I held Emily in my arms as we watched the end of the day. I knew I would hold the memory of Hanna in my heart. In that way, her death only released the physical part of her.

"Ready?" I asked the kids. They handed me the urn they carried. Emily turned to me, and her tears soaked into my t-shirt. I choked mine back.

I rolled over the side with Hanna's spirit for our last dive.

I watched her cremains drift away with the evening current. A school of curious zebra fish tasted her and spat. Kneeling in the sand 40 feet beneath crystal waters of the Caribbean, I knew she would appreciate my choice for her final resting place. This whole tragedy started underwater; it was only fitting that it ended the same.

An eel stuck its head out of the reef, exhibiting fearsome teeth as it breathed, and looked at me as if to question my reason for invading its territory. I lingered a moment as I remembered her first encounter with an eel.

Destiny is a superstitious explanation for the thermodynamic driving force of the universe. Her destiny was an early, violent death. I had known about Blue Death and the threat Kelly's Reef posed to the world long before I reacted. Had I foreseen that in time, would she still be alive to share this dive with me?

The government, of course, denies everything. Many who knew my role are dead. Ramón killed the puppet master, but too late. Those of us who remain can't prove it. We move forward just as Hanna's ashes drift with the current.

As I released her, I wondered if the world would ever be sane again. Kelly's Reef no longer existed. Djibouti was a distant memory of deception and death. Roswell remains a conspiracy. All the players in this *Danse Macabre* have taken their curtain call.

Above me, a spinner dolphin breached into the sunset. Thousands of miles away, a hungry lionfish awaits her next goldfish meal as she silently guards three small blue globes in an aquarium.

ABOUT THE AUTHOR

James R. Burke, a retired OB/GYN, lives with his wife in Oregon where he writes and is active in community volunteer activities.

His debut novel, Kelly's Reef, is loosely based on a love of scuba diving, adventures in the Navy, and many friends throughout the years.

Contact the author at:

Kellysreef@burkeworks.org

Made in the USA
San Bernardino, CA
17 August 2016